D0875873

THE
JADE
ALLIANCE

THE
JADE
ALLIANCE

by

Elizabeth Darrell

G. P. Putnam's Sons
New York

Copyright © 1979 by Elizabeth Darrell
All rights reserved. This book, or parts thereof,
must not be reproduced in any form without
permission. Published simultaneously in Canada
by Longman Canada Limited, Toronto.

Library of Congress Cataloging in Publication Data

Darrell, Elizabeth.
    The jade alliance.

    I. Title.
PZ4.D2235Jad   1979   [PR6054.A697]   823'.9'14   79-14342
ISBN 0-399-12342-3

Printed in the United States of America

To My Husband—With Love

THE
JADE
ALLIANCE

PROLOGUE

A small movement of icy air sent a powdering of snow from the roofs of the houses and stirred the branches surrounding them. They moved in leaden fashion, weighed down by the frozen covering that had been there all winter long, on a tree-lined street that lay deserted. There were gashes in the snow where sledges had passed earlier in the day, but at that hour of early evening most of the travelers had either reached their destination or were still preparing to set out.

It was a long street glistening in the pools of light from numerous lanterns; a street that looked proud and arrogant. Tall railings protected the residences of the wealthy, surrounding formal gardens and ending in gilt-topped and crested gates that were opened only when the coachmen of visiting nobility rang the bell and were identified.

Those to whom admittance was out of the question were often to be found when darkness fell peering through the bars at the great houses that had lights blazing at every window, just visible at the top of long driveways. These nocturnal dreamers would try to imagine the interiors as they pulled shawls or cloaks closer around their shoulders and tried not to shiver. Some marveled at

9

wealth great enough to allow a lamp to burn in every room, whether occupied or not. Other thoughts ran riot over furniture made of gold, ceilings studded with rubies, and walls covered in silver-threaded brocade—a picture more breathtaking than the interiors of the great cathedrals of St. Petersburg. They gazed at the beauty out of reach across the snow, then returned to their hovels brightened and warmed as children are at the sight of glistening rainbow bubbles, or as ascetics sustained by greedy study of works of art behind glass.

But in that February of 1905 there were other kinds of faces that pressed against the railings after daylight had gone . . . faces that saw profanity in the lighted windows and degradation beneath the walls of the elegant buildings. These white faces darkened with passionate recollection as they stared at the virgin snow inside the railings and saw again the dark spreading stain of spilled blood in front of the Winter Palace only the month before. These watchers who had nothing left in the world to live for imagined that same scene within those railings that kept them out.

The Brusilov family lived at the favored end of the street. There were lamps burning in every window of their mansion, shining out a welcome to the two men of the household who had not yet returned. In the grand salon the family, with the exception of the three younger children, were waiting not only for the head of the household and his son, but for someone who regarded lateness as her right.

Nadia sat straight-backed on the crimson sofa and reflected that her mother might be forgiven if she were visiting the sickroom where Catherine, Charlotte, and Constantin were recovering from a lowering fever, but she had done nothing except send in posies of winter blossoms by way of maternal comfort.

As usual, there was that tension in the room that would flee on a sigh of relief only when light footsteps were heard on the stairs before crossing the marble of the hall—tapping heels and the alluring rustle of stiff skirts as they slid over the stone.

In an effort to take her mind from the tightness of her corsets which were new and unyielding, Nadia looked at all those sitting in unrelaxed expectation in the room and tried to guess their thoughts. On the high-backed chair to the left of the fire Catherine, Nadia's grandmother, gazed at the flames that symbolized the brightness of her youth. She was now seventy-three and the brightness had gone—dimmed prematurely by a daughter-in-law beside whom any woman must ill compare.

Yet, it was not really anything to do with beauty. Catherine Brusilova had been a *grande dame* who reigned on a plane above physical attraction: She had not gained a daughter but lost her son as irrevocably as if he had gone to his grave. What had broken her completely was that he had continued to live in her house, only *she* was the ghost he could neither see nor hear. Small, silver-haired, infinitely sad, she wore a dress of black watered silk with the family pearls around her neck. She wore no other color these days, yet Nadia wondered if she was the only one in the family who guessed the real reason.

Sitting close to Catherine, who blocked the warmth from the fire, was Aunt Marie. Always in someone's shadow, always deprived of warmth by those who obstructed her path, her aunt might make only an insignificant glow beside those who dazzled, but it was constant and brave. Not quite pretty, not quite slender, not *quite* in the height of fashion, she trembled on the brink of being a social nonentity. Unable to compensate for the lost son, Aunt Marie refused to believe her mother had no use for her whatever, even when the fact stared her in the face.

The round bun-face broke into a smile when she saw Nadia looking across at her. The girl smiled back and asked herself yet again why such a natural mother had been destined to remain barren when another had been blessed with numerous children she did not want. This cruel fact had been alleviated by pouring love and care onto those children, but the bittersweetness of such devotion was tinged with the knowledge that they could be taken from her by a mere whim on the part of the true mother at any time. Everyone knew this would never happen, but Aunt Marie trembled on nights when her dreams tore the young ones from her arms.

Uncle Misha would have made a doting father, and perhaps the responsibility of a family of his own might have stirred him to do something with his life. Coming from a good but impoverished family, he had been allowed to marry Marie Brusilova only because it was thought unlikely she would receive another offer. The couple loved each other in a grateful kind of way which strived to extend to mutual understanding. By the rules of nature men were incapable of realizing fully the pain of a barren woman who yearned for children, but Uncle Misha did his best even when his own virility was put to the doubt by those who were sure of their own.

In the silent salon he was the only person not obviously on edge, yet he had the most cause for being so, thought Nadia. A large gentle man with soft hair falling across his face and eyes as blue and boyish as young Constantin's, there was that about him that aroused contempt in the woman for whom they were all waiting. To Nadia's perceptive eyes it could only be because he was the utter and complete opposite of her own father.

After the marriage Uncle Misha had moved in with his wife's family and been there ever since. He spent a great part of his day in the study writing snatches of his thoughts and observations, or merely meditating on life and nature. He was going to be among Russia's greatest poets one day, he assured them all, and they let him live his pretense merely because it kept him out of the reception salons when visitors called. Nadia had never really decided whether he was serious about being a poet—some of his verse was arresting in its sadness—or if it was just the excuse of a lazy man for not employing himself in more taxing occupation.

At that point in her study of those in the room Nadia thought she heard a door close far off in the house. In the vaulted salons it was possible to hear echoes from distant regions of the great house. Her great-great-grandfather had been a passionate lover of music—and women also, by all accounts—and had designed the house so that the grand hall acted as an echo chamber. There he would pay a group of peasant musicians to play the music of his beloved country all night long, and be able to hear it in whichever—or whoever—room he might be.

Quite plainly, her ancestor's lusty temperament had jumped two generations and come out in her father, except that his passion was centered on one woman only . . . and hers on him. Anna Brusilova had been just seventeen when she met a young lieutenant of the Imperial cavalry. It was the greatest love match of the decade, which had lasted through the next. Seven children had sprung from the union—the last, twin daughters, had died soon after birth during the great winter of 1901—and been mourned by neither parent. The five surviving might well also have perished at birth for all the pride and affection they aroused in the pair who saw them only as the inevitable outcome of passion between a man and woman.

Society saw the couple as romantic, beautiful together, almost immortal, but it took someone untouched by their aura to take a shrewder view of two people who lived only for each other. As their eldest daughter, Nadia saw the ruthless arrogance in her father's personality and the slight narcissism that reveled in the worship of a beautiful woman. In consequence, she had no more than respect for a man with steel nerves, pride of heritage, and ideals of greatness.

For her mother Nadia experienced wariness bordering on apprehension. What others chose to call great romantic love she saw as a frightening kind of obsession. Far from seeking maternal affection, she held aloof, feeling that to draw near might mean entering a steel cage from which there was no escape.

The sound of footsteps was growing louder as Anna descended the stairs, and Nadia's gaze swung next to sixteen-year-old Katya. It did not linger long upon her young sister. Already showing signs of their father's arrogance and their mother's beauty, the girl was not particularly lovable. Beside her sat Ivan, Nadia's twin, nineteen years old and destined to hurt her. As close as most twins they shared sympathy and understanding on everything but the subject of their parents. Excluded, like the younger ones, from their all-absorbing love, they were affected by such neglect in different ways. Nadia stood safely distant: Ivan never ceased trying to draw close. An introspective boy, he found it difficult to reach his father's inflexible standards and, standing on the threshold of manhood, was blinded to his mother's neglect by her aura. Nadia would not allow herself to guess his thoughts in that silent salon, but she knew his face would turn eager when their mother walked in.

The tapping of heels on marble told them all she was almost

there, and the sigh of expectation was almost audible. It did not surprise Nadia that her mother was immediately concerned over the lateness of her husband, and several in the room gave opinions on what could keep not only Andrei but his father so late at their duties. The cavalry barracks was not far, and surely Boris had concluded state affairs for the day. If they had intended being late, why had neither sent word to the family?

Speculation came to an end at that very moment. A commotion echoed around the walls of the great hall—servants' voices raised in horror and Andrei Brusilov's baritone edged with a chilling unidentifiable tone it had never adopted before. A sixth sense told Nadia disaster was near; in what form or how it would affect her she could not know. She watched in growing fear as her father entered, a ghastly sight in the midst of graciousness and elegance. His head was cut and bleeding, crimson was splashed across his cloak and on his hands. His face was livid against the dark green of his uniform; his bright hair sticky and matted with blood.

The girl felt suspended within that scene, the one person immobile amidst the activity of the others. Catherine was on her feet, clutching the shawl of Aunt Marie who had gone to her in instinctive need for mutual consolation; Uncle Misha had run to instruct the servants to heat water and bring liniments. Ivan was at their father's side in an instant, but was pushed aside as the older man went straight to the only person he saw in that room. They clasped hands so tightly between them their knuckles showed white. It was as if they had been apart for an eternity.

He spoke only to her, and the things he said fell upon Nadia's ears like stanzas from one of Uncle Misha's more dramatic verses. Boris Brusilov had been shot on the steps leading from the house of another member of the Czar's administration. Grandfather was dead! The entire family was marked down to die at the hands of those who witnessed the massacre of peaceful unarmed workers outside the Winter Palace to petition the "Little Father."

Nadia thought back on her grandfather's account of the tragedy. The Czar's soldiers had formed up in defense of their ruler, silent and still, confronting a crowd of starving people who had reached the limit of their endurance. Suddenly, the word had been given, and rifles felled men, women, and children who died with disbelief still on their faces. During the screaming, clawing turmoil that followed Andrei Brusilov had led a charge through the tangle of those trying to get away, and those advancing in the grips of the madness of grief, holding dead infants in their arms. His sword had slashed as cruelly as those of his men; the hooves of their horses trampling the dead and dying until the snow was a frothy pink.

The whole disaster had been due to a misunderstanding on the part of one nervous young officer who thought he had been ordered to open fire. The first rifle shot had started an unstoppable atrocity . . . and those who had been there would never forgive. They went back to their underground communes remembering the faces and insignia of those who had given the commands. For a whole month they had been watching and planning. Now the time for vengeance had come. The head of Andrei Brusilov's family had died first, then it had been the turn of the cavalry officer himself.

Nadia had turned intensely cold sitting still on the sofa while the nightmare went on around her. It was as lurid as Uncle Misha's lines on death and suffering. She could not believe the filthy half-animals who manned the factories would dare to kill a man close to the Czar, then attempt to drag his son from his horse and cudgel him to death. Yet her father stood battered and bleeding before her eyes and spoke of it as the truth.

His words were sharp, clipped off short, full of commands that had a hint of desperation in them. He had escaped the murderous mob by using his saber; several were dead. There was no time to lose. They must all get away immediately. He brushed aside the servants with their bowls of water and bandages for, whatever else he was, Andrei Brusilov was a strong man. He sent them instead for furs and rugs.

Aunt Marie was crying silently, tears rolling down her cheeks as she went across to hold Katya's hand in protective gesture. Grandmother was displaying true breeding by leaving aside grief for her husband while she suggested to her son that she should take the three young invalids to the nearby convent run by her cousin, where they would all be safe during the danger. Uncle Misha was white and shaking, speaking in a voice high with fever. Ivan stood back, outwardly calm, but betraying his shock in eyes

15

that never left the united figures of their parents.

Nadia told herself it was unthinkable for Brusilovs to run from a few lice-ridden gutterlings, yet that was what they were about to do. The frozen breath of sudden disaster still encompassed her as she donned her furs and prepared to depart with the others in the horsedrawn sledge. They were to cross the border and stay at their *dacha* in Finland until the assassins were caught. Servants would follow with all they would need; the only possessions they would take with them were their jewels.

The whole family had fallen silent after saying farewell to Catherine. There was no time for a word with the young invalids upstairs before going out into the icy night where the family traveling sledge was drawn up. The sudden freezing temperature pinched Nadia's nostrils together and bit into cheeks that felt stiff. She pulled the fur-lined hood further across her face, wishing it was a whole comforting nest into which she could nestle until the nightmare had passed.

The four women were tucked in with furs and soft rugs; Ivan and Uncle Misha sat up on the box with guns. Andrei Brusilov, showing no weakness from the bludgeoning he had received, mounted his horse and prepared to bring up the rear. Then they set off into the night.

To Nadia that ride was almost macabre—her father covered in blood riding to protect them from attack, and her uncle and brother armed with rifles normally used for hunting. They had gone through the streets of Petersburg on so many occasions when the lamps had set glistening stars in the snow, and the mystic hush broken only by the squeak of pressed ice and the jingle of harness bells had aroused excitement in her. So many times her heart had beaten so fast at the thought of the party to which they were going, and so many times she had returned wreathed in dreams of a handsome face or a voice that had whispered sweet things during a stolen moment. Tonight's ride was almost a desecration of those other times.

The grand streets ran into a square, and others leading from it were narrower as they headed for the river Neva, which had to be crossed in order to reach the Finnish border. St. Petersburg was silent and almost deserted at that hour between the activities of the day and the festivities of the night. The snorts of the horses, the muffled beat of hooves, and the pretty ringing of silver harness bells had settled into a rhythm that made mockery of any suggestion of danger; yet, as the runners glissaded across the frozen surface past the great walls of a warehouse beside the canal it was suddenly there, in the form of three dark figures barely discernible in the shadows.

A shout sent Nadia's head turning swiftly and she saw a rag-wrapped creature pointing a finger at the crest on the side of the vehicle—the proud emblem that betrayed them as the Brusilov family. In a minute they had shot past, but her father swung round in a vicious turn that had his horse scuffling for a foothold. Suddenly, Nadia saw through the wisps of fur lining her hood a multitude emerge from nooks and crannies in all parts of the building.

Andrei Brusilov was just drawing his sword when a whistling twisting blade cut through the air to enter his throat. There was no cry from him, just a silent agonized jerk of his body before he toppled from the saddle to land face down in the thick snow. The multitude began a concerted advance on his still figure.

The sledge slewed to the right as the driver instinctively reined in. Someone was shouting: It was Uncle Misha. Ivan got to his feet like a person risen from the dead and raised his rifle. Nadia's nerves twitched in expectation, but the shot did not come. The fur covers were thrown back as Anna flung herself from her seat, staggered, and nearly fell before running back toward the man on the ground. She gave a terrible cry that rent the air with a sound the girl had never heard from human lips.

As they swung in a dizzying turn Nadia saw everything at once. . . . Ivan standing like a statue with the gun to his shoulder, unable to lower it yet prevented from firing by the running woman; Aunt Marie praying with eyes closed tightly; Uncle Misha and Katya screaming. Incredibly they were telling the man to drive on. A whip cracked, horses whinnied shrilly as they tried to change a check into a forward movement. Nadia was thrown against the side of the sledge as the driver obeyed his orders.

Swaying wildly from side to side the Brusilov sledge rushed on towards the boarder, leaving behind a woman trying desperately

17

to reach the man without whom life would be worthless. Four feet from his she was felled by a club wielded by those surrounding her husband. Her progress continued on all fours. Next minute, the travelers had rounded a corner cutting off all further sight of something so swift and terrible it seemed never to have happened.

With the icy winds freezing strands of fur against her wet cheeks Nadia turned to her brother in instinctive appeal against the pain that had taken place in her body. Ivan was lost to anything but this final evidence of rejection. Now he could never earn his father's approval; his mother would never love him. Even in the face of death they had seen only each other, and he was in the throes of shock.

She turned away from the nakedness of his expression. He gave her no comfort in that terrible moment. Just before the corner had been turned she had seen her mother lying flat on the snow reaching out an arm to its fullest extent in an effort to touch his hand before eternal darkness fell. Their fingers were but a few inches apart, and Nadia would never know if those two who could not live apart had died united. She who had always held aloof now felt the anguish of life and love as the sledge crossed the bridge and rushed toward the border.

ONE

A house with a garden built along the midlevels was a sign of success not only to those who passed the ornate gates, but to everyone on the island of Hong Kong who kept his sharp eyes open for rivals or possible collaborators. A house of substance, with pale colonnaded facade, wide airy verandahs, graceful steps to the arched entrance, and storm shutters that folded back to give views across palm trees to the vivid waters of the harbor beyond: garden extensive, sloping away from the house and green with lush foliage that flourished beneath tropical rainstorms.

Nadia saw it all with a lift to her heart on the day they moved in. Within ten months they had achieved what many struggled for in this colorful colony. She went from room to room in the new house, pride filling her breast. Suddenly she knew what Ivan kept locked within him; had tried to maintain during those first dreadful months after leaving Russia. Now they could hold up their heads again. The name of Brusilov was of some consequence once more.

She leaned on the windowsill of the room that was to be hers and breathed in the warm air that was sweetened by the scent of damp blossoms. It was so totally different from Russia, from the life she had always known . . . yet she felt part of it. Even at the beginning she had been aware of a rapport with her surroundings, had believed their future would be good in a place such as this. Perhaps it had been the result of a subconscious rejection of what had happened in her own country, or maybe the pulsing surge of thriving commerce, young men struggling in the cut-and-thrust world of business enterprise, and an indigenous people growing alongside their overlords yet remaining proudly individual appealed to the newfound awareness of life that had been born as the sledge rushed away into the night.

The first weeks after their arrival had been a severe strain on them all. Uncle Misha anxious and still possessed by fear; Aunt Marie treating them all as small frightened children; Katya petulant and difficult; and Ivan doing all he had to do with an air of burning resentment. Their surroundings had seemed completely alien. They knew no one but Uncle Misha's cousin who had settled in the colony several years before when his mercantile company had collapsed through political pressure. It was this cousin who had helped them to decide to use Misha's collection to go into the jade business, and once the decision had been wrested from all members of the family, it had been a concerted effort. Admittedly, Aunt Marie had done no more than make a comfortable home for them, and Katya had complained about anything and everything, but Uncle Misha worked harder than he had ever done in his life, and Ivan was determined that if they had to become merchants they would do it on the grand scale. Nadia had ignored his protests and insisted on helping with paperwork and bookkeeping—like her twin she was good at figures—and her feminine advice on decor for the premises was invaluable, as Ivan was forced to admit.

They had succeeded, each member of the family taking it as the result of maximum effort on his own part, but Nadia suspected a lot of it was due to curiosity. In a colony like Hong Kong, a group of exiled aristocrats was sure to stir up feelings beyond those normally applied to new arrivals. The European element watched them like hawks, the aristocratic section glad to welcome them at their dinner tables to add spice to insular life that tended to pale after a while. Those others who had come up the hard way from low origins regarded anyone who had wealth enough to start near the top of the ladder as pretentious and unworthy of their success. The British who ruled the colony also split into two groups—those who regarded their Russian nationality with suspicion, believing their nation to have unwelcome designs on the Far East, and those in whom the idea of aristocrats becoming the victims of a peasant uprising brought out the same chivalry that led their ancestors to bring out the French during their revolution. The British were past masters at fighting for the underdog, but it did not mean they regarded him as their equal. There was a patronizing benevolence about their interest but, once launched on this tide of anglicized curiosity, the venture gained strength from sheer good management and flair. Now, six months later, they were able to take over a house left vacant by a departing American businessman. They were established colonists.

It was new and exciting, thought the girl as she looked across the dark green curving fans of palm leaves to the busy waterway of Hong Kong harbor. Merchant ships from all over the world came there, and the great junks plying along the China coast rode the waters with elephantine gracefulness, their brown sails rising up in the sunlight like curved ribbed curtains. There was an air of opportunity mixed with established dignity about Hong Kong that made it unique.

The mixture of races produced a colony of colorful unexpectedness. Grand houses of western design rubbed shoulders with Chinese temples; British engineering skill resulted in a hill railway that ran alongside graveyards where the bones of Chinese ancestors were taken out and polished in ancient rituals; Portuguese traders entertained French merchants to dinner, then tried to cut their throats over business deals; American, Portuguese, French, and British shippers used every method known to them to reduce the length of their runs yet increase their cargoes, keeping an eye on their competitors under a guise of friendship.

The social scale was well defined and known by everyone. The

British administrators topped it, with varying strata within their own ranks. British and colonial businessmen came next, then the white foreigners according to their wealth and social standing. Asians were not really included: They had a scale of their own from princes to coolies and were regarded as entirely separate from the western community.

To Nadia it all seemed entirely reasonable. The social system in her homeland had been well defined and strictly observed. That she had been in the top echelon was due to her birth, but that she was a little lower in the scale in Hong Kong did not worry her as it did Ivan and Katya.

Nadia sighed a little as she heard voices along the corridor approaching her room. It was like being a mother to them all, this obligation to bolster them all up in their separate needs. Aunt Marie had joyfully taken over the family she had always wanted, but her mothering was the cough-syrup and pat-on-the-head variety that satisfied her own maternal yearnings more than anything else. It was left to Nadia to encourage the elderly couple when they had doubts, mollify her precocious sister and, most difficult of all, keep Ivan's spirits up with constant praise and calm reason. If there were times when she longed for someone to relieve her of the burden, they did not come very often and were put aside with determination.

The voices were drawing nearer, but Nadia stayed by the window looking out at the view that would be hers. The sunshine, the beauty of hills sweeping down to a sea of deepest blue, the cheerful hotchpotch of cultures, and the exotic plants beneath her windows were as far from her memories of Russia as she would ever find. She did not want to look back. The shock and horror of that last night colored her past . . . a life that now seemed pale and cold.

Here in Hong Kong they were a family as they had never been before, with freedom from those two who had dominated the great house in St. Petersburg—had dominated every place to which they had traveled. All that was behind her. She wanted a future, like any young girl of just on twenty. For too long she had been in the wings watching the principal players hold center stage. They had gone now, and she was ready to walk on.

The door burst open without ceremony beneath Katya's

imperious hand. "You must have heard us calling. Why didn't you answer?" she demanded.

"I was telling myself how lucky I am—how lucky we all are—to live in a house like this with such beautiful vistas in every direction."

"The house in St. Petersburg was bigger—and much grander. I do not care for open shutters everywhere, and verandahs. There is no privacy."

Nadia refused to budge from her window, saying, "Then you will have to spend most of your time in the central hall. No one will see you there."

Aunt Marie entered at that moment. "There you are, *golubchik,* I wish you would give me your opinion on the rugs I have instructed to be put in the small salon. Vanya approved immediately, but you know what a wicked boy he is when one wants a serious comment from him on domestic matters. I suspect he agrees with anything just to escape from me."

Nadia smiled, knowing her twin well. "He has rather more serious problems on his mind, you know."

"Yes, yes . . . of course," said the other with fondness. "I sometimes wonder if it is not too much for one so young."

The girl left the window reluctantly. "He is twenty—has been since last week. I think he has been absolutely splendid in the way he has coped with something entirely new to him. Having believed for years that he would follow Papa into the army, he found his training did nothing to help him in the world of business. However, I see no signs that it is too much for him." She touched her aunt's hand gently. "Within a year he will become head of the family. He is no longer a boy, *tyotushka.*"

The soft round face looked stricken for a moment. "It seems no time since you were both little ones coming to me for sweetmeats. Time goes past so quickly. If only Constantin and the small girls were here."

"Time will bring them, no doubt," said Nadia with repetitive comfort. "Grandmother will not let them join us while she still lives. You must try to accept that."

A small sigh. "Yes, I suppose I must be grateful for those of my children that I have."

Katya walked around the room looking at it critically. "This is the best bedroom in the house. I suppose that is why you chose it for yourself."

"Naturally," replied Nadia firmly. "Yours has only a view of the side of a hill which, since it is uninhabited, will provide you with the privacy you want so much."

The younger girl plonked herself onto the pretty white cotton cover on the four-poster bed and leaned back on her arms, looking at her sister and aunt with chin raised in superior attitude. "Make the most of it, Nadia. When Vanya is twenty-one he is taking us back to Russia."

"No . . . we cannot go back," cried Aunt Marie sharply.

"I am not sure he includes you in the plan," the girl replied with one of the little bursts of cruelty that seemed to delight her.

All atremble the poor woman tried to protest further. "But we have the business."

"*He* has the business," Katya cut in sharply. "It is Brusilov money . . . all of it."

"Be quiet," said Nadia angrily. "You speak of things about which you know nothing, Katya."

The young girl let herself fall back onto the bed and lay looking at the swath of curtains above her. "Vanya told me himself. We often discuss it."

Shaken, Nadia responded as best she could. "You should not believe all he says. He has dreams, like all of us, but that is all they are."

Katya rolled over so that she could look at her sister through the bedposts. "Because you are twins you think you own him, Nadia," she said spitefully. "He is no longer a boy, as you have just pointed out. He is a man with a mind of his own and he is the only one amongst you who is not afraid to return to Russia. When he goes I shall go with him. That is where we belong—not in this outcast of a place where nobody acknowledges who we are."

Aunt Marie was vocally upset, and Nadia tried her best to pacify her. She could have smacked her sister for deliberately baiting the woman who had dedicated her life to them all. The pretty creature lay there in an attitude of contemptuous martyrdom, forgetting how she had screamed in fear for the man to drive on while their parents were being battered to death before their eyes.

Yet, even as she assured her aunt that Ivan loved them all far too much to break up the family, Nadia felt a clutch of apprehension. Her twin was unhappy and spoke wildly about going back, but if he meant what he said it would do just that. Perhaps, as Katya suggested, she should make the most of this life while it lasted, for how could she remain if he said they must return to that place that cast too many shadows?

Even after three and a half years the sight of the English entertaining in Hong Kong still amused Andrew Stanton. Sweeping green lawns; ordered flowerbeds; gravel paths raked and watered meticulously; regimental band playing softly; marquees pegged out with disciplined correctness; ham, pâté, and cucumber sandwiches; tea in delicate china cups; officials smiling to order, then turning away to ease the tightness of their collars in quick furtive movements; gentlemen in morning coats, and ladies in pale dresses whose skirts dragged the ground as they swayed along beneath lacy sunshades and hats that should have been framed and hung on the walls as works of art. It could have been a garden party in any stately home in England, but it was in the grounds of Government House on the island of Hong Kong. The English did not adapt; they preferred to take England with them wherever they went.

Andrew was present in his official capacity as a liaison officer between the police and the government civil department, but was able to enjoy the sights and sounds of this annual affair. It was held for what the stiff-necked colonials called "the foreign element," which meant any white person who did not hail from the mother country or her colonies. Even so, the guests had to be of some consequence to rate an invitation: foreign diplomats, banking giants, influential merchants, or professional men of good standing. Andrew had vetted the guest list and checked on those whose names appeared on it for the first time. Now he was busy putting faces to names.

He stood with a colleague in government service who was apparently required to know every person in Hong Kong by sight

25

judging by the ease with which he identified each strolling guest from a distance.

"That fellow admiring the roses is the new American vice-president of the finance company I was speaking of earlier this afternoon," said the mine of information. "He's got a dashed alluring wife who will need some watching, in my opinion."

"Really?" Andrew was not interested in the man's opinion on another's wife.

"That's the charmer . . . there in yellow with the big black hat." The speaker became animated. "By jove, I'll bet she sets some ostrich feathers quivering by the end of the afternoon. You have to hand it to these foreigners. They liven up the jolly old place. Makes a nice change after the lavender-and-lace Lady So-and-So, with her demure and delicate daughters in white lace gloves." He chuckled. "Daresay they even sleep in them, what?"

Andrew gave him a pained glance. "Must you always be so confoundedly jolly, Barnham?"

"It's the only way to survive these affairs, old boy." He touched Andrew's arm and pointed to the left. "That group by the ornamental fish pool—the Brusilovs. Russian, you know. Very distinguished. Distantly related to the Imperial family, I hear, but they all say that."

"Brusilov?" repeated Andrew, mentally reviewing the guest list. "Jade, isn't it?"

"Yes. Been in Hong Kong some months and have built up a solid and reputable business—plus a sizable profit, if their style of living is anything to go by. Of course, they might really be related to the Czar in some obscure way, which would account for their wealth," he added reflectively. "The showrooms are impressive. A young, rather touchy fellow and his uncle own the business, and the jade is top-quality stuff. Young Brusilov has the business acumen and his uncle, by the name of Zubov, has real flair for recognizing good pieces. The family has a private collection of considerable value, so I am told. Don't know much about the stuff personally. If it's green and shiny it's jade, as far as I'm concerned." He leaned nearer and said in a warm tone, "The girl in the pale-blue hat is Brusilov's twin sister—about twenty is my guess—and there is another of tenderer years bringing up the rear. The young one is a real corker. Pity she's not French."

"Why?" asked Andrew abstractedly, trying to get a clearer view of the family as they chatted to a French wine importer.

"You can have a flirtation with a French girl, but the Russians are almost as stiff on protocol as we are—especially the high-born ones. Besides which, Sir Goodwin does not believe in close relationships with them. He firmly believes the Russians mean to get their hands on the Far East by hook or by crook, and says they will not be content with Port Arthur." The young man grinned. "He would see a dalliance with one of those beautiful Slavic girls as undermining the British stand against their effrontery. Was he ever young and virile, do you suppose?"

"My uncle is not a bad sort, really," Andrew told him. "He means well."

Barnham groaned. "How many people get away with all kinds of things under that excuse? However, I'll present you to the Russian family when they come this way. You would have met them before if you hadn't been in Shanghai so long. But you have surely seen their premises in Queen's Road."

Andrew shook his head. "I've been down with fever since I got back. Shanghai is a hellish place, and I was there at the worst time of the year. I've never known. . . ." He broke off as his alert eyes noticed a guest leaving. "Hold on, Barnham, there's old Dourier making signs for his sedan chair. If a mad Chinaman or a member of the Triad gangs makes an attempt to assassinate him as he walks out I must place my body between him and the killer." With a perfectly straight face he added, "And if a young Tanka girl rushes at him with a wrapped bundle calling him Papa, I have to claim the child is mine. Excuse me, old chap." He walked off feeling he had nonplussed his young colleague for once.

It was basically true that he should ensure the safety of guests while they were at or in the vicinity of Government House, and was glad of the excuse to avoid being presented to the Brusilovs. The young aristocrat and his uncle must certainly be cultivated, but he had no interest in pretty young girls, Russian or otherwise. As he crossed the lawn with hasty strides, a memory of Cissie's blond curls and wide blue eyes disturbed him once more. He cursed. It was the fever that had brought it all back again just when he believed it all behind him. Delirium always dragged up memories buried deepest in the mind.

Monsieur Dourier departed without being assassinated, kidnaped, or presented with a Chinese bastard, and Andrew decided his duties might be over sooner than expected. In the direction of Kowloon clouds were gathering fast, and experience told him it would be raining in fifteen minutes. In expectation of a great rush for sedan chairs and rickshaws when that happened, he decided he had earned a cigarette before the downpour.

He took a path that wound through the wilder and, in his opinion, more attractive section of the gardens that were not used by guests. He knew every inch of them. Men had been posted there out of sight on occasions that demanded it— intruders in a quiet world of palms and ferns splashed here and there with the yellow of bananas and vivid red cannas. In these green ways the heat hung heavy with the scent of the tropics. Crickets rattled their legs in continuous whirring, broken only when Andrew sent them leaping from beneath his feet, and iridescent lizards, posing bravely on the warm flatness of stones, turned and vanished quicker than his eyes could follow them.

The tranquillity of such solitude heightened his sudden feeling of melancholia, and he was swamped with the pain Cissie had brought him. He smoked the cigarette slowly, watching a butterfly colony through eyes narrowed against the sun. Their exotic colors put shifting blooms on the greenery, reminding him of Cissie's transient beauty as she had fluttered before his eyes from man to man, never staying long enough to reveal the falseness of her vividness.

His thoughts jumped to those days at war—the heat, the endless African veldt, day after day riding around in circles after tiny groups of Boers who always remained a day ahead of them. He had seen men at their best and at their worst. He had known hunger and nearly died of thirst. His friends had died bloodily; he had killed others the same way. There had been comradeship and hatred, but it was the latter that had lived with him when it was all over. He could not forget the way they had looked at him, especially the women who watched their farms being burned— enemy eyes full of hatred.

It had been an attempt to forget it all that had sent him with his friends on a mad jaunt around London's West End during those first weeks following his return. Cissie had fixed her great blue eyes on him and walked past the other stage-door johnnies straight into his waiting carriage—and into his arms at the end of the evening. She was fresh, very pretty, smelling of flowers and full of laughter. She made him forget those other women a half a world away, forget the sickness and death, the noise of battle, and the fear.

They were married within a month. He could still remember that scene with his parents, and how he had walked out with such arrogance, a protective arm around Cissie's shoulders. It had taken him only the following month to realize they had been right. She had been heartless and greedy and ambitious. But what had been impossible to forgive was the fact that she was common. The stunning stage costumes, the generous admirers, the indiscriminate borrowing of others' property had given her an air of class and opulence, but beneath it all she was a true product of her birth. She had flirted with any man in sight, shamed him before his friends, returned to the theater immediately after the honeymoon, and spent his money with cruel delight.

Life had been so full of pain and regret he had made it bearable by drinking himself insensible night after night, and it was on one such occasion after a party that he had insisted on driving the carriage himself and charged headlong into a wall. If it had not been so completely dark, so black a night, he might have seen it in time.

Cissie's funeral had caused a traffic jam around London's theaterland, and men were seen in tears at the graveside. He had not cried. The guilt of knowing he had rid himself of the blight on his life was too terrible for tears. His family had rallied round. He was only twenty-one, young enough to start again and forget it had ever happened . . . but the scandal made it impossible to remain in England.

Aunt Maude, his mother's sister, was married to a man who could get Andrew a decent position in Hong Kong. It was one of the farthest-flung outposts of the British Empire, and there was a boat sailing in two weeks. Colonel and Mrs. Stanton breathed a sigh of relief when it left the jetty, and so did their son. All that had been well over three years ago. Society had agreed to forget, and he was expected to make amends . . . only life was not that simple. Pain, guilt, disillusion, all left scars. He had closed his conscience to guilt, and his heart to women.

He had come to a halt in his walk, staring at the undergrowth but seeing nothing. It was that damned fever! After all this time he had believed it behind him, yet at this moment he could feel the humiliation and despair as if she were still part of his life. He sighed heavily. She always would be. Those six months were there within his soul whether he liked it or not. Stubbing out the cigarette with angry movements, he walked on along the path, lost in the past.

Nadia could have cried with vexation. If only she had not felt so irritated with Katya, or so exasperated with Ivan; if only Aunt Marie had not bored everyone with her endless chatter about children, and Uncle Misha on the subject of jade! But her predicament was her own fault, if she acknowledged the truth, because she should never have wandered off alone away from the milling guests, no matter how badly her sister behaved or how much her brother imagined himself insulted. *"Bozhe moy,"* she muttered and stamped her foot. "What am I to do . . . oh, whatever am I to do?"

It was such an undignified and ridiculous situation to be in. The more she wriggled and turned the faster her hair became entwined in the branch of the tree. It had taken her all of half an hour to coax her maid to arrange the swaths and coils of rich brown hair into the complicated coiffeur she had considered suitable beneath the wide-brimmed muslin hat, yet in a matter of seconds her impulse had resulted in the ruin of elegance—and of her reputation also, if she did not pull free very soon.

She grew flustered and irritable standing in the midst of fragrant shrubs with her hands up to her hair. Unable to see the tangle, her fingers could only wind and unwind in experimental fashion. Another attempt to move her head told her she was held as fast as ever. *"Bozhe moy,"* she cried again, and further vented her feelings by reciting all the Russian oaths she had ever heard.

"May I assist you?" asked a voice in French, and her head swiveled round smartly to look between her upstretched arms at the man who had approached unnoticed. The movement pulled at her tender scalp, bringing tears to her eyes so that she saw him through a blur. He was in white, starched and suggesting a uniform of some kind. Wishing the earth would swallow her up she turned away, hoping he would disappear.

He did not. In fact, several paces brought him right up to her. "I think you would be wise to put yourself in my hands. I can see the cause of the trouble, and you cannot."

Mortified at being discovered like a ewe in a thicket by an Englishman who spoke fluent French, she lowered her arms and stood helpless while he looked at her hair and said "Mmm" several times in tones that wobbled with laughter.

"You find it amusing, it seems," she said stiffly in English. "That is not very polite."

He sobered immediately. "I beg your pardon. The . . . er . . . originality of the situation took me by surprise. You speak English very well," he commented as he reached up to the branch above her head.

"We had an English governess in Russia."

His hands were lowered again. "Russia? Oh lord, you are the elder Miss Brusilova, aren't you?"

She looked sideways at him. "You know me? We have not been introduced. I should have remembered."

Yes, I should have remembered, she added in silent emphasis as her vision cleared and she gazed into his face only inches away from her own. He was young, strange yet somehow familiar, as if she had known him once long ago in her girlhood. Without warning there came a shaft of alien emotion, a sense of vital reciprocation with him that left her breathless as he said, "We haven't met in person, but I was introduced to your hat by Reggie Barnham just a short while ago. It is very attractive."

Trembling slightly she asked, "You have an eye for hats, Mr. . . .?"

"Andrew Stanton. It's part of my job. Some hats are so large they are easier to recognize than faces. Please . . . if you look at the ground it will enable me to see the problem far easier."

She looked down in a daze. There was something about standing close to him, encircled by his arms, that took her unawares. His fresh starch-laundered jacket added novelty to that indefinable smell that signified masculinity. Uncle Misha combined cigar smoke and vodka fumes with the warm whiskery scent of drooping moustaches; Ivan was a mixture of boot polish, open air, and office ink. This man was different altogether. Something about the faint whiff of cigarettes on bleached linen, the tangy pureness of good soap, and the warm incitement of sunbrowned skin set up a tingling response in her. It grew almost unbearable when she felt his hands on her hair. Such intimate contact between them caught at her senses, swirling them around until she felt off balance.

"How did this happen?"

The warmth of his breath stirred on her neck as he spoke, and a tremor ran through her body. Her answer was vague. "It was a butterfly . . . so lovely a blue, yet green in the sunlight. I followed to see it."

"Ah, yes. They are much prized for their wings which are set into rings and brooches."

"How cruel!" Looking up swiftly she met his glance angled down at her.

"The butterflies are dead at the time, you know."

"That is not the point."

"Oh?"

"When something is so beautiful we should not try to take that beauty for our own adornment. Surely you must agree?"

He gave a slow smile that crushed the breath from her. "I certainly have no wish to adorn myself with butterfly wings."

Her cheeks grew warm. "But you would give them to someone else?"

"Not after this . . . no."

For a time-suspended moment their glances seemed locked and unable to break away, but he frowned slightly before raising his head to study the tangle of her hair once more, leaving her studying the lines of his face. What had put such tautness in his jaw and hollows in his cheeks? He was a big man, strong and muscular, yet there was a wariness in the deep blue of his eyes and the timbre of his voice that suggested vulnerability. His next words seemed almost to emphasize the fact, since they took refuge in officialdom.

"You would have been wiser to keep to the official paths, Miss Brusilova."

"Am . . . am I trespassing?" The words were independent of her thoughts.

"Not exactly . . . but we prefer guests to remain in the area that is roped off."

He sounded so formal, so aloof, she felt a tremendous disappointment overtake her. He seemed intent on unwinding her hair, so she said, "I took off my hat to cover the butterfly—not to kill it, of course, but to keep it for a while to look at it closely. Then I backed into a tree I did not see. The more I tried to escape the worse it became." She sighed with the sadness of a moment that had gone as quickly as it came. "It was the penalty for taking forbidden paths, I think."

He looked down swiftly, and the contact was there again as something darkened in his eyes and banished the wariness. Their faces were a mere twelve inches apart as they stood as lovers might, he touching the softness of her hair as she gazed wide-eyed up at him.

"Forbidden paths are the most exciting," he said almost under his breath as his hands stilled.

The seclusion of musk-filled foliage, the pulsating drowsiness of late afternoon put a charm upon her. Nadia had never felt such an overwhelming urge to surrender her soul to another. In that moment he was the father stroking the hair of his child, the mother making everything come right. He seemed to take away the burden of the past and the demands of the present. He dismissed Katya as immature; he made her a single person instead of a twin. But, strongest of all, the dreams of handsome faces and troika rides after the ball flitted away on the feet of girlhood as an aching limpness filled her limbs.

For a timeless moment they stood motionless, almost touching yet holding back as if afraid, until he seemed almost to shake himself from a trance. His hands fell to his sides as he stepped back.

"There . . . you are free," he said in a voice that echoed the pang of loss she felt at his withdrawal. "With your hat pinned in place no one will ever notice."

She could not recover as quickly as he. His words had meant nothing to her. She still stood as if held by her hair to the branch, her eyes taking in the pleasure of sunlight on his springy fair hair that set a halo of shining strands shimmering in the slight breeze. It put a glow on the brown face and heightened the ocean-blue of his eyes. He stood waiting, and she might never have let him go if it had not been for the butterfly. The flash of blue-green caught her eye, making the one movement in the midst of stillness.

"Do not move," she whispered. "It is there on your sleeve."

He looked down quickly, then stretched out his arm with infinite care until the creature was only a short distance from her face. She put gentle fingers on the back of his hand to steady it while she watched in delight what had become a symbol of that afternoon.

"It is quite, quite beautiful. Do you not think it worth all the trouble we have been through?" she asked softly, willing him to agree.

But the butterfly afternoon had ended. With a zigzag path of color the creature was off, out into the sunshine to dazzle other eyes.

"I am afraid we are in for a downpour," Andrew said breaking into her mood. "May I escort you to shelter?"

She followed the direction of his nod and saw the black clouds nearly overhead. He was holding out her elegant hat which he had picked from the ground. She took it, but made no attempt to put it on.

"There is always a downpour to spoil every perfect moment, do you not find?" she asked him.

"Yes, yes, I'm afraid there is," he answered slowly, looking as lost in thought as she.

TWO

When the guests had departed there were still things to be done by those who had been on duty, so Andrew did not arrive back at his uncle's house on the Peak until late. He changed for dinner hurriedly, then went downstairs to the verandah where sundowners were always ready on a side table. His aunt and uncle were already there, and he greeted them before offering to forgo a drink in order not to delay dinner any longer.

"To tell the truth," he confessed with a grin, "Barnham and I cracked a bottle before we left Government House. Had to have something to drown the taste of all that tea."

His aunt gave her "fond nephew" smile; Sir Goodwin merely grunted. They went into the dining room that commanded a fine view of the city and harbor. By day, it gave a vista of green sweeping slopes that were scarred by the rich reddish-brown earth of the island and dropped to the spread and rooftops on the lower slopes and the harbor.

At night, as at that moment, the view from the open windows was a close contestant for perfection, since any ugliness that might be revealed by daylight was disguised by the sparkling lights way down that gave one the feeling of seeing a star-filled

35

sky above and below. Andrew paused for a moment by the window, then went to his chair where Lee, the Chinese boy, was waiting to push it into place as he sat.

"On a night like this it would be easy to imagine myself back in South Africa," he said reflectively. "From Table Mountain the view is much the same—lights scattered everywhere reflecting in the water—and the nights can be hot and still, like this. But Hong Kong has a smell of its own. There's something about a mixture of damp undergrowth, joss sticks, fried rice, and temple incense that is unique."

"Really, dear, need you speak of such things at the dinner table?" protested his aunt, her plump face wrinkling with disapproval.

He gave her a wicked grin. "You *smell* them at the dinner table, Aunt Maude . . . something much worse!" He glanced up at Lee, who was serving him. "A little more of that soup." He grinned again at his aunt and explained, "Cucumber sandwiches are all right for ladies to nibble without appearing indecorous, but they hardly provide real sustenance. I think men should be excused garden parties."

"My dear Andrew," said his uncle heavily, "there was more goodwill dispensed this afternoon than one could manage in ten dinner parties."

"And more diplomatic advice," he added slyly. "Come, sir, admit it. We government servants seized the chance to sound out our guests with a view to getting some idea of their intentions in the Far East. You cannot tell me your long chat with the French Consul concerned yesterday's cricket match."

Sir Goodwin broke his roll with strong fingers. "As a matter of fact, he was vastly concerned over the sinking of the *Diable* last week."

"Understandable," agreed Andrew. "Piracy is on the increase again."

"We have all accepted that pirate junks still operate along the wilder parts of the coast, despite our vigilant gunboats. It's rather more serious than that. The owners of the vessel have been salvaging what they can of the remaining cargo and found a dozen bodies of men who were not members of the crew." He

36

frowned at Andrew. "Since the *Diable* had come from Japan the French suspect those men were revolutionaries."

"Damnation!" exclaimed Andrew, then added automatically, "Sorry, Aunt Maude. You know, sir, De Montfort up in Shanghai told me he had heard Wong Fu was active again."

Sir Goodwin gave a thin smile. "Well, he is active no longer. The French believe he is among those drowned with this ship. They are awaiting positive identification by one of their men who knew Wong Fu during his association with the Boxers."

Andrew whistled through his teeth. "I'll have a word with Cardew tomorrow. He had better concentrate more of his police boats in Junk Bay for a few months. When one reovlutionary leader dies, two more spring up in his place. Nothing inflames zealots more than one of their number dying for the cause— although Wong Fu hardly did that." He waved away the house-boy who was offering him ice. "No, Lee, it ruins the taste of the wine." Then he turned back to his uncle. "One cannot help feeling sympathy with them. Anyone with knowledge of the present system must see that the dynasty is rocking prior to its fall. What is not so easy to see is the ideal to replace it. Is a people's revolution the answer?"

"I trust you are not expressing those views seriously, Andrew," said Sir Goodwin in stern tones. "And you had better not express them at all among your colleagues, if you value your career."

Andrew looked over the rim of his glass in the act of taking a sip of wine. "Oh, come, sir, I am well aware of our official policy, but it surely does not mean one must turn a blind eye to all other considerations. If you were a Chinese wouldn't you harbor a burning grudge against the Manchus who ruled your country so arrogantly?"

"They have been doing it for over three hundred years" was the dry answer.

"That much longer for the grudge to harden into revolt." He waved the glass in his uncle's direction. "If Napoleon had taken Britain a century ago would you now live docilely under French rule and never dream of driving them from your country?"

"That is a hypothetical example," snapped Sir Goodwin.

"But one you understood enough to avoid a direct answer.

Look, sir, my professional knowledge tells me a revolution would be disastrous for China at this stage. With a dozen other nations fighting to take bigger and better stakes in the land, internal strife would leave them defenseless, but because I am a member of the Crown's administration, it does not mean I close my eyes to the point of view of the ordinary Chinaman."

Sir Goodwin dabbed at his mouth with a starched napkin and regarded his nephew with a patronizing expression. "My dear Andrew, the 'ordinary Chinaman,' as you call him, *has* no point of view. Apart from ensuring that he and his family have daily rice and some kind of hovel in which to shelter, he is uninterested in what goes on around him."

Andrew looked up sharply from pouring gravy over his cutlets. "That same mistake was made over the Boers."

"You are surely not making a comparison with . . ."

"No, no, the Boers were not oppressed in the way these people are," he said, "but their resentment of us burst into revolt eventually, and the tragedy of that war was due to the same complacent view that they were nothing but simple farmers content with their lot."

"*Andrew,*" cried Lady Halder after her prolonged silence. "How can you speak like that?"

"Because I experienced their passionate defense of all they held dear," he told her quietly.

"That is just my point," went on the flushed and indignant lady. "They were our enemies."

"They were certainly that," he agreed reflectively. "But because I fought them for three weary years it did not mean I could not see why they hated us, or admire their courage and loyalty to a cause they believed in. War in not all hatred, Aunt Maude, or we should simply slaughter each other until mankind was extinct."

Ignoring his wife's high color, Sir Goodwin renewed his attack. "The Boers are European and Christian, Andrew. We are dealing here with barbarian races. Young Marchant came in from the New Territories only yesterday with his arm in a sling. He had a riot on his hands after condemning a case of *Mui Tsai*. He was stabbed in the arm by the father who had just sold his fourth daughter. How can you sympathize with *that* point of view?"

"I do think that is a terrible custom," exclaimed Lady Halder at once. "It cannot be called anything but slavery. Those poor little girls are sold and bought quite openly, and turned into drudges. For all their protests at being civilized people, the Chinese have some very pagan customs."

Andrew helped himself to peas, then glanced at his aunt. "Maybe, but if those girls were not bought by wealthier Chinese, most of them would be found floating in the harbor. Surely a more pagan custom."

The lady was distressed. She sat on several committees dedicated to helping the heathen, but never came into actual physical contact with those she wished to help. Plain truths upset her peace of mind.

"Need we speak of all this at the table?" she begged her husband and nephew, feeling she had had quite enough. "You both spend so much time at your office, I should think you would wish to relax when you are at home." She cast large reproachful eyes at Andrew. "You have not even inquired why the Andersons are not dining with us tonight, after all."

With his fork halfway to his mouth Andrew looked at her in resignation. "Sorry, Aunt Maude, I had forgotten they were supposed to be coming."

The older pair exchanged glances. "That's not very flattering to Lavinia, dear."

All at once, he knew what they were up to and tried to remain casual. "Is there any particular reason why I should flatter Lavinia Anderson? She has no influence in high circles, neither is she related to royalty. I cannot see any advantage in cultivating her acquaintance. Anderson is an old dodderer who will climb no further in the Civil Service, and Mrs. Anderson is a frail little mouthpiece who echoes every word her husband says. I am surprised you bother with them."

"We do it for your sake, Andrew," said Lady Halder in a hurt tone.

"Then you are putting yourself out unnecessarily," he told her firmly. "As far as I am concerned, you can send them packing."

"That is a little uncivil, to say the least," put in Sir Goodwin in the tone he used when speaking to a young subordinate in his department—as Andrew was.

"I'm sorry. Perhaps I was a little too blunt."

Silence descended, but Andrew's appetite had gone.

"It *is* more than three years, Andrew."

"I beg your pardon, sir."

Lady Halder looked a little flushed, but spoke on her husband's behalf. "Several years have passed since it happened. Surely long enough to put it behind you?"

His resolution vanished. He *was* angry. "It?" he queried. "Why don't you say 'that dreadful affair' or 'that tragic night'? Or even 'your scandalous action'? I'd prefer any of those to 'it' spoken in a meaningful tone, Aunt Maude. And need we discuss it now? Even in South Africa sitting in thick mud beneath the shelter of flapping canvas, we banned certain subjects during meals."

"I think we must discuss it now," insisted Sir Goodwin. "Unless you are rude enough to leave in the middle of dinner, it seems the only time you are likely to sit still and listen. You have always avoided facing the issue before."

For a couple of seconds Andrew almost did get to his feet, but he hesitated long enough for Sir Goodwin to embark on his speech. "The unfortunate events leading to the death of that young woman took place nearly four years ago. Enough time has elapsed to satisfy convention—if it should be considered at all, in this case—and you owe it to your parents to make amends. Naturally, they would like to see you suitably settled and starting a family." He cleared his throat rather pompously. "We are not trying to force anything on you, as you seem to think, but Lavinia Anderson is just one of many suitable English girls who would make you an admirable wife. Your aunt has gone to much trouble to introduce the right kind of young woman to you. Is it too much to ask that you consider them seriously?"

Andrew's jaw tightened. "Yes, I think it is too much. How can you know who are the 'right kind' of young women for me?"

"You certainly do not. That much has been proved all too tragically," snapped his uncle, taking offense at his tone.

It was a hit below the belt. The minute it was said Sir Goodwin apologized, but the damage had been done. Lady Halder, softhearted and susceptible, looked extremely upset, and signaled Lee to clear the plates. In the interim between the main course and the arrival of the pudding, Andrew did his best to

40

swallow his anger along with a full glass of wine. No good would come of losing his temper further. They meant well, but by God, life was not as simple as they had always found it.

With the pudding before them Lady Halder said hesitatingly, "Beatrice Meades is back from Australia looking prettier than ever. I . . . I think she is hoping you will take her to the Sailing Club ball, dear."

"Well, I won't," he said immediately. "She wears white gloves all the time—probably even in bed."

"Andrew!" It was a plea rather than an admonition.

"Reggie Barnham's words, not mine, He's right though. All the ladies at today's garden party were much more imaginatively dressed."

"They were *foreigners*, Andrew."

"But ladies, nevertheless," he pointed out dryly.

Sir Goodwin signaled Lee to refill his wineglass, and Andrew did the same. "I was not aware that you were well acquainted with Miss Brusilova, Andrew."

It was slipped in casually, but it did not fool him for a moment. He now saw the reason behind the previous conversation. He had been seen coming from the shrubbery with a flushed and disheveled girl on his arm.

"It's my job to know who's who, sir, as you have often told me," he said easily. "She's very charming, don't you agree?"

Sir Goodwin ignored the question. "Pity about her background. Had to get out of Russia in a hurry. Her father was concerned in that barbarous affair outside the Winter Palace. He massacred dozens, so I am told. They caught up with him and threatened to wipe out the entire family. Old Brusilov was shot, and the girl's father was dragged from his horse as he tried to run away across the border."

"I heard the mother went mad and flung herself from the carriage as it went over the river," said Lady Halder in shocked tones. "They dared not stop to pull her from the water, and those poor girls had to watch her struggling and calling their names until they were out of sight. Think how it must have affected them."

"They're all rather unstable—it's a national weakness," pronounced Sir Goodwin. "Damned excitable lot, the Russians. There'll be a bloodbath there before long, take my word, and all these exiled aristocrats will find themselves dispossessed."

"Don't worry, sir," said Andrew with bitter flippancy. "I only offered Miss Brusilova my assistance, not my heart and rather sullied name."

Andrew might have forgone his sundowner, but he made up on "moonuppers" as he called them when Sir Goodwin and Lady Halder retired that evening. Venting his feelings by savagely attacking mosquitoes with a lighted cigarette he stood on the verandah with a decanter of brandy as a companion.

"But where were you that night," he challenged the moon. "It was so hellish dark. . . ." He tossed back the brandy in one gulp, remembering the black rushing night, the shriek of dying horses, and the terrible splintering cracks as the carriage broke apart just before he passed out.

Afterwards, they told him she must have died instantly—her neck snapped in two—with no time for thought or pain . . . and then the nightmares had started. Cissie laughing with her head thrown back—laughing at him. *My dear Andy, what a terrible stuffed shirt you are! Relax and have fun with my friends.* Then, she was standing with blond hair unkempt, rouge still on her cheeks at ten in the morning—standing in the doorway of their bedroom in a gaudy wrapper. *Oh for God's sake. You make three hundred pounds sound like a fortune. You're rolling in it, and you know it.* And himself saying tautly, *I wouldn't mind so much if the coat had been bought for my benefit . . . but that spineless cad Hemmings. . . .*

For your benefit! That's a laugh, it really is. Rudy Hemmings knows how to give a girl a good time. All you ever do is pull long faces and stiffen that already rigid backbone of yours. The war is over, Andy. Nobody thinks you're a hero now—just a bloody spoil-sport! The door had slammed in his face.

Night after night he had relived scenes like that in his mind, or saw her again covered in blood, her head lolling at a sickening angle. Now standing above the lights of Hong Kong three and a half years later he saw it all again as vividly as before. It was worse than he had known it for some time, and he began to sweat as her

42

sharp pseudo-genteel voice rang in his ears once more. She had been taunting him that night, on and on in the high-pitched tone she adopted at theatrical parties. The guests had been predictable in their vulgarity and insincere caperings. Cissie had kissed every man in the room and metaphorically offered her body to any one of them who might further her career.

He had begun drinking early in the evening. It might have been no different from a hundred other evenings if one of Cissie's adolescent entourage had not stumbled over Andrew's feet and spilled a glass of champagne in his lap. He had immediately lunged at the fop and pushed him down, then several of the chorus boys had held him when he would have piled into the lad again.

They still held his arms while Cissie helped the other to his feet and brushed him down. Her face had been pale and furious. She could not have guessed she was about to sign her death warrant when she began a brittle and cruel piece of theatrical destruction. Holding center stage she ridiculed everything Andrew valued, painting a picture of him as a pompous thick-skinned cavalryman who was only happy in the company of horses. She retold those things he had confided in the first days of their relationship, when war still haunted him. She turned deeply dramatic experiences into comedy, parading his emotions during battle as if they had been adolescent attacks of fright.

The whole room had echoed with laughter. He had grabbed her wrist and dragged her from the room, telling himself he would stand no more. Ordering his coachman from the box he had climbed up in inebriated bravado telling his wife he would show her he was no weakling, and set the horses forward at a gallop. The night had rushed past. Cissie was crying. He had seen the wall only when it was three feet from the horses.

His hand gripped the glass tighter and tighter, until he realized this was Hong Kong and it had all happened long ago. For a few moments he stared at the glass. Drinking again, and far too much! In a savage movement he threw it onto the stone verandah. Damn his uncle for bringing it all up again tonight.

But he knew it was more than that. Walking the length of the verandah he leaned on his hands against the balustrade, looking in the direction of Government House. That incident with the Brusilova girl had been mostly to blame. She had been as near as dammit in his arms. Her scented warmth and soft fronds of tawny hair had reawakened awareness of how long it had been since he had held a woman against him.

He turned away from his contemplation of the scene of the garden party and straightened up. Clouds were beginning to cover the silver perfection of the moon. *There is always a downpour to spoil every perfect moment.* A girl and a butterfly! Instinctively he felt she was all the things Cissie had never been, yet something told him to pursue her might lead to another disaster. Society wanted penance from him and demanded that he obey the rules. Foreign girls were out of the question. With a last look at the spangled hillside leading down to the harbor, he turned and went indoors.

The air was hot and dry, full of dust and the odor of charcoal fires. Noise abounded, echoing in the narrow streets edged by tumbledown buildings. Hawkers cried their wares in nasal staccato phrases; women haggled excitedly over baskets of dried fish; ragged children poked sticks in innocent cruelty into cages crammed with chickens and set them cackling with fear and desperation; pigs lay in piles, embalmed in wicker baskets, trotters sticking out pathetically, and grunting in vain for their plight to be relieved.

Further on a hypnotic perfume hung over a kaleidoscope of blooms that filled a narrow street with a living garden across the tops of stalls and barrows. Singing birds in minute cages poured out their hearts in a plea for freedom; vividly painted paper lanterns hung from wooden poles; kites jerked and tugged in the breeze that tried to take them up and away over the ramshackle rooftops.

Down a small alleyway tiny black-haired children were squatting on their haunches, absorbed in the study of a dead rat lying in the damp refuse that gathered in the nullahs. Sensing food, a pi-dog turned into the alleyway and headed for the group, squat face alert for a flying clog or a rival who might try to prevent his taking the prize.

At the end of the sloping street another crossed it at right angles, wider and influenced by the Europeans who had built it and made it their own. Here, smart westerners were borne along in sedan chairs with the bearers varying in number according to the status of the passenger, or they sat in rickshaws if the slow bouncing motion of the sedan chair did not suit their need for haste. Rickshaw boys in loose flapping tunics and trousers ran with the wheeled chairs, bare feet pounding the ground for mile after mile to earn a daily bowl of rice.

Nadia sat in her rickshaw, holding a sunshade open to protect her head from the afternoon heat. She looked at the passing scene, but her thoughts were elsewhere with a tall fair-headed Englishman whose blue eyes held a bewildering mixture of warmth and wariness. A week had passed since that meeting—a week of feverish brain-racking and plotting—until she had found a way of making their paths cross again. Something told her he might not take the matter in his own hands, and there would not be another garden party until next year.

Andrew Stanton had been unlike any man she had known. At almost first glance she had noticed the way his hair rested against his temples in beautifully cut straight lines; the solid strength of a throat that had none of a woman's curves to make it graceful; a mouth that even when smiling was firm and determined.

Even more revealing had been the discovery that his close proximity set up an excitement within her that brought with it awareness of his superior height and strength to emphasize her own weakness in delightful comparison. His hands gently entwined in her hair had merely transferred her captivity from the tree to himself. In those glorious moments of discovery she had known the desire to belong to him, and the denial of that desire had left her breathless.

Instinct told her he had also been affected, despite his control of the situation, and it might have been only her first experience of overwhelming adult desire if it had not been for the butterfly. Andrew had lifted his arm, offered her the beauty of the creature in a gesture that took her beyond physical attraction. Their eyes had met, and there had been a moment of commitment before the blue butterfly had gone, and he became the polite official

45

once more. She could not forget that moment, could not abandon its promise, fleeting though it had been. Only if they met again and he denied it had ever happened would she believe there was no hope.

It was to this end that the outing had been instigated, but it had taken a deal of patience to persuade Aunt Marie, who disliked venturing out during the afternoon. For once, Nadia would not give in to the foibles of the simple soul and, with Katya on her side in unwitting collaboration, she cut short her aunt's protests and ordered the rickshaws for a visit to the family business premises.

Galerie Russe was situated in the select part of Victoria. The white stone colonnaded building had been the premises of a passenger-shipping line before the business expanded, and it lent itself beautifully to its present purpose. An arcaded entrance allowed rickshaws to draw up under cover so that visitors would not suffer the inconvenience of being drenched by rain when they alighted. A young Eurasian dressed in Russian costume (Uncle Misha's idea) acted as doorman to bow the way into a cool dignified interior.

High ceilings, slowly rotating fans, and cool marble floor provided that air of hushed distinction demanded by Ivan in return for his collaboration in a business venture that offended his pride. The ground floor comprised some five or six rooms separated by arched ways, in which the jade was exhibited in glass cabinets according to value or dynasty. In each room was a black-coated supervisor to answer the questions of visitors, then call Misha Zubov when expert advice was needed. People did not *buy* things at Galerie Russe, they viewed them, conducted negotiations for purchase with either of the proprietors, who then arranged for the piece to be delivered suitably packed on receipt of a draft for the agreed amount.

The three ladies walked in and were greeted with great courtesy by the supervisors in each room, until Uncle Misha spotted them.

"My family, my family! Your charming presence dims the beauty that surrounds me," he greeted in his usual flowery manner, kissing the hand of his wife. "Come, you must meet Mr.

Corville Ransome, an American gentleman who has just selected a black horse of considerable rarity. It is so sad. The figure has been here so short a time I cannot bear to let it go."

To Nadia the time spent talking to the American collector was so much time wasted, but eventually they all went up the curving staircase to the mezzanine floor where the administrative offices and pieces of particular value were situated. Uncle Misha immediately led the way to the treasure room to show off his latest prize, and Nadia took the opportunity to slip into the office, not wishing to hear a eulogy on the virtues of jade. Poor Uncle Misha regarded everything he bought with jealous possessiveness and parted with it reluctantly. How could they all have known his fascination with the family collection would prove so invaluable?

Ivan was sitting at his desk writing, but looked up when the door clicked. A smile transformed his set expression at the sight of his twin sister, and he left his work willingly.

"The one happy event in a miserable day," he said, kissing her cheek. "I am glad you did not tell me you would come. Surprise makes your visit even better, *sestrushka*."

"Not too miserable a day, surely," she replied lightly. "An American dealer has just decided he cannot live without a beautiful black horse Uncle Misha has shown him."

"Ah . . . sales, offers, orders . . . that is all he thinks of."

"He does very well."

He nodded listlessly. "He has a mercantile mind."

"And you have not?" she teased.

His dark eyes grew intense. "If we had not left Russia, I would have been a cadet officer in my father's regiment now, serving the Czar, not . . . a . . . jade merchant!"

She gave a deep sigh. "Will you never forgive him for bringing us here?"

His good-looking face grew bleaker. "It is myself I cannot forgive. I should have refused to leave . . . to let you and Katya be separated from the rest of the family."

She touched his arm. "Vanya . . . no. It was a nightmare—you know it was. People do strange things under such circumstances. He was left with an instant family who were all in danger. It could not have been easy for him."

47

"He was afraid." It was said with contempt.

"Who was not? Remember Katya—she was terrified and screaming." Having said it all before she turned away from him with "Life is not always the way we want it . . . or expected that it would be. If it cannot be changed we must accept what we have and be glad it is no worse. I like it here. We have a good life, you cannot deny."

He made no answer, but his expression showed her she had not won him over. She sat on the small chair by the wall and looked at him frankly. "Within the year we shall come of age. You will then be head of the family. All decisions will be yours to make."

He flung her a challenge. "What if I say we return to Russia?"

Her heart fluttered. "Then we shall go."

"What of all this?" He waved a hand to cover the expanse of the room.

"Uncle Misha will stay. He will fail without you . . . but he will stay."

"And Aunt Marie . . . what of her?"

"*Mily,* do not ask me," she begged. "She believes us her children now. What mother can abandon them without breaking herself?"

"*Our* mother." It was said with brutal bitterness that set her on her feet again with angry words.

"She could not abandon what had never been hers. They lived only for each other. When will you accept that? That she left us in order to die with him is something you cannot understand. Neither can I, but I accept it . . . and pray to God I never feel such love for any man. It would destroy me the way it did her."

He was full of immediate remorse and went to her, taking her hands. "Forgive me. I am so selfish . . . always concerned with what I should do. Yet it is you who hold the family together . . . yes, it is true. What should we all do without you?"

She regarded him with exasperated fondness. "So serious. Why do you not enjoy being young? So soon you will be twenty-one and the family will depend on you. Until then, make the most of your life here. Galerie Russe is a great achievement—everyone says so. In such a short time you have established a business of some merit, which will grow and gain distinction. We now have a fine home that is the envy of many; friends in plenty. Perhaps we are not as we were in Russia, but perhaps Russia did not want us that way."

He frowned. "Are you so sure Hong Kong wants us? The British make it plain that we are second-class residents."

"They regard us with suspicion because of our advancing army in China. It is the same with the French and Germans, to say nothing of the Americans who speak their own language. We are foreigners."

"So are they," he countered quickly.

She smiled. "Yes . . . but they built it. Does that not make it theirs?"

He shook his head in mock despair. "So much common sense in a girl so pretty. Does your heart ever rule your head, I wonder?"

She colored slightly, knowing it was at that very moment. At any time the others might join them, so she broached the topic that had brought her there with such determination.

"How are the arrangements for the exhibition? Have I interrupted your work on them?"

"Yes, and I am glad you did." He walked to his desk and sat on the corner of it, looking at her ruefully. "Uncle Misha is right once again. I have been forced to agree that the collection should be displayed in four rooms, after all. That is the only way to do it justice."

"Have the invitations all been sent?" She tried to make it casual.

"Most of them." He nodded toward a lacquered table on which were several piles of white gilt-edged cards. "If they all come Galerie Russe will be full to overflowing."

"Why should it not?" she demanded, her heart beating faster now. "Vanya Brusilov is a man of consequence."

Clouds passed over his face again. "I wonder, Nadia. Tell me, *rodnaya moya,* is there anything of the father in the son?"

What a question! But she could not answer in the way he hoped. "Very little. The man who is my dear brother has doubts of himself, and that will make him the greater of the two, in time."

49

He did not believe her. She knew he was disappointed, but their privacy was fortuitously broken by the entry of the family, all talking together, as usual. Nadia used the disturbance as cover while she edged toward the table in the corner. Suppose there were no blank cards upon it? With her eyes on Katya her left hand closed around a pile of them behind her back. A quick downward glance was enough. Heaven be praised! Just one she took and slipped it into her white net purse. All that she could do now was pray he would come.

"What are you doing in here?" asked Katya of her sister, at last. "It was because of you we came, yet you vanished when we got to the treasure room. You said there was a particular piece you just had to see."

"Yes, yes," beamed Uncle Misha, "I know what it is. The red hind I spoke of last night. I knew you would be excited about it."

"That is the one," agreed Nadia, loving him for giving her the way out. "Why else should I be so anxious to come?"

Ivan Brusilov was unhappy and worried. He had chosen to walk to the hotel so that he would have an excuse to leave the gallery earlier, yet he now regretted the decision. The smell of rotting vegetables mingled with that of burning joss sticks lodged in his nostrils, and the Chinese shouts and the hawking of passersby only increased the desperation he felt. It had begun slowly and deep down, growing more insistent until it seemed like a hysteria that would burst from him when the strength to hold it down failed him.

Sidestepping a legless beggar he went full-tilt into a barrow containing fruit. Some overripe mangoes fell to the ground in orange squashy lumps, and he threw a Russian oath in the direction of the peddler who looked at him with venom. From round a corner came a coolie carrying huge blocks of ice wrapped in sacking suspended from each end of a bamboo pole across his shoulders. The pole bounced up and down with the peculiar running gait used by such men, and water dripped from the ice across Ivan's shoes as he passed. It was only a little thing, but enough to make him stop at the street corner and try to take hold of himself.

How he hated the life he led! In his opinion, Hong Kong was dirty, a meeting place for outcasts of society and those who wished to make a fortune quickly. The hotchpotch of nationalities was too great to draw any good from each, yet seemed to highlight the bad only too well. The British rulers lived as they always did in their colonies, with themselves as infinitely superior, the native people childlike but devious, and all others as embarrassing intruders with designs on areas of land. It was intolerable that a Brusilov should be part of it. In Russia, the family was proud and respected; here, they were merely foreign merchants.

Sick at heart he continued his walk with slower steps. His father would never have abandoned his homeland; his mother had been a greater lady than any of these haughty-faced creatures living in mansions on the Peak. He acknowledged that his uncle and aunt had been left with the responsibility of three young people in a fearsome situation, but only a weak man would have run away so far and in such a panic. Aunt Marie cared only for the fact that she had a family of her own, at last; Katya had been so terrified it did not occur to her what a distance they were to travel; Nadia had, for once, seemed unsure of herself. We were both stunned, he told himself yet again, or we would never have agreed to it— never have turned our backs on our rightful inheritance.

Legal affairs had been complicated, since Boris Brusilov and his son had died on the same day and Catherine was still alive in Petersburg. Until Ivan could claim his small fortune there was a desperate need for money when they first arrived. Nobody had guessed Misha Zubov, genial, overweight, and prepared to live off the family into which he had married, would have had such flair for buying and selling jade. It had never occurred to the members of the family that he had spent so many of his indolent hours studying the Brusilov jade collection, and following up that study in books and museums.

All Ivan's pride had risen up at the suggestion of becoming a jade merchant, but it had risen higher at the thought of poverty. So Galerie Russe had been conceived. His own aptitude for business must surely have grown from spending much time with the family estate manager during his holidays, and Uncle Misha's artistic nature took care of that side of the business. They had succeeded and were respected by other businessmen in the colony, but Ivan burned with protest during every hour spent in his office, every day Galerie Russe continued, every time the British colonists spoke to him in their easy cordiality reserved for anyone unfortunate enough not to be as good as they.

When Katya provoked him he spoke bravely of going back when he was twenty-one, but that day just under a year hence stood in his mind as a testing time. As head of the family could he ever reach the strength and command shown by his father? Would it be better to stay as he was then risk failure in the eyes of his countrymen by going back?

His familiar procession of thoughts had so occupied him the hotel steps appeared before he was ready, and he had to collect himself for a moment or two before entering. The interior was hushed and dim after the street and smelled of damp ferns, polish, leather cabin trunks, and French perfume. He walked across the fan-cooled foyer, past the reception desk, and through the short corridor leading to the garden. There he should find the Portuguese rival who was selling up and returning to his mother country because of the death of his wife and small daughter in a riot in Macao. Waiting unobtrusively on one side should also be Ho Fatt, his comprador, who would act as interpreter between himself and the Portuguese.

The Chinaman had lived, until recent years, in Macao and spoke Portuguese as skillfully as he spoke English. He had appeared one day during the infancy of the gallery to offer his services, and Ivan had never regretted taking him on. Ambitious, competent, a linguist, he had greatly helped to make Galerie Russe what it was, yet Ivan knew no more about him than he had the first day. During working hours he was as westernized as it was necessary to be; at the end of the day he melted away into the inscrutability of the East.

The hotel garden was immensely green, almost cloistered by the great spread of curving palm branches. Ivan spotted the Portuguese at a table near a stone pedestal-bowl full of geraniums. The man rose at his approach, hand outstretched. Ivan gave a stiff bow, heels snapping together with precision, then looked around for Ho Fatt. There was no sign of the man, but Ivan's annoyance had no time to rise because his attention was taken by a small figure who materialized from between the trees.

She approached swiftly on tiny feet encased in black slippers and bowed low before him. "Mei-Leng, daughter of Chuan Ho Fatt," she said in delicate English. "My father offers a thousand apologies for his unforgivable absence. An illness of burning nature makes the ground impossible to walk on. He sends his most unworthy daughter to speak Portuguee if the Master wishes it."

Ivan was dumbfounded. He stood trying to size up the situation, staring at the girl who was still bent almost double. Then, conscious of the other man's slight amusement, he felt himself growing hot with embarrassment. He put out a hand beneath the girl's elbow, but she came up hesitantly keeping her eyes lowered even when standing erect.

Words were out of the question. The girl was exquisite, an echo from his past when Mongol entertainers had come from the eastern stretches of Russia traveling from town to town, visiting large summer estates in the country to perform their exciting songs and dances. As a boy he had admired and tried to imitate the men who leaped and stamped in their high boots; later it had been the women in their vivid costumes who had drawn his eyes in their dignity of movement and dark serene beauty. Now, in the middle of this place he hated, she had appeared to heighten the memory of those people of Russia.

He felt his eyes filling from the ache her beauty brought to his breast. The trousers were black, the high-collared tunic she wore was of palest yellow silken brocade, edged with black and fastened down the left of the tunic with beautifully worked frogging. In the coils of her black hair was a flower as creamy and perfect as her skin. He could not see her eyes for the lashes covered them, but they were slanted and wide-set like those oriental dancers of his homeland. She was submissive, petal-fresh, reticent. She could have been a princess.

How long he stood silent there was no way of telling. She would do nothing until he spoke, and he found it impossible. Only when the Portuguese said something in rapid irritation did Ivan manage to collect his wits and mumble his wish that she should assist him.

All through the business discussion Ivan had to fight the desire

53

to turn his head. It was tormenting to hear her clear high voice and be unable to see her, for she stood unobtrusively behind him, as befitted her station. Unable to concentrate, he brought matters to a swift conclusion, accepting a price that was generously high for the man's jade pieces. With his head in a spin he refused the man's offer of a drink to seal the bargain, rose, and bowed stiffly once more before wishing him good morning.

When he turned it was almost a relief to discover she really was as perfect as he had first thought, although her downcast eyes still prevented his seeing her as he wished to. The Portuguese was dismissed from his thoughts instantly.

"Thank you," he said with great courtesy. "You translate every bit as well as your father. I will tell him so."

She made no answer, just stood meekly before him looking the personification of dejection and misery. Thinking she had misunderstood his words he followed up quickly with, "You have done well. Ho Fatt has an excellent daughter."

To his great dismay and bewilderment a tear rolled down her cheek and her shoulders drooped even further. Glancing up he realized they were in a conspicuous place, and he drew her toward the overhanging palms which formed an arbor. She went unresistingly, but when he asked gently why she was crying she would not answer. His voice grew sharper. "You *will* answer me," he said. "Tell me what has made you so sad!"

His aggression did the trick, but the words smote him with their genuine grief.

"My honored father is disgraced. This unworthy daughter is not fit to live."

Shocked at such intensity on her part he could only stare helplessly. She had seemed happy enough at first. Why should she suddenly speak in such drastic fashion?

"Are you in trouble?" he asked wildly. "Can it be that your father is more ill than I understood?"

No response.

"Is Ho Fatt in trouble?" he probed. "The fever you mentioned—was that untrue?"

The tears were flowing faster, sliding down her cheeks to soak into the material of her jacket, and Ivan felt himself shaken by an emotion new to him. An unbearable urge to touch her, shake the girl, make her answer him, left him angry and imperious.

"Look at me. Answer when I speak to you!" he demanded in a loud tone.

As if by magic her head came up to look full at him for the first time, and the urge to touch her took a new, more exciting direction. Small perfect mouth in a face of eastern shape and line, jet-black eyes, slanted and softened by moistness set him struggling with himself not to put up a hand to caress away the tears making a silver runnel on each cheek.

"My father is disgraced in the eyes of his master by a wretched and worthless daughter who tries to copy his great knowledge of other tongues. No punishment is too great for such treachery."

Suddenly, it was Ivan who could not produce an answer. All he had heard about the Chinese began to make him understand what she was telling him, although it was as senseless to a westerner as many European customs were to the oriental mind. Daughters were counted as nothing in Chinese families, compared with the blessings of sons. Many were given away at birth, and in poor families they were either sold as little slaves to a richer family or drowned in order to leave food for the male mouths of a large household. Those who stayed with their parents worked hard for their keep and knew their place amongst their male betters.

This lovely young creature had been brought up in this belief. By complimenting her he had suggested that she had been boastful; by saying her knowledge of language was as good as her father's he had unwittingly made Ho Fatt "lose face" at the expense of his daughter. To a Chinese girl it was a disaster from which there was no escape. Her distress would be equivalent to that of his sister Nadia if it had been she who had betrayed their father to his murderers.

Somehow he had to save the situation and, aware that she could not go until he dismissed her, took his time working out the best way around it while she stood before him in an attitude that made it hard for him to remain silent. At last, he began a speech he hoped would be sufficiently unkind to satisfy her oriental mind.

"Mei-Leng, I am an important man in Hong Kong, respected by all those in influential circles. In consequence, my servants must be of the best. This Portuguese does not know of your father, Ho Fatt; he sees only that *you* come to serve me. Afterwards, it was necessary to pretend that I was pleased with you. If he should think I am not well served by those I employ I should lose face with him. My esteem would be lowered in his eyes." He paused, unwilling to go on. "Now he has gone I can say your father was right to send a thousand apologies with his daughter. Several thousand would be more fitting for the disappointment and trouble you have caused me."

It disturbed him to say such words to her, and it disturbed him more to see the smile of relief break out on her face. Castigation expunged the guilt like magic. Having striven for all of his twenty years in vain to gain his father's approbation, he thought it particularly cruel that this girl must be denied, on pain of eternal disgrace, ever seeking it. Even more he felt the longing to touch and console her.

Yet there was no longer any need for consolation. Happy that she was an unworthy replacement for her father, the tears had dried and she stood waiting for his next instructions. He could not bring himself to send her away just yet, but they could not continue standing in the hotel garden.

"I have to visit the Lap-Sun printing company," he told her quickly. "Will you guide me to that place?"

His breath caught in his throat as her glance came up to meet his for a brief tantalizing moment. "Anything the Master wishes."

She moved off in her little black slippers, and he followed with his mind and body in a ferment.

56

THREE

Galerie Russe was closed for business on the day Marcel Bris-
saud's priceless jade collection was on show to those who rated a
preview invitation. Ivan and Uncle Misha had disagreed over the
handling of the occasion, then compromised, as usual. Ivan,
striving endlessly for dignity, refused to allow the premises to be
turned into a pseudo-Chinese temple interior, with their atten-
dants dressed as mandarins, but Uncle Misha, thwarted in his
artistic exuberance, insisted that they should make some special
effort at impressing the guests who were amongst the most
influential in the colony. In the end, they charged Ho Fatt with
arranging tasteful floral decorations in oriental style and that,
plus champagne served on the mezzanine floor, was as far as Ivan
was prepared to go. He saw the event as something unsuitable to
the dignity of the family Brusilov, and no one would persuade
him otherwise.

It was, however, extremely important for business that it
should be a success, and Uncle Misha grew so agitated he
resorted to the bottle and woke up with a hangover on the
morning he most needed his wits about him. Aunt Marie scolded
gently and fussed around straightening his cravat and brushing

imaginary specks from his coat as if he were one of her children instead of her husband.

"Please . . . *please*," he begged in his soft poetic voice, "come with me now. You and my little flowers . . . do not wait until later . . . eh? Please."

"You are like a big bear . . . a dancing bear. So fierce you look—but only on the end of a chain," his wife told him in exasperated affection. Then she nodded. "We shall come with Papa."

Nadia watched them together and sighed. Both a little ineffective, they found strength in unity and the pretense that they guided their adopted family. What would become of them if Ivan took herself and Katya back to Russia next year . . . and what would her own future be if Andrew Stanton took up her invitation today?

She had no time to develop those thoughts further, for Katya protested she was nowhere near ready and rushed off to her room. Nadia followed, knowing the girl would deliberately force a delay if she could, so that their uncle would have to go on alone. It was typical of her young sister to create agitation for the pleasure of proving her knowledge of another's weaknesses.

As Nadia coaxed and insisted, she was most careful to lay emphasis on the importance of the day for all the family and for their future, being most careful to let drop no hint of her own feeling of facing destiny that day. Everything rested on the invitation she had secretly sent to Andrew Stanton. If he ignored it there was nothing more to be done with the memory of a butterfly afternoon. If he accepted. . . .

They did all accompany Uncle Misha very shortly afterward. Nadia was glad as the guests arrived promptly. Uncle Misha forgot his headache and nervousness in the pleasure of discussing jade in all its aspects to people who looked upon him as a dilettante; Ivan stood aloof letting visitors approach him instead of the other way around; Katya tried to copy him, but soon abandoned the pose when she found it did not suit her liking for impressing people. Aunt Marie fluttered around like a moth seeking an open window, and Nadia soon gave up her attempts to keep her company.

She stood for a while in a quiet alcove between two salons, watching those already in the gallery. There was no reason why Andrew Stanton should be amongst the first arrivals but, oh, the strain of uncertainty and the thud of her heart each time the door opened!

"Who is the special one who has not yet arrived?" asked Ivan softly in her ear, making her jump. He smiled. "You have been at such pains to appear uninterested in the swing of the door, it is all too plain to me you are expecting someone very particular. Confess, *sestrushka*."

For several seconds she tried to look indignant, then decided Ivan would see through her pose of innocence. He always read her mood correctly, as she did his. It was the penalty of twinship.

"You are remarkably lighthearted on an occasion you condemned as undignified and unnecessary," she countered, to avoid an answer. "Did I not see you chatting to Sir Hugh Featherly for longer than the three minutes you claimed you would allow any one visitor?"

To her surprise he frowned. "He is something of an authority on Chinese customs and beliefs. I found his remarks interesting." Then, as if coming back from a long distance, added in a lighter tone, "He has a brother in Burma who is something of an authority on jade. The British can be found in every corner of the world, it seems, and manage to be authorities on something or other. I have handed Sir Hugh over to Uncle Misha who will provide a more garrulous tongue for a receptive ear."

She shook her head in gentle impatience. "There is nothing disgraceful in a Brusilov discussing jade. Papa was proud of our fine pieces ... and Fabergé presents jade eggs to the Grand Duchesses each Easter. What could be more acceptable than that?"

Her brother answered with a touch of reflectiveness. "Papa *collected* jade; he did not sell it."

"You cannot compare our situation with Papa's," she reminded him shortly.

"No. Perhaps I have made that mistake for too long. The child should never try to equal the father."

It was such a strange remark for him to make Nadia was

59

certain she was frowning when Andrew Stanton stopped before them with a slight bow. Her heart sank. It was all wrong! She had had no time to prepare herself, and Ivan would surely guess he was the one for whom she had been waiting. Moreover, he would wonder how an invitation had been sent to someone he did not know. In something of a fluster she met Andrew's polite greeting with a rise of color and a quick nod.

"I am afraid the cloudburst put paid to my intention of making your acquaintance at the garden party, Mr. Brusilov," said Andrew easily. "I've been in Shanghai for the past few months, which is why I am a little out of touch with things in Hong Kong. It was good of you to invite me along today."

"Not at all," replied Ivan, stiffer than the relaxed Englishman. "Are you a collector, Mr. . . . ?"

He gave a rueful smile. "I confess myself a mine of noninformation on the subject. I was hoping you would enlighten me."

"I am sorry. Jade is the love of my uncle's life, not mine. I take it you are not in the business."

Nadia saw her long-awaited moment being trampled on by her brother's insensitive remarks.

"Mr. Stanton is with the Governor's staff," she said quickly, and turned to Andrew. "Forgive my brother. Housing such a valuable collection here is a great responsibility. Is it any wonder his mind is a little abstract today?"

"Very understandable," Andrew agreed with a nod. "But if all I hear is correct there is no better place in Hong Kong in which treasure of this nature should be housed. Your gallery has acquired something of a reputation, Mr. Brusilov."

"Indeed?" he answered in a tone that suggested Andrew had just insulted him.

Nadia was in despair. The speaking looks she had thrown her brother failed to impress themselves upon him. He was taking all Andrew's comments the wrong way, and growing more aloof by the minute. It was so important that they should like each other, it seemed imperative that she should part them before they did the reverse. She turned to Andrew and took the plunge.

"I cannot promise to make you an expert on the subject, Mr. Stanton, but my slight knowledge might serve as an introduction.

60

If you would care to accompany me I will show you the most interesting pieces in the exhibition." Heart thumping with the hope that he would follow, she began moving away from her brother toward the furthest room, a quick glance at Ivan showing her the dawning enlightenment in his eyes.

"I think we should start over here where there are some fine tablets," she told Andrew over her shoulder, praying she could avoid the remaining members of her family for as long as possible.

They made their way through the visitors until they reached the first case, where she began a short speech on the virtues of its contents.

"To really appreciate jade you should know that the Chinese regard it with great reverence. They believe it more precious than jewels, more valuable than gold, and. . . ."

". . . more beautiful than love," he finished for her.

No longer able to resist meeting his eyes she turned her face up to his. It had not been merely a garden illusion; he was the man she had been unable to forget—strong, yet with an indefinable suggestion of barricaded vulnerability.

"You see, Miss Brusilova, I do not know much about jade, but I have studied the culture of those among whom I have lived for the past few years."

"Of course," she murmured, thinking how incredibly blue his eyes looked against the brown of his skin.

"On the other hand," he continued, "there is much about the Russian people that remains a mystery to me. How is it that a man can send an invitation to another, yet have no idea who he is when he arrives?"

He knew what she had done! In that moment she realized what her action would suggest to him and took refuge in formality. Walking to the next case, she tried to remain in control of the situation she had created.

"Here are the most significant items in any jade collection. That one is Pi, representing the earth. Here is Ts'ung, heaven. Those arranged around them are the four symbols for the points of the compass."

"No," he said, so close behind her his mouth stirred the tendrils

61

that stood up from her piled hair. "There is nothing as simple as that to the Chinese. North, South, East, and West are deities who can control events and destinies." He came round to stand beside her. "As a person with a penchant for the romantic, that should appeal to you, Miss Brusilova." He studied the curve of her cheek and mouth for a long moment. "You look rather grand today. I almost didn't recognize you."

Knowing she had lost her control of the situation she could only remember a shaded grove on a hot afternoon. "You were rather grand that day, reading me a lecture about remaining in the roped-off area," she told him, forgetting the jade and well-dressed visitors around them.

"You must have thought me very pompous."

"No!" It was said too quickly, and her color rose. "How could I have done when you were so kind?"

He smiled, just faintly but enough to soften the rigid line of his jaw. "It's part of my job to rescue butterfly hunters in distress."

She was completely lost after the sweetness of his smile. "Is it written in your duties?"

The shake of his head was mock-tragic. "Alas, no. It happens so seldom we are expected to use our own initiative—that's what they called it in the army."

She was surprised. "You have been a soldier, Mr. Stanton?"

"For a few unforgettable years." His expression had grown bleak.

"My father was in the cavalry," she said to cover the moment.

"I know. It's a very tragic story."

"You know about my father?" The question was sharper than she intended.

"Hong Kong is a small colony, and there are a lot of people who haven't enough to occupy them," he explained with a trace of apology. "New arrivals always stimulate interest and speculation."

"Especially to someone like yourself—on the staff of the Governor?"

"I certainly am required to keep track of influential new colonists—especially those who are not British."

"That is part of your job also . . . to delve into the secrets of

62

their past?" Why did she feel angry with him?

"I . . . er . . . Miss Brusilova, I thought you were giving me a lesson on jade," he said firmly, putting a hand under her elbow. "Shouldn't we move on?"

"You do not make an attentive pupil, Mr. Stanton."

"My headmaster said the same thing," he murmured, nodding to a passing Portuguese. "I promise to read my catalogue from cover to cover this evening. Will that do?"

Suddenly, her interest in him shifted into a new plane. Not only was he a fascinating challenge, but a mystery to be unraveled.

"You have been in Hong Kong for some years, Mr. Stanton?" she asked.

"Nearly four."

"What did the colonists discover about you—the secrets in *your* past?"

It was more in Katya's style, she knew, but his reaction shook her out of the unfamiliar approach. The barricades hovering in his expression went up immediately, and his jaw tightened.

"My past is no more secret than yours. You may hear it from anyone in the colony—in four different versions, no doubt."

She put a hand on his sleeve in immediate regret. "I'm sorry. I am not normally so impertinent."

There was a quick deepening of the blue of his eyes as he struggled with himself. Then he smiled faintly. "And I am not normally so ungracious—at least, not with defenders of the blue butterfly."

"I am forgiven?" she asked, as breathless as at their first meeting.

"There is nothing to forgive. But I really think we should keep away from forbidden paths," he added with slight roughness deepening his voice. "They invariably lead to disaster."

Before she had time to absorb his words she was hailed and found the rest of her family approaching. In a turmoil of emotions she made the necessary introductions, cursing the circumstances that had sent them her way just at that moment.

Andrew handled the situation with easy competence.

"The exhibition is a great success, sir," he told Misha politely.

"This is surely the perfect setting for such beautiful pieces."

"Ah, but I would have made it *extra* perfect." He humped his shoulders up and down with emphasis. "My nephew has not an artistic soul, Mr. Stanton. He remains so unemotional."

Andrew smiled. "Just as well in business, surely? You make the perfect combination, which is borne out by the reputation you have acquired in so short a time."

Uncle Misha's head lolled from side to side, happy with such praise. *"Gospodi!* You have taken the words from my own tongue. Yes, indeed."

Aunt Marie was beaming, her face flushed with the pleasure of an occasion that allowed her to be seen with her children.

"I have always felt that beautiful things should not be shut away," she confided in her thick Russian accent. "It is like keeping children in a nursery when they should be running in the sunshine. Do you have children, sir?"

He shook his head briefly, and Nadia caught her breath. She had not considered that he might be married. "No, ma'am, I am a bachelor."

Katya was studying him with large bold eyes. "I have seen you before," she declared in her pert fashion. "I know I have."

"At the garden party, perhaps. I remember your hat covered with roses."

She flushed. "You should have been presented to us."

"I should have presented myself," he said easily, "but I was detained on important duty in the shrubbery. A crisis only I could handle," he added with a straight face.

Nadia felt her confusion deepen. By his reference to a meeting only she knew about he implied a bond he had just suggested they should ignore. It was as if he felt the same compulsion as she but was fighting it. Why?

"Your niece has been instructing me in the art of appreciation," Andrew was saying to Aunt Marie. "Where I have previously just liked what I have seen, she has been revealing the finer points of good jade. It is fascinating."

Uncle Misha's moustaches twitched and quivered, scenting a quarry. *"Ay, ay, ay,* dear sir, you do not tell me that a gentleman like yourself has little knowledge of jade?"

64

"Quite reprehensible, I agree, but I hope to put it right one of these days."

"One of these days! *One of these days!* My dear Mr. Stanton, that day has come. No, no, I cannot rest until . . . *gospodi!* . . . to think you. . . ." He tried to put an arm around Andrew's shoulders, found it was nearer his waist, and abandoned the Russian gesture. His face had grown pink with enthusiasm.

Nadia held her breath. He could be the instigator or trampler of her happiness. She prayed he would play into her hands.

"We have in our home a very fine collection of jade which we brought from Russia, Mr. Stanton," he boasted. "If you would but honor us with a visit . . . here is not the time nor place. We could take the whole evening—several evenings. The Brusilov jade is very fine," he ended, almost on a note of pleading.

"It is very kind of you, but I hardly like to trespass on your valuable time," Andrew told him, his attention seeming to be more on a group of people in the next room.

"What is time?" quoth the artist in full flow. "Value is reckoned in a man's mind, not on the clock face. Now, what do you say?"

Nadia breathed again as Andrew agreed to the visit, although with a disturbing hint of reluctance. Was Uncle Misha too pressing?

"Wonderful, wonderful! Mama, you must send an invitation to dinner very soon," he instructed his wife.

Aunt Marie was as excited as he. "A family evening! We shall make it a family evening in real Russian style, Mr. Stanton. There is nothing like having young people all together around the samovar."

Andrew smiled, instigated more by politeness than delight, Nadia thought. She began to worry. His interest had faded. She could not help noticing the way his eyes kept returning to the visitors in the next room. Had her family frightened him off with their eagerness? Why had he changed so suddenly in the midst of a happy group? In an attempt to coax him away from them she said in a formal voice, "I have not yet shown you the prize piece of the collection. The most remarkable carved vase in pale yellow. It is said to be almost impossible to put a value on it."

He turned almost dutifully to her. "Then I must not leave

without seeing it." He bowed to the other three and said politely, "It has been a pleasure meeting you."

Uncle Misha folded his arms around his vast stomach, well satisfied with himself. "Until we meet again very soon, my dear sir . . . eh?"

"Yes . . . until then." He held back to allow Nadia to go ahead of him, and something began to flutter deep inside her breast. He wanted to leave. Then, as if to shatter what remained of her pleasure, Katya declared her intention of going with them to see the vase and fell in beside them.

"I still cannot think where I have seen you before," she began.

"I was wandering about the grounds of Government House most of the afternoon, you know."

"No, it was before that. It is quite remarkable, because I feel that I know you well. Have you been to Russia, Mr. Stanton?"

"To my regret, no . . . and I was in Shanghai for the early part of this year. In any case, if we had met before I should certainly have remembered you, Miss Brusilova."

It was said with polite gallantry, but Katya took it as a deep personal compliment that she felt was her due. Her dark eyes flashed provocatively, and a smile curved her lips into an expression of breathless delight that was not lost on Andrew, judging by the smile he gave her.

"Then, you must remind me of someone else," declared the girl. "It is the only explanation."

They saw the vase, but even that seemed less beautiful to Nadia now that Katya was taking Andrew's full attention. Their earlier rapport had gone. He was abstracted and formal, and she had not realized just how beautiful Katya could be when excited. Even so, the girl did not manage to persuade Andrew to accept the offer of champagne, and he made to leave soon after.

"Goodbye," he said to Katya. "It has been most interesting."

But the girl's interest was caught by two people across the room.

"There are Sir Goodwin and Lady Halder, Mr. Stanton. They have been trying to catch your attention for some time. Do you know them?"

"My aunt and uncle," he replied shortly.

Katya was impressed. "Your . . . I did not know. I think they wish to speak to you."

"I am afraid it will have to wait until tonight. I am rather pressed for time right now."

The girl laughed seductively. "Are you trying to avoid them?"

"Something like that," he admitted. "Although I do have an appointment for luncheon. Please excuse me."

"Very well," she told him as if granting a royal boon.

But Nadia had a last precious moment that deepened her perplexity. He bowed and looked right into her eyes with an echo of his earlier mood. "Thank your brother for his kind invitation, Miss Brusilova, and please tell him I have seldom enjoyed a morning so much."

When he had left Katya was agog. "I suppose the Halders are quite important. Is he in direct line of inheritance, do you think?"

"I really have no idea," replied Nadia.

"You appeared on remarkably friendly terms with him," said Katya. "How is it you have met and I have not?"

She lied easily. "Vanya introduced us."

"Mmm, the nephew of Sir Goodwin Halder! Do you suppose he has been on some diplomatic mission and passed through Russia at some time? The Crimea, perhaps . . . or could it be Finland?"

Nadia spoke with only half her mind on the conversation. "No, he was in the army before."

"That's it!" cried Katya excitedly. "That is where I have seen him before. I remember him quite clearly in a uniform of green with yellow facings."

Nadia was more than usually irritated with her sister. "That is a Russian uniform, Katya. I should think it rather more likely that Mr. Stanton was in the British army," she said tartly.

The girl fell silent for a moment, looking intently at her sister. "Well, I suppose it must have been a young officer in Papa's regiment that I remember—someone who tried to flirt with me." Another pause. "He is very attractive."

Nadia kept her lips firmly together and walked on.

"Do you find him attractive, Nadia?"

"I expect there is hardly a female in Hong Kong who does

not," said Nadia coolly. To herself she added, *and his luncheon appointment must be halfway across China if he has to set out at ten-thirty in order to get there.*

Ivan watched Ho Fatt over the top of a ledger he was supposed to be inspecting. The Chinese used characteristic unhurriedness as he moved among the small boxes being unpacked by the coolies. A consignment of jade had arrived from China that morning from an exporter in Peking, and the best pieces would be selected by Galerie Russe before selling the remainder to small dealers and curio stores in Victoria and Kowloon. Uncle Misha should have been there to make his choice, but it would have to be delayed a day. Yesterday's preview had taken its toll of him and kept him in bed with an ice pack on his head.

Ivan had no great urge to see what the crates contained. He trusted Ho Fatt to make a good deal, and there was no point in employing a comprador who could not do so. But there was another urge within him that kept him away from the unpacking area. For days he had fought against it, but it had mastered him in the end. He felt the shame of acknowledging his own weakness, yet was excited by it.

Before long he would be head of a noble family. All his life he had known it would come someday; tragedy had seen to it that it was sooner than expected. The Brusilov men were known for their strength, courage, honor, and virility. In the normal way he would have tested his manhood before becoming a cadet in the officers' school—it was an unwritten qualification for entry—and there were peasant girls galore on the Brusilov estates. His had not been a traditional life, and events had seen to it that it was interrupted before that very necessary experience had been his. Hong Kong was not a Russian summer estate, but he was twenty now—a man in name only. It was these facts that he blamed for his present state, but knowing the cause did not ease the desire. He was haunted by a petal-smooth face, downcast almond-shaped eyes, and dainty submissiveness. The longing for his homeland centered itself on her: She treated him with the respect those in Brusilov service had done. He burned as if with fever. Somehow, he must see her again.

68

An altercation broke out by the packing cases. Ho Fatt was gesticulating and speaking in angry tones to a young coolie who nodded now and again to show his agreement. Nearby another coolie was gathering together a quantity of shavings he had spilled from one of the cases accidentally overturned during unpacking. The remaining contents, a snuffbox and several fans, were safely cushioned from damage. Ivan watched for a while, wondering why his comprador ignored the clumsy man in his great conversation with the other.

At length, the Chinaman walked over to his employer. He halted before the table, a small figure in a long gray tunic and black round hat. A bow preceded his words.

"Many pardons for such carelessness, sir. The jade is unharmed, and I have dismissed the man."

Ivan frowned. "You have censured the wrong man. There is the culprit."

Ho Fatt bowed again. "Quite so, sir. I have told his companion that the Master does not tolerate servants who are not worthy of his name, and would send away in disgrace any of that description. I also told him that I, Ho Fatt, would be humbled in the eyes of the Master if the work was less than of the greatest perfection, and would not wish again to set eyes on any man who so humbled me." Ivan could not tell if he was angry or apologetic. His tongue was left to tell what expression did not, but even then it was difficult to discover his true feelings. "The unworthy one will not come again, sir."

"Because of a hint to a companion?" It seemed a little vague to Ivan. "Are you certain? Should you not dismiss him directly?"

Ho Fatt looked neither resigned nor abashed. He was supremely negative. "It is necessary to explain to you, sir, the custom of Chinese people. If I chastise a man before another who is younger or of lesser consequence he loses face, but if I tell another man in his hearing that I would be displeased or upset if he acted in such a manner, then the guilty one knows of my displeasure and makes amends. He will not come again, sir."

Ivan shook his head. "It is a good thing you are here for such things. I find it very confusing."

The Chinaman bowed again. "Not confusing, sir. Chinese

customs make life very simple. Civilization makes rules—men not break rules."

Ivan privately thought his philosophy rather too simple to work, but marveled again at the great dependency on "saving face" that ruled these people. Such thoughts naturally brought him back to those that governed him lately, and his pulse began to thud.

"I am interested in your civilization, Ho Fatt. My family all expressed a great desire to see the temple of Kwan Yin. They have heard there is to be a celebration in honor of the goddess on Tuesday next." It all came out as he had rehearsed it. "Is it possible to see this?"

There could have been the faintest shadow across the comprador's face, but Ivan was too tense on his own account to ponder it.

"The celebration you speak of is performed in many temples, sir. Kwan Yin is widely worshiped."

Knowing he must not lose his chance Ivan tried to prise the information he wanted without arousing suspicion. "My sisters . . . would they be permitted at the temple?"

"It is a festival celebrated mainly by women, sir. Kwan Yin is the Goddess of Mercy."

Ivan felt he was getting nowhere. Ho Fatt was answering without telling him what he really wanted to know.

"Does that mean men do not attend? Shall you not wish to go to the temple that day?"

Ho Fatt still stared back with tranquillity written all over his sallow face, but the eyes as black as the small round hat he wore filled with momentary fire before turning mild once again.

"My daughter will take chickens and a roast pig to the temple early and remain there until nightfall. I shall offer my thanks to Kwan Yin when she returns. One has need of great mercy during the hours of darkness. It is said that a sleeping man is the prey of all evil."

It was one of those inexplicable comments Ho Fatt used frequently. Ivan suspected they were designed to put an end to conversation. The Chinese was a strange uncomfortable person, but he worked with such devotion and skill they could not have

70

run the business without him. His manner was always respectful, and if there were times when it seemed there might be a murmuring volcano beneath the gray silk of his tunic, Ivan put it down to the pagan blood that ran in his veins.

This day he was less concerned with the man's inner self than his own. Mei-Leng had told him she would be busy at the temple of Kwan Yin, and he had wanted to know where he might find her that day. She would be alone—without her father—and all he must do was discover the temple that lay nearest the village in which she lived. Kwan Yin would be merciful indeed if he found her there.

The smell of paint was still too strong for comfort, but Andrew had been so anxious to move in he was not prepared to wait for another two days. The men had finished placing his furniture ten minutes ago and departed. At last, he was master in his own house.

He wandered from room to room, footsteps ringing on the stone mosaic floor in irregular bursts between rugs. He gazed at his retreat as he went. A retreat it might be, but he liked to think of it as an advance even though the white stone house built on the lower slopes of a hill running down to a tiny bay could only be described as a secluded hideaway for a man who wished to get away from it all. It was basically true in his case, but a man could get away in order to get *to* something else, surely? That was what he had done.

As he looked at the white walls, sharply colored rugs, and dark carved furniture, he threw off a few of his shackles. In a place like this he could entertain those with whom he really wished to spend an evening, stretch out in loose pajamas with a book and a brandy and soda, or listen on his prized gramophone to the dramatic and sensitive renderings of poetry and prose by England's leading actors—words that had sent Cissie into one of her peals of insincere laughter when he had read them to her.

Walking through the airy rooms and onto the graded terrace from which steps ran down to the beach, he felt complete freedom. It was midafternoon and the stillness was like a drug, softening his senses, dulling the unpleasant in order to heighten

71

the aesthetic. He took a deep breath. He could have taken to opium—he had seen many poor devils who had—and believed it the answer to everything, which it was for a while. He had been tempted many times. It would have been so easy for someone in his position, for the Triad gangs gladly bribed officials with any amount of the drug in return for a blind eye to their activities. It would have been just as easy to take the other drug—women. Prostitutes abounded in the colony, mostly owned by those same gangsters. But he had preferred to fight his guilt and despair his own way, and Aunt Maude and her husband had been wonderful props. Now, they would not see that he no longer needed help.

He gazed out to sea. The bay curved in a half-moon shape with sand providing a pale edging between the beauty of the sea and the splendor of rock-scarred slopes. A small fishing village clustered below. Joss sticks and fried rice, he thought ruefully, just to remind me that this is not paradise. Fishermen's nets crisscrossed on the sand; children ran with hop-skip-jump actions, their pi-dog shadows behind them; the women gossiped as they sat cross-legged beneath enormous basket hats. Out to sea several junks with brown sails bellying in the breeze moved toward Hong Kong harbor, whole families living amidst the cargo year in, year out.

A soft footfall interrupted his thoughts, and he turned to find his houseboy, Kim, a young Christian Chinese who had been passed on to him by an old army acquaintance who had been stationed in Hong Kong until recently. The relationship promised to be rewarding, for Kim had inherited the happy-go-lucky charm of his race combined with their ability to keep a house spick and span. His smooth round face beamed as if he had just heard a joke.

"It is four o'clock. Time for the making of tea, I should hazard a guess, if it is all right by you," he said in phrases picked up from a succession of army officer employers. "Would it be jolly on the terrace, sir?"

Andrew grinned broadly. "Exceedingly jolly."

"For just one, sir, or are there other fellows dropping by later?"

"Just one, Kim."

"Right-o. I make it chop-chop," he assured Andrew, and went

off in happy style, jaunty feet splayed as he went.

Andrew let his glance travel over the beautiful lonely vista and sighed with contentment once more. After the correctness of his uncle's mansion this place was perfect . . . and Kim's Anglo-Chinese personality was part of it. It was in a mood of almost boyish defiance that he threw aside his jacket, and rolled up his shirt sleeves while he relaxed in a cane chair to drink his tea.

"My God, what a view," he breathed, then gave a short laugh as he imagined the expressions of his aunt and uncle if they could see this house built for a Javanese painter, who had recently committed suicide in a fit of artistic depression. There was not all humor in his laugh, for he still felt the strain of his departure from their house.

Unfortunately their personal differences seemed to be affecting their professional relationship. There had always been slight discord between them. Sir Goodwin, who was one of the upright pillars of the Empire, would willingly die for his principles and those of his country, but tended to apply long-standing solutions to problems that required deeper insight. Andrew had fought under men like his uncle and suffered the punishment of using age-old methods against an enemy who did not. The experience had made him aware of wider issues his inflexible senior blindly ignored. The two men had clashed more than once over incidents peculiar to that part of the world. Andrew had learned the language and studied the culture of the people he helped to govern; Sir Goodwin remained the lofty administrator.

Only that morning their differences had been apparent. Andrew had been called into his uncle's office to discuss the Kowloon-Canton railway that was still having teething troubles. The British section that ran through the New Territories was pushing a tunnel through the hills, but coolies had stopped work because of *fung shui*, a common problem met with by construction men.

It needed only the slightest mishap or a storm at a crucial time to persuade the Chinese that the *fung shui* was wrong, and they would put down tools and refuse to continue until advice was sought. It was infuriating to western engineers who had done extensive work on siting their projects, but without coolies

73

completion was out of the question. Many highly qualified men had been forced to grit their teeth and draw up new plans that would not offend the gods, dragons, or mythical beasts who had shown anger at the way the building had been progressing, simply on the word of a *fung shui* man hired to consult with mystical forces.

On the subject of the railway Sir Goodwin had been out of patience. "Those damn coolies have been put up to it, Andrew. The revolutionary elements in Canton are not averse to using any means to undermine our authority here."

"Oh, surely, sir," he had replied, "the average coolie has no understanding of political undercurrents."

"Has he not!" snapped Sir Goodwin. "He will understand anything if it means meat with his rice, or an extra pipe of opium. That tunnel is halfway finished. At this stage it would be excessively difficult—dangerous even—to reroute the excavations. What's more, it would add thousands of dollars to the cost."

Andrew had given a faint smile. "It is the last that is causing the greatest protest, I imagine."

His uncle had glared. "Please, do not be flippant, Andrew."

"Sorry, sir."

"Hmm . . . yes . . . well, I am sending you over there to deal with it."

"Me, sir? I should imagine Crossland is well able to cope with the situation. He has been out here for ten years and is familiar with the *fung shui* problem."

"Yes, yes, he has dealt with these crafty devils on many occasions. His big failing is that he is so damned slow-winded. Time is money on this railway link with Canton. It is of the utmost importance to our influence in the Far East." He had fixed Andrew with a penetrating glare as he leaned back in his chair. "The French and Russians—to say nothing of the Americans—have their eyes on China, and even the Germans are gaining a firmer foothold here in commerce and industry. You do realize what it will mean if any of those nations wins the tussle for China?"

"Of course." His reply had been indignant. "Whoever controls China commands the Far East."

"Quite . . . and since the Franco-Russian alliance ten years ago it has been more than ever important to protect our hold on Chinese influence if peace is to be preserved. Those two powers arm-in-arm suggest formidable opposition. They have been our traditional enemies too often to feel relaxed in their present amiability. They need watching—very careful watching."

"Yes, sir," Andrew had agreed patiently, "but international politics are not really our direct concern. We have quite enough to handle on internal law and order without getting involved in multipowered machinations in Peking."

"Yes, yes, but when revolutionary elements start rousing the populace it does concern us. This trouble on the railways is an offshoot of such activities."

"*Fung shui* is as old as Confucious," protested Andrew with a trace of amusement. "You are not suggesting that dragons are now joining the Chinese Revolutionary League under Sun Yat-sen?"

Sir Goodwin, seeing no humor in the words, snapped, "That remark is typical of you, Andrew. You never take responsibility with the seriousness it requires. There happens to have been an abortive uprising in Kwangtung, and the Viceroy claims the ringleaders crossed the border into the New Territories, where they are sheltering under our protection. I think you will agree that is no lighthearted matter . . . and if that does not convince you of the seriousness of my words, perhaps this will. In the shacks housing the coolies working on the railway, Crossland discovered revolutionary leaflets that had been printed in Japan and brought across to the colony. From here they are being smuggled into China and finding their way into every town and village. You see the position in which it places us?"

"Good God, yes. This is our direct concern."

Sir Goodwin had leaned back with smug satisfaction. "As I said ten minutes ago."

"I have had extra police boats out since the *Diable* foundered. Men have been boarding all vessels from Japan, but found nothing. How in heaven's name are they bringing the stuff in?"

Andrew thought about the problem again as he drank his tea that afternoon. Away from his uncle's disapproving approach it

75

was easier to keep a clear train of thought on the subject. It was one hell of a problem—the whole future of China was one hell of a problem—and his own country's stand was a precarious one.

For over a century the British had fought with words and guns to establish a permanent presence in the East, not only for trading purposes, but because military and naval bases in that part of the world were essential for the protection of the Empire. They had made no attempt to add China to it—the country was too vast and the people too hostile—but Hong Kong had been ceded to Britain in 1841, and Kowloon plus the large area inland from it had been added to the colony some seven years ago. Three short and savage wars in alliance with France had gained the two western nations direct access to the Celestial Throne in Peking, and the Americans, Germans, Russians, Italians, and Japanese also staked their claim to diplomatic recognition.

With such a vast underdeveloped land lying helplessly before their eyes all the nations found the prospect for advancement irresistible, and a complicated jostle for supremacy had begun. At the turn of the century the Boxers had staged a rebellion designed to drive out all foreigners—including their Manchu rulers, if possible—but they were like a rat against a unity of dragons.

One drastic outcome of the rebellion was that the Russians had taken massive reprisals for the slaughter of their own subjects by the Boxers in Manchuria, and attempted to take the whole area under the Czar's rule. Britain had allied with Japan to prevent this and had supported the Japanese in their war with Russia that had ended but a few months ago. In the present scramble for settlements under the peace treaty, every other major nation stood ready to pounce, ostensibly to protect the Chinese Empire, but mainly to ensure no one nation took a bigger bite than another.

It was in that role that Britain was pledged to oppose any revolution within the land that lay ripe for despoilation. The dynasty was dying and in its death throes seeking to survive by devising reforms to keep the encircling powers happily slumbering. But this blatant pandering to the hated foreigners put the seal on the Manchu fate. The threat of revolution was now a real one, and every nation with interests in China knew that the end of the dynasty meant the end of their hopes. When the Chinese people rose as one it would be to take their country for themselves.

Knowing the importance of the China trade to his own country's economy, and the need for a military base between India and Australia, Andrew strongly supported the policy dictated by London, but he opposed the revolution for other reasons his uncle would probably not consider.

For centuries the Chinese people had suffered under the yoke of warlords; beneath the Manchu rulers they had been reduced to subordinate citizens in their own country. The Boxers, in the name of "China for the Chinese," had slaughtered thousands of their own number who had taken the Christian religion, and whoever rose next in national fervor would see the need to massacre even more in the name of their cause. The long-suffering simple citizens of the Celestial Empire would be the victims yet again. A revolution was dearly bought with the lives of those who did not even know why they had to die.

The same thing was happening in Russia. Deep-rooted fear, a sudden mistaken command, and hundreds were dead outside the Winter Palace. And families like the Brusilovs were forced to run for their lives. Revolution was invariably a bloody business!

Andrew gave a sigh as his thought pattern led him to Nadia Brusilova, and to the reasons for taking this house above the bay. After the day of the jade exhibition Sir Goodwin had made a point of repeating his disapproval of the Russian family and the length of time his nephew had spent with the elder girl. Unsure of his own feelings, yet knowing he would take up the invitation offered by Misha Zubov, Andrew felt it was time he found a place of his own where he could live without accounting for his activities to his relatives who were supposed to be "keeping an eye" on him.

The Halders had taken his decision badly and forced him to resort to bluntness that further persuaded them he was about to go off the rails again. Every time he had a brandy and soda they looked at each other as though he had downed a whole bottle, and when he returned after a night out they looked up as if he

77

was about to announce that he had married a Portuguese belly dancer. He had moved into a hotel for a week until this house was ready, a move that earned condemnation for creating a situation designed to arouse gossip amongst the Halders' friends and the colony in general. Altogether, it had been an uncomfortable period, happily ended that day.

Still Andrew frowned into his teacup and returned to thoughts of that morning's interview with his uncle. After the main subject had been thrashed out and his plans made for the trip to the railhead where the revolutionary pamphlets had been found, Sir Goodwin had deftly approached his other talking point.

"I had luncheon with Orlov yesterday. He has always been a man to beware. Full of Russian bonhomie and Slavic expansiveness, but I don't trust him—don't trust him, at all. He was sounding me out about the trouble on the railway."

"As you sounded him out about the Trans-Siberian. No *fung shui* problems there, I'll wager."

"No." The clipped voice had grown abstract as Sir Goodwin changed from official to personal matters. "He tells me you are a frequent visitor to the Brusilov house."

"Not *frequent,* exactly," Andrew had told him, suddenly wary. "Old Zubov invited me to see his jade collection. I have been a couple of times."

"Do you think it wise?"

"I think it is natural to visit someone I like. He is a cultured man. We discuss literature and the arts in general. The old boy knows what he is talking about on those subjects."

"Mmm! I am surprised you are so welcome. Since we backed Japan in the war last year the Russians are cooler toward us. I noticed the change in Orlov."

"Young Brusilov finds it difficult to be more than icily polite to me, but the remainder of the family treat me as a friend. I find them charming, and refreshing among so many protocol-conscious colonists."

"That's as may be . . . but Orlov is not particularly happy about it, and I have heard comments from our people. Official and diplomatic contact with Russians is fine, but men in your position do not make friends of them. You must see what construction can be put upon it by both sides. I believe your aunt and I warned you of foodhardiness connected with that family."

Andrew had felt himself growing angry. "A friendly conversation is hardly foolhardiness, neither does it make me a diplomatic risk. I cannot see why there should be such consternation from all sides."

Sir Goodwin had attacked in another direction. "What about the elder Miss Brusilova?"

"I . . . find her cultured and very intelligent."

"Oh, come now, Andrew, I know your weakness for a pretty face." Sir Goodwin had drummed his fingers on the desk nervously. "At the garden party you emerged from the shrubbery with the girl on your arm looking flushed and abashed. At their gallery you caused conjecture amongst the guests over the warmth of your manner toward the young woman. Your aunt and I saw for ourselves that you were conducting an open flirtation with her. You deliberately avoided us and slipped away in the most furtive manner. I would call that foolhardiness of a serious nature, my boy."

"I really fail to see why." He had been deliberately provoking.

"Think of the consequences, for heaven's sake. You cannot take a young woman like Miss Brusilova as a mistress."

"I have no intention of taking anyone as a mistress," he had replied hotly, "least of all Miss Brusilova. She comes from a highly respected aristocratic family."

"Just my point . . . and Orlov's. Any association with her must be strictly honorable."

"Are you suggesting mine is not?" he had snapped out.

"I am suggesting that you remember she is Russian and, therefore, out of the question in matrimonial terms."

"By God, all I have done is visit her family several times . . . at *their* invitation, I might add."

"Do you deny that your main reason for going is to see that young woman?"

"I think it is no affair of yours who I go to see," he had said ill-advisedly, for he walked straight into the trap set for him.

"That is where you are wrong—it is very much my affair. As your superior I am entitled—no, compelled—to issue a serious

79

warning. If you value your career you must obey the rules. Members of the Crown's administration earn their promotion according to their observance of what is expected of them, apart from natural ability. I used my influence to get you this post, but I admit that you are excellent for the job. You have a fine future ahead of you in Hong Kong, and the chance to compensate your parents for your earlier mistake. If you continue with this liaison I shall wash my hands of you . . . and do not be surprised if the department does the same."

Sitting in his chair on a peaceful terrace overlooking the bay, remembering that conversation, Andrew had to admit the justice, if not the truth of their suspicions. By their rigid standards he was showing all the signs of irresponsibility once more. This house was isolated and dramatic, hanging on the edge of a bay from which a depressed man had just drowned himself. To their minds, breaking away from established respectability was the first sign of slipping the traces that led to downfall. Isolation led to introspection . . . and that could lead to heavy drinking.

He thought back on those months with Cissie, and still felt the despair. No, he would never revert to that phase in his life but, in this house away from those who had helped him through a terrible period in his life, he would have to come to terms with his future. To pursue Nadia Brusilova was playing with fire, but he was strongly drawn to the flames.

FOUR

A week after moving into his new home Andrew set out for the house on midlevels to take dinner with the Brusilovs. The house was grand, even by his uncle's standards, and furnished with extreme formality at great expense. It echoed their pride and background, yet there was one room that bore the stamp of family life against a background of sofas, scattered occasional tables, and enormous leafy plants that moved in the stir of air created by an overhead fan.

The overstuffed sofas generated heat that made Andrew's shirt stick to his back, he found the tables extremely hazardous to the pleasure of stretching his long legs, and the dank overflow of ferns suggested a jungle clearing, but it was in this room that he found his greatest pleasure. These people, he discovered, were true intellectuals, lovers of the arts, and great conversationalists. Only Aunt Marie remained apart, happy to sit in her family circle and preside over the samovar. Andrew discovered that Misha Zubov really did have knowledge of jade and the ability to transfer his own enthusiasm to another. That he was something of a poet was debatable, but his familiarity with literature in

Russian, French, and English instigated many a lively conversation with his English guest.

Ivan was also well read and intelligent, but Andrew thought it a pity he lacked the ability to bend from his rigid standards or accept others who did not conform to them. He made very little secret of the fact that he did not approve of Andrew, either as a person or as an Englishman. Luckily, although strictly the owner of the house, his youth made him indecisive enough to allow his uncle and aunt to behave as host and hostess.

It was during those happy argumentative evenings that he grew close to Nadia. Being with her in a relaxed and natural atmosphere had shown him a girl who had, as he had guessed, all the qualities lacking in Cissie. She was loyal and devoted, the cornerstone of her family, with a depth of perception unusual in a young girl. She could be sad with an echo of the tragedy behind her, or laughing and witty when she teased her brother. But the teasing was warm with affection, never cruel as Cissie's had been, and in all she did there was the indefinable air of breeding. Perhaps his feelings were heightened by the fact that they were never alone. Aunt Marie's fantasy of family life ensured they all remained in a loving group, and no one seemed aware of the throbbing tension between Nadia and himself.

That evening she was in a dress of yellow-bronze that lay against her breast in deep scallops and encircled her shoulders with enticing modesty. The skirt was drawn back into fashionable fullness that fell in godets beneath an enormous bow of bronze gauze, and the bodice clung tightly to a waist so slender he was filled with an immediate urge to feel the curve of her body beneath his hands.

"It is kind of you to come so far to visit us," she said, blushing. "Now that you live on the other side of the island, I suppose you have to make a voyage to Victoria when you receive an invitation from your friends."

He laughed softly, knowing he was being teased and enjoying the intimacy it brought. "I will admit my house is off the beaten track. . . ." He put out his hands in a mock gesture of surrender at her provocative smile. ". . . All right, isolated in an unfashionable and scarcely accessible part of the island, and I daresay I am now considered an eccentric . . . but I assure you there is a road from Victoria to my house—primitive, but a road, nevertheless." He smiled again. "However, using a boat for the journey isn't a bad idea. Think how novel it would be to greet my guests on the beach. I could arrange to have red carpet stretching from a jetty to the steps of my house."

"You cannot be serious, Mr. Stanton," said Ivan stiffly.

"Perfectly serious," replied Andrew, unable to resist the temptation of baiting the young Russian.

"But the ladies . . . one could not expect them to—"

"Oh, Vanya," said Nadia with deliberate interruption, and a glowing look at Andrew that said volumes. "Do you remember the *dacha* beside the lake that we went to as children? When Mama and Papa held a party their guests came across on boats decorated with flowers."

"How long ago," said the boy now grown. "I can see them now—ladies in white dresses sitting on log seats, and gentlemen in pale suits smoking their cigars and talking endlessly beneath the trees." He closed his eyes momentarily while he relived the memory, then smiled at his twin sister. "There was a group of musicians on a raft whom Papa had hired to play during the afternoon. The wind sprang up, and the raft began to sink. They all had to be pulled from the water, spluttering and holding their instruments above their heads."

Brother and sister laughed, and Misha chuckled good-naturedly, but Andrew noticed the bleak look that had settled on Aunt Marie's face. It was always the same when the young people spoke of their youth with their parents. To cover the moment he said, "I can remember a boating party on the Thames when two of my friends tried to serenade their partners with a tune on their banjos and forgot to see where they were heading. The boat went aground and they were rescued two hours later in the midst of a summer storm. The young ladies refused to speak to them again."

Everyone laughed and Nadia said, "We are not so different really, are we?"

Was it an appeal, an example set before him to bring him closer together? It did the opposite, in reminding him of their differences and the dangers of growing too close to this girl. All the same, a moment of unbearable contact hung between them until it was broken by Aunt Marie urging them all to go into the dining room for the meal.

Andrew looked around him and asked where Katya was that evening.

"A little headache as a result of the sun," he was told by the fond foster mother. "I have tucked her into bed and given her a posset."

Nadia smiled at him as they took their seats at the table, and he thought immediately how right it seemed to have her opposite him. "My sister was sad to miss your visit. I think she enjoys sharpening her wits against yours."

"Ah," he said in sudden recollection, "I have brought with me that ancient Chinese puzzle I promised to show her. I was on the mainland during the week and saw one on a stall. That will sharpen her wits more than any words of mine." He smiled. "People have been known to go to Bedlam trying to find the solution to it."

"And you?" prompted Nadia challengingly. "Are we to assume you solved it with no difficulty?"

"I wish you would . . . but I have to confess I gave up before I went completely mad."

They laughed, and the meal began with a spicy soup which was followed by a dish of seasoned fish covered with a thick cabbage sauce. Andrew had viewed it with suspicion on the first occasion, but it proved to be very tasty and he began on it this time with relish.

"I might find a boat very handy," he said, reverting to the original subject of his new home. "The journey is long, so I find the only solution is to take home much of my office paperwork. There is a snag to which I have not yet thought of a solution. Kim is first class, but I can hardly expect him to take on the duties of office assistant, also. I have a cook, a wash-amah, two gardeners, and a groom. What I really need is someone with intelligence who can keep my study tidy without throwing away important papers."

The conversation ran on about servants in general for several minutes, and Andrew was about to ask them if the recent outbreak of cholera had affected the coolies at Galerie Russe when Ivan broke his period of silence.

"Perhaps I might help with your problem, Mr. Stanton."

"Problem?" repeated Andrew, at a loss.

"Someone to assist with your work."

"Oh, really . . . do you know of such a man?"

Ivan looked very uncomfortable as he said, "Not a man. The daughter of my comprador speaks English and Portuguese very well. She could deal with your books and papers easily enough once they were explained to her."

Andrew considered the idea. A Chinese woman in such a capacity? "I think it might involve a few snags. Has she a family?"

"Only her father. She is very young."

"Mm . . . I suppose. . . ."

"They live near your house, as it happens, so there would be no need to provide accommodation." He was watching Andrew with surprising sharpness. "I could easily speak to her father on your behalf."

Andrew frowned, not because of the proposition, but the way the young man had paled since broaching the subject. Did the comprador hold too much sway in that business? Young Brusilov was an unwilling merchant who might have allowed the Chinese too much authority, and now found himself unable to curb him. Brushing it aside as none of his affair, he said politely, "It might be a good arrangement if the girl fitted the bill . . . but I think I should have to meet her before I made any decision. Go ahead and speak to the father, if you like. We'll take it from there."

The evening followed its usual pattern except that Andrew declared that he must leave earlier than usual because of his long journey home. They settled in the family room while Aunt Marie slipped upstairs to see her youngest, and Nadia poured tea from the samovar.

"Do you not feel lonely living in such a place alone, Mr. Stanton?" she asked him.

"Very often . . . but it is better than being surrounded by people who have no conception of the realities of life" was the answer that surprised him, for he had not intended saying such words.

85

She took him up on it. "Your uncle and aunt were like that?"

"I . . . ." He wished the subject had not been raised. What could he say now to cover up his hasty comment? He looked across at her sweet face and recalled her saying: *There is always a downpour to spoil every perfect moment.* He wanted to tell her that there in her home surrounded by her family he felt a real person as he had never felt with his aunt and uncle. But that would be fatal. Suddenly, he knew he must leave and put her and her family out of his mind.

"I . . . enjoy living alone, Nadezhda Andreyevna," he told her in an impersonal tone. "My work takes me away a lot, and demands my presence at any hour of the day or night. I have an ideal arrangement, because I am free to come and go without upsetting the plans of other people, or feeling that I must hurry back for their sake. It might be out of the way, but my new home is an ideal bachelor establishment."

It hurt him as much as it hurt her. Her hand shook as she held a cup beneath the tap of the samovar, and there was time for him to recognize the pain of rejection in her eyes before she dragged her glance from his face. He sat drinking automatically, feeling his own treachery like a lump in his throat.

Just then Aunt Marie entered in some agitation, calling upon Nadia to go with her to Katya, who was asking for her sister. The girl rose at once. Time passed, and Andrew fretted at the absence of the two women. He could hardly leave until they returned; that would be too brutal. He grew annoyed with Katya. An hour had passed since Nadia left the room!

Misha rambled on in his usual fashion; Ivan was as pedantic as he could be, on occasion. Suddenly, Andrew found them boring. Without a girl with bronze clustering curls and greeny-brown eyes that lit with laughter and enthusiasm, the room was empty and the conversation dull.

Then she was coming into the room, flushed and wearing a frown. He rose, sensing that she was deeply concerned, and saw again a girl who held together a volatile and emotional family with her quiet strength. She went straight to him, and there was no sign of anything but honest friendship in her eyes.

"Forgive us for neglecting you, but I think we must stay with my sister. The heat stroke is more severe than we thought. She has fever and great pain."

He nodded sympathetically, although surprised that the girl should be suffering so badly on a day of moderate temperatures and overcast skies.

"A cool cloth on the back of the neck will relieve the pain . . . and dimmed lights."

"The pain is not in her head, but here." She put a hand on her stomach. "She is crying out with it."

He frowned. Heat stroke did not usually give such severe abdominal pain. "Are you sure it is the result of too much sun?"

She looked at him wide-eyed with uncertainty. "What else could it be?"

"Any number of things. Would you like me to take a look at her? I saw a great deal of sickness in South Africa. I might recognize the symptoms and advise you. If she needs a doctor I can recommend one."

Her decision came quickly. "I suppose she will not like you to see her like this, but please come. It might be that we are not helping her recovery."

Neither Ivan nor his uncle made a move, plainly feeling the sickroom was a female domain, and Andrew was angry. Could they not see Nadia was worried? She went off ahead of him, her silk skirt rustling with her quick steps. The stairs were curved and shallow, edged by a marble balustrade, and he followed her without a word.

Aunt Marie disapproved of the presence of a gentleman in a young girl's bedroom, but Andrew heard Nadia speak in her own language to her aunt in a tone that brooked no argument. Then she asked him to go inside. He smiled reassuringly at the older woman, but she was past knowing who he was or understanding his assurance that he had seen a great deal of illness in the past.

There was a pungent smell in the room that told him Katya had been vomiting—a symptom of heat stroke—and her faint moans could well have been a result of stabbing pains in the head. He moved toward the bed that was shielded by a screen, remembering the many times he had entered a field hospital in South Africa to visit sick or wounded friends. This was the first time he had seen a female patient. For a flash moment he saw again the marble-white face of his dead wife as she lay in the bed, then thrust it away as Nadia led him around the screen.

He knew the truth the minute he saw the girl and everything in him cried out against it. The beautiful features were gray and glistening with the sweat of her agony as she lay twisting from side to side in an attempt to escape the gripping pain. Cholera! There had been a small outbreak amongst the junk inhabitants in the harbor, but this was the first case amongst the Europeans of which he had heard.

He turned to Nadia with swift urgency. "At what hour did she first complain of feeling ill?"

"This afternoon . . . four o'clock, perhaps." In the dim light her eyes looked black. "You know what is wrong?"

He nodded, working out in his mind the length of time the virulent disease had had to take hold of her. Six hours! A long while . . . but he had known men succumb within two. Putting his hand beneath her elbow he led Nadia away toward the door, ignoring the other woman who went straight back to the bedside.

"I will send for a doctor—he is a friend of mine," he told her in a low voice. "Is there somewhere I can write a note for your servant to take?"

"Yes, of course." She spoke in quick Russian to her aunt, then took Andrew along a landing, down the stairs and into a study, calling to a passing servant to wait by the door. His note was brief and to the point. Unless the girl had instant medical care she would die very shortly. Folding the paper and sealing it in an envelope, Andrew instructed the servant on where to take it and told him to hurry.

Nadia seemed to loath to return upstairs or to her uncle and brother, just stood in the doorway of the study staring after the departing servant as if hope had gone with him. Andrew saw the line of youth in her face and body with infinite pity. Getting to his feet he went up behind her and said in gentle tones, "Please don't be so anxious. My friend is very clever."

She turned, and it was almost a repetition of that first afternoon, with his hand resting on the door frame above her head and she looking up at him as helplessly caught as she had been on that occasion.

"I think you do not know yourself very well," she said in her soft accent. "I read your face in the room, and the look is still there. She is very ill."

Disturbed that he had revealed his thoughts too clearly, he slowly slid his hand down until it rested on her arm. "Yes, she is very ill."

"You know what it is?"

"Yes."

For a short while she questioned him with her eyes, but she seemed to be asking much more than his honesty. "Will she die?"

"I don't know. There is always hope."

"I . . . I am afraid," she whispered. "It is weak of me . . . but I am afraid."

Moved beyond words he touched the bronze fronds curling against her temples with gentle fingers, remembering that this same girl had watched her parents battered to death before her eyes not more than a year ago.

"I am here this time," he said huskily.

"Will you stay?"

"Just as long as you wish me to."

Katya's death, instead of drawing them all closer, separated the family as never before. Aunt Marie shut herself away grieving for a child who had been hers so short a time, yet whom she had loved all her life. It was impossible to console her, and Nadia gave up trying. Uncle Misha, feeling inadequate to the situation, turned to morbid composing as an escape. He appeared not to be aware of his nephew's hostility, or chose to ignore the implication that he was the indirect cause of the girl's death by bringing the family to Hong Kong. Ivan himself grew even more introspective, this tragedy caused by a resident disease completing his hatred of the colony.

Without Andrew, Nadia would never have known how to survive those first weeks after the funeral. He gave her a sense of hope when life seemed so difficult and dark. Even so, with a touch of guilt she knew it was still not enough. Despite her mourning for Katya she wanted passion from him—passion that would ease her loneliness and satisfy the ache that had begun at their first meeting.

At times, she sensed a reciprocal feeling in him as he watched her, yet the barriers remained up to protect his vulnerability. Common sense told her he was respecting her sorrow for a dead sister, that convention ruled out any suggesting of romantic advances at such a time, but because of her loss she needed what he would not give. Time and again she asked herself was he using convention as an excuse, or did he really mean to remain no more than a comforting friend? Her instinct told her otherwise, but events gave her no encouragement.

After six weeks she could stand no more of the atmosphere at home and waylaid her brother as he was leaving the house rather later than usual one morning. At the sound of his name he halted in the large square hall, then took a few steps toward her, smiling with the sadness that touched him these days.

"I thought you were in the garden. You spend so much time there, *sestrushka.*"

She went across to him. "Only because the house no longer has the joy in it that it once had. Vanya, I ask only to delay you a short while. We must talk . . . *please.*"

He nodded and began walking back into the room from which she had just come, his arm across her shoulders in an affectionate gesture from the past.

"*Rodnaya moya.* Always you have tried to be the mama to us all."

"No," she told him quickly, "Aunt Marie has been that. I only wish to be myself."

He stopped and turned to face her, not more than an inch or so taller than she and therefore almost eye to eye. "Who are you—have you decided?"

"No, that is the problem."

He looked away and sighed. "That is the problem of us all. We do not know who we are, or what we should be." He began pacing the floor, walking between the carved inlaid tables and around the green velvet chaise longue. "Are you asking me to give you the answer? I do not know it. Am I the son of Andrei

Brusilov or a Hong Kong jade merchant? If the former I take you back to Russia to rejoin our brother and sisters, where we should have been all this time. But, in doing that, I take away the reason for living of a woman who does not know if she is a mother or not. You see what she is now, having lost one. Do you think she will survive our going?" He reached her again and took her hands, drawing from her, not giving. "I think I know what is right . . . and then I look at her and wonder."

He had taken her moment of togetherness and used it for himself, but she recognized his torment and put aside her own feelings.

"*Mily,* in eight months, when you come of age, it will be clear to you what you must do. All decisions must be left until then. It is useless to . . . ." She broke off at his despairing gesture. ". . . Yes, Vanya, I truly believe the future is out of our hands. Surely, we have had evidence enough of that."

"It does not have to be."

"Then help me now to make a start. This home has become a house of separate people. Perhaps you do not realize what it is like. You spend so much time away. Where do you go?"

She did not notice his sudden tenseness, the paling of a face browned by the sun.

"Like you, I cannot bear the house these days. Katya seems to be in every room. There are places of great beauty on this island, you know, I go there for peace and time to think. I am seeking my own consolation." .

She longed to cry, do you think I am not? but said instead, "Yes, there are places of great beauty on the island—something you seem only now to have noticed. We should visit them—all of us together. Only by helping are we ever to get Aunt Marie to put aside the tragedy, and bring *dyadya* from his dark thoughts. They must see that the world goes on. Vanya, our blood is the same. Our unity is never likely to be needed more than it is at this time."

Her words came out tinged with desperation, and once she had allowed her emotions their rein they began to master her. "Remember the time we set Papa's horse free because he had given orders for Zoblenski to shoot it? We did not know it was suffering, but Mama made us suffer more by telling us how it

91

would have to die so slowly. You were ill, and I cried as much for you as for the horse." Her eyes filled with tears at the memory. "That great house in Petersburg was only warm because I had you. The family has scattered. Has it changed between us? Will it ever be the same again?"

His grip on her hands had grown tighter and tighter as she spoke, and the pain of his thoughts softened the rigid lines that had dominated his expression for too long. Youth was struggling with emerging manhood. Moved by the fervor of his race all resistance broke as he became again the brother sickened by his mother's description of a dying beast. With a swift movement he took her in a hug, matching his own tears with hers.

It was fully an hour later that he set out, and Nadia felt that the sun might shine again on the family Brusilov. They had talked, heads together as they used to, planning a new start that would unite the family once more—a smaller group, certainly, but a warm one. She walked to the door with him and stood on the step as he climbed into the rickshaw.

"I will plan some outings," she told him as he settled back in his seat. "We could go to Repulse Bay on Saturday. Now you are prepared to support me it will be a lot easier."

His face took on the unhappiness of uncertainty she saw there so often. "The twins were wrongly blessed," he said sadly. "You have the strength that should have gone to me."

She went to him quickly and took his hand. "No, *bratishka,* I am not so strong. Without Andrew these past weeks would have seen me in despair."

It was meant to console him, show him she shared his grief, but it brought a surprising response. "As you say, now I shall support you. There will be no need for visits from that man . . . a foreigner, an Englishman. He should not have come without an invitation from me. With our uncle in a state of melancholy, he should have applied to me before calling. We have shown our gratitude for his actions at the death of our sister. Now he should respect our mourning and leave us *en famille.* I trust the association will now cease."

His conversation with Nadia hung heavily on Ivan throughout

the day. She had appealed for help and he had felt inadequate to give it. He had never been really close to Katya, but her death had hit him hard. It emphasized his own weakness in allowing the family to be brought half across the world to escape a few peasants driven by temporary madness. It was his duty to go back, yet his dearly loved twin was happier here than she had ever been, and a well-meaning elderly couple would be torn apart by such a decision.

By midafternoon he was in so feverish a state he could concentrate on shipping orders, papers of sale, and letters of introduction no longer. It was humid, and one of Hong Kong's light mists had settled over the island. Deep depression settled on him and, shortly afterward, came the usual surge of physical torment that accompanied his longing to see Mei-Leng. She was the balm, the cure for his inadequacy. She did not demand from him, but gave. He was the Master, wise, infallible, commanding infinite respect. When he was with her he became all a man should be.

Yet, he was also the slave. Her compact beauty kept him awake at nights. He traveled in erotic fantasies in which she became part princess, part prostitute, driving him to sexual arousement with the oriental arts of pleasure. She alternated in his mind from demure eastern maid to one of Russia's traveling dancers, enticing him, making his blood pound with the rhythm of her stamping feet.

The weeks had passed, and his celibate existence laughed in his face. He could have gone to a Tanka girl or a reputable house patronized by Europeans, but there was an almost masochistic determination to delay his initiation. The pride that governed his personality balked at the thought of a frowsy harlot who would sell him satisfaction in fifteen minutes between the patronage of a French seaman and a German engineer. A Brusilov should take a virgin . . . and Mei-Leng possessed the immaculate innocence that promised the earth, and heaven too. Yet, was she as blushingly innocent as she appeared? Her demurely downcast eyes held secrets that set him alight, and the uncertainty of her true thoughts made her even more exciting.

When he had found her at the temple of Kwan Yin, had she

93

really believed he was interested only in the customs of her race? She had shown him the shrine and explained the legend of a beautiful daughter who had come back from the dead and cut pieces from her own body to give to her dying father who had murdered her. Since then, she was renowned as the goddess of mercy. He had thought the story bizarre, but Mei-Leng was sincere in her worship. She had given him roast chicken, sweet almonds, bamboo shoots, and tiny rice cakes, which he ate with sticks, as she had done. Then, he had watched her bow before the shrine and light joss sticks for favorable times ahead.

She had had flowers in her hair to match the pink silk tunic she wore, and he had thought her more beautiful than before. Every moment with her was a delight of sensuality. Andrew's need for someone with just Mei-Leng's qualifications had seemed providential. He had introduced them, and the scheme worked. Using the excuse of checking to see the arrangement suited both parties he had seen her again at Andrew's house. She was happy, and he knew where she was on three evenings a week. He also knew what time she set out along the road from her village to the bay.

All at once, he knew he had to see her. Turning from the window he went out of his office and down through the gallery, calling to his uncle that he would not be back that afternoon.

It took only a short while to return to the house, where he went in cautiously to avoid meeting his sister, and made for his room. With a mounting sense of freedom and excitement he threw off the suit and starched collar, dressing instead in breeches, and Russian shirt belted at the waist with full cuffed sleeves. He postured for a moment before the long mirror as he settled a round tassled cap on his head. Yes, if he had been fair instead of dark, he would look every inch the son of Andrei Brusilov. Sturdy, square-shouldered, feet firmly apart in high polished boots, silk shirt embroidered with the family crest, dark Cossack breeches.

To reach the bay where Andrew lived it was possible to ride along the lower slopes of the hills to join the road some two miles on, and thereby avoid going down to the center of Victoria. With this idea in mind he swung into the saddle of his horse and set off down the drive and thence up to the wooded slopes that ran behind the house. If the occupants of sedan chairs stared at the young man who resembled a Tartar brigand as he rode with panache through the swirling grayness, he did not notice them.

His heart was swelling with the return of his identity and, once in the trees, he gave the horse its head, letting it stretch its stride to the full as he galloped flat out, bending low beneath the overhanging branches and negotiating hazards that loomed in the mist with the skill and iron nerve of a natural horseman. For the moment, he was back in Russia racing after the hounds and the great red deer, dreaming of the day he would proudly don the uniform of a cadet in his father's regiment.

But it was not a Russian forest. It was a typical Chinese landscape, with occasional small temples standing back amidst the trees, inhabited by idols with yellow faces and bodies curiously twisted. He rode on through the eerie ambience, past the village of mudbrick houses that had been built on each side of the stream, then on past them to an orchard of mango trees. He saw the lower terraces of paddyfields where the villagers were cultivating rice, and trestles supporting beehives all in a row.

Children ran happily on the dusty road between houses, or splashed with noisy abandon in the stream. Poultry ran spread-winged with indignant cackles at his passing, and he tried to shake from his mind that Mei-Leng was part of this village. His fantasies did not place her here, in oriental poverty. Yet her father's house stood at the end of the collection of houses, with carved lintel and stone gryphons guarding the entrance, as befitted his importance—but it was supremely Chinese in style.

Half a mile on he saw her, and all introspection fled as he dug in his spurs. She turned just as he drew level and leaped from his saddle in spectacular Cossack style, bouncing high in the air again with one leg flung out as he dragged the horse to a standstill. One glance at her face was enough, and he laughed as he swept the tasseled cap from his head and clicked his heels smartly.

"You gave me instructions on your customs, now I show you something of mine," he told her, the exertion of the ride plus the success of his mission making him a true Brusilov in that moment.

The abruptness of his spectacular arrival still held her away from tradition. There was wonderment, admiration, and traces of apprehension in her shining black eyes as she continued to gaze up at him. His pulse quickened further. It was the first step to ravishment, this forcing from her the emotions she normally hid. It established a sense of mastery, and he tried to maintain it.

"In my country, it is a measure of a man's greatness that he rides a horse well, not that he has many bearers for his sedan chair. So you see that I ride even when it is possible to mistake a man for a tree, a house for a temple."

Her lashes came down then, and she gave the bow her upbringing demanded. "Truly you are a great man."

"As my father and grandfather before me," he said, knowing what would impress her Chinese mind. "For many generations my ancestors have ruled over vast lands and owned many servants."

She straightened, but kept her eyes lowered. "Will the Master one day go back to the land of his ancestors?"

"Yes," he said with absolute conviction. "Soon, I shall return."

"How many moons?" It was asked in a tone that whispered with the fear of hearing the answer.

All at once the braggart vanished, and he was trapped by her destiny that dictated she should expect nothing and receive nothing. His own culture cried out at such treatment.

"Perhaps thirteen moons yet," he told her in a gentler tone, and put out a hand to tilt her face upward. "Will it sadden you when I go?"

Already there was a luminous sheen in her eyes that brought back the longing to touch her that he had felt at their first meeting. His hand moved from her chin to rest lightly on a cheek that was smooth and warm, with the silky softness of a female's skin.

"Will it sadden you, Mei-Leng?"

"One is always sad to lose the moon and the sun," she said simply. "It is only possible to look from afar, but that does not make the day and night any less black when they have gone."

Almost breathless with the accelerated beat of his heart, Ivan inched nearer as his fingers touched the flower fixed above her ear, then the coils of black hair. "In such a case it is wise to look upon them as much as possible before they are gone. There will be many times that I shall pass this way. It might be that we shall meet."

Almost without his being aware of it she moved back and bowed again. "If it is the wish of the Master, we shall meet."

"It is very much the wish of the Master," he told her.

"Then it shall be so."

Ivan realized he had just accomplished what he most wanted as easily as if she had been a peasant girl on the further boundaries of the family summer estate. Yet the simile was not a good one. A Russian shepherdess would have flashed her dark eyes boldly at him, given him messages with the movements of her body, laughed softly when she promised to meet him as often as he wished. He would have kissed a peasant girl and smacked her round bottom as she turned to go.

With this girl it was different. She used no seduction, seemed unaware of her own body, and withdrew into dignified subservience from his sexual overtones. But she was caught by him; it was in her eyes no matter how she tried to hide it.

His earlier bravado returned. He felt like flinging his cap in the air in triumph. Ahead lay the delights of her irresistible attraction. A peasant would go giggling into a hayloft with little persuasion, then he would want to find another. With Mei-Leng the game would be extended, each step tantalizing and unexpected, with the final victory a glittering peak from which he would surely survey the entire world.

She still stood away from him, quiet, restful, a magnolia in a wild garden. With a swift burst of energy he jumped into his saddle, brought the highly bred horse round in a trotting circle before bending to pick up the Chinese girl in one arm, as he had done with his brother and sisters so many times. He held her before him on the horse, his right arm tightly round her waist as he urged the beast forward.

"Mr. Stanton will be displeased if you arrive late," he said with exultation, "so I must take you there."

She sat meekly against him, more like a child than a temptress, yet his entire body was aware of her slight pliancy as they moved together in rhythm with the horse. The scent of the blossom in her hair filled his nostrils to add an even headier quality to the misty afternoon. Filled with a spear of rare happiness he gave the horse its head. He was Ivan Brusilov, son of Andrei and defender of the Czar. The jade merchant was forgotten.

Ivan kept his promise and, during the following week, Nadia glimpsed in him a confidence that was surprising. It was no easy task breaking into a pattern of grieving that had become almost a pleasure to those who indulged in it but, with Ivan's determination and her own compassion, Aunt Marie was shown that she was still needed by the living, and Uncle Misha was coaxed from his dark stanzas.

Yet Nadia felt no closer to Ivan. If anything, she acknowledged a wariness she had not previously experienced. A twin was closer than a brother, with shared understanding, yet he had trampled on her love for Andrew with words that had held no sympathy for her feelings. With the passion so strong in her, how was it possible he had not guessed her secret? Had the mystical union of their spirits gone forever?

From the start Ivan had been at his most ungracious with their English visitor. Nadia knew he did not like the British, as a race, and spoke often of their great-grandfather who had fought against them in the Crimea, and their recent stand when the Japanese forced the Czar's troops to admit defeat. Still she had hoped Ivan would respect her feelings, instead of insisting the relationship cease.

The strain of that problem on top of all the others took its toll of her spirits. Each time she gazed from her window at the sun-washed roofs and brilliant blue, she remembered Katya saying on that first day: *Make the most of it.* It was all out there waiting for her, yet she felt chained down and unable to reach those things she so badly wanted.

So restless did she become, it seemed a sign of Providence that Andrew called one morning when she was seeking peace in the green cloisters of the garden. She was on a seat that gave an uninterrupted view of frangipani trees, the overhanging foliage giving shade, and the white blossoms a heady perfume that soothed her senses. But at the sight of the houseboy leading the visitor down the path, she rose to her feet with a quickened heartbeat. The moment had come, and she was still uncertain what she must say to him.

He presented his official appearance—white starched suit, gun belt, white pith helmet—as if he had called on business. He looked strained, his jaw taut with tension.

"Forgive me for disturbing you," he began in formal tones. "I cannot stay long and did not wish to bring you all the way up to the house."

"It is kind of you to call when you have your duty to attend to," she replied with an echo of his strange formality.

"How is your aunt?"

"Much improved."

"And Mikhail Sergeyevich?"

"My uncle, also."

"I'm glad."

It was as if she did not know him. He seemed taller in the helmet with its brass spike. His face was shadowed by the stiff brim, and the thick leather gun belt around his waist suggested all she had overlooked in her love for him. He was English with an allegiance to a country that had a history of enmity with her own.

Even his voice sounded alien, but its tone was nothing to the shock of the words. "I have to go to Canton . . . tonight. I have come to say goodbye. I have no idea when I shall be back."

He had done it for her— broken the bond that should never have been allowed to grow between them. The decision was made on her behalf, and it hurt more than she had imagined.

"I see."

"It's nice to know you are all beginning to recover from the tragedy. I am sure things will be easier for you now." He hesitated, twisting the short brass-nosed swagger stick in his hands. "Of course, if I can ever be of service again, please do not hesitate to call on me."

Raw inside she heard herself answer, "No . . . you have already been more than kind." She turned away from him and walked the few yards to the garden boundary where her world ended and that of the Chinese began, praying for an assurance that would allow her to let him walk away without guessing.

There was a sultriness in the air that hung with the weight of portent over the island. A storm was coming, but it was not only the elements in conflict at that moment. As her senses tried to accept what Andrew was telling her, she stared at the scene below.

The road wound down in a long drop to the center of Victoria, and there was a constant human stream in both directions. Tradesmen with carts; coolies in loose clothes, their wares in wide pans slung from a bamboo pole across their shoulders; Eurasians or wealthy Chinese leaving exertion to the bearers of the sedan chairs in which they rode; women in enormous basket plate-hats who worked on road-laying; emaciated men clearing rubbish from the nullahs so that storm waters would run away; soothsayers walking endlessly on pilgrimages; maimed beggars squatting helplessly where relatives had left them, hoping for a handful of rice, or a fish head; children in ragged clothes, chattering loudly; women clattering back and forth with pots and pans, airing their grievances in loud nasal voices.

Watching it all from her few acres of Russia-in-exile, Nadia was suddenly filled with desperate sadness. She did not belong here, after all! Turning from it swiftly, she caught Andrew unawares. Gone were the barricades, the protective barriers that kept him aloof. The deep pain in his eyes made nonsense of all that had just passed between them. He was as vulnerable as she.

"Are you really gong to Canton?" she flung at him before she could stop herself.

"One of our men has been killed up there by revolutionaries. Yes, I have to go."

There was a painful silence then, she wishing he would go, and he hovering on the brink of saying more. Eventually, he gave a sigh and took off his helmet, wiping his brow with the back of his wrist. It made all the difference. He did not then seem so tall, or so formal. Standing with the soft sunlight on his hair, his face no longer shadowed, he was so much the man she loved, her hands gripped the railings behind her to ease the surge of renewed longing for him.

Walking up to stand beside her he kept his gaze on some point beyond the garden boundary. "Duty is a harsh master," he began,

100

as if embarking on a rehearsed speech. "In the army it was supposed to be clear-cut. Orders were given and one obeyed without question. But it was not easy to push on with an advance and leave a friend crying in agony. Nor was it possible to burn down people's homes before their eyes and not question why."

He half turned then and looked down at her in a manner that left her breathless. "One's duty to family might not be as severe, in comparison, but it can still demand a heavy penalty. You know something of that, and so does your brother, who will find it pulling him in opposite directions when he comes of age." His mouth tightened, and he beat the side of his hand softly with the stick. "I defied it, and several people paid a high price for my action. Since then I have obeyed the rules. It might not be what I want, but it is the only thing to do." He cast her an intense look from beneath fair lashes. "A man should never make the same mistake twice."

His body was only inches from hers. She could smell the clean starched linen, the soap-scrubbed warmth of his skin. It was like being back in the shrubbery of Government House . . . and she could stand it no longer. She began to run, knowing anything was better than hearing any more of his reasons for rejecting her. Perhaps she did it with instinctive seduction, to make him pursue—she was too new to passion to know—but he responded immediately. Halfway along the path she was caught and turned to him, held in strong hands. He was ablaze with what had previously only smoldered.

"Do you understand any of what I have been trying to tell you?" he demanded. "Have you any idea why I have been fighting this? You are already crying. There would be oceans of tears, I promise. Tears, anger, and hostility."

Worn out by grief over the death of her sister, exhausted by her efforts to keep the family together, she saw only that the one steady support in her turbulent life was pulling out and leaving her to fall.

Trying to pull free of him she cried, "Go, then. Go and do your duty!"

He shook her in sudden loss of control. "What do you want from me? Would you be happy if I went down on one knee and told you I cannot see a life without you," he said savagely. "Is that what you want . . . what will take that desolation from your face? I will do it. I will shout it from the top of Victoria Peak; I will gallop on horseback all round the colony bearing it on a banner . . . but you would be snubbed in the streets, spoken of behind hands, and at mess tables." His chest was heaving. "It is because I love you that I am doing my duty."

Riding on the same wave as he, she cried, "Say that again . . . say all of it again."

Her tears stopped flowing beneath the shock of his kisses. Passion might be new to her, but the tide of desire filling her limbs made her responses fiery and demanding. She challenged him to make a mockery of his goodbye, of all he had said about duty. She discovered a wayward and exciting ability to draw from him words he had tried hard not to speak, and to whisper against his lips secrets she had not known lay within her.

At last he held her away, saying unsteadily, "Forbidden paths again. I warned you!"

Stunned with the pleasure-pain of physical arousal she spoke in Russian. *"Nenaglyadny moy."*

He touched her temples with caressing fingers. "Love on the wings of a butterfly."

"Niet . . . no!" she cried, putting her fingers swiftly against his mouth. "A butterfly rests for only a short while before flying away again."

He took her fingers and kissed them one by one. "Not this time. I am going away for a few weeks, not forever."

After he left Nadia walked back to the garden from the drive where they had said goodbye, unwilling to break the spell. She wandered dreamily until she caught sight of a butterfly, brown with speckled wings. "I was like you a short time ago," she whispered to it, "but now I am iridescent blue. He has done that to me."

The storm broke half an hour later. The rain was an immediate curtain of warm water that drenched her in seconds. Caught at the far end of the garden she took shelter in a tiny pavilion while the rain thundered onto broad curving palm leaves, slender bamboos, flowers of strange and vivid style, and the earth that was always thirsty. As she watched from her wooden shelter the paths, the paths turned to streams, mud-colored and surging down the slope toward the boundary railings; the grass grew greener by the minute. Over the garden hung a mist of rising heat, creating a sensation of having stumbled on a scene from long ago—a secret place that had materialized from the mist after a hundred years. So it seemed to Nadia as she stood in her tiny shelter . . . but any place would have seemed enchanted that afternoon.

When the rain stopped she hurried to the house, keeping to the grass to avoid ruining her shoes in the mud, and holding her blue-and-white striped skirt above her ankles. She laughed softly, finding in the action an echo of childhood that had finally vanished in Andrew's arms. Being a woman was a heady state.

Standing inside the hall to wipe her feet and shake the worst of the rain from hair and skirt it was a little while before Nadia became aware of her aunt standing on the threshold of the parlor. Her hands stilled in their tasks. Aunt Marie looked at the point of death, her face gray with shock, her eyes like those of a madwoman, haunted and bruised. She made no attempt to speak, and Nadia was too far in her own happiness to accept what she saw immediately. For a moment or two they stared at each other, then the girl felt her afternoon tilt disastrously. *Duty is a harsh master.*

"What is it, *tyotushka?*" she forced herself to ask as she went to her aunt, still crying out against this intrusion into her lovely dream state. "Are you ill?"

Aunt Marie heard the voice, but did not appear to see her niece. Nadia reached her and supported the woman with her arm. "Whatever can have made you so upset? Tell me what ails you."

The gray face turned to her. "Anna is here."

Nadia was as gentle as she should be to a person who did not know what she was doing or saying. "Anna? Anna who?" she asked encouragingly.

It came out in a monotone. "Anna Brusilova. She is alive. She did not die. Anna Brusilova lives . . . she lives . . . *dear God, she lives!*" A paroxysm of weeping began to shake her from head to foot so that Nadia had to tighten her hold. "She has come back to claim you—to claim my children!"

FIVE

On the surface, life continued as before, yet the return from the dead of Anna Brusilova brought undercurrents of emotion that ended the unity of the family forever. Her dramatic reappearance without warning was a severe shock to those who had believed her murdered as they sped through the snow that night ... a shock that took varying forms. Everyone heard her story with the compassion it would draw from any listener, yet instead of falling upon the sufferer with tears and embraces, there had been silence and set expressions when she had finished speaking. Entering that door with her had been guilt, despair, and animosity—each one singling out its victim and settling upon him.

The only one who had withstood the shock and remained relatively unchanged was Nadia, reflected Ivan as he sat at his desk at the Galerie Russe a week later. There was even a new happiness, a glow about her since that day which suggested she was not as untouched by her mother as they had all supposed. Perhaps, being the one who had always held herself aloof, she was now able to accept her back with the gladness of detachment, unmarred by other feelings.

He gave a heavy sigh. The prayers he had said, the candles he had lit at church would not expunge what was in his soul; the Great Father would know only too well. Putting his head in his hands he made his confession—to whom it was not certain, but the truth had to be brought into the open.

God help him, he had been glad that the cudgels had knocked her to the ground—not at the time, but afterward, when he realized what it meant. It had been the end of a lifetime of rejection, of seeking approval that was never there, of seeing the worship of a man he was unworthy to follow. Her action that day had set him free, given justification for his feelings of resentment. She had finally abandoned her children, her duty, her human unity with the fruits of her passion—denied six souls for the sake of one. Who would not condemn her?

For nearly a year he had vindicated himself with that thought. Although he had been driven by the need to become a copy of his father, she had no longer been there to make the comparison. The road ahead lay easier before him by that fact. Now it was a stony one again. He felt her watching him, testing the son against the memories of the father, forcing him to his limits. She was there when he had believed himself a free man. The endless striving and endless rejection must go on.

A tapping on his office door brought him back to the present and, physically shaking off the mantle of gloom, he rose and went to open. Ho Fatt stood outside.

"Sir, it is time that we should go."

"Yes, I am ready," he said heavily, and fell in beside the Chinaman. "If this man speaks the truth we are fortunate. Have you any reason to doubt him?"

"The man who doubts not is a fool to himself and those who believe him" was the reply.

Ivan told himself he should have known better than ask such a question and said no more as they walked through the gallery and into the street. The comprador had rickshaws waiting, and Ivan stepped in and sat down on the hard seat, giving instructions for the hood to be unfolded over his head. He disliked being pulled through the streets in such a manner, but when it was the only alternative to walking insisted on using the partial privacy of the hood that was similar to that on a child's perambulator.

Rickshaw runners were individualists who held vigorous arguments with anyone and everyone preventing their passage and, when jammed tightly between stalls and teeming throngs, as they invariably were at some point in their journey, Ivan had no intention of being stared at like a prize exhibit whilst his runner gesticulated and shouted curses at everyone around.

The hood made the interior hotter, but the shade was welcome. Through the framework he saw Ho Fatt give instructions to his own runner and both rickshaws set off. The Chinese sat in happy majesty in his seat. He always appeared to take pleasure in being pulled by one of his own race and never had the hood up. A small upright figure in gray gown, he could have been an emperor from the way he sat reviewing the passing scene with such implacability. It could be that he dreamed of being an emperor as he journeyed along, but Ivan would make no guess at the man's thoughts. As an agent he was faultless; as a man, an enigma.

Not so his daughter. A quick stirring of excitement moved in his breast at the thought of his secret meetings with Mei-Leng. She was his consolation and release from a life that threatened to batten him down. At first, she had talked only of her life and the ways of her people, asking him about his homeland and customs. But at their last meeting she had trembled when he took her hand to help her through the long grass on the headland where they talked, and there had been the shimmer of tears in her black eyes when he left her. He knew Ho Fatt was ignorant of the meetings. When asked, she had replied that an unworthy daughter did not burden a father with her own words, but listened to his.

The rickshaw ran into the predictable jam of bodies and vehicles, and he was jerked from his thoughts by harsh noises that splintered the pictures of a blue-water bay, paths through

107

long grasses, and a girl who made him a king without yet becoming his queen.

Ahead, that girl's father sat erect ignoring the shouts and cries around him as if his ears were too precious to hear such sounds. Ivan tried to copy him and was unsuccessful. The din grew and he covered his ears with his hands. The cause of the holdup was a funeral procession heralded by the customary crashing cymbals and banging sticks.

The coffin, draped with an elaborate cover embroidered with gold and bright trimmings, was borne on poles resting on the shoulders of a dozen men. Following it were the official mourners and close family of the deceased, who seemed to set up inhuman wailing at given intervals. Behind them came a prodigious line of distant relatives and friends bearing banners filled with holes. Bringing up the rear was a stretcher bearing paper replicas of all the things needed by the departing soul in the next life to which it was going—a house, chairs, tables, a bed, livestock—as well as bowls of fruit and rice so that the spirit would not feel hungry on its journey.

At the back were large baskets of paper pieces printed to look like money, into which the relatives plunged their hands and scattered to the winds as a temptation to devils who might be following the coffin in order to snatch away the soul of the departed one. The crashing gongs and cymbals at the head frightened away any devils lying in wait, and any who still persisted in their evil intents lost their way as they tried to find a way through the holes in the banners. The safety and comfort of the dear departed was assured.

The procession passed slowly, creating a havoc and a dreadful din, yet the watchers seemed unmoved by it. Death was inevitable and a happy event. The next kingdom was full of joy and plenty. Those left behind were glad that the day had come for the one who was lost to them. After the burial there would be a great feast and a get-together, then life would go on as usual. Thus, while Ivan felt saddened by the sight, it left unmoved those concerned only with choosing a piece of dried fish or strip of fat pork to give flavor to the day's rice.

The rickshaw jerked: He was on the move again. But the

passing of the coffin had reawakened memories of Katya, and he found tears hovering as he recalled the lack of emotion with which his mother had received the news of her daughter's death. She had merely said that it meant nothing now she had been so near death herself.

He wondered yet again at the will of God that had kept beating the heart of a woman who so dearly wished to die. The murderers had fled thinking her lifeless, but she had lain bleeding and broken in the snow until a passing woman saw the two bodies lying close together and saved her.

Nuns from a nearby convent had taken her into their hospital, and for weeks she had lain reaching out to the Angel of Death, as she had to her husband, her fingers not quite touching his. Her body mended, but her mind was still broken. It told her ways of oblivion, and the nuns were forced to take away all knives and sharp articles from her room. They brought her back when she ran into the river; they waylaid an old man bringing her a potion. She was never left alone. Months passed while they taught her to pray for the one she had lost. Slowly she grew quiet, but any suggestion that she should leave the convent worried her.

A new holy sister joined the convent, and it was she who brought about the maximum recovery possible. Concentrating on the son who would be taking the responsibilities of the family upon his shoulders in such a short while, the nun told her patient she could best serve her dead husband by guiding the son in his image. Since Captain Brusilov had given his life for their sake, it would be a vain sacrifice if the family did not live up to his memory. With constant repetition, this theme was enough to persuade the sick woman that she must follow that half of the family containing her elder son. Since the elderly Madame Brusilova had banished her daughter-in-law from her mind and considered her mental experience something which should be kept secret and confined within the convent walls, the nuns felt the journey to Hong Kong was the only salvation for their patient. Not knowing the history of the family, they enthusi- astically made arrangements for her to travel in company with two Sisters of Mercy who were going as missionaries to China, believing her arrival was expected. Anna had had only one aim in mind, however—to return to Russia with her son. He must learn by the image of his father. The rest of the family did not matter. She had no more interest in them than before.

Gazing blankly at the scene on the wharves as the rickshaw reached the harbor area, Ivan knew there was greater conflict in his breast than before. His brave assertions that he would go back as soon as he became head of the family now melted away. He felt like a man digging his heels into the soft earth in order to pull up a runaway stallion that threatened to drag him forward. He would not go back as her puppet . . . yet was there an alternative? The rest of the family were watching and waiting, he was sure. Waiting for his move.

"We have arrived, sir," said Ho Fatt beside the rickshaw, and Ivan dispatched his thoughts with a nod. But they did not go far enough away to give him the clear head needed for business, and he followed his comprador with reluctance.

The air was pungent with the combined odors of fish, rotting animal carcasses, oiled rope, spice, sewage, rancid fat, and the inevitable joss sticks. Ivan turned his head away from the breeze that blew across the wharves, but it made little difference. The heat fermented the smells that permeated the wooden staging and the hulls of the crowding junks that filled the basins. Riding the filth-strewn water were the merchant vessels of the Chinese and other oriental traders. Some of the cumbersome wooden sailing ships with their distinctive flat ornate bows were part of entire fleets owned by taipans, others were hired by merchants to carry cargoes down from China along the treacherous rugged coast from Shanghai. More often than not, they were the floating homes of entire families who lived their lives packed between decks along with livestock, and meager cargoes of rice or flour that had turned sour; cheap tin dented or distorted from shape; bales of silk ruined by seawater or corrosive stains. There was always a market for such things; a certainty of earning an extra bowl of rice or a pipe of opium.

Ivan hated this part of Hong Kong harbor, but it was to these wharves that his consignments of jade came, and not where the great ships from the West landed their passengers.

"Was it really necessary for me to come here?" he asked

irritably. "Surely you could have persuaded him somehow to bring the jade up to the gallery."

The man walking half a pace ahead of his employer to clear the way nodded serenely. "Most regrettable, but necessary, sir. If a pig is worth eating, the chase is little effort."

Ivan scowled. "You know this man well?"

"He knows me well" was the infuriating answer.

The comprador always spoke in proverbs or with oriental evasiveness, but that afternoon it increased Ivan's ill humor. He strode across the planking where water slapped against the sturdy wooden piles, feeling angry that the distant view of green, sun-washed Kowloon across the channel of heavenly-blue water should present such a contrast to the squalor at his elbow. He liked things cut and dried, conforming to accepted patterns. This British colony cheated. Just when the pagan, odorous, alien atmosphere became overwhelming, Hong Kong slipped in a palliative in the form of breathtaking scenery, exquisite creatures and flowers . . . and Mei-Leng.

Desire washed over him, increasing the heat of his body and pounding in his temples, but he was forced to subdue it, as he did so often lately, when Ho Fatt led the way onto a junk of substantial proportions. The merchant was awaiting them on the deck, smiling with the insincerity that accompanies purely business transactions, and bowing obsequiously to hide the look of satisfaction in bringing a European to him, instead of the other way around. Ivan felt his gall rising but decided on a show of haughty indifference to the man. It was the only way to handle the situation if he really wanted the jade this man was offering. He could only guess the man had already offered it to a Chinese rival and felt the price too low, otherwise Galerie Russe would never have been given the chance to see the pieces.

The merchant was almost the opposite of Ho Fatt in appearance. Weatherbeaten skin more brown than yellow, round face with fat-lidded eyes, taller and carrying the weight of good living, he gave an appearance of joviality and good nature that was found frequently in his race. But Ivan knew the impression to be false. His business shrewdness had taught him to trust the Chinese merchants no further than he would a Russian who was

111

full of vodka. In his opinion, they would as soon cut his throat as trade with him and only did so for their own ends. All the same, they were even harsher with their own countrymen.

This man bowed to Ho Fatt and Ivan, but they were robbed of dignity because his enormous stomach prevented his doubling forward very far. A swift exchange between the two Chinese was punctuated by jovial nods and approving noises from the merchant, then he waved an arm to indicate a table and chairs. The drinking of tea was a ritual that must be observed. To approach the subject of business immediately would be very bad-mannered and suggest that the visitor was not welcomed for the honor of his presence, but for the host's convenience. It was time-consuming and not a little boring, in Ivan's view, since the ritual of inquiring after his own health and that of all his family, and wishing him prosperity, long life, and favorable joss was all conducted through Ho Fatt and translated for the benefit of both ritual well-wishers.

At length, several coolies brought into the cabin the crates containing the pieces claimed by the merchant to be part of treasures found beneath the ruins of a pagoda in northern China. He could, he told Ho Fatt, obtain the remainder if the voyage was financed by the purchaser. He was a poor man, and there were still pirate ships along the China coast which plundered the cargoes of honest merchants. It would be a dangerous and expensive trip, entailing the hiring of many coolies to carry the crates overland to Shanghai.

He told a long and complicated tale, as was usual, and it took a good while for Ho Fatt to translate the remarks of both negotiators. Finally, Ivan agreed to back the venture if his uncle studied the jade carefully and found it to be genuine. The cost of the voyage would be borne by Galerie Russe, but the man must hire his own coolies. That would ensure he did not employ six and charge Ivan for twenty.

Having given his terms to the comprador, Ivan left the two to argue it out, amusing himself with observation. The merchant appeared to physically deflate, the grins and nods carrying less and less joviality until they disappeared altogether. Ho Fatt, on the other hand, remained an austere figure, his triangular face expressionless. It was his eyes that could give him away if a person watched carefully. The mildness was broken by lightning flashes of contempt that vanished in a second suggesting that they had never been there. The merchant might know him well, but Ho Fatt knew his man better. Vanquished, the fat man promised to deliver the crates to the gallery for inspection the following morning, and tried to look delighted with the outcome. He was probably getting much more than the deal was worth, but less than he had hoped.

Ivan said as much to Ho Fatt as they went back along the wharf, and praised his bargaining powers. "It was as well you were not the merchant and he my comprador," he concluded. "You did well. I shall reward you handsomely."

"The man who seeks reward is not worthy of it; he who accepts when it is given will never be denied it," he replied obliquely. "My family is much favored by you, sir."

Ivan understood that part and his pulse quickened. "Is your daughter happy with Mr. Stanton?"

Parting a group of coolies as if they were tall grass, Ho Fatt walked between them with unconcern. "If a man be blessed not with sons, he can hope for little. Mei-Leng brings me no more than frugal comfort. If she serves Mr. Stanton with satisfaction I am saved from complete sadness."

Once again Ivan felt irritated by flowery speech from a man who gave nothing of himself away. He had answered the question with an eastern philosophy; he cared nothing for his daughter's feelings.

The parallel with his own life set up an ache of sympathy that was impossible to resist. The bobbing boats in the harbor, the beckoning beauty of the Peak rising up to his right, green-clad and promising seclusion in foliage, all filled him with the need to go round to that lonely bay. Andrew Stanton was away, but she went to the small headland just the same, in case he went there to their meeting place. With roughness deepening his voice he told the Chinese that he would call on a friend in Kowloon, and sent him off in a rickshaw.

But he turned away from the Kowloon ferry and went to a tiny jetty, threading his way between fishing nets, baskets, cooking pots, squatting infants using the sea as a lavatory, and an assortment of ugly dogs continually on the offensive. The sampan colony ignored him, apart from bold-eyed Tanka girls who offered him their charms in phrases learned from British soldiers with strange accents. He caught a word here and there—enough to understand the erotic pleasures they promised—and his step quickened. Their laughing chorus increased his desire to see the girl who was so modest and fresh in comparison. He prayed the young boy would be there with his boat.

He was . . . at the end of the jetty. Catching sight of Ivan the boy grinned.

"Hallo, all along," he greeted. "You wanchee along go see? I takee you go now, allight?"

Ivan jumped into the boat and awaited while the boy swept from the plank seat the remains of his tattered washing that was spread to dry. His grin was perpetual; life was one long joke for him. Slapping a young lad into action and hauling on the collar of a toddler in danger of falling into the water—his brother and sister for whom he was the sole provider—he took the long pliant pole and began moving out into the harbor with expert ease.

"You come soon see missy, then all along home chop-chop," he said chattily. "Englee master all same likee."

Ivan was not listening. He sat watching the distance draw nearer with great impatience.

It was good to be back in Hong Kong. Thirty-five days in Canton were thirty-four too many, Andrew reflected as he walked on the sand below his house after a swim. Wanting to prolong the sunset hour he slung the towel round his neck and stood looking out to sea. There was a poignancy about the evening beauty that stirred the yearning in his soul.

Nadia. He said the name softly. He longed to see her, yet had made no attempt to contact her since his return two days ago. Admittedly, he had spent the first mostly in bed catching up on his sleep, but there had been time enough since then to send a letter by hand. The Brusilov house was not far from the building that housed his department.

Truth was, he was still uncertain how to handle the situation.

114

That day in her garden he had confronted a girl who was more than a match for him. He had gone there steeled against the necessity of hurting a young girl in love for the first time. His defenses had not been geared to the kind of sexual challenge his words had brought from her.

For the past five weeks he had been using wit and muscle in the heat of Canton, following up information regarding the whereabouts of the revolutionary group known to be responsible for the murder of several Europeans, one of whom was a man in Andrew's department. It was difficult now to know which were political killers, for many of the secret societies that had flourished for centuries through the brutal crimes of slavery, prostitution, opium smuggling, and assassination had allied themselves with the nationalist groups. A Triad or Tong killing was always recognizable; the motive for it no longer was.

His mission had not been entirely successful. True to form, witnesses had either been too afraid to speak, or agreed to anything to avoid further questioning. He had spent half his time in a stuffy office and the rest conducting equally frustrating interviews in those villages thought to be used by revolutionaries opposing the Manchu overlords.

However, they were fortunate enough to come upon one shack housing an old man and several boxes of leaflets calling upon the Chinese people to rise against their oppressors. The frail old coolie claimed he had been threatened with death if he did not allow them to use his hut. When questioned further "them" turned out to be a group of young students, one of whom was, to his eternal sorrow, his own grandson.

The Chinese officials had clubbed the victim around the head and charged him with violence against the emperor. Then, ignoring Andrew's protests, they had dragged the old man off to suffer his punishment. Helpless to prevent such injustice, Andrew had remained in the village long enough to question some children who had unwittingly betrayed a young man of the village who went for meetings to the hut. From that information the culprit was caught. Under torture he confessed that his comrades had recrossed the border into the New Territories.

It had been left to Andrew to send messages to all District

officers in the colony's newly acquired area to search for the men, collect his murdered colleague's effects for the wife in Hong Kong, and make the tedious journey back. In Canton, he was merely a guest, allowed on the fringes of the investigation only because an English official had been killed. Chinese cooperation was unwilling, and he had no sway over the fate of anyone taken by them. Life was cheap, punishment swift. An example must be set to any other who sought to speak against the Emperor, or his Manchu officials.

But Andrew could not help sympathizing with men who were courageous enough to stand against the tyrannical system. The murdered Englishman left a widow and three children who would be sent back to their homeland to face life as best they could. He had liked and admired his colleague: the sight of his mutilated body had angered him deeply. Yet he could not forget an emaciated old man in a filthy hovel, who had been battered and dragged away to his death. Surely a nation could not be expected to bleed forever?

The problems of duty had occupied him so fully there had been little time to think of Nadia, except at night, when he had remembered the afternoon in the garden with an ache of pleasure. It was only on the journey back to Hong Kong that he fully realized all that afternoon now entailed.

He had declared his love, kissed her with great passion, spoken recklessly of all she meant to him. But the facts had not changed because of it. She was still Russian; he was still in the service of the Crown. As his uncle had pointed out, there was no question of conducting an *affaire* with her. There was only one direction their continued love could take and it would be difficult, if not disastrous, for them both. The sensible answer stared him in the face as plainly as before. He had taken a giant step in the wrong direction. Now he was back in Hong Kong, some kind of decision must be taken.

For a few seconds more he gazed at the red-and-gold beauty of the dying sun, then pulled the towel from his neck in sudden exhilaration. He would write to her, arrange a meeting . . . and to hell with the consequences. Blood pounding he turned and ran up the beach, taking the steps two at a time until he reached the terrace of his house. There he paused for breath, holding the back of a chair for support while his heart pounded.

"Damn fool thing to do," he told himself huskily. "Five weeks up-country lowers the stamina."

Kim appeared from around the corner and grinned broadly. "Will it be tea, or a noggin or two, sir?"

Andrew looked at him, panting. "Eh?"

"After such exercise a gentleman always needs refreshment," said the cheery houseboy. "You are a pretty damn fine fellow to run like that and still stand at the end. Very curious thing too, but *pukka sahibs* great fellows."

Straightening up Andrew said, "Kim . . . the British army should . . . take you into its ranks."

"By jingo, thank you, sir," replied Kim with a beaming smile. "What shall I bring?"

He thought tea would be most sensible, and Kim went off saying, "Right o, chop-chop."

Relaxing on his terrace, drinking the cooling tea, Andrew let his thoughts return to Nadia. They would have children, he thought, who would run on the beach leaving tiny footprints on the sand as they chased after him. He would carry the girls on his shoulders, and swing the boys through the waves, letting them feel their growing strength as he held them. God, he would be proud of them—proud of watching them grow into fine men, or girls with gentle eyes and bronze hair.

Kim hurried around the corner again, breaking into his faraway visions. "There is a visitor, sir." He handed Andrew a card.

"Damnation!" cursed Andrew, sitting up and reaching for his robe. "I can hardly pretend to be out now." Getting to his feet he went on. "Does he look set to stay the whole evening?"

"He is not in mess rig, sir." It was Kim's way of saying the visitor was not in evening clothes. "Shall I show the old boy onto the terrace, or will you have sundowners in the study?"

"The 'old boy' is my uncle, Kim. I hardly think he would approve of my garb if I met him in the study and, since he won't take kindly to waiting while I change, it will have to be out here. Bring the brandy out."

117

Kim looked doubtful. "Brandy with tea, sir? You will feel pretty damn queasy."

Andrew laughed. "Yes, I daresay . . . but it is for Sir Goodwin. My uncle won't want tea."

The young Chinese looked relieved. "Ah, frightfully much better for my uncle." He leaned forward conspiratorially. "You want me to come in twenty minutes to say cook-boy is taken ill?"

"What on earth for?"

"If cook-boy is ill there is no dinner . . . and visitors go, chop-chop," he assured Andrew.

"Your previous employers were a wily set," he commented with amusement, "but I can make my own excuses to my uncle."

Sir Goodwin was in a dark suit, impeccable cravat, starched shirt, and carried a silver-knobbed cane. He did not approve of what he saw.

"You've grown damned casual, Andrew," he greeted. "It comes of living out here, I suppose." He looked down his high-bridged nose at the wet towel flung over the back of a chair. Andrew removed it.

"Sorry, sir, but it would have meant keeping you waiting if I had dressed first. I have been swimming."

"So I see" was the heavy comment as he frowned at Andrew's robe.

"Won't you sit down? It's all right . . . that chair isn't wet."

Kim brought the brandy, cast a meaning glance at Andrew, then hurried off. Sir Goodwin watched him go.

"Wherever did you pick up that boy of yours?"

"He has lived almost exclusively with the army—was born in the barracks, I gather. He's excellent. A military friend of mine passed him on to me when I moved. It wasn't easy getting servants to work here after the suicide. *Fung shui,* and all that."

"He has a dashed strange attitude. No respect at all." He looked pointedly at his nephew. "A man is known by the servants he keeps."

Andrew began to bridle. "Kim suits me very well. I find him refreshing after the formality of the office."

"Yes, but what about when you entertain? It's all very well for army types—they're all a bit casual. Comes of serving in damned heathen countries. But you have a reputation to maintain."

With great determination Andrew checked his temper. "I wish you had let me known you were coming, sir. I could have entertained you better. I have invited you and Aunt Maude several times, but you always have other engagements."

"Yes . . . well, this is a devilish difficult place to get to by road, and we could hardly come by boat. Your aunt does not enjoy the best of health, as you know, and this is a little . . . um . . . uncivilized." He cleared his throat and fixed Andrew with a stern eye. "She is still upset over your sudden departure, of course. Put yourself in her place. As your mother's sister she feels a responsibility—mistakenly, perhaps—but a responsibility a woman of her compassionate nature takes to heart. Your parents sent you out here on the understanding that we would help you through a difficult period in your life, and I think you cannot deny we did our utmost in that direction. It's only natural that your aunt was . . . hurt . . . that you should pack up and move into a place like this after all she has done for you. She has put off writing to your mother, because she is afraid Charlotte will feel she has neglected her duty."

"That is quite ridiculous," cried Andrew. "I am a man of twenty-six. Aunt Maude cannot be serious!"

"She is perfectly serious," snapped Sir Goodwin. "When it comes to duty she is very diligent."

"I know," he said, trying to dilute his annoyance. "She was marvelous to me when I arrived, but I could not possibly expect her to play wet nurse to me any longer. I have written to my people explaining why I moved out. I'm sorry Aunt Maude is still upset." He sighed. "Is that the reason for your call?"

"No, not really. I've been visiting the reservoirs and thought I'd have a look at your place as I was passing. Heard you were back, but haven't had time to read your report. Bad business, that! Let's hope our fellows up-country ferret the rascals out. Those years in South Africa were valuable training, Andrew. I always said so to your aunt, but she wouldn't have it. Women have no time for wars. Don't understand the politics of it."

"Another brandy, sir?" Andrew hoped he would refuse, but he did not.

"Thank you." His pale eyes surveyed the Chinese village in the bay. "Awful smell from that place. I wonder you can stand it."

Andrew gripped the decanter hard as he poured. "It's no different from any other Chinese village."

"That's what I mean," said Sir Goodwin, taking his refilled glass. "All frightfully smelly." For a moment or two the two men stared out at the darkening scene, then the elder one said, "I hear you have a Chinese girl here—young. A *secretary*, or some such nonsense. Very unwise, don't you think?"

"Not really," replied Andrew, holding on to the shreds of politeness.

A thin smile stretched Sir Goodwin's lips. "Look, old chap, I'm a man of the world. It's four years since . . . well, it stands to reason a young man has to. . . ." He tugged his moustache self-consciously. "This is not the way to do it. Set her up in a little place in Victoria, but to have her here is madness. Already the lower echelons of the service are buzzing with it. Once the mamas get wind of the setup. . . ."

"To hell with the mamas!" Andrew exploded. "I don't give a damn what those precious creatures think." He got to his feet, unable to contain himself any longer. "Just to get the 'lower echelons' straight, you may tell them Mei-Leng is a most virtuous young woman with multilingual talents who helps me with translations and my library. She does not sleep here. Her house is in the village between here and the gap, and she returns there with her honor intact—despite the fact that I have been a widower for four years."

Sir Goodwin had also risen, rather flushed and not a little out of his depth. "I beg your pardon, Andrew, but it comes of living out here, you know. Gives you a reputation for unconventionality. What are people to think when a native girl turns up out of the blue?"

"She did not turn up out of the blue . . . the Brusilovs recommended her. She is the daughter of their comprador, who is a middle-class and very respectable Chinese. I mentioned my difficulties, and young Brusilov kindly arranged for me to meet the girl. *He* did not appear to think I wanted a mistress, I am pleased to say."

Sir Goodwin flushed darker and snatched up his cane in an angry movement. "So you have ignored my recommendations to dissociate yourself from that family."

"I saw no reason to do so," snapped Andrew, really roused by now. "They are extremely cultured and well-bred—attributes you generally applaud."

"They are *Russians*, Andrew. That is all I can consider . . . and so should you."

"No, sir. Unlike you, I have the ability to see below the surface of life. Where you look at Kim and see an unconventional servant, I see a young man of oriental charm and sincerity. Where you find my house bizarre, I see it as freedom from rigid and confining attitudes. Where your code of narrow-minded rules makes Mei-Leng a victim of lust, I am happy to allow a young girl of undoubted intelligence the opportunity to use it to the advantage of us both." He faced his uncle across the terrace, unable to stop himself now he had started. "You refused my invitations, then call on me unexpectedly only to find fault with every aspect of my life. I have borne your criticisms of servants, home, the way I am dressed, and the heartless manner in which I have treated Aunt Maude . . . but I will not stand for your condemnation of my friends—Russian or otherwise."

With a set face he began walking toward the house to signify that he wished his visitor to leave, but Sir Goodwin had not finished.

"You will not have heard the latest concerning your *friends*. The mother has turned up after all these months. She has been in an asylum, it appears, not clubbed to death by revolutionaries."

Andrew stopped and swung round. "But they saw her . . . her and her husband . . . right before their eyes." He felt shocked, in some way, as if he were part of the family.

Sir Goodwin's mouth twisted. "We only had their word for that."

"I . . . I don't understand. How could she . . . good God, what a terrible shock for them all."

"Indeed it was, by all accounts. The aunt has lost her mind, I hear . . . and Zubov is to be found in hotel bars drinking excessively and making a fool of himself with hysterical stories of supposed attacks by hordes of ragged peasants. Young Brusilov is hardly ever to be found on his premises, and the girl has been seen *serving in the shop*. Now, do you see the reason behind my warning?"

The biting superiority in his uncle's voice was lost on Andrew. The words were not, however, and all he could think of was Nadia trying to hold together her family once more. He had seen for himself how they reacted over Katya's death, and the toll it took on her courage. Just as they were beginning to recover, this blow would be enough to cause all Sir Goodwin suggested . . . a blow, because the joy of the mother's survival would be over-shadowed by her mental state. If ever Nadia needed him, it was now. He became aware of his uncle's thin disapproving face and realized he was still speaking.

"Their whole history is probably lies. It would not surprise anyone to hear the father was killed in a drunken duel, not defending his family from revolutionaries, as they claimed. The whole family is unstable and extremely suspect."

Gripping the edge of the table Andrew heard himself say, "Don't you think they could say the same of us? *Andrew Stanton killed his wife in a drunken rage. His parents had to get him out of the country. His grandfather had previously caused a scandal by trying to rear his Indian bastard son. The uncle, Sir Goodwin Halder, has never had a child, bastard or otherwise, and one can draw one's own conclusions. Lady Halder suffers terrible headaches. There's no history of insanity in the family, so they say, but one never knows with the aristocracy.*" He slammed his hand down onto the table. "There! See how easy it is to turn a normal family into a group of monsters."

The older man had gone as white as death and had difficulty in getting his next words out. "I will try to forget you ever said that, or I think I could never speak to you again." He walked past Andrew and into the sitting room.

The Brusilov house was well lit. Andrew rode straight to the stables and handed his horse to the groom, who greeted him with apparent pleasure. For once, he had no word for the cheery Indian. He strode round to the front entrance, still breathing heavily from the exertion of his gallop.

Inside the large reception hall he greeted the servant by name, and was about to ask that Miss Brusilova be informed of his arrival when he heard his name and looked across at the staircase. Misha Zubov was hurrying down, arms outstretched to greet him.

"Mr. Stanton . . . *Andrew* . . . how good of you, how very good of you to come." He pattered across the mosaic, a rotund figure in evening clothes and small patent shoes. "I call you Andrew as a token of my esteem and affection." The smell of vodka wafted to Andrew as the Russian reached him and flung his arms around him in Slavic emotion. "To have friends at such a time is a great happiness. There is so much sorrow, so much pain. It surrounds us . . . yes, truly it does." He dabbed his moist eyes with a crimson handkerchief. "We have missed you, dear friend."

"I have been in Canton," he supplied, noting how his host had changed in those five weeks. His moustaches drooped in ragged untrimmed fashion, his eyes were doleful and red-rimmed. Even his stomach had lost its cheerful obesity, hanging like a weighty and unsightly feature of a very sad man.

"Yes, Canton. I know. That you had to go at such a time . . . tsk-tsk!" His hands clapped Andrew's arms again with emotional fervor. "But you are here now . . . you are here, *slava Bogu!* Come, come, we are in the salon."

Andrew held back. "No. I am not dressed . . . I rode over as soon as I heard. I had hoped to. . . ."

"*Gospodi!* Do you think we would deny a dear friend because he wears riding clothes?" He tucked his hand through Andrew's arm and began leading him toward the salon in which the family usually gathered before dinner. "Fine trappings can disguise a fool besides adorn a nobleman," he quoted wagging his head from side to side, and Andrew began to wonder just how much vodka he had consumed.

All such thoughts flew when they entered the room, and he saw Nadia rise from her chair, looking at him with the faint blush of pleasure. As he returned her gaze he realized how inadequate his memory was. It had missed the glowing promise of love in her eyes that made them larger and more arresting; the tender lines of a mouth curved by her compassionate nature; the glory of hair

123

piled softly around a pointed face, springing into tendrils at her temples and nape. After his long absence from her the slightly accented voice fell upon his ears with seductive charm.

"I did not know you were back. How—how good of you to call."

How calm she appeared after her uncle. "I did not mean to intrude," he heard himself say as he indicated his boots and breeches. "I called only to. . . ."

"A pity you did not let us know of your proposed visit, Mr. Stanton," said Ivan from his stance before the fireplace. "We would have delayed dinner. As it is. . . ."

"He will stay," declared Misha expansively, "of course he will stay. When has a Zubov denied his friend a seat at his table?"

"No . . . no, I have work to do," lied Andrew, disappointed at the outcome of his visit. He had wanted to talk to Nadia alone. Now he was standing like a gamekeeper in the midst of a fashionable salon full of dinner guests. Unable to approach the real reason for his unorthodox visit, trying to deduce the situation from what he saw, Andrew felt he had acted unwisely. His contact with the girl he loved could be no more than polite civility.

Obliged to turn to his hostess, he smiled and murmured conventional words. She did not return his smile or show a spark of interest in his presence. Her reply was automatic, and she sat like a sad little outcast, her once beaming round face pinched and pale. Ivan was pale, also, and looked no more than a boy who had been allowed to join the adults for dinner.

He felt like shaking them all. Aunt Marie giving the world away, Misha taking his courage from a bottle, Ivan playing the adult rather than becoming one. Their temperamental behavior did nothing to help Nadia or the situation. If the mother was now an added responsibility, a half-demented creature back from the dead, they would do better to unite in strength. All except Nadia appeared to have bowed beneath the weight.

Determined this visit would not be entirely fruitless he turned to Nadia and tried to convey with his eyes what he could not say to her.

"My uncle told me of Madame Brusilova's miraculous survival.

If there is anything I can do, please do not. . . ." There was a rustle at the doorway, and he turned his head involuntarily. His words tailed off as he forgot what he had been about to say, forgot everyone in the room, forgot who or what he was as he gazed at Anna Brusilova.

She stood framed in the wide doorway against a backdrop of white walls, like a cameo in reverse. The dark red dress was cut severely without decoration, molding her body to the hips, then sweeping up into a beautiful waterfall of puffs and flounces that spilled into a train spreading along the floor behind her.

Almost stunned, Andrew was unable to take his eyes from a woman whose face combined such pride, sensuality, and breeding. Her cheekbones were high and pronounced, creating hollows beneath to echo the tragedy behind her, but her mouth was curved with the generosity of passion still lingering to tantalize the beholder. Black hair drawn back and up into a pile of gleaming swaths added height to her slender arrogant stance and contrasted with her creamy skin.

Around her throat was a dazzling collar of diamonds, but Andrew hardly noticed them. He was totally drawn by the brilliance of her eyes, wide-set, oblique, and silver-green against the thick dark lashes. She was not beautiful—she was magnificent!

Oblivious of all else he began walking toward her, but he had taken only three steps when the figure in red sank to the floor in a faint. There were exclamations, movements around him, but he was already there bending to pick her up with hands that shook. It was difficult to get his thoughts straight as he carried her to a sofa, marveling at the pliancy of her body, and cradling her head against his arm to prevent it dropping back.

With great care he laid her against the gold upholstery, then knelt beside the sofa, watching the smudge of black lashes against her cheeks, waiting for her eyes to open. Someone, he did not notice who, put a smelling bottle in his hand, and he passed it gently back and forth beneath her nostrils. She looked as pale as death.

His heart was hammering with the suddenness of all that had happened, not understanding how the moment had turned into drama in an instant. The lashes quivered, then her eyes opened to look full into his as he bent over her.

Their brilliance increased as they widened, and he caught his breath at the blaze of living passion in their depths. It set him on a throne, knelt at his feet, and proceeded to consume him. Even through the swell of tears it burned like mesmeric fire as she put up a hand to touch his pale hair, then his mouth.

"Andrei," she whispered. *"Andrei!"*

It was late—very late—but he remained on the terrace staring out to sea. He had been there for two hours, or more, but time meant nothing. He kept hearing that rapturous whispered *Andrei* and knew it would be a long time before he forgot the whole incredible evening.

Reaching the end of the terrace he stood with his hands on the rough stone and put back his head in a gesture of unease as he remembered those trembling fingers on his lips, and his own unsteady voice telling her she was mistaken. He had known the story, but paid no heed to the man's Christian name. His own English version of it had increased her state of fever.

He began pacing again, burning with the memory of her struggle to accept the truth. He had hardly ever been witness to such emotion before. Yet, it was her eyes that truly haunted him, if he was honest with himself. They had worshiped him; given him her whole life, *made* him Andrei Brusilov.

So little had ever been said by the family of the parents who had been murdered in Russia. Respect for their loss had prevented him from asking questions. If he had it might have come out that Nadia's mother had been a bride straight from the schoolroom. He had gone there expecting a stricken matron.

Even now, it was difficult to believe what he had seen on looking across at her entry. Anna Brusilova *was* Russia—exotic, proud, a magnificent combination of cultures and races. She had nobility yet the wild splendor of the people of the Steppes. In her face there was suffering and exultation, Slavic passion and eastern mystery. And her eyes . . her eyes had seen in him all she wanted in life, and claimed him. No, dammit, she had claimed Andrei Brusilov!

126

Fever-hot, he flung off his jacket and went down onto the beach where the moon put a silver frosting on the wet sand at the water's edge. For five weeks he had held a memory of Nadia in his mind and heart, yet all he could remember of her this evening was her face as if miles away across the room as Ivan, with surprising assurance, asked him to leave. For once, the young Russian had been more in command than he, and only now could he remember bidding a general goodnight to unhearing ears. Aunt Marie had been crying, her husband trying to comfort her with soft-spoken despair. Nadia had been a shadow behind the sofa, holding a bottle of smelling salts in her hand. Just before he had turned from the room he had seen what was written in her face.

He reached the line where the receding tide sent dying waves onto the beach in frothy surges. They went over his riding boots and sucked around the depressions made by his weight, but he still stood with hands deep in his pockets, gazing out across the bay at the moon.

After a long time, he escaped from his thoughts enough to acknowledge his lunar friend. "You are not to blame this time, dear lady," he murmured, "but I hit another wall tonight that I could not possibly have forseen."

SIX

It was wonderful to get out. As the rickshaw bowled along the tree-lined avenue, Nadia took a deep breath of the warm blossom-scented air and put her head back to look at the serenity of the sky through the lace of her parasol. Since last night the house had become unbearable.

With determination she had let her mother's return change nothing of herself, holding aloof as she had always done. Yet, those around her had changed like the little two-headed mandarin from Paris she had once been given as a present. Depending on which way the head was placed on the body, the figure changed from a serene smiling advisor to a frowning and angry official.

Aunt Marie's pretense at motherhood was shattered by the return of the natural mother, and she had surrendered to her sister-in-law something the woman did not want—had never wanted—before withdrawing into the shadows of eternal regret leaving the position vacant.

Uncle Misha had changed his face from that of a voluble enthusiastic man of culture to one of guilt and inadequacy. He

128

had screamed *drive on* leaving behind a woman he had thought dead, but who had returned to challenge him with cowardice. He spent a lot of time in his study riffling through his oppressive verses with a bottle at his elbow.

As for Ivan, he changed faces with bewildering speed. One day he was plunged into introspection over their mother's plans to return to Russia which she made without consultation with him. Another day he would arrive home bursting with elated assurance that suggested he had reached a firm decision on the stand he would take. Yet it seemed to have nothing to do with his future. The renewed closeness that had followed their resolution to end the mourning for Katya had gone again. Nadia did not understand her twin at all these days.

From the day of her mother's return those three had fallen into their old roles as if their life in Hong Kong meant nothing, and she had watched, telling herself they were providing their own misery. Nothing had really changed. Aunt Marie still had the love she had always received from her "children"; Uncle Misha had lost none of his success and reputation as a jade merchant; and Ivan was forced to make a decision only a few months earlier than expected.

She had seen all this from her safe immunity and despaired for them all, but it was different now. Last night her own happiness had been threatened, and in a way that left her feeling bereft and fearful. Having remained supremely untouched by each other for twenty years, her mother had now entered her life in the most bizarre manner. A stab of apprehension pierced her again, and her hands clutched the embroidered bag on her lap until she could feel the clasp biting into her flesh.

The rickshaw was held up while an enormous ritual dragon, on poles held by twenty men along the street, undulated breathing smoke through its garish nostrils and rolling huge thick-lashed eyes at the revelers. It was a common sight in Hong Kong, a noisy colorful procession with a mixture of fire and fun attached to it, but today Nadia saw only the macabre side. The great brightly-colored head swayed in her direction, symbolizing the chimera that was born last night while she had watched like a patron reviewing a new theatrical drama.

Her eyes closed to shut out the pagan street scene, but the one she saw in her mind's eye was worse. All night she had seen that tableau—her mother lying on the sofa, and Andrew kneeling beside her. The pain of what had happened increased as Nadia recalled the hand touching Andrew's hair, his mouth, his throat ... and the Russian words *My heart, my body, my soul!* She had ravished him with every word, every sight, every touch of her fingers.

Looking back, Nadia realized she had done nothing but watch the scene unfold, gripping the smelling bottle as if it had been a lifeline. She vaguely remembered Ivan touching Andrew's shoulder and suggesting that he leave. There had been sounds of crying, and Uncle Misha's voice murmuring deep consolation, but it had not been her mother who wept. She lay in a spread of dark skirts upon gold velvet, gazing at the departing Andrew as if she had only that moment come back from the dead. Not until he reached the door had Andrew looked her way, and the pain in her breast had increased.

Numb and shaking, she had helped Ivan guide their mother upstairs to her room, where she had moved unsteadily to a tiny drawer and taken from it an ivory miniature of a blond young man with eyes as blue as a summer day, and a smile lingering on his mouth. It could have been a picture of Andrew Stanton, except that he wore a Russian uniform, green with colored facings. Through her disbelief Nadia remembered her sister insisting that she had seen Andrew before. At some time she must have seen the miniature and remembered it at the back of her mind.

Sleep had evaded Nadia for most of the night, but when she did succumb she was haunted by nightmares of their escape from St. Petersburg. But this time, it was Andrew who was slipping away from life and herself who crawled through the snow reaching for him with outstretched fingers. When morning came it was like coming out of a future which she had already lived.

Incredibly Anna had been serenely calm, as if Andrew's visit had never taken place ... yet Nadia could not remember when her mother had looked so beautiful. It was then she realized it was no longer possible to stand aloof.

The increasing noise of central Victoria made Nadia aware that they were nearer the gallery, but she looked around her with a heavy heart. The rickshaw boy pounded along beside gracious colonnaded buildings that housed the British administrators, wealthy merchants' offices, grand hotels, and large finance companies.

They had come to a halt at Galerie Russe, and the runner dropped the yoke to allow her to alight. The Eurasian doorman hurried forward, and she steadied herself on his arm while gathering up her cream serge skirt.

The interior of the gallery was refreshingly cool, the dark cabinets and hushed atmosphere pleasant after the brilliance of sun on white buildings. She went straight through to the large alcoved section where her uncle sat with clients while negotiations for purchases were made. It was discreet, quite apart from the showrooms, yet gave a comprehensive view of the gallery. It was not their business policy to press visitors to buy, but when they showed serious interest in one particular item, Misha would stroll from his office alcove to chat with them.

Since her mother returned, Nadia had been going almost daily to the gallery, earning not only her brother's disapproval, but that of many colonists who were shocked at a girl of her station playing shopgirl. She was not, in effect, doing anything of that nature, but Uncle Misha was so unreliable now, he could not be depended upon to be there when needed and, since the supervisors were not qualified to make sales, some member of the Brusilov family had to be on hand. Nadia knew little about jade, but was charming and helpful, fetching Ivan from his upstairs office or explaining with smiling regret that Mr. Zubov was unavoidably detained but would be glad to call upon them at home or in their hotel, if they so wished.

It was difficult, sometimes, when gentlemen came in alone and Ivan was also away from the premises, but something had to be done to keep the gallery from losing its high reputation, and Nadia argued fiercely with her twin before firmly defying him.

On the whole, she enjoyed the freedom her new life offered—enjoyed watching the teeming life of Hong Kong pass the windows—and closed her mind to the occasional rudeness and derision of regular colonists who wandered through the gallery just to see if what they had heard was true.

Nadia went in that morning feeling the need for escape more than ever before. She put her parasol and bag on Misha's big desk and gazed at her hands as they moved slowly over the polished surface. She had glimpsed a whole blazing world in Andrew's arms that afternoon . . . but what now? He had appeared without warning last night to change the sad lament of her heart into a soaring triumphant aria. Then he had looked up and. . . . Her hands gripped the wood hard. Anna Brusilova had found her Andrei. May God help him, for no one else could!

Movement behind her sent her around swiftly. He stood just inside the glass-partitioned alcove, the sun through the fanlights catching his hair with a flaxen gleam. His eyes were bluer than the waters of the harbor, and as deep with some emotion she could not recognize. The remnants of last night's drama were still visible in the tightness of his jaw and the rigid way he held himself.

"You looked at me that way when I left last night." His voice was husky, lacking its usual gentle authority. Her fears bobbed up again like corks on water; an ocean seemed to divide them.

"How did you know I would be here?" Her face felt so stiff it was amazing she could speak at all.

He came nearer, putting his helmet on the corner of the desk. "My uncle told me you spend a lot of time here these days." He searched her face with an intent look. "As soon as I heard it seemed imperative to see you, offer my support. That is why I rode across as I did. *To see you.*"

He was telling her nothing she did not know. It just seemed unimportant now.

"Nadia, this is very difficult," he went on in the same husky tone. "If I had known she was so . . . so. . . ." He sighed deeply. "It caught me on the wrong foot—completely unprepared."

"Yes, of course." She was being frostily polite. Had they ever kissed in her garden like lovers who could not bear to say goodbye?

"How is your . . . how is she now?"

"Outwardly the same as usual. None of us has ever known what

132

she feels beneath the surface." She was tonelessly blunt.

"I shall be prepared next time."

She seized on his words with passion. "Next time? You are already speaking of coming again?"

His jaw tightened further and the darkness of his eyes blazed. "This must not be allowed to change anything."

"It has changed," she cried. "Already you are different."

"Only because you are," he flung back. "You looked at me last night as if I had betrayed you. It is still there on your face—an accusation."

"And it is still there on your face—the same look he always wore." All at once the excessive emotion of the past twenty-four hours, the nightmares and fears, proved too much. She turned away from him, hands to her temples. "It made me dream . . . oh, terrible things. It was as if you had . . . become *him.*"

He was behind her instantly, drawing her back against him. "Nothing has changed. *Nothing has changed.* How could it?" Turning her around he kissed her fiercely. "I love you. I thought I made that clear enough before I went to Canton." His hand caressed her cheek, a brown hand full of strength. "You are my peace and my future."

When he drew her into his arms she went with wild relief. Their love was so new, so desperately precious, she had been afraid for it. She had believed him lost to her already.

"Forgive me," she whispered between his kisses. "It was the dreams. They seemed so real."

"I know, I know," he murmured. "I have had dreams, too."

After a while she gently disengaged herself from his arms, smiling up at him. "Do you want the whole of Hong Kong to see us and start gossiping?"

"They will do that soon enough." He took her hands in his, growing serious. "There is so much we must talk about. You do see that we cannot let this . . . unfortunate affair keep us apart?"

"Yes . . . but Andrew, you do not know her," she said with a return of her fears.

"I have thought about this for most of the night," he told her firmly, "and there is only one answer. It is important for her to accept me as Andrew, and not. . . ." He sighed rather than say

133

the name. "The sooner she sees me again, the sooner she will forget last night. She has been very ill; I was a stranger. For some reason she identified me with your father. If I stay away she will continue to do so."

"We can meet in so many other places," she said quickly. "There is no need for you to come to the house."

He dropped her hands in an angry gesture. "You have not understood at all. How can I avoid her forever?"

She seized his hand and closed it around her own again. "It is you who do not understand. After you had gone she showed us a miniature. It was of . . . Papa, as a young man. It was a picture of you."

He was shocked, she could see it in the way he frowned, and by the quick indrawn breath. On the surface he seemed untouched, but the huskiness in his voice had returned.

"I see. All the more reason for proving that I am myself. I daresay there are many people who could be said to look alike in a portrait or photograph that catches a certain expression. Once they are identified as separate personalities the likeness fades. It was the shock of that first meeting that created the illusion. She will not be like it again."

"And if she is?" she asked, knowing how a man could be held by a woman who lived only for him.

"If we are to have a future together, how are we to keep that from her?" He pulled her back in his arms. "Oh, my dearest, it will be difficult enough as it is. This is the only way, I promise." His kiss was tender and full of a message that reassured her. In consequence, she only half-heard him say, "I have no intention of letting a ghost take me over. I have already lived with one far too long."

Andrew had been gone only a few minutes when Nadia was faced with another complication she found difficult to accept. Hardly had there been time to settle herself than Ivan walked round the glass partition and stood there before her, pale and angry.

"What did that fellow want?"

She was conscious of her flushed cheeks, and knew the color

deepened at his attitude. "He wanted to see me."

"Then he should have called at the house, where you could have declined to receive him." He cast a quick glance at the showrooms and lowered his voice somewhat. "You refused to listen to my objections to your presence here. Now you see the danger of exposing yourself to that kind of cavalier behavior. I only saw him as he was leaving, or I should have soon sent him on his way. Coming here day after day is doing your reputation great harm. *Now* will you listen to me?"

She rose from the heavy wooden chair, trying to placate him in his absurd display of formality. *"Mily,* how could he have come to the house after last night? He came to enquire after Mama."

He wavered on the brink of disapproval. "I see. If he had not appeared in that manner—uninvited and casually dressed—it would never have happened."

"Yes," she insisted. "Whenever Mama first saw him it would have happened." She sighed with the memory of it. "Vanya, how is it we did not see the likeness?"

He was brusque in his dismissal. "It is only there in that early miniature, a passing expression. We knew Papa as a mature man with big moustaches, an officer of the Guards, serving the Czar. Stanton is an Englishman through and through, young, a minor official. There was nothing to link the two, in my mind."

"Nor mine. Papa was cold," she reflected. "A man who almost frightened me."

"Papa was a man of courage. He died to save our lives. Never forget that."

"He died to save Mama." It came unheralded, but she knew it was the truth.

Ivan grew paler. "Great men often appear cold and frightening. They have to hide their emotions."

"He did not hide them from her." Why was she suddenly so passionate, so full of the need to destroy the picture her brother was building in his mind? She looked at his face, so very like her own in many aspects, and struggled to reach him again.

"Andrew Stanton has been a good friend to us all. Why do you dislike him, *bratishka?"*

The reply was unexpected. "When he was twenty he was

fighting a war. What am I doing? I sense that he is asking me that every time we meet."

"*Chepukha!* He speaks constantly of the success of Galerie Russe."

Ivan curled his lip. "You think that is praise from him? He speaks of a fact; he despises me for doing something I hate."

"You despise yourself, that is the truth of it," she cried.

He would not face her, but walked across to the window to stare from it as if at the future. "It is easy for you. You will marry, rear a family, serve your husband with loyalty and devotion. But me, I have to tread in Papa's footsteps. I must be Brusilov of Petersburg. Ivan Andreyevich. *Ivan—son of Andrei.* Do you know what that means? What Russia demands of me—what *she* demands of me? No, it is easy for you, *sestrushka.*"

All her tension and fears from the night before made her fly into a rare temper. "So, it is easy for me? Can you, for once, forget your own feelings and consider mine?" Gripping the back of the chair she went on, "When we first came to Hong Kong I was left to smooth the feathers of everyone in the family. The older ones were afraid you would go back; you were too proud to try to accept this life at least until you were in a position to leave it; Katya was only happy when she set you all against each other." Her hands moved on the warm wood. "It was the same for me. It was no easier for me to settle here without friends, and with the young ones across the world in a convent with Grandmother. There were times when *I* was lonely and afraid, uncertain of the future. But there was not one of you in whom I could confide. You all demanded comfort from me. That is how easy it has been for me."

He had turned to face her while she spoke, and the pain of her accusal was written across his features. She felt her temper die, as the old protective affection rushed in. She went to him, holding his forearms as she looked up into his face.

"Vanya, *golubchik*, I know what it is like for you, believe me. Have I not always known?"

He took her in a great hug, saying, "Forgive me, *sestrushka*, my dearest friend, my blood and my heartbeat. Without you I am

136

nothing." He kissed her brow, and she smiled into his moist eyes.

"Yes, you are Brusilov of Petersburg—Ivan, son of Andrei. One day Russia will compare the father with the son, not the other way around. You will see."

He hugged her again, overcome with emotion that he would only display before a twin who shared his secret self. In a flash the old bond had returned, and Nadia felt instinctively that it was the moment to tell her brother of her own secret self. Taking his hand she began with the garden party at Government House, and went on to describe how Andrew had declared his love for her on the day he went to Canton.

"The shock of what followed that day—of Mama's return—kept me from telling you. He came as he did last night because of me. Vanya, he is the rock to which I can cling . . . but it is more than that. He makes my day bright, and my night a siren song of dreams. You will not understand that yet, but you will, *bratishka,* you will when it happens to you."

At that point she realized he was standing unnaturally still. She drew away. "Vanya, what is it?"

"I thought he was merely an acquaintance—a friend of our uncle. It did not occur to me . . . *Poberi!* why did I not see? It is out of the question . . . a foreigner, and Englishman . . . have you thought of that? Have you truly thought of that?" He was beside himself with a new kind of passion to any she had seen in him before. "Would you turn your back on your heritage, your country, your church? Will you sacrifice all that?"

She felt stricken. "It . . it has not come to that yet. He has been in Canton since that day. There has been no time to talk. He . . . this morning, he said he will invite the family to his new house very soon . . . all of us. Perhaps then he will speak to you, to Mama. There has been no time. Of course he will speak to you."

He pushed himself away from the window and headed for the gallery without another glance in her direction. "He will be wasting his time." For once he looked like a young man who knew his own mind very well indeed.

Sir Goodwin stood up when he went in, which surprised

137

Andrew. The surprise was extended to the silver tray with brandy and glasses, and the box of cigars, all reserved for important visitors. There must be a senior official due at any moment.

"You wanted to see me, sir?" he asked cautiously, it being the first time they had come face to face since his uncle visited him at his house.

"Yes . . . yes. Come in and close the door, Andrew," blustered his uncle with unusual informality for the office. "Make yourself comfortable. Brandy and soda?"

"Thank you." He grew suspicious. What was going on? Sir Goodwin was pulling at his moustache, a sure sign that he was about to embark on something he did not relish.

He accepted the drink. "Shouldn't we wait for our guest?"

"I beg your pardon?"

"Isn't this laid on for someone of importance?" he asked, waving a hand at the tray.

"Er . . . no . . . although Captain Smethwick will be coming along in a moment. This is something of a private discussion, my boy."

Andrew grew more suspicious. "My boy" in the office!

"Your good health," the older man said, taking a pull at his brandy.

Andrew waved his glass vaguely by way of a return salute and drank with his glance still on his uncle. Sir Goodwin remained standing, completely unrelaxed for what he had implied was a private and informal discussion. When he began speaking it was as if his nephew sat somewhere just outside the window, a habit he always used when tackling tricky subjects.

"A man is often called upon to do many things he does not like under the call of duty, Andrew . . . and while it might be that he has certain principles that he feels unable to forgo, circumstances often prove greater than his scruples. It does not mean that he is any the less honorable." He cleared his throat noisily. "No doubt, you found such instances during your time in South Africa."

Really on the defensive by now Andrew answered warily, "Yes, sir . . . but I have to say that, circumstances or not, I found it hard to accept that I had not lost something of my integrity by obeying such calls of duty. Each time I came face to face with a

Boer I knew it was him or me, but I lost something of myself each time I pulled the trigger." He had suddenly had enough of walking around the subject. "What is this particular 'call of duty,' sir?"

Sir Goodwin turned from his study of the view from the window and frowned. "You will not have heard, because I kept the report back for a day. A Chinese junk was boarded by officials from Kwangtung province, and the vessel was found to be carrying cases of literature, both leaflets and journals banned in China, that preached revolution. One of the sources of this distribution has at last been discovered."

Andrew rested his glass on the corner of the desk. "Splendid! I only wish our own men had been more vigilant. The vessel must have passed through our own police patrols."

"Yes . . . but the master of the junk was well-known to our people, and the search was waived, in consequence."

"Good God . . . who was the man?"

Andrew whistled through his teeth when his uncle revealed the culprit to be a man of good reputation who plied the China coast as a carrier of cargoes on commission from wealthy merchants, but Sir Goodwin's next words gave him the first clue to what was to come.

"The vessel was heading for Shanghai . . . on a round trip for jade. The voyage was commissioned by young Brusilov."

At that point wariness became aggression. His uncle's words hit him hard. "You are surely not suggesting that he is in any way connected with it? It is not only out of the question, it is the supposition of an ignorant man . . . and you are not that."

Sir Goodwin pulled at his moustache ends again. "You have very foolishly become emotionally involved with that family, but try to look at this with detachment, Andrew. I asked you to my office so that you could come to terms with the situation before Smethwick arrives. We are considering facts. The voyage was financed by young Brusilov ostensibly to collect and bring back jade from Shanghai. He paid a great deal of money for a straightforward carrying job, far more than an astute merchant would pay."

"He is not much more than a boy, new to the colony. You

139

cannot compare him with Jardine, or Dent," Andrew said at once. "He is bound to be fleeced now and again by men like Yang."

"How do you account for the fact that the cases containing the leaflets had the trademark of Galerie Russe stamped on them?"

Andrew got to his feet. "Anyone can steal packing cases from a warehouse. Yang probably asked for them to pack the pieces in when he picked them up." He paced the floor once or twice in his mood of defense. "The whole notion is ridiculous. Brusilov would be the last person to back a revolution in China. Dammit, he and his family only just escaped murder by revolutionaries in his own country. You don't know him as I do. He is an imperialist through and through." He paced some more. "God in heaven, the entire family is devoted to the Czar. Old man Brusilov was a court administrator, and the father was a . . ." he hesitated, remembering silver-green eyes, and a hand touching his lips in adoration,". . . the father was an officer of the Imperial Guard."

Sir Goodwin remained silent, allowing his nephew ample opportunity to say all that was inside him.

"All that boy thinks and speaks of is getting back to Russia to follow his preordained path. He is full of aristocratic notions that have been drummed into him since childhood. He has no interest in the Chinese—has never attempted to understand them or their way of life. It is absolutely ludicrous to attach anything of this nature to him. In his mind, there is only one nation in the world, and one race of people."

Sir Goodwin broke in at that juncture, because he saw the perfect lead-in to his next point.

"What you have said, in effect, is that Brusilov is a fervent advocate of Russian supremacy." He refilled Andrew's glass and handed it to him. "Just listen to me for a moment with the impartial mind of a man in your position. The Brusilovs are one of the great families of Russia, pledged to live and die for it. You are only too well aware of the Russian drive to expand in the Far East. One way to combat revolution in their own ranks is to strengthen their overall power as a nation." He was warming to his theme, but Andrew stood motionless, the drink in his hand untouched. "Unrest in China, the kind of unrest no other large nation wishes to encourage, could help their cause. The Chinese

140

people are not yet ready or equipped for a successful revolution, so while world attention was focused on scattered minor uprisings, Russia could advance its interests in the north of the country without too much notice being taken of such movements."

Andrew stared at him. "Are you suggesting that Brusilov would involve himself in such despicable diplomatic activities? He has hardly yet come to terms with the murder of his father and grandfather. He is a boy still struggling to become the man he feels he is expected to be. I say he is incapable of even thinking of such involvement in world affairs."

"Yes, possibly, but men like Orlov are not."

"You think . . . but the Russians profess a policy similar to ours, surely?"

"Officially. But there are always men who seek personal gain with the advancement of their country—men in positions of trust and authority, who will not hesitate to enroll pawns like young Brusilov. From all you tell me he is ripe for that kind of activity. Burning with love for his country, it would only need someone to whisper in his ear that there was a way he could fulfill his destiny and serve Czar and country, and he would do it."

Andrew was halted in his defense. It was quite true. Such connivance in the fate of the world had altered its course many times in its long history. What his uncle said made sense . . . but Ivan Brusilov was too transparent to be doing what he suggested. Andrew would stake his life on it.

"No," he said shaking his head emphatically. "In theory it is sound, but I will not accept that boy's involvement."

"It is his business that is involved, like it or not." Sir Goodwin turned as the door opened to admit a tall dark-haired Englishman in light suit and soft hat. "Ah, Captain Smethwick, come in and take a seat. You know my nephew, of course. Brandy and soda?"

"Thank you, sir," said the new arrival. "Hallo, Andrew. The last time I saw you was at the opposite end of a cricket pitch. That was a wicked ball you sent down at me."

"Hallo, Chris." Andrew did not take up the comment about the cricket match and the police official came quickly to the reason for the meeting.

"Sir Goodwin has told you by now that we have a very touchy situation on our hands, Andrew. The Viceroy of Kwangtung is in one hell of a rage over the incident." He made a face. "My boys are to blame, because they let the bloody junk past. I understand the entire crew was punished in the usual manner before we even knew about it." He shifted in his chair and eased his collar. "Damned hot, today! Anyway, His Excellency in Kwangtung is making diplomatic noises that sound suspiciously like accusations of the colony's involvement with revolutionary activities. Those damned tracts came from Japan, and from here on their way up-country." He let out a puff of reflective breath. "Seems we bloody well let them in and out again without suspecting a thing."

"We can't search every vessel that uses the harbor, and it would be impossible to even keep track of the millions of small boats and sampans plying between the island and the mainland," Andrew pointed out.

Chris made another face. "Don't I know it! All the same, it does mean the old boy in Kwangtung has a case against us that he can interpret into anything he likes. There is no doubt of that jade gallery being the source—one of the crew confirmed it before he lost his head." He smiled briefly at Andrew. "It really is a blessing that you are acquainted with that family and can save our bacon."

"Actually, I hadn't got around to explaining that yet," put in Sir Goodwin hastily.

Andrew experienced a sudden lurch of apprehension. "Explaining what?" He looked from one to the other. "What is this meeting really about . . . this bonhomie amidst the brandy?"

Chris smiled again, innocent of what he was about to do. "A bit of softening up before the call to duty, old fellow. But then, you chaps in this department always work in strange and devious ways. We want you to use your connection with that Russian fellow to investigate his activities; find out more about his business and Chinese friends; check if he has links with the secret societies. It should be easy enough to get a good look at his premises under the guise of friendly interest, and you might find out about his general comings and goings from the rest of his family. Women are usually much more garrulous than their

142

menfolk; they could give you valuable information without knowing it."

Something inside Andrew exploded. He banged his glass on the desk and stood up to face his uncle. "You have done this. By God, you really do have a low opinion of me! If they were English you would not dream of asking me to do something so contemptible."

"I am not asking you, Andrew. The order has come from the Governor personally." Sir Goodwin spoke with genuine apology. "It appears one of his close advisors knows you have visited the Brusilov home several times, that you are acquainted with the uncle, and so on. He knows you rendered the family a service when the young girl died so suddenly. It was on the strength of that information that he issued these instructions."

"But you know it is more than that," cried Andrew. "By God, they are all coming to my house to dinner tonight."

"Excellent," said Chris Smethwick. "A perfect opportunity to sound out young Brusilov on that junk he commissioned."

Andrew rounded on him. "I intended to sound him out about something quite different. I am in love with his sister."

There was a moment of silence while the police officer absorbed Andrew's statement. "Oh lord, that does make it somewhat complicated."

"Complicated!" raved Andrew. "I won't do it, and that's that."

Sir Goodwin sighed. "You have no choice, I'm afraid. This is a direct order from the top, and the Governor is not likely to consider your reasons for excusal. We have a very serious situation on our hands. Our relations with the Chinese are shaky enough, at the best of times; we cannot allow them to deteriorate into a state of national aggression. The Viceroy has dealt with his countrymen; he expects us to deal with a fellow-European who falls under our jurisdiction." He walked across to Andrew. "We have no option but to comply ... and there is no doubt of Brusilov's involvement."

Andrew looked at his uncle in despair. "Would you do such a thing to your friends?"

There was sympathy in Sir Goodwin's face as he looked at a

143

young subordinate rather than his nephew. "I understand that your sense of honor protests at this . . . but in our profession, one cannot afford to have friends in the enemy camp."

The dinner party that night was a disaster despite the careful preparations that had been made for it. There were painted Chinese lanterns strung along the terrace, a meal chosen with great care, flowers floating in bowls at each place setting, matching the jugs full of blossoms all over the house, and a boat hired to bring the guests and take them home again. Mei-Leng had willingly extended her duties to act as maid to the ladies, and Kim had organized everything to the last detail, assuring Andrew that "he would eat his hat if his master did not feel jolly perky after his guests had said toodle-oo."

Unable to cancel the evening at such short notice, and weighed down by the events of that morning, Andrew had greeted the family with false heartiness and a smile dragged up from somewhere in his past. But they were impossible to entertain.

Ivan was even more than usually aloof, pale and imperious, and curiously fascinated by Mei-Leng. Misha drank too much, his Slavic charm turning to maudlin expansiveness as the evening wore on while his wife sat with uninterested resignation.

Nadia watched him from the moment she arrived, but he could do nothing to reassure her questioning anxiety. He knew now that he would have to let her go—there was no other way—and the knowledge made him sick at heart and evasive with her.

Then there was Anna. There had been no repetition of the fainting fit when she saw him, but her reaction was even more disturbing. Her eyes still burned with the same obsessive adoration, and he was held in shock from the moment of greeting. He knew there was no other person in the room for her but the man she called by his Russian name, Andrei. She presided over the evening with compelling supremacy, everyone at the dinner table knowing she held them all in her hand. It made Andrew angry with them all, and yet he could not forget her for one moment however hard he struggled against it.

With a determined effort he broached the subject of a recent jade forgery with Misha, saying, "It is the end for Wah, of course.

144

A reputable merchant only ever sells one fake. I know him personally, as you do. He is old, but years usually add to an expert's wisdom." He smiled in a somewhat strained manner. "He once told me his failing eyesight made no difference; the jade 'spoke' to him when he handled it."

Uncle Misha put down his wineglass, leaving his moustache dripping bubbles, and waved his hand in exaggerated fashion. "This time they spoke the wrong words, hey?" He laughed over-loudly. "My friend, he was a foolish man. As we say in Russia, he who runs with the wolves will howl like a wolf. I have watched him for some time. He buys from men who are rogues. What can he expect?"

"How is one to know who is a rogue and who is not?" asked Ivan. "In business there is not one man who will not deceive another if it means bigger profits. Is it any wonder I do not enjoy being a merchant?" He frowned. "I should be in my father's regiment. A soldier is honorable. To his fellows he is a true and trusted companion."

Andrew looked at him for a moment. "True enough, but rival armies are not content to deceive each other. They kill. Being a soldier is not all horse-riding and bonhomie, Ivan Andreyevich."

Uncle Misha continued as if they had not spoken. "It is not difficult to produce a fake, but very difficult to detect it if it is done by an expert. Ancient jade has a certain amount of discoloration from being buried for many hundreds of years, but this can be produced by baking in ovens and treatment with liquid mud that stains the surface in identical manner. It takes an expert to detect it. Wah was a fool. He does not deserve to be a merchant."

Andrew put down his knife and fork and leaned back. "He followed the profession for fifty years. He cannot have been too much of a fool." He continued casually. "I suppose this means you are in a stronger position in Hong Kong. The closure of his business must mean an increase in yours."

"Perhaps," said the other with a shrug, "but we did not need this. Galerie Russe has a reputation second to none. Where did Wah buy this jade? That is where a reputation is built, my dear friend . . . in the source."

Hating himself Andrew asked, "Then your source must be of the best, would you say?"

"Assuredly," nodded the older man. "I see many things when I am about in Hong Kong, and Vanya—this boy who will have none of being a merchant—has arranged a voyage to Shanghai for—"

"I think Mr. Stanton does not wish to hear of our business affairs on a social occasion such as this," put in Ivan coldly.

"On the contrary," said Andrew through stiff lips, "I find it all fascinating." He turned to Misha. "I have often wanted to ask you if I might visit the gallery and see your treasure room, but felt you might see it as an impertinence."

"Imperti . . . my dear friend," exclaimed Misha, going pinker than ever. "There is nothing would give me greater pleasure. *Gospodi!* To think you would not ask such a thing of me. Am I so ungracious that you did not know I am happy to do anything for you? You have been so good to us all . . . yes, on many occasions . . . there is no one more entitled to my consideration. Come tomorrow . . . whenever you like. Mikhail Sergeyevich Zubov is at your service."

"That's very kind of you," said Andrew woodenly, and added silently, *exit Judas.*

The meal ended at last, and Andrew offered to show them over his house before they took coffee on the terrace. Nadia went to him at once, putting her hand on his arm like a gesture of appeasement and saying, "I cannot wait to see this room that hangs above the sea. Is it really so beautiful?"

The deep hurt in her eyes, half accusation, half plea, increased the trauma of that evening. He had had no time to recover from the blow of the Governor's orders, to assess the repercussions of what he had been told to do. He had just taken the first step in the betrayal of a friendship, and his senses were being bombarded by a woman who wanted his body for the soul of another man.

All he could do was look back at Nadia like a man who was drowning. He was helpless that night, caught in a sudden tide that had swept away all he had been.

146

"I thought the room was beautiful, but tonight it might be different," he heard himself say. "Things change so quickly."

The enormous room surprised them, even though he had described it enthusiastically during his first days of occupation. They went through a curtain of red, yellow, and blue beads while he deliberately kept the room in darkness. It was as if one side of the room had not been built. From floor to ceiling it was entirely glass which, in the nighttime, gave the impression of not being there at all. The spread of shimmering stars, the huge hanging moon, the silver pathway of its reflection on the water, and the glow-lamps of passing junks all lay before them like a scene in a magic-lantern show.

They all moved forward with a chorus of delight, seeing their way to the window by the moonlight flooding through it, and he moved up with them. A faint movement, a breath fanning his cheek made Andrew aware of the girl beside him.

A hand reached for his, sliding warmly against his palm, fingers twining around his own in an exciting intimacy. Then she eased forward, dragging his arm until it was behind her waist as she leaned back against him.

Suddenly, the despair of his love for her weakened him, tensing his body with awareness and locking his fingers to hers. It was almost unbearable to look out on a night that should have been theirs alone. In that darkened room he longed to turn her to him, feel his strength melt her against his body, cover her mouth with his own. He stifled a sigh, brushing her hair with his lips as his hold tightened. There, in that room on the edge of the world, he imagined lying in his bed seeking a surrender she gladly gave.

Yet, even as the desire flared in him, he knew it was a vain dream. He could not play a two-faced game with love. Cissie had done it with him, and the results had been too tragic ever to do it to this girl he had won and must now lose.

The exclamations had stopped; the room was now silent. He put Nadia from him with brutal suddenness, and lit a frosted-glass lamp before pulling heavy brocade curtains.

"The previous owner was an artist," he told them all, avoiding

147

Nadia's eyes. "This was his studio. He found the wild beauty too much to bear and walked into the sea one night to become part of it."

"Sometimes, it is the only thing to do." The comment in heavy accent surprised the group. It was the first time Aunt Marie had spoken since the fish course. There was a spate of comment to cover the strangeness of her remark, and they all looked at the exquisite Chinese carpet with a design of cream, bronze, and turquoise, until their attention was gradually drawn to a figure standing apart. Anna was near the door, still and absorbed, holding a photograph in a silver frame.

Andrew walked across, saying, "That is the only picture of my horse, Chukka, that I have. He was killed three days before the end of the war."

He put out a casual hand for it, but she held it against her and looked up at him, alive with a passion that took away his breath.

"It is beautiful, Andrei," she whispered.

In an instant, it was there again—the contact that took him from himself and made him another man. He forgot the others, the room in which he stood, the whole of his life. At the end of a day in which he had been made vulnerable to violent emotions, she looked into his eyes and promised more. Looking at her he felt an echo of snowy wastes, brooding dark castles, savage emotions, and love-unto-death. In her eyes there was the worship of a serf, yet the command of a queen. Her hands on the photograph seemed to be holding him a physical prisoner, a prisoner she set on a throne.

"May I see the picture," said a clear firm voice breaking into the moment. Nadia was gazing at him with enormous greeny-brown eyes—eyes that were sad, and not at all those that made him unwilling to see anything else.

The girl's hand took the photograph and she studied it. It showed Andrew in military uniform of elaborate design astride a light-colored stallion. Against a landscape of flat-topped hills he looked young and dashing, representing the romantic side of war.

She looked up at him, her face pale. "It is just like him."

*   *   *

148

He stood on the beach after the boat had disappeared round the headland, kicking viciously at the sand with the toe of his polished shoe. He stayed there a long time, unable to bring himself to go back to the house. Along in the village there was a death ceremony taking place, and crashing cymbals mixed with the wails of official mourners in sackcloth, and the mourning chant of the priest spinning around like a dervish.

The morbid sounds worsened his depression and, on impulse, he stripped off his clothes and went naked into the sea. Rolling onto his back he floated on the surface, hoping for mental absolution. But the great scatter of stars high above him brought back the poignancy of that moment when he had held Nadia back against him. She was peace and salvation, yet he must deny it.

Turning in the water he began swimming with furious energy, hoping to drive from his mind and soul all that haunted him. When he finally headed for the shore it was to emerge with chest heaving and limbs full of lethargy, a weariness that would surely ensure the banishment of ghosts. Yet, as he walked unclothed across the sand, he was conscious of his own strength and the way his body moved with healthy ease. Immediately, he saw again the face that had gazed up at him above a photograph.

This is beautiful, Andrei. He heard again her husky voice that turned prose into poetry, remembered the superb body in vivid green silk, but mostly the eyes that promised a world beyond the one in which he lived. She had not referred to his beloved horse, but himself at his most physical. What kind of man had Brusilov been to have commanded such passion from a woman like Anna? Had he ever swum naked, then run across a beach to her? Had he been wild like the men of his past ancestry?

Andrew found himself in his sitting room without knowing how he had reached it and took up the decanter as he passed through to the stairs, still lost in thought-realities that would not let him go. *Andrei.* The voice was husky, enticing. . . .

In his bedroom the lamp was still alight and burning low, making his reflection in the long mirror shadowy and almost mystic. He drew up, unable to take his eyes from the young man he saw. *Andrei.* The voice seemed to echo in the room, and it held his life in that one whispered name. In vague dream-memories he rode like the wind through the snow, fought battles in savage lands that were quite unlike Africa, saw her watching dressed in furs, as if through a misty window.

Somewhere below a door banged in the servants' quarters, bringing him back from another's identity. Heavy as if he had been drugged he turned from the mirror shaking his head to dispel the strange mood that had settled in it. Shaking with cold he pulled on a dressing gown and downed two brandies in quick succession. Still cold he poured another and was halfway through it when he noticed the space on his dresser. The photograph in the silver frame was gone!

SEVEN

At 6 A.M. brother and sister came face to face in the garden and halted in surprise. For a moment there was concern, a conflict of decisions in their expressions, but Ivan was weary and the bond of twinship triumphed.

"So, here we are, two troubled souls who take furtive walks at dawn," he said with rough gentleness. "There was a time when a problem was immediately shared." His sigh accompanied the affectionate gesture of an arm around her shoulders. "Each has caught the other out, eh? There is nothing to do but confess, *golubchik.*"

She smiled back, but wistfully. "If confession could make everything come right, how easy life would be. I have prayed, I have consulted the icons . . . but I believe one must do more than that." She allowed him to fall into step beside her, still protecting her with his arm as they walked down the path to the boundary.

"The Chinese have this great faith in joss," she went on. "Do you remember Andrew telling us about it? It is a mixture of luck, fortune, evil, and fate . . . an abstract kind of icon, I suppose. Yet they do not leave much to chance. They have gods, idols, dragons, spirits, mythical beasts to take care of almost anything in case their joss fails them. I feel as they do at this moment. My prayers are fervent, but I am afraid they will not be enough. I cannot stand aside and wait."

She stopped, and they turned to face each other. Beneath the heavy foliage in the sharp white light of a Hong Kong dawn Ivan saw for the first time that his sister was no longer the young girl he believed her to be. Written in the lines of her sensitive face was a new awareness. Wrapped in his own problems though he was, he knew what ailed her, and his pride was angered once more. Hong Kong cursed them, in his opinion. One by one they were reaping the harvest sown for them by one man's weakness. If they had stayed in Russia Katya would be alive yet . . . and Andrew Stanton would never have entered their lives.

"I think you must put your trust in prayers, *sestrushka*. No good will come of trying to change what will be."

She challenged him with the hurt in her eyes. "If that is so, why are you also walking here at this hour, unable to sleep? Such philosophy should have you soundly asleep in your bed with the prayers still on your lips."

The moment of understanding was fading. It was impossible to say to her what must be said without widening the gap already appearing between them. Perhaps it was because his motives were double-edged, but he truly wanted her happiness at the end of it . . . happiness away from Andrew Stanton.

"You have not answered me," she prompted, and he shied away from the real issue, telling her instead of his other problem.

"Prayers alone will not balance the books, as many businessmen have found to their cost." He began walking again. "We are losing money at the gallery."

She looked at him swiftly. "But why? It has been such a success."

"Perhaps there is a limit to the amount of trade one can do in a colony of this kind. We seem to have reached that limit. Business is quiet; it has been for several weeks. Surprisingly quiet."

They reached the boundary, and Nadia turned by the railings to question him further. "It will pick up when the next big ship comes in. That alone would not have you walking here at this hour. Is there more that you have not told me?"

He sighed heavily. "Some weeks ago I financed a merchant to bring from China some very valuable jade. I heard yesterday that pirates had taken the junk on the outward voyage. There is nothing to be done, no way of disputing it. The merchant could be a genuine victim, or a rogue who took my money and shared it with the corsair."

Nadia touched his arm with sympathy. "How could you have known? Anyone might do the same. At least you did not lose the jade."

He patted her hand and took it from his arm to swing in his own. "Perhaps it is as well the jade did not arrive."

"You speak in riddles, Vanya," she said with her usual concern for him. "Tell me what keeps you from sleep."

He had meant to be strong, keep his worries from her, but she drew him out, as she had always done. "You know it was difficult for us, at first, to live here in Hong Kong. The money was in Russia; the inheritance had to be divided according to Grandfather's and Papa's wishes. As they both died on the same day the normal processes were further complicated by the fact that I was in another country. It took some months, and we started Galerie Russe in order to live in the style that was our right. You knew and understood all that."

She nodded. "Yes."

"You also understood that I kept all the property in Russia and Finland—the house in Petersburg, the summer estates, the villa in the Crimea."

She nodded again. "You were determined to return, and they are part of the Brusilov inheritance. Vanya, perhaps I have reasons for wanting to stay here, but you are right to think of going back. It has not been easy for you to accept this life. You are a true Brusilov, and all the property in Russia is part of you and what you will become. Papa will have a worthy successor."

"No," he said with swift anger. "The child should never attempt to equal the father." Into his mind came a vision of Mei-Leng standing wretched and ashamed because she had done just that.

"You are wrong. How many strong men would have been wasted if it were so."

He pursued his original line. *"Rodnaya moya,* it takes a great deal of money to maintain the estates, but nothing . . . *nothing* . . . will induce me to sell any of it. Galerie Russe is our support in Hong Kong, but it has probably not occurred to you that its success is far more important than ever before." He sighed at her puzzlement. "No, Mama would not speak of it to you, of course. As you know, Papa was a man very conscious of family honor and pride, but he was also a man who loved only one person in his life. All the property is entailed, but he willed a great part of his fortune to his widow—and Mama has now returned to claim it back from me. Galerie Russe must make enough money to keep us here, for the estates take all I have left. So you see, I am not certain that we can now afford to buy the kind of jade for which we have acquired our reputation, and if business does not pick up soon the problem will become serious."

His words had visibly shocked Nadia; he saw it on her face and in the sudden tension of her shoulder. Suddenly, it seemed right to broach that which he had avoided a moment ago. They were alone at an hour when confession came easily to the lips. The chance might not come again. He leaned back against the wrought-iron bars, gazing back toward the house. It was a fine building, a symbol of prosperity and consequence, but it gave him no sense of pride.

"It seems to me the time has come to go back—take up the old life in Petersburg," he said. "The young ones will have a home again, and Grandmother. Aunt Marie loves the children; she will be happy." He turned to her then, and if his voice took on a note of pleading he tried to ignore it. "We are Russians—Brusilovs. We do not run from a few peasants. How do you think we appear before those who still remain?"

"You mean 'how do *I* appear,' do you not?" she asked in hollow tones.

"Perhaps . . . yes," he returned awkwardly. "It is different for you. I am now Brusilov, heir to Andrei."

"You will become a cadet officer in Papa's regiment?"

"Yes. It will all be as it was before."

"It will never be as it was before," she cried. "You have made no mention of my part in this plan to return—no mention of *my* happiness."

Hurt and guilty he said quickly, "You will marry a fine man—a Russian. You will have Russian children and be mistress of vast estates. You will be happy."

"I would never be happy back there. You speak of fairy tales, as if you could wave a wand and make everything come right. I am not a little girl to be dazzled with the promise of happy-ever-after." She jerked away, wringing her hands with passion. "I will not go back with you. You know why I will not."

Ivan was suddenly shaken with anger. "You renounce your family, your rightful future for *him?*" he cried. "Do you know what he is like, this man you claim to love? Then I will tell you. It was my duty to search into his past, and Orlov was only too quick to tell me what does not surprise me. He is a weakling, a man of dishonor. He married a woman from the bourgeoisie, turned his back on his family. He mixed with people of her class, took to drinking heavily, and finally killed her when driving his carriage home from a wild party. The scandal was so great he was sent to Hong Kong in disgrace, where the uncle and aunt were to see that he behaved."

He saw the pain blooming in her face, the girl who had been part of him since the womb, and because of it his words were even more brutal. "You see what he is. While he speaks his words of love to you, he lusts after Mama. If you did not know it that first night, you must have seen it at his house. He looks at her as Papa looked at her . . . and she at him!"

He had not known what it would do to her. He expected tears and a seeking of comfort from him, but she withdrew into a world of passions that took all color from her cheeks and bruised her eyes into blackness.

"You know nothing of life yet, Ivan Andreyevich Brusilov," she told him in a tone not much louder than a whisper. "You think that what you have just told me will wipe him from my heart and soul like a damp cloth over a blackboard—as if he had never existed? How little you know me; how little you have lived life. It is not what is in his past that matters to me, but what is in his future. I love him, and because of it am not proud before him. What he has done cannot be undone, but I can help him to forget it." She backed a few paces. "As for Mama—yes, I have seen how they are together, but I will fight to prevent her taking him from me. It is time someone stood his ground before her. None of you will, yet I am the only one she truly threatens." She backed further, caught in her onslaught of passion. "You are no longer my twin, the brother of my blood. You understand nothing, you feel nothing, or you would never have been so cruel. You have broken the bond. *Do svidaniya bratishka!*"

She turned from him and walked away up the path, and he was the one with tears blinding him. He gripped the ornate railings with hands that were searching for support, and bowed his head with the weight upon it. How could a man strive so hard, and for so long, yet fail in all he did?

His father had brushed him aside as insignificant. He had been wrenched from country and inheritance by a weakling who did not even bear his name; he fought his battles with pen and ink rather than the saber. The family was dissolving around him. In an effort to protect her he had just alienated the one person he loved best. But all that was bearable, he realized, in comparison with this ultimate rejection. From the night she had set eyes on Andrew Stanton his mother had forgotten he existed. The plans to return to Russia had been abandoned; the reason for her return to health and sanity, the voyage to Hong Kong to fetch her son—all that was cast aside. There was now only one person in her life once more; she lived only for him. Andrew had taken her as surely as his father had done. Her own son was nothing.

Perhaps, in his youth, his father had looked as the Englishman did, but only a young girl who had pledged her life to him could see him like that forever. But it was there, a link between those two men, that he recognized in that moment. They had an air about them, an air of experience and assurance. They had seen life and proved themselves men. He was a mere boy, in comparison. There, in that Hong Kong dawn he knew the moment had come for him.

A Chinese village awakes early. The young women are up and about, fetching water from the stream in containers swinging from a pole; feeding babies at their breasts; helping the men in the fields. The older women sweep the mud floors, shake the sleeping mats; castigate toddlers left in their charge; go to market. Everyone is busy. Old men with long gray beards discuss village policy in lengthy meetings; their counterparts sit in the shade sewing garments with gnarled fingers no longer swift but still skillful.

It was like that when Ivan rode through that morning, but he saw only one thing, the house at the far end with stone gryphons guarding the door. Ho Fatt was away for two days visiting a sick uncle on the mainland. Mei-Leng would be there alone. He saw nothing of the glances cast his way by ancient sages; black eyes raised from their study of the paddy fields to watch from beneath plaited basket hats.

From the time he had set out Ivan had cast off the present. He donned the clothes of his true identity, and he had galloped like the wind through the trees and along the road. All the while he pictured her sweet face, the shining black hair, the slender body that would be unequal to his strength. This was his hour, at last.

She was not at the house. He called, but the rooms rang with the sound and produced no one but a wide-eyed servant girl. Then he saw her, along the road where the beehives stood in a row, squatting down to seek the honey. The image increased his hunger. She was seeking the sweetness he sought.

Exultant, he jumped into the saddle in spectacular style, setting the horse forward in the same movement. The hoofbeats announced his coming, and she stood shading her eyes against the sun to watch.

He sat straight in the saddle looking down at her, which intensified the flavor of worship in her upward glance as she took in the splendor of his Russian clothes. Her cheeks took on a deeper color as she stood motionless beside the horse, and there was a world of emotion in her eyes that he did not stop to analyze.

"Are you surprised that I am here? You did not expect me at this hour?"

She gave her little bow. "It is always joy when you come," she told him softly. "When the sun and moon have gone it will be very dark."

He urged his horse forward, bent down and picked her up in his arm. She made no protest, just settled against him knowing

157

where he would take her. Ivan said nothing, too full of her nearness for words. Time enough for those afterward!

The morning was full of blues now the sun was on the rise, and the road running toward the headland and Andrew Stanton's house gave a breathtaking view of distant mountains and the deep cobalt-blue sea that lay sparkling and vivid below them.

It was growing warm with the seductive lulling of one's senses a tropical morning can bring—a heaviness that softened the edges of doubts and conscience leaving only a desire for sensuous pleasure; a lethargy that finds it easier to obey instinct than caution. Ivan dismounted at the spot where they usually parted and lifted her down. Tying his horse to a tree he took her hand as they walked along the path that led down to the foot of the headland where she waited in case his boat came on the evenings she worked for Andrew.

The girl went with him trustingly, her small hand in his, her little black slippers jumping over the ground in an effort to keep pace with him. Full of the power of his virility he strode through the trees, finding pleasure in her need to run to keep up, until they thinned and gave way to rocks along the water's edge. Around the promontory lay the bay and Andrew's house, but this place they had made their own was a narrow inlet hidden from view by any except those who might follow the same path down. Here they had spent wonderful moments of mutual escape from the distress of their lives in talking to each other, and exploring the sensation of attraction in its most restrained form. For Ivan the restraint had gone.

Mei-Leng sat on the rock she always used, and he stood beside her, one booted foot resting on the rock as he leaned on his knee studying her. He felt a sense of mastery again as she looked up at him, waiting.

"I have come to say goodbye," he said deliberately. "I am going back to the land of my ancestors."

What a fool he had been to expect a show of distress; instant surrender in the hope of holding him. He had forgotten he was dealing with the East.

Her whole body grew still until it seemed she had even stopped breathing; her lashes lowered over her eyes to hide what might lie in them.

"The master once said thirteen moons. There are but four that have passed."

It was said in so desolate a tone his swagger melted. She sat docile and wretched, accepting what he told her as she had been brought up to accept anything that came her way. She must hope for nothing and receive nothing. In a swift moment of clarity he saw in her a vision of himself—sitting motionless while events buffeted him—and his lust changed its form. Tilting her face to his with gentle fingers he saw the shining wetness in her eyes. She had never looked more beautiful than at that moment . . . nor more full of nobility.

"Mei-Leng, you are the flower of the fourth moon."

Her lips were soft beneath his mouth, and grew softer as he felt the power of manhood extending the embrace. Sinking onto the rock beside her he tightened his hold until she was against him small, yielding, passive. But the wetness of her tears broke them apart. She looked again the girl he had first seen in the hotel garden, broken by his praise, and a fierce upsurge of protective anger swept through him.

"I *have* to go," he said urgently. "For a man it is different. When the father dies he must return to honor his name. Do you understand that?"

She nodded, the rising sun glinting on the tears on her cheeks. "I understand all things, but understanding does not make the darkness any lighter. The sea will be empty when there is no boat to come; the road will go on forever when the horse does not pass along it; the moons will have no significance when there is no reason to count them." She seized his hand, bent low, and kissed it. "The father's name must be honored, but the son is honored more."

Shaken by her fervor, Ivan cradled her head with his hands and raised it up tenderly. As he did so, the flower fastened in the coils of black hair fell to the ground and lay at his feet. He stared at it, feeling the symbolic incident bring a return of desire.

With a hand that was unsteady he took the combs from her

hair one by one, until it hung to her waist in an exciting tumble. The gesture was so intimate, the driving passion returned with a force that would not be denied.

Jumping to his feet he tore open the fastening of his Russian shirt, tugged it free from the leather belt, and pulled it over his head with urgent movements until he was standing bare-chested before her. But she read his actions in a way that took him by surprise. Kicking the black slippers from her feet she walked down and into the water, still wearing her pink silk clothes, and turned to wait for him, the curtain of hair floating out around her on the ripples her entry had made on the water.

Ivan stared in delight. She was living the erotic dreams he had shared with her. She wanted to prolong it, tease him with the arts of her race. But the final triumph would be his!

Laughing he tugged off his boots, then took a running dive into the sea. Uncertainty, fear of failure, damaged pride were all forgotten as Ivan reveled in his own strength and prowess before the worshiping eyes of the young girl.

At some point it ceased to matter who it was who watched him—identity took second place to touch, sound, sensation in that ritual between man and woman—and Ivan performed his water-courtship with gathering desire as the sun burned down upon his body and set shimmering pinpoints of light around the girl's exquisite face above the water.

He dived yet again, plunging into midnight-blue limbo that set a roaring in his ears and in his body, and when he burst through into the golden day above, shaking the blinding drops from his eyes, she was emerging onto the rocks. He shouted to her in Russian, the triumph of the moment clear in his words.

She was standing on the rocks when he reached them and began to climb out. His heart started to pound with more than the exertion of the swim, for the wet silk of her suit clung to her body outlining it as if it were naked. He saw the line of her tiny breasts with their dark centers, the small waist, and swell of her hips as she waited tranquilly for him unaware of the sensuous picture she made.

Unable to take his eyes from her he pulled himself out of the sea to stand, water running over his bare chest like caressing fingers, as he held on to that moment on the frontier of passion. Next minute, he pulled her to him and began kissing her with mounting violence while his hands felt the warmth of her body through the wet silk. It was not enough. His hand slipped beneath her tunic searching until he found a swelling breast that quivered beneath his caressing fingers.

She began to twist and turn, beating him with her fists on his back, and he felt the joy of male strength as he kept her against him still. But her struggles grew until she somehow twisted free completely and began backing away. She whispered pleading words in her own tongue and clutched the thin tunic with tense hands.

Ivan was past the stage of level thought. He would not lose the moment now it had come—*could* not! She cried out when he seized her again, and the cry increased his urgency. Beneath the dappling leaves her body revealed all the secrets at which he had only guessed, and not all the days of waiting had prepared him for the heady anguish of physical passion. The girl's tears were part of it, her high sobbing entreaties. But, most exciting of all, was her eventual surrender leading to wild urgent response that sent him soaring into the realms of conquerors.

Only when it was over and he lay back spent and exhausted did it register once more that the girl was Mei-Leng, daughter of his comprador, Chinese . . . and very frightened.

There comes a time in every crisis when, failing help arriving from outside, the person caught in it has to find a solution or succumb. To Nadia that same measure recommended itself the following day and, after a day and a night of serious and feverish thought, she told the houseboy to call up a rickshaw and set off at midafternoon for a house overhanging a bay.

A large ocean liner had docked the previous evening, and the streets were filled with the passengers eagerly viewing the goods on display in the shops. Rickshaw boys were much in demand, charging twice the usual fare for the journey, and many ladies were experiencing the rather more gracious form of travel in sedan chairs.

Looking at them as she passed, Nadia remembered her own

first days in Hong Kong, well over a year ago. Now she took for granted the rickshaw; the cry of street vendors; Chinese faces wherever one looked; the sound of Mah-Jongg pieces clicking in upstairs rooms; sampans jam-packed along the waterfront; and cockroaches and centipedes side by side with fragrant flowers and vivid paper lanterns. It was all so very different from Russia yet, despite the problems confronting her, she still had no wish to leave and return to her homeland.

She knew that where Andrew was concerned she had no pride. At his house she had shown him that quite plainly. He had responded—how sweet and stolen had been that moment—yet he had gone away from her just as quickly, and it had happened before her mother had seen the photograph and held him in her aura.

That whole evening had been strange and haunted by the fears of everyone in the room, but Andrew had taken on a guise she did not recognize or understand. As on that day he went to Canton there had been a suggestion of deep emotion suppressed beneath the facade of officialdom. Yes, that was it, she now realized. He had behaved like a polite colonial administrator entertaining foreign guests. Only in the darkness of his bedroom while they had all watched the stars had he betrayed himself as the man she knew and loved.

Since that evening over a week ago she had heard no word from him and could stand the silence no longer. It was not the thing a lady should do, but in her new mood of determination she was going out to confront Andrew. Waiting at home for a word from him might be considered, by society, the only course open to a young woman neglected by her lover but it would not do for her.

The road was long and distant from the European influence of Victoria, but Nadia was surprised to find it busy. There were a number of Chinese returning to their villages, a long line of black-clad coolies. If they were surprised to see an elegant Russian woman in cream dress with a striped cummerbund and tie and a flat straw hat, they made no sign of it. But Nadia knew from her short experience that little escaped their notice, however impassive they might look. I can be as impassive as they, she thought.

Even so, her heart was hammering against her ribs as she paid the boy at the top of the narrow path leading down to the house, and began to walk between rows of high bushes, holding her skirt in her hand so that its fullness would not catch on the sharp twigs. There was no guarantee that Andrew would be at home, but such was her determination she vowed to wait until he returned. Fate would not be cruel enough to send him up-country again so soon.

The Christian Chinese houseboy answered her ring, and his was one eastern face that did register his thoughts and feelings. Its cheery roundness was plainly astonished at her sole presence.

"Good afternoon, madam," he greeted politely, standing aside for her to enter. "Will there be others toddling along in a moment?"

"No," she said in a voice that sounded nowhere near as confident as she wished. "Mr. Stanton is not expecting me, but it is a matter of some urgency." She waited in the hall with its mosaic floor while he closed the door. "Is your master at home?"

Kim grinned. "Oh yes, he cut along home early today. He has not been hitting it off with my uncle lately. The old boy can be a crusty devil." He led the way across the hall into the vast sitting room that opened onto the terrace. "Would madam find tea jolly at this hour?"

Nadia found him difficult to understand, for he spoke in a strange manner. But tea would give her something to do, so she said she would like some and hoped he had been offering it to her. "Mr. Stanton does not already have a visitor, I hope," she ventured, seeing that Andrew was not anywhere in sight.

"Oh no, madam. It has been very quiet here since you came to dinner, and he has been sunk in his boots."

"I see," she replied.

"If you will take a seat I will go pretty quick onto the beach, chop-chop. He is taking a dip, don't you know."

"A dip?" she repeated curiously, but he was halfway from the room.

163

Feeling out of her depth she wandered onto the terrace just in time to see Kim take a dressing gown from the back of a chair and hurry splay-footed down the steps and onto the sand where a tall man was just emerging from the sea. He wore a black bathing suit that left most of his arms bare and his legs from the knee down. The wet material clung to his body showing its muscular lines, and Nadia grew breathless as she realized the danger of going alone to such an isolated house.

Andrew went to Kim, picking up a towel from the beach and rubbing his hair. The Chinese boy was speaking, holding out the dressing gown as he did so, and it was clear that Andrew was unprepared for the announcement when it came. As she watched, he stopped the vigorous toweling and looked sharply across at the house, not even seeing the robe held out to him. He stood so long staring at her across the distance she knew it was a mistake to have gone there. He did not hurry across to her as a man in love should; he did not attempt to wave. From across one hundred and fifty yards she could tell he was not even smiling.

A raw feeling spread across her chest. Swiftly turning she walked back into the sitting room and stood in the center of the carpet. Coming up from the past flashed a memory of being taken to see a grand review of the army, and her ten-year-old brain had marveled at the Czar riding onto the enormous square quite alone to be met by his generals—so small a figure in all that space. She had felt his isolation, and the memory chose an apt moment to return. Like the Czar, however, there was no question of evading something on which she had already embarked, and she realized the blind eye and facade of pretense would have to be adopted, after all.

He came in from the terrace, but had swiftly dressed in a light suit and spotted cravat that emphasized the fresh browning of his skin by the sun on the water, and the darker hue of blond hair still damp from his swim. He brought in the salt smell of the sea, and an echo of virility that shook her flimsy rice-paper screen of protection. She saw at once why he could not smile at her.

On his face was written all that she felt, all she longed to tell him. In his eyes was the pain and pleasure of all the moments they had spent together. At that moment it came to her that if he were dying she would forsake all else and run to him, crawl on her hands and knees, lie on her face in the snow, reaching with desperate fingers to touch his in eternal unity. There, blazoned on his face, was the knowledge that he would do the same. Yet they remained where they were, trying to find a way of approaching each other.

"You should not have come here alone," he said at last.

"There was no choice. You would not come to me."

He sighed, shadows crossing his face. "I intended to come when . . . I am not the man you think," he began slowly. "I rushed into a declaration I should never have made."

"I know about your wife," she said steadily. "I have only heard one of the four versions you said were probably circulating the colony, but I cannot believe the other three are more explicit. Andrew, that is all in your past. The man I know is not like that."

He looked shaken, and watched Kim enter with a tray of tea as if he saw something he did not understand.

When the servant had gone Nadia added gently, "Did you think I would not still love you, that your past sadness would make me add to it? How little you know me." Despite her words, the scene was putting a thunder of pulsebeats in her temples and weakening her legs. "I accept it, but do not understand. Tell me the true version so that I shall . . . please." She sat on a chair by the tea tray and waited until he began in a faraway voice.

"A man might be a natural warrior in that he does what he is trained to do to perfection, but few are natural killers. When it comes to the point of driving a sword into another, most men know a split-second's hesitation." He ran his hand through his damp hair. "They called me a hero, but those three years of war sickened me to the point of desperation. I could not forget the smell of death, or the blaze of hatred one human could feel toward another. I dreamed of blackened landscapes and the whistle of bullets." He frowned, lost in his narrative. "She was a showgirl, pretty, gay, full of smiles. Watching her on the stage was like looking at life through entirely different eyes. She sang and danced only for me; she wore beautiful things and smelled of French perfume. She made me forget what I had left behind. I married her within a month. My family refused to accept her,

165

and I took her away in the misguided pride of youth."

It hurt unbearably, even though she had known what was to come. She sat perfectly still, watching the spiral of steam rise from the spout of the teapot. He had given himself to another woman in love. Whatever the outcome, nothing could change the pain of that knowledge.

"She nearly broke me," he went on doggedly. "She took away every shred of pride I had, betrayed our marriage, destroyed the image I had glimpsed from my seat in the stalls. It lasted six months, until I drank too much at a party and drove our carriage into a wall. She was killed instantly, and I was sent to Hong Kong to avoid the scandal."

He stopped, and in his glance there was vivid feeling. "My people had reckoned without my conscience, however. For four years I lived with it as a constant companion, until that day at the garden party. I knew at once that you were everything she had not been. I also knew the dangers. But in my all-embracing desire for the truth after falseness I turned a blind eye to them. Now, I know how wrong I was. As a member of the Crown's administration I am expected to abide by certain rules."

"But they have accepted you in Hong Kong after . . . knowing of your past. It is the same with me. Andrew, I love you. There is no need to alter anything you have said to me." She rose and went to him, taking his hands. "I understand . . . I truly understand."

If anything, his expression grew more distant. He carefully loosened his hands. "You *don't* understand. It is not my past—I would have explained all that to you, in time—but my future. Just think. In the eyes of the closely knit, self-absorbed majority of the English set here, I would be considered a traitor to love a Russian girl. Those with marriageable daughters would never never forgive me, or accept you. They would turn away when we passed."

"It would not matter to me," she cried. "I will turn away, also."

"Doors would be closed to us."

"They have always been closed to *us*," she told him passionately. "We are a proud and aristocratic family, but your uncle and aunt never invite us to their home. Your friends are happy to chat with us, but return to their own circle alone. The doors of your clubs are closed to us, also. I have lived without those things since I arrived here. I should not miss them."

"But I should," he said with the coldness of complete dismissal. "To continue to see you would endanger my career. After the disgrace of Cissie's death they would see me as unsuitable. If I should be dismissed from the service, I could hope for nothing but a menial job in a backwater. I could not even go back in the army except as a private soldier."

She stared at him, unable to accept or believe in what he was telling her. "Why . . . why should they do that? Society, yes—the mothers with English daughters, yes—but how could I endanger your career?"

Dusk was falling outside, bringing a vivid glow to the scene outside the window. He made a tall outline against it, and it was no longer easy to discern his expression.

"Your country is viewed with suspicion by mine. You are Russian."

"I am a Brusilov," she cried fervently. "Let no one forget that."

"I have never forgotten it."

"Until now." She felt her cheeks flame. "I thought you were different, but my brother was right."

"About what?" It was a tight-lipped challenge.

"At the first opposition you join those who cannot forget they are British."

"Can you forget you are Russian?"

"He is right: There is no honor in you." She pushed past him to go quickly onto the terrace where the approaching evening had brought a brisk breeze to catch at her hair and skirts. The wildness of the seascape and the utter silence of the bay heightened the desolation that now filled her. He came up behind her, but she would not turn to look at him.

"If dishonor means protecting you from insult, distress, and poverty—if it means denying you the right to move in those circles to which your birth entitles you— then your accusation is true. I could not ask you to lead that kind of life."

Her hands gripped the balustrade as she thought of that other woman who had destroyed him once, and her love pushed through the tangle of their quarrel to override all else. Turning she looked at him through a mist of tears.

"I am a Brusilov, yet I have no pride before you. Take me as your wife, and you will see that nothing else matters. I am not like that other one. I love you, *serdechko moyo*. I shall not care what you are, or where we must go. The world does not matter if I have you."

His face looked dark and angry in the fast-fading light, and the rising wind blew his hair up into a fan on the crown of his head.

"The world will always matter," he said with deep emotion. "It is eternal, and we are only pawns upon it."

He was rejecting her! She had thrown away her pride, vowed to face anything for his sake, begged him to take her as his wife. She had lifted her face to his, and he had struck it. Suddenly, it was all too clear why. He had known what he must face if he loved a Russian girl—had known from the start—yet had continued to declare his love, until. . . . The love running through her veins so hotly turned into ice. She began retreating down the steps to the beach, and he grew taller and more monstrous with every one.

"Now I see what it is," she whispered. "It is because of her— because of Mama, who wants you in place of her Andrei."

She turned and ran for the boat moored at the jetty, knowing she must get away from him. The tears that had been so nearly shed now flowed down her cheeks as she stumbled through the sand that closed over her feet with every step. Night was closing in fast, but she could still see the line of white breakers and the dark shadow of the landing stage.

"Nadia . . . wait." His hand caught her arm, but she shook it off and stumbled on.

Three paces later he caught her again, his hands holding her so that she could not escape.

"No," she begged, turning her face so that he would not see the tears, know that she cared so much.

"You are wrong—so wrong," he cried above the sound of the waves, holding her struggling body with difficulty.

"Yes. Ever since that first night it has been different." She felt the wind catch her straw hat and tear it from her head, leaving her curls tumbling down one cheek.

"Of course it has been different . . . not just for me. She has changed the whole family."

Her feet were sinking into the sand, and the skirt of her cream dress was wrapped around her legs by the force of the wind. "You admit it? You do not deny she has come between us?"

"Yes, I deny it," he shouted, his eyes blazing in the light that was almost gone. "But she has made everyone unhappy, I will not deny that."

"Unhappy? You do not look unhappy when you gaze so deeply at her. I have seen you forget all else in the wonder of her eyes."

With a savage twist she flung herself from him and tried to run, but the deep sand and long flapping skirt sent her headlong to her knees. Next minute, he was there kneeling beside her, taking her arms and shaking her with unconscious fervor. Her hair was caught by the wind and blown back in a stream of bronze; she felt the salt spray mingle with the tears on her cheeks.

"It is something I do not understand, cannot seem to handle yet, but I am fighting her." His voice was husky and rough with the urgency of making himself heard against the orchestra of the elements. "I am fighting her . . . which is more than your family seems able to do."

Struggling to her feet she cried wildly, "You are not fighting. I have seen you when you look at her. You do not want her to let you go. I have seen it before, and the trap will close around you forever. She is like *La Belle Dame sans Merci*. You have made her live again. She will not die a second time."

Once more she set off toward the jetty, but he caught her one last time and swung her round to face him. The roar of the sea was all around them, but his voice was low and hollow.

"If you truly believe that, there is no more to be said between us ever again."

"I believe it . . . *Andrei*," she cried, wanting to destroy him as he had destroyed her.

Slowly he let her go, gazing at her as if to capture her for all time in his memory. "I wish to God I had never set eyes on the Brusilovs."

"You do not wish it more than I do," she whispered back.

It was over, the passion spent, the promises broken. Love had flown on the winds that crossed the China sea. He walked to the jetty, shouting awake his own boatmen who slept beneath the planks. She took his hand to step into the small rocking vessel, but did not look at him. As they drew away from the shore he turned and walked back into the darkness, leaving her to the desolation of pale yellow lamplight in the tiny cabin.

EIGHT

Both young men were products of the same background and environment, but one was a theorist, the other had learned through experience that human frailty made nonsense of many theories. Apart from that, they did not like each other, and each had an axe to grind.

They stood in a mudbrick house consisting of only one room. It had a shelf bed of crude design, a table and two chairs, wooden altar shelf, and a lavatory bucket provided solely for the English visitor. There was no ceiling fan, and the two men sweated in the airless heat of a room letting in only little light from the one small window.

"You should have stopped it," Andrew said heatedly. "By God, you were told to use every delaying tactic in the book until I could get here."

His companion sneered. "Sir Goodwin's nephew to the rescue! Apart from confiscating every sharp weapon in the place, what else could I have done?"

"That might have been a good start. You are supposed to wield some authority here, you know."

171

"What would you have done in my place, tell me that? What did your uncle expect you to do? My dear Stanton, when one white man stands opposed by a Chinese official who is surrounded by armed henchmen, it is no use whatever telling the yellow devils that he wields the authority around here. Ewing was up-country sorting out a village riot, and those of the police detachment that were left were not prepared to act under my orders. I can't say I blame them. The locals are as rough a set as I have ever seen, and liable to take reprisals."

Andrew threw his pith helmet onto the table in disgust. "If that's your attitude, no wonder you got nowhere with him. This is going to raise a hell of a row in the department. Our relations with the Chinese are very shaky at present over that junk we let through. An incident like this will undermine our reputation completely. We are supposed to administer the New Territories. What kind of administration is it that will stand by and let a minor village headman summarily behead eight men without trial?"

"Look here," said the other. "I did all I could."

"Well, it wasn't enough," snapped Andrew. "So much for our policy of fair and just rule. The execution was barbaric, and that . . . that . . . *exhibition* outside is an obscenity."

"But a powerful deterrent, surely? Eight heads in baskets on display in the marketplace would discourage all but the most determined revolutionary."

"They had not been proved revolutionaries," pointed out Andrew trying to hold on to his temper.

"Oh come, you went to Canton and routed out one of them yourself. These men answered to the names given by him."

"Under torture. A man is liable to say anything that will stop his agony."

The younger man mopped his brow with a silk handkerchief and went to the tiny window in the hope of finding more air. "I don't understand all this bloody brouhaha. Eight men have been executed before we gave permission for them to die—that is what it amounts to, isn't it? Whether they were revolutionaries or not, the colony is well rid of them."

"By God, you're a cold bastard, Brotherton!"

"Yes. I have been told I shall go far . . . and not as a result of nepotism," he added slyly. "Look, I know this was your case, that you dashed up to Canton when old Smythe was murdered, but I just happened to be the man on the spot when they walked into our police net. How was I to know the local bigwig had a personal score to settle with them? Or that our police chap would be deep in the jungle and completely inaccessible? I still say we are well rid of them."

"Yes," said Andrew sharply, "that is just about your level of understanding. British rule is reputed to be based on authority and justice. It just isn't good enough to back down when it seems the easiest thing to do. What do you think would have happened in Peking if our ambassador had cleared out and left the Boxers to do as they pleased?"

"I suppose you were there to advise him," sneered Brotherton.

"No. I was fighting in South Africa."

The good-looking face lost its sneer. "All right . . . but we are talking about a parcel of cutthroats from one of the secret societies active in all kinds of vice. Dammit, they were responsible for Smythe's death. Yet you defend them."

Andrew let out his breath in a heavy sigh. He was very angry, and anger did not mix well with oppressive heat in a small jungle hovel.

"I am defending a principle," he said wearily. "If you cannot see that, you have no right to be here. I have learned in a harsh school how to accept orders, and it makes me highly resentful when I see men like you brushing them aside with such damned arrogance. When we annex new territory we rule it our way—and that means we do not allow local headmen to take the law into their own hands whenever it pleases them."

Brotherton strolled across to a chair and dropped onto it, tilting it back onto two legs as he surveyed Andrew with an insolent smile.

"My god, a true imperialist, if ever I heard one. Go ahead. Since you were sent here by your uncle to put me straight, give me a full and precise account of how you would have dealt with this, old chap."

Andrew sat on the edge of the table and threw his riding whip down beside his helmet. "Very well," he said grittily. "You speak no word of any Chinese dialect, and have limited your knowledge of the people to sessions at the popular brothels. You were sent up here to gain experience, believe it or not, so listen carefully. I could have stopped the execution by speaking to the man in his own language and denying him the opportunity to pretend he did not understand me. I would have quoted the precise regulations, and ended with the threat of dishonoring his ancestors by lack of understanding of simple things when he held a key position in the village. At the same time, I would have put the greatest fear into him by suggesting his action would cause the displeasure of the Celestial Throne. After saying all that I would have placed a chair in the doorway of the captives' hut . . . and sat on it! Contrary to your theory, *old chap*, when one white man stands opposed to a Chinese official and his henchmen, it *is* of some use to tell the yellow devils that he wields the authority."

Brotherton was silent for a moment or two, then let out a short laugh. "Bravo! Men like you have formed the Empire, Stanton . . . but you have inherited one of the old school's greatest failings. Underneath that starched coat you are fatally human."

"What does that mean?" demanded Andrew.

"You came out here after a scandal with a showgirl, and benefited not a jot from the experience. Russians are out, don't you know?"

Andrew stiffened and stood up. "My private life is none of your concern."

"Oh, but it is. When your career ends, mine takes a jump forward. It's all round the colony that you are getting far too chummy with that family. No one is under any illusions as to who you go to see on your many trips to Galerie Russe—showgirl to shopgirl is a natural step, I suppose." He curled his lips. "Now there is this added complication. Madame Brusilova seems intent on checking your intentions where her daughter is concerned, for she seems to appear in your company more often than a mother should. Does she know her daughter visits your house alone? Now, don't look at me like that, old chap. She was seen getting off your boat one dark evening. The news didn't go down very well, I hear. You see, Stanton, I might not know much about the Chinese but I appear to know more about my brother than you do. Watch your step. This time, your uncle might not be able to come to the rescue."

With quick deliberation Andrew hooked his foot around one of the back legs of Brotherton's chair and pulled. Taking up his whip and helmet he addressed the man picking himself off the filthy pressed-mud floor.

"As an old Etonian you should know better than to try to play school bully when you are still wet behind the ears." He held out the man's helmet. "Shall we go and do something about those heads in the marketplace? I'm sure you will do your best to talk our friend into removing them, *old chap.*"

The trip to the New Territories took five days and gave Andrew cause for much thought. Brotherton's blunt words stayed with him to increase the heaviness that weighed him down of late. No duty had ever caused him so much heart-searching. For a while he had told himself he was doing it in order to clear the family—prove that what he had said about Ivan Brusilov was true—but even that did not dispel the feeling of treachery each time he faced them.

He had been twice to the gallery in his new guise—once at Misha's invitation, and then again to take them by surprise—but had found nothing of a damaging nature either time. On both occasions Nadia had been absent. The first time his visit had been planned and she must have remained at home; when he had gone in without warning she had left the place while Misha had still been greeting him, and he had seen her emerging from a tea shop across the road as he walked away from the premises.

The memory of that day she had visited his house still filled him with self-disgust. He had come to terms with having to reject her and had thrashed out in his mind the best way to send away the love that had so nearly been his salvation. Her unexpected appearance had caught him unprepared, and from then on his careful plans had been useless. Somewhere inside Nadia a passionate and vital woman had awakened from a girl with peace

175

in her eyes. It had made her infinitely exciting, a wild surprise kicking away the gentle dreams with a promise of intoxication. But it had come too late.

How could he have guessed she would counter his every argument with a generosity that made his rejection doubly agonizing? He had only been able to present a picture of a man clinging to feeble arguments to hide the real reasons—which he had been. But it had not occurred to him that she would translate it in the way she had. In time she might have accepted and forgiven his fears for their future facing a hostile society, but this thing would eat into her permanently. To be replaced by another woman was bad enough, but this woman was her mother.

Once having thought of Anna, he could not then put her from his mind. She was unlike any woman he had ever come across. Sweeping away all conventional relationships between a man and a woman, she was dedicated to one theme only and pursued it with unbelievable and shattering results. He did not yet understand it or have the least idea how to counter it. Hong Kong had the main city of Victoria, and Europeans of the higher echelons invariably congregated in those places considered as their own. It was inevitable, therefore, that their paths should cross a great deal.

At a party given by the Russian consul she had sought him out quite deliberately and openly; twice when walking through the Botanical Gardens she had approached to introduce a friend and kept Andrew there until passersby had begun to stare. He never knew when he would glance up in a restaurant to see her looking at him across the tables; or when he would take the Kowloon ferry only to find her standing on the decks.

On each occasion she took him by storm. She threw a full battery of sexual artillery at him when he was unarmed, yet commanded a kind of imperial reverence that was above basic desire. She changed from wanton to countess without his knowing which she really was; she challenged his manhood in a way that was more than an expression of passion, because it demanded the dedication of his whole life to her.

Nadia had been partially right. From the moment he had seen Anna standing in a doorway, he had been fascinated against his will. But he was fighting the ghost of Andrei Brusilov quite desperately.

As he dressed prior to setting out for the Dragon Boat festivities on the day following his return from the confrontation with Brotherton, he knew a feeling of deep reluctance. The Brusilovs were certain to be there, and he wished he had not to come face to face with them. Misha was almost piteous in his avid friendship: Marie was colorless and silent, hardly noticing anyone. Ivan switchbacked between icy haughtiness and a curious concern over Mei-Leng, who had been sent to Kowloon to nurse a dying uncle. The boy was showing ridiculous signs of responsibility to the man who employed her at his recommendation. He had even called twice at Andrew's house to discover if she had returned. Andrew missed her services, but not to the extent the young Russian seemed to imagine. It was all rather tiresome and irritating.

Knowing he must still cultivate a relationship with all of them, it was small wonder he would rather avoid the festival if he had not to go there on official duty. Word was out that there could be trouble over the beheaded revolutionaries. The secret societies that indulged in any activity that caused unrest in the British colony might choose such an occasion to show their strength. Antirevolutionaries could also plan a demonstration of their beliefs by attacking known supporters of the nationalist cause. In short, both factions could disrupt a festival that would be full of happy-go-lucky celebrating and part of a culture the British had no wish to change.

The water carnival, as it really was without the pagan overtones, was an occasion for everybody and the whole colony appeared to be there that afternoon on the shore—the Europeans in a special enclosure with seats, the wealthy Asians in elaborate mat sheds, the ordinary citizens strung along the beach in an excited, babbling, moving crowd that covered every inch of sand.

Andrew looked at it through narrowed eyes as he discussed the arrangements with the chief police officer, and agreed it would need sharp eyes to spot the beginnings of a disturbance in the mass of jubilant humanity. His own job was to take care of the

177

Europeans present, and he was conspicuously armed for the occasion. To help him he had been given an English officer and four Chinese constables to mingle with the crowd while he remained at the entrance to the enclosure.

There was a large number of white foreigners besides a larger-than-usual detachment of English people. Due to the presence of several Royal Navy warships accompanying the visit to the colony of a royal duke, naval officers and seamen abounded. The military, not to be outdone, had produced a major general and elaborate escort to swell the crowd. It did not ease Andrew's job, but he was concerned with his own problems and took the rest in his stride.

Although the main attraction was to take place in the harbor, there were all kinds of sideshows to entertain the crowds and make money for the owners. For an early June day it was excessively hot, and Andrew was already sweating as he began the long walk with the police chief along the extent of shore covered by early revelers.

Beneath the shade of the trees food barrows were drawn up to provide meals and sweetmeats for the Chinese spectators. The heavy smell of frying oil hung in the air, and smoke from the large shallow pans over charcoal fires shimmered several feet above and wafted extra heat across the two men's faces as they walked laboriously through the sand. At one there were *dim sum* being cooked—tiny dumplings stuffed with pork or fish, or even plain vegetables. At another a man was shoveling shrimps in a blackened pan. Deep-fried rice, strips of fat pork dangling from strings, bean shoots, chicken wrapped in rice-dough pastry—all these delicacies were being prepared and consumed by those who were having a picnic before the main excitement.

For the children there were sweets, ginger balls, sugared almonds, little moon cakes, and to amuse them, tiny colored-paper sunshades, straw frogs, brightly painted papier-mâché figures on sticks and, favorite of all, kites to fly above the heads of the crowds, the eyes painted on them enabling the child to see what his own could not.

Around the stalls milled the customers, many dressed in the

pretty traditional costumes they kept for festivals, but it was not only food that drew them beneath the trees. Seizing the opportunity all kinds of peddlers and tradesmen had carried their simple necessities to that beach knowing more than a few would take advantage of their services. Barbers set out stools, took up their scissors, and satisfied customers within minutes; letter writers sat on one box and used another on which to rest their scrolls while writing the words the customer dictated. Fortune-tellers sold happiness in red envelopes; traveling physicians offered to cure leprosy, boils, venereal disease, bad temper, and limping, all with much the same ointment. Moneylenders stood discreetly behind trees lest their clients "lost face" by being seen, and there was even a marriage broker on hand for those parents who decided the joss that day was auspicious for making inquiries on behalf of their sons.

Right at the end was the strongest competition to the fascination of the boat races—an open-air Cantonese theater performing one of the marathon folktales in lurid and melodramatic fashion. The two Englishmen halted at the back of the dumbstruck audience and gazed up at the bamboo staging where the performers in elaborate and costly costumes went through their lines in high piercing singsong voices while moving with symbolic gestures that told the story much more vividly than words ever could.

Andrew could not follow it—the language was ancient and formal—but he thought yet again how compelling such drama must seem to those who lived their lives in dismal poverty in the back streets of Chinatown. There was nothing left to chance: The villains wore hideous masks and the virtuous were unmistakable. At that moment there was a confrontation between a green-and-black silk-clad villain with a lizard's head and a girl in gold jewel encrusted robes who was clearly standing on her dignity while defending her virtue. It was all slightly macabre to western eyes—lizard-head was too hideous to be taken seriously, and the girl's face painted dead-white with heavily emphasized eyes and mouth looked uncomfortably like a wax doll that had taken on a roving human spirit and come to life.

179

"I don't know about you," Andrew remarked to his companion, "but these would give me nightmares if I watched them too often. No wonder the Chinese work so hard at keeping on the right side of the spirits. A fate worse than death if one fell foul of one of these characters, I should say."

The police chief winced. "A fate worse than death to have to listen to it, in my opinion. I don't think we need worry about this area, Mr. Stanton. The Triads are not likely to start anything in a crowd that is completely overawed. It's my guess they'll choose some innocent trader as their excuse, if they do decide on trouble."

They turned and began walking back along the beach where the boats were drawn up on the sand ready to be launched. Being a keen amateur sailor, the policeman extolled the virtues of the long narrow craft whose bows swept up into an ornate dragon's head painted in vivid and eye-catching fashion, and whose sterns narrowed into ridged tails.

"I'd like to see one of those at Henley," observed Andrew with amusement. "There'd be a few hats falling off with astonishment."

"Outrage, more likely," returned the other. "It's strange to reflect that what we regard as a common sight is completely unknown to our compatriots in England."

"More's the pity," said Andrew with sudden sharpness. "They might be a little less insular."

Back at his post, as time wore on Andrew found the heat more and more trying. The noise was growing as people poured onto the beach prior to the start of the races, and floating on the air was the shrill sound of the Cantonese opera players and the crash of cymbals as the white-faced girl defied the temptations of evil.

Then, before he had had time to prepare, they were there walking toward him in a group, standing out as foreign against the British spectators by the clothes they wore. He noticed nothing more of them, for his attention was taken up and commanded by Anna as she came toward him. The trampled sand strewn with cuttlefish and dried seaweed could have been the marble floor of a ballroom from the way she walked across it, the skirt of her champagne-colored dress sweeping behind her.

The moving figures of the Chinese revelers blurred into a vague dark shifting shadow; the shouts and laughter, and singsong wail of the actors faded into distant sounds borne on the wind of some faraway bay as Anna Brusilova made the curving trees into cathedral arches, the squalid foodstalls into a picturesque folk scene, the surrounding gentry into members of her court.

He felt that pressure in his chest that accompanied acute exertion, so it was with an automatic action that he took the helmet from his head in salute as she reached him. Standing there bareheaded before her he felt a moment of helpless irrevocability, as a knight pledges his life to the service of a beautiful woman. The features molded by pride and passion were shadowed beneath the large hat of champagne-and-brown ruched ribbons and curled feathers, but her superb oblique silver-green eyes gazed up at him through the net veiling with possessive fire. He could not drag his own from them as he kissed the hand she offered.

"Andrei," she said softly, "it has been so long. Every day I have waited for you to come."

"I have been away," he told her in a voice deepened by breathlessness.

"There was conflict; you were troubled." She clung to the hand that had taken her own to his lips. "Am I not right?"

"How . . . how could you know?" he murmured.

"Ah, I felt it—here I felt it." She placed his hand lightly against her heart, and he felt the excitement of her curved breast for a moment before she lifted the hand to rest against her cheek. Incredibly, her eyes were shimmery with tears. "You must never go away again without telling me." The deep collar of fiery opals blazed with all colors in the sun as she slid her hands along both his arms, tilting her head back to look deeply into his eyes, as a woman looks at her lover. "Andrei, you must not be cruel . . . *please*," she entreated in a husky voice that suggested desperation. "Do not make me suffer more than I already have, *serdechko moyo.*"

"We have come to watch the boats, have we not?" The heavy expressionless sentence plunged through the gossamer threads being spun around him, breaking the hold of a pair of silver-green eyes.

Andrew stared at Aunt Marie as if he could not believe what he saw, then gazed around him to see that he was surrounded by people staring. With a lurch his breathing became normal, and the Russian woman's plain features shifted into focus. Beside her stood her husband, his gaze wandering restlessly over the distant scene. Behind him were the twins. Ivan was staring at him with heightened color and such vicious intensity Andrew was shocked. Nadia was as pale as her brother was flushed and two paces behind him as if already in retreat. He dared not put an adjective to what was written on *her* face.

Clumsily, as if moving for the first time after years of immobility, Andrew put his helmet back on and stood aside with an arm out to indicate the way into the enclosure. His wits were jumbled and crying out against what had happened. There, in front of the whole family, Anna had made a mockery of all he had ever said to Nadia—and he had offered no defense. How it had happened he could not now say. She had walked toward him, and the rest had faded away. Even now the remnants of those suspended moments made him move like a man in a daze, and speak without being aware of the words.

Somehow he blustered through an introduction to a visiting diplomat before conducting them to their seats. Only then did he attempt to face Nadia. She tried to slip past him, but he put a hand on her arm to halt her. She looked up at him, still pale. Their glances locked for a short time as they tried to think of a question that would fit the plain answer.

"Let me pass, Andrew," she whispered at last. "What is there to say? All the world has just seen that she has her wish—you in place of him." She joined the others and took her seat, leaving him conspicuously alone.

Obliged to return to his post and leave her in the midst of her family, he was not so dazed that he could not see eyes watching his progress, white gloves held to mouths to cover scandalized asides, and several of his colleagues who found sights of absorbing interest to study when he passed.

The races began, with the dragon boats pushing through the

water like great sea serpents rearing up from the spray as the crews paddled in mad competition. The shouting and cheering rolled in crashing waves against his ears, and the rhythmic pounding of drums to encourage the oarsmen matched his pulse. He stood tensely, knowing a sense of traveling back in time. It was South Africa again, with the roar of battling men and thunder of guns.

He watched the bowmen of the dragon boats casting the ritual dumplings on the water for the hungry roving spirit of the honest official of long ago, who drowned himself after failing in his attempt to prevent corruption and cruelty at the Emperor's court. Chinese beliefs were so reassuring. There was always a festival, a shrine, a prayer to cover any situation. His own spirit was roving, at present. Where would it eventually find a resting place?

Finally, it was over. The Europeans began to move away; the Chinese went back to the stalls and sideshows where the feasting would continue to the accompaniment of the inevitable fire-crackers. A festival day was celebrated right up to its last hour with as much zeal as its first.

Ivan, deep in conversation with a Swedish banker, walked past Andrew as if he were not there. The rest of the family had been detained by a family of Turkish wine merchants. Andrew tried to keep them in sight through the movements of the crowd, but an old army acquaintance took his attention and entered into a long and enthusiastic account of what he had been doing since the war, and pressing Andrew to name an evening when he would dine in the Mess at Kowloon.

It was not the best place for an involved conversation. Europeans were pressing forward from the enclosure, chattering loudly; Chinese children were running in laughing pursuit of each other; revelers shouted across from one group to another in harsh unmusical voices; the boat drums were still thudding; the open-air opera had only reached its second act; and firecrackers were exploding with deafening rushes of noise.

Parasols twirled amidst a bobbing sea of paper lanterns and puppets-on-sticks; elegant muslins moved through a shamble of coolie-dark suits; the aroma of sizzling fat was augmented by that

183

of Havana cigars. There was an ache growing behind Andrew's eyes as he half-listened to his army friend but watched the milling scene alertly. Then, suddenly, his body tensed as acute training of the senses warned him of danger.

In a flash, he was running, pushing his way through those jostling back and forth with the friendly impatience of eager celebrators. He shouted a warning to a Chinese policeman some yards away, but it was swallowed up in the din. Still running, he drew his pistol and fired into the air to alert his colleagues, but firecrackers exploding all around ensured that his shots created no attention.

Struggling against the flow of humanity, he lost his helmet somewhere beneath their feet, but pushed on toward that which had caught an eye that had seen violence too often not to recognize it. In the general air of celebration a small group of young men were in a circle that was actively hostile. Andrew feared the worst and knew delay was out of the question if he was to stop the violence from spreading.

He burst through the crowd and raced for the group who were plainly attacking something or someone encircled by them. Yelling in Cantonese he fired his gun at a tree beside them. The sounds were lost, but the whistling breeze of a bullet passing nearby gave a message all of them knew. They fell back, hesitated for a moment, then began to rush into the trees. Andrew had a brief impression of broad evil faces before they were off leaving a man lying on the ground.

Carried on by the impetus of his run Andrew leaped over the body and made a grab at a laggard, but the young Chinese swung round, and a blade flashed in the shaft of sunlight penetrating the branches. The knife caught Andrew's upper arm and sliced through his jacket into the flesh. Military training prevented his losing hold on the man and led to him firing at point-blank range. It also enabled him to leave his victim and go back to the one lying on the ground with no hesitation over what he might find.

Blood was spread in thick rusty pools over the black jacket and already matting the springy brown hair, the pale face was turning faintly blue with bruising, and several bloody smears were swelling to distort the features. He looked to be in the hands of death already, and Andrew felt the swift pain that had always accompanied the loss of a fellow soldier. This time it was more poignant. The one on the ground was Ivan Brusilov.

Andrew went down beside him and felt for his heart, sadness for a boy who might never become a man causing his hand to shake slightly. People began to gather around, the vibrations of tragedy having penetrated the happiness at last. Two policemen pushed through, and Andrew looked up sharply.

"Find a doctor immediately. He's still alive."

Then everything happened at once. The English officer appeared and organized control of the crowd, sent someone for Ivan's family, another for a horse ambulance.

Meanwhile Andrew looked at Ivan carefully without disturbing him more than he could help. There were serious knife wounds in his chest and abdomen, besides injuries from heavy blows with cudgels. This was not a case of Triad disturbances. Ivan Brusilov had been intended to die quite brutally, and Andrew could not understand why.

There was movement, and he looked up. They were all there— the family that had suffered so much from violent death. Anna walked straight to him as he got to his feet, and there was terror haunting her features now. It seemed to Andrew that she did not see the boy on the ground, only the spreading bloodstain on his own sleeve. Her Russian words sounded like a prayer, but the agonized murmur was cut through with a more terrible sound.

The woman who had taken the children into her keeping when no one else wanted them now saw another of them lying before her on the brink of death. It was too much. Sobbing, half-crazy with grief, she had to be forcibly restrained from flinging herself onto the blood-drenched figure on the ground, and her awful cries rang out even above the continuing din of bangs, explosions, and shrieking Chinese opera.

In the midst of all that noise, horror, and confusion, one figure stood alone, still and silent, gazing at the wounded boy as if there was no one else in the world at that moment. On her face was the look she had worn just before Katya died, only this time it was unbearable to watch. Half of herself was dying before her eyes, and she plainly felt Ivan's agony in her own body.

Andrew knew he must reach her before she entered the realms her aunt had already reached. Uncaring and unheeding of Anna's fervent concern over his own injury he pushed her roughly aside, his gaze fixed on the broken Nadia. Her whole body was swaying like a branch before it snaps, her hands hung limp and lifeless beside her. He took them in his, gripping them tightly and willing the life back into her.

"Hold on," he said thickly, "for his sake, hold on. I am here with you."

Slowly she drew her gaze from Ivan and looked up into his face. The tears began to run down her cheeks, but she went with him when he began to lead her gently away.

NINE

Everything was shimmery-hazy, floating on cushions of sound that made no sense because they ran into their own echoes with confusing volume. Each time the pale light began to appear he fought to retreat as pain and anguish always accompanied it. But there came a time when it was no longer possible to retreat, and he cried out in protest until hands were laid on his brow in soothing fashion.

Words sailed in the air above his head. None of his questions were ever answered: Those who seemed to be beside him were never there. There was a sense of utter desolation that terrified him, yet beckoned with the irresistible promise of escape from the wraiths and demons chasing him. The most persistent came in two forms. One was Mei-Leng standing naked on a rock, with her face changing in horrifying manner into that of a man even as he took her in his arms and, instead of the ecstasy he expected, driving agony through his body. The other version was of his father galloping across the fields of their summer estate, an arresting figure in a proud uniform, yet when he ran out to meet him it was Andrew Stanton's face that laughed down at him with triumphant mockery. With both visions came a frightening suggestion of inhuman voices, high-pitched and singsong, like something he had once heard that was associated with fear.

It was when these voices started that light began to grow and, miraculously, at last there was a voice he knew, words he could understand, the scented presence of reassurance.

"Vanya," whispered the voice, "brother of my life, do not be afraid. Here is my hand. Take it and stay with me."

He felt fingers against his and tried to grip them. *"Sestrushka?"*

"Izvini." Something wet trickled along his hand. "The bond is not broken. Forgive me, forgive me. It can never be broken."

He opened his eyes, and everything was clear in the shuttered room. Nadia was sitting in a chair beside the bed, weeping. He saw the sheen of tears on her dear face that had grown thinner than ever. The narrow bars of sunlight pushing through the shutters striped her hair with bronze and brown, and highlighted the large shining eyes. He thought he had never seen anything more wonderful and tried to tell her so. The words drowned in the tears gathering in his throat.

"I have prayed, Vanya . . . before the icons I prayed. You were close to death, but now you are back with us again."

With an effort he curled his fingers around hers and pressed them. But he was tired and his eyelids closed over the one vision he knew had not been a dream. When he opened them again she was still there, but wore a dress of pale silk, and a lamp was burning in the room.

"You should not spend your time sitting here," he told her with slow words. "A sickroom is no place for a pretty girl."

She smiled with such joy it gave her a radiant beauty. "So, my brother is well enough to scold, is he? That is the very best of signs."

He smiled back wearily. "What is the use of scolding a sister who has never paid any heed? If I had been born first, perhaps it would have been different."

She took his hand lying on the coverlet. "Five minutes to change your whole personality? I think not, *bratishka.*"

They looked at each other in silence for a while, then he asked, "Do you come alone?"

Her nod hurt him, but she softened the news with "Aunt Marie is herself ill. The shock of seeing you has made her remember Katya, and Papa—all those things that make her unhappy. Uncle Misha spends much more time at the gallery now he no longer has you to attend to business. I have hardly seen him."

He thought she had finished, but she added after a pause, "Andrew has been every day, I understand."

It was not what he wanted to hear: It made the pains in his chest and abdomen worse and reminded him of his dreams. "Andrew!" he murmured contemptuously, and turned his head to gaze at the washstand and basin in the corner.

"He saved your life."

It was not easy to accept. He wished she would go away until he had come to terms with it. How could one hate a person to whom such a debt was owed? A Brusilov must honor any man who gave him life.

"Do you remember it, Vanya?" she asked gently.

He nodded, still with his eyes on the washstand. "Not . . . *him.* Just saying farewell to Lars Svenson, then looking around for you and the others. There were so many people, such a crowd. I did not realize they were edging me toward the trees until I felt a sharp point in my back." Recalling it for the first time, he turned back to face her with something akin to relief. "I was not afraid, you know. I fought."

"Of course you fought. You have no need to impress that upon me. Sometimes I think I know you better than you know yourself, *golubchik.*"

He had to know the rest, but it was with a perverse sense of mortification that he asked, "There were four or five. How . . . how did he do it?"

It was her turn to avoid his eyes by studying the washstand, and he knew she shared his obligation to honor the man who had so affected their lives.

"I was not a witness until later. They say he ran at them with his pistol. One is dead, and he has a knife wound in his arm." She looked down at her lap at that point and admitted she had not seen Andrew since that time, an astonishing ten days ago. "He comes to the hospital when I leave."

189

Ivan did not pursue the matter. He had relationships of his own to sort out. "I suppose it is part of his job to find the men," he said half to himself.

"I think he comes out of concern for you," she said quietly. "There is a police officer waiting to talk about the men."

After she had left with a promise to return the following day, the English police officer was allowed in to ask him questions about the affair. He was a tall man, spare and with smooth dark hair and clipped moustache. He had that English air of cool superiority, and Ivan took an instant dislike to him.

"Did you recognize any of your attackers, sir?"

"Recognize . . . why should I recognize them?"

Eyebrows rose, but the cool calm prevailed. "You have never had any personal dealings with any of them?"

Ivan was irritated. "The only Chinese with whom I deal are wealthy merchants. Those men were cutthroats."

"Quite so, sir, but I felt it wise to establish right at the outset that this was not a case of vendetta by an employee or small trader who felt he had been ill-used in some way."

"As I just said, I do not deal with such people. My comprador is employed for such a purpose."

Dark eyes looked frankly into his. "He's all right, is he?"

"I do not understand you."

"You trust him, do you? Ever caught him out at side-dealing—anything like that?"

"Side-dealing?" He was growing angry. "Perhaps you are not fully aware who I am."

"Yes, I think so, sir."

"Then you should know that 'side-dealing' in top quality jade is out of the question."

The man did not bat an eyelid, just sat upright on the chair completely at his ease. "I was referring to *kum shaw* from merchants. It's very easy for a comprador to earn a commission by recommending one man in preference to another to a business man like yourself, Mr. Brusilov. Quite a lucrative business, in some cases, but the merchants get the money back by charging higher prices for their merchandise—which means *you* pay the commission."

190

He resented the man's suggestion and said so. Then added, "Even if it were true, I cannot see what bearing it would have on this affair."

The man looked at him frowning for a while. "I have been in the Hong Kong police for ten years, Mr. Brusilov, and seen a great number of violent disturbances at Chinese festivals. More often than not, the Triads start a general fracas to disrupt the festivities while they indulge in pocket-picking and a general exhibition of their power as a warning to anyone who might oppose them in the future. Occasionally they use the cover of a crowd to kidnap ransom victims, or girls for brothels. Alternatively, such public occasions are chosen by fanatics or desperate men to take revenge on a particular person they feel has wronged them." He shifted slightly in his seat. "However, this case is slightly different, sir. Unless the assailants made a mistake in their victim, there is no doubt you were intended to be left for dead—no doubt at all. Isolated murders at such public occasions are rare—especially murders of Europeans. It suggests to me. . . ." He broke off, and Ivan prompted him sharply.

"Well, what does it suggest?"

The man looked him sternly in the eye. "Strange as it sounds, it suggests that the killing was planned to take place beneath the eyes of your whole family. You see, sir," he explained, "the Triads don't usually come into the open over something as serious as this. They are more likely to waylay a European in a quiet part of town if they intended to kill him. That they chose that moment in a public place where you were surrounded by your family and friends gives me the uncomfortable feeling that there is a dedicated and calculating mind behind the attack."

Ivan lay staring at the face that seemed to him to be suggesting something quite preposterous.

"Perhaps your ten years of experience has led you to read sinister intentions into something quite uncomplicated. It is easy in a colony such as this," he said stiffly.

The dark eyes gazed back unabashed. "Perhaps. What is your explanation, sir?"

"Explanation?"

"Well, sir, if Mr. Stanton had not noticed what was going on and dashed to your rescue, you'd be dead. If I were in your place I'd be damned curious to know why—if there wasn't an obvious reason, that is."

"What are you implying?" he demanded, for some unaccountable reason finding a heartbeat of apprehension fluttering in his breast.

The man rose and picked up his helmet with nonchalant ease. "Look at it this way, Mr. Brusilov. You are a highly respected businessman and member of the community. You tell me you have had no business quarrels with the Chinese, and that you think I am reading sinister intentions into something quite uncomplicated. Well then, since you were the person five Chinese tried to hack to death within reach of your family and friends, what do you think made them do it? Perhaps you'd give it some thought, and I'll come in again tomorrow." With a meticulous salute he went out.

Ivan had not long to brood on his words, for a nurse entered shortly afterward. It had been an exhausting day, and he needed fortitude to counter the treatment and rebinding of his bandages. Yet, when all was finished and the lamp dimmed, his mind raced in many directions preventing sleep. Why, oh why had it been Andrew Stanton who had faced five times his number in order to save his life? Why had Nadia avoided any mention of his mother when explaining why she was at the hospital alone? Why should anyone in Hong Kong wish him dead? He knew no Chinese thugs, had never given anyone cause to wish to harm him.

Yet, as he eventually slid into unconsciousness, the nightmare of a little Chinese girl covering her nakedness with a crumpled silk tunic came back to torment him.

Chris Smethwick was already in the office when Andrew opened Sir Goodwin's door two days after the Dragon Boat Festival. He gave a curt greeting to them both.

"Ah, Andrew." Sir Goodwin smiled as he went to put a hand on his nephew's shoulder. "How are you feeling?"

"Quite all right. It is these damned bandages on my arm that suggest I am at death's door."

192

Another broad smile. "Doctors always tend to be overcautious. It was extremely good of you to come in at my request, all the same."

"Not at all. I fully intended asking for an interview with you."

"Oh . . . about this Brusilov business?"

"Yes. I want to hand it over to someone else."

The smiles faded. "You know that is not possible."

Andrew's long-held temper flared. "I don't want to know about 'possible.' Under the circumstances, you cannot expect me to continue my investigation."

"I understand your feeling, Andrew. That was a nasty gash."

"I am not speaking of that," he interrupted angrily. "I faced worse than a knife wound in South Africa. I am talking about integrity, betrayal of trust, and ruined reputations." He fixed a belligerent stare on his uncle's face. "You cannot have failed to hear what is being tossed around the colony's gossip courts. Miss Brusilova's name is being mentioned in connection with mine in the most vicious manner. Even Brotherton in the distant jungle suggested she was no better than my dead wife."

"*Andrew*," said Sir Goodwin, shocked.

"Yes, the wife I killed," he repeated, beyond caring what he said. "You remember her, sir—a cheap showgirl masquerading as a lady. How dare anyone compare her with Nadia Brusilova? And there is more. There are stories that she visits my house alone—that we are conducting an amorous liaison behind the glass cases of Galerie Russe, because of my constant visits." He gripped the edge of the desk. "Please do not insult my intelligence by shaking your head like that. You, of all people, would have been certain to hear every nasty little whisper." He swung round on the other man. "Do you deny hearing it, Chris?"

The dark-haired man shook his head. "No . . . it's all over the colony."

Feeling even angrier at the confirmation of his words, he turned back to his uncle. "You see! I happen to know from Zubov that business is falling off—English customers are few, if any. They must also be feeling social repercussions. You are asking me to destroy them!"

Sir Goodwin walked to his large curved chair, sat, and

regarded Andrew calmly. "Very well, Andrew, I admit to hearing all this . . . but I cannot accept such an unpleasant outburst of protest from you. Until a month or so ago, you were preparing to put Miss Brusilova through all this voluntarily. I warned you what would result from an alliance with a Russian girl. As I remember, you were unforgivably abusive."

Andrew was taken aback, but not silenced. "This is rather different. My intention was to conduct an open and honorable courtship that would have protected her from this kind of thing."

"Mmm . . . open and honorable, eh? Would you say that is what that family has been toward you?"

"How do you mean?" asked Andrew sharply.

Sir Goodwin looked across at the other man in the room. "Captain Smethwick," he invited.

He stood up and went across to Andrew, his polished shoes ringing on the stone floor where it was not covered in rugs. "I'm sorry we have put you in this position, truly I am, but I think your protection of this family is slightly misguided. This attack on young Brusilov is the proof positive that he is up to his neck in activities that have nothing to do with being a jade merchant. You happen to be in the perfect position to get information for us without arousing their suspicion, and we have to ask something further of you." He lit a cigarette, then continued.

"There is now a new angle to consider. Madame Brusilova has withdrawn a massive sum of money from the family account since she arrived in Hong Kong, and has also had the Brusilov jewels brought from St. Petersburg by special courier."

Andrew narrowed his eyes against the smoke from the cigarette and asked cautiously, "And the new angle?"

Chris breathed out some smoke and watched it for a moment before answering. "She has been seeing a great deal of Orlov."

"He is Russian. Isn't that natural?"

"Yes. But he was a great friend of Boris Brusilov . . . who was on the staff of the department dealing with Sino-Russian affairs at the Czar's court."

Andrew could see immediately what his friend was suggesting, but found himself unable to answer right away. He walked to stare from the window at the antics of two lizards on the flat roof

194

beyond. They took his attention for no more than five seconds. Then, he was back in imagination on the beach where she had walked toward him and made all other awareness drop away. It came back so strongly to him, the present slipped away also until a voice brought him back to it.

"Well, Andrew?"

"She couldn't be dabbling in such a dangerous game." His voice sounded husky, and he still stared from the window at a fading vision of silver-green eyes.

"Why not? A woman like that would want Russia to be all-powerful."

"There is only one aim in her life," he said automatically.

"What is that?"

Shaking his head he turned slowly. "You don't know her. She has no interest in politics."

"That's what you said about her son," reminded Chris apologetically. "She is using that money for something, and we want you to find out what. Brusilov is going to be in that hospital for several months, so you will be able to concentrate on the mother."

"No, I can't do it."

"Why not?" asked Sir Goodwin. "They have encouraged your friendship yet, behind your back, they are conducting activities that are designed not only to give Russia predominance over us, but to bring the administration of this colony—and the British, as a whole—into direct conflict with the dynasty." He rose again and walked round to stand beside Chris Smethwick. "Andrew, for four years you have been steady, reliable, and an asset to the colony. Your work is only a little short of brilliant and there is no doubt you have an attractive future in Hong Kong. Are you going to throw it all away because of a foolish sense of loyalty to a family that seems to have bewitched you in some way? I would have thought saving that boy's life would be enough service to any family."

The two men stood looking at him, and he finally said, "You don't know what you are asking me to do."

Chris said, "We are following up the case of the attack on young Brusilov in the hopes of finding tangible evidence of the traffic in revolutionary literature. All we are asking you to do is

195

keep an eye on Madame Brusilova with a view to discovering if she is passing money to Orlov . . . or anyone else, for that matter."

Sir Goodwin then laid his bait. "You covered yourself with glory in South Africa—offered your life for your country. This is a little thing to do for it, in comparison."

His defense was destroyed, and he was walking out of Sir Goodwin's office with Chris, having agreed to their demands. He was silent as they walked along the corridors.

"This sort of thing is never pleasant, even when one is not emotionally involved," murmured Chris sympathetically. "I take it you have given up all idea of marrying Miss Brusilova?"

Andrew did not look at him. "Since I am virtually spying on her family for evidence of diplomatic treachery, I have no alternative. It hardly makes for mutual trust, does it?"

"No." Chris seemed embarrassed. "Perhaps it's all for the best, Andrew. You could hardly have a Russian wife out here—not in your position. Apart from the political objections, there would have been an outburst of horror from our set."

"There already is. I am running the gamut of public disapproval already."

"Mmm. It's the price of doing one's duty. It will all be forgotten when the truth comes out."

"Will it?" Andrew felt a surge of bitterness wash over him. "I don't know that I can just forget it. Too much damage will have been done." He walked on for a moment, then decided to tell his friend something he would know sooner or later. "I had a note from the president of the club this morning, suggesting that I might care to resign my membership. It seems too many members' wives have complained of my behavior."

"Ahhh," said Chris, going rather red because he was a member himself. "I knew there was . . . but I mean, I had no idea they would take such a strong attitude. It was that incident at the Dragon Boat Festival. If it had been Miss Brusilova they might not have kicked up such a dust, but it looked remarkably as if you had some kind of liaison with the mother, as well. The scene was rather . . . *warm*," he added tentatively.

Andrew swallowed. "Thanks to your 'new proposals' every one of those sharp-eyed rattle-tongues will shortly feel smugly justified. Oh God," he sighed, "I think I would sooner be back in South Africa. At least, that cause was clean-cut and defensible . . . and I knew then exactly what I was doing."

Mother and daughter passed each other along the corridor, but continued walking with no exchange of words or glances. With Nadia it was deliberate, but Anna always went about the house as if she alone inhabited it. The only time she acknowledged her family was when she had something particular to say to them. For the rest of the time they might not be there.

On that afternoon she was dressed for going out in a striking damson-red silk dress with matching hat of dyed feathers and veiling that heightened her dark perfection. It was new, like many of her clothes since she arrived in Hong Kong, and the ropes of pearls lying against her breast were of superb quality and sheen.

Nadia found it impossible not to be angry. Ivan was struggling to keep them all in grand style while maintaining the estates in Russia, but their mother selfishly spent the money she now claimed as Andrei's widow and gave no thought to her son and family. It had been so much easier when she had stood aloof from her mother, Nadia realized. Now, through Andrew, she lay open to hurt, anger, and humiliation at her hands.

Once in her room Nadia became prey to the thoughts she put aside in front of the others. With Ivan she tried to appear bright and confident; with her aunt as gentle and understanding as her condition demanded. With Uncle Misha drinking more heavily than usual she felt it was necessary to bolster his confidence but, at the same time, take a firm line with him. She sighed. If ever she had needed his masculine support it was now, but he was very little help during this critical period in her life. Before her mother she determined to show no sign of the desperation she felt. Not that Anna would notice if she did.

There was one person who would have been her salvation, if . . . but it was pointless to torment herself with memories of that day at his house. On her return, she had believed herself so steeled against him nothing he did would ever touch her again. How wrong she had been!

Restless, she pushed open the shuttered windows and went

onto the wide shady verandah and stood looking out. The vivid blue sea suggested escape from this house that had become so full of unhappiness, and she longed for the joys of an uncomplicated courtship.

Clutching one of the graceful wooden pillars she gazed at the sea that could take a boat round to his lonely bay. There was no escape from loving him. He had saved Ivan from certain death; he had given her back the other half of herself. He was now linked to her for eternity. Since the day of the Dragon Boat Festival two weeks before she had seen nothing of him. She thought back to the day of the festival. The memory was dominated by the terrible vision of Ivan lying in a pool of blood, his face almost unrecognizable. But it was now possible to remember the rest of the day, hazy though it seemed, in comparison.

Their arrival had been shattering, with her mother holding Andrew in thrall, just as she had Papa. There was something about the way Anna Brusilova walked *anywhere* that made all else fade into insignificance. Nadia had seen Andrew's face then, his eyes that were held, against his will, by the most beautiful woman in Hong Kong—held for as long as she wished.

That same look had been almost constantly on her father's face. She knew that, like Andrei, Andrew had been unable to see anyone else in that moment. It had crushed her, it had been so public. Yet, he had come to her after saving Ivan. At the time, she had been too anguished to notice anything but her brother's torn body, but later she had remembered Andrew's sleeve covered in blood, his hair tousled and damp, all dazed brilliance gone from his eyes. He had been completely hers, then.

She closed her eyes to shut out the beauty of the day, the rise of hills that sheltered a lonely bay with a house that hung above the sea. *Andrew!* So short a while ago she had told Ivan she had no pride where Andrew was concerned; that she would fight for him—yet she had surrendered in the first skirmishes.

Her words to Ivan had been vain; her pride had not withstood even the slightest setback. It did not compare with Andrew's dismissal of it after their disastrous arrival at the festival. He had led her away, and she had clung to him, telling all her fears, her anguish over the quarrel she had had with her twin. She had gripped his arms, uncaring of the blood that had run over her hand, and confessed that her soul would be in torment forever if Ivan died believing their bond of blood broken, as she had said. So many things she had confessed to him that day. How could she approach him now? For love there was no longer a chance, but she could not bear this complete severance. Somehow, she must make an opportunity to show him she had the courage to be his friend, even after all that had been between them in the past. Anything would be better than the situation as it now was.

The thought was still with her when she went to her aunt's room for her usual visit. The Chinese woman sitting inside the door smiled, bowed quickly, and slipped out to wait in the corridor. Nadia experienced her usual pang of sadness before going forward to smile at the woman who sat by the open shutters enjoying the sunshine.

"*Tyotushka,* I declare you have as fine a view from here as I have from my window," she said gently.

The face that turned to hers was plain as ever, but the years seemed to have dropped away leaving her innocent and curiously appealing. A wrinkled hand caught at hers as Aunt Marie smiled.

"They are gathering in the harvest. The boys look so brown, and the girls are taking them loaves in their kerchiefs. Soon, they will be singing." Her face saddened. "I wish I could go out there with them."

Nadia sat on a lacquered stool beside her. "You have not been well. It is too soon to go out. But you are getting better every day." She regarded the plump figure in brown silk. "Do you remember being ill, dear?"

"The harvest will be a good one—everyone says so. We are to have a picnic on Saturday. Have you been invited?"

"Yes . . . yes, I am invited. And Vanya. He has been ill, too, but will soon be coming to see you again."

"That will be nice." It was said with no indication that she had really registered what her niece had said, and Nadia sighed.

"There was a letter this morning from the little ones. They write very well of their occupations. At the end they send very special greetings to you, and warmest love."

199

"Do you think this dress is suitable for the Markievs' party? Mama will not let me have a new one." She leaned forward and said confidentially, "Sergei Markiev is so very handsome, I would like just once to catch his attention. Think of the gratification if he were to ask me to dance beneath the glares of the Smolensky sisters." Her expression changed to one of infinite desolation. "But it will not happen."

Nadia rose quickly and leaned against the windowsill, filled with a sadness that cried out for all young girls and their dreams. Young Marie Brusilova had been plain and, therefore, neglected at parties and balls. How must she have suffered when young— even fathers gaze with a fonder eye at pretty infants—how grateful must she have been to the penniless poet who was principally after a life of ease and a dowry! But the one great gift she desired, a child, was denied her, and it must have been almost unendurable when her handsome brother brought home his bride who was blessed with everything.

Nadia felt an absurd rush of tears blur the view of green-clad hills beyond the northern confines of the garden. How unfair life had been to her aunt, taking the little she had from her piece by piece until she was left again with the fervent wishes with which she had started out.

"I think she has a young man." The voice made Nadia start, and she turned back from the window to look at a face that was flushed with excitement. "I would not tell Papa, but I have taught her a lesson for keeping it from me." For a moment the excitement died. "She never tells me her secrets."

"Who is this?" asked Nadia softly.

"Anna, of course. I have seen young men looking at her in that certain way, but this one is special—an officer of the Guards. She keeps his picture by her bedside."

A strange tightness began to grow in Nadia's throat, making it difficult to speak. "How do you know that?"

"I have seen it."

"You have been to Anna's room?"

An uncomfortable slyness crept over her round face. "She does not know of my visits. I wait until she goes out."

"But how do you get out? Does Loi go with you?"

The slyness increased and Aunt Marie rose, beckoning with her hand. "Come along."

She led the way into her bathroom where the lavatory cubicle stood open. At the rear was a half-door which opened onto the verandah to enable the servant to cleanse and attend the unit.

"Do you remember how we used to play follow-my-leader all through the house? I can still do it, you know, but I go on my own. It is much more exciting. See what I did today after she had done." Laughing she went back into the cluttered room and straight to a closet on the wall where her icons hung. "It will teach her to tell me her secrets, in future."

Reaching beneath some camisoles she brought out a photograph in a silver frame. "That is the one—an officer in the Guards."

Wincing a little from the pain of what she was witnessing, Nadia could only gaze at the picture of a man on a horse while the tears she thought had gone returned.

"He's very handsome, isn't he?" giggled Aunt Marie.

"It's . . . it's Andrew," Nadia managed, at last. "He showed it to us at his house. Do you remember?"

Her distress registered on the older woman, who immediately thrust the picture at her. "He is your young man. Oh dear, oh dear, I did not know or I would never have hidden it from you." She jabbed Nadia with the picture. "Go on, take it before she comes back." She walked back to her chair by the window, bowed down by a sudden reversal of mood. "I might have known it was not really hers. She is always taking things that belong to other people." She looked swiftly at Nadia. "I hate her, you know."

The girl went quickly to put her arm around her aunt's shoulders, but the woman seemed to be more of the comforter than Nadia. Putting up a hand to wipe away the young girl's tears with fingers that had always been gentle, she said, "There is often a worm in the apple, and then one must get rid of it. You must do it soon, *golubchik,* or there will be no apple left."

TEN

The following day Nadia went, as usual, to the gallery, but she went with a determined intention of trying to improve the financial situation and find means of attracting customers back. With her limited knowledge of business it seemed a high goal for which to aim, but her thoughtful hours of the previous day had produced a new sense of optimism. It was of no use reflecting on unhappiness. What was out of reach must be forgotten. Her intention was to find fresh happiness elsewhere, and she would not achieve it with inaction.

For once, she did not notice the stares of fashionable ladies as they passed in rickshaws or strolled along the streets with their skirts sweeping the ground. On reaching the gallery she found her uncle busy with several visitors—probably from an American ship that had docked overnight—and was forced to linger by the display cases. She thought of another time when she had tried to give a lesson on jade to a man who looked all the time at her instead. She pushed the thought away.

Eventually, it was possible to approach her uncle, but her heart sank when he greeted her. There was a flush on his cheeks and the smell of vodka on his breath. He was far too hearty.

"The prettiest face in my gallery! My own niece—daughter of my heart." He threw his arms around her with great exuberance and kissed her heartily on the cheeks. "Come . . . come . . . I have something very exciting to show you, *golubchik*. I believe there is no other of its kind. See . . . look here." He pulled her across to a small case that housed special pieces, and she saw on the velvet a table screen of white translucent jade etched with carvings in jade of all the varying colors of green to create a picture of night-dark creatures against the moon-shimmer sky of the background. It was a work of great skill and patience executed by a craftsman with artistry in his fingertips. It was plainly worth a fortune!

"It is superb," she breathed.

"Superb . . . superb. Is it not superb?" he chanted. "I, Misha Zubov, have acquired it for my gallery. See how perfect are the animals carved upon it. It represents the assembly of the twelve beasts who govern the Chinese years, when Buddha summoned them at the beginning of time. The stand is of eaglewood—the only possible resting place for a child of beauty such as this."

He mopped his forehead with a bright handkerchief, then brushed his moustache which was moist with the effusiveness of his speech.

"How did you come by such a treasure?" she asked, beginning to feel apprehensive the longer she studied the small screen. He gave a sly smile. "Ah . . . aha! The merchant Wah who was caught selling fake jade is ruined. Now in prison, he has lost face before his sons, who cannot now continue the business that was his. Your uncle has gone very quickly to the family, who were so ashamed before another merchant of impeccable integrity they gladly let their best pieces go for less than their value." He turned his back to the case, but tapped it with his fingers. "Had I known this beauty was resting within the treasury of that shop I would have lain awake at nights." He seized Nadia's hand and pressed it firmly. "Your uncle is to be praised for discovering this. He is not the black sheep, the man of no distinction, hey?"

It was a plea for approval, and Nadia sighed. Would he never have faith in himself? "It is certainly one of the most exciting pieces we have had in the gallery—and one of the most expensive, no doubt," she added, sounding him out.

He moved away restlessly. "Ah, what is money? We do not need it when there is such wealth in beautiful things."

She followed him up to press her point. "We need it to buy them. Was this the right time to purchase Wah's stock?"

"There was only one time to purchase it—when it was for sale."

"But Vanya told me the gallery is losing money, that customers are fewer than before. Could we afford such a piece as the table screen?"

He turned round red in the face. *"We* . . . who are *we?* I, Misha Zubov, decide what we shall buy. Have I been wrong . . . huh? Have I? Fewer customers—*chepukha!* See . . . look, look." He waved his arms wildly. "There are customers—in every room there are customers. Vanya is a boy, he does not know about jade. He should not tell such things to you—a girl—his sister." He twirled round, sweeping the expanse of showcases with an elaborate gesture. "Could we afford these? No . . . but they are not for us. Soon, someone will come and buy them. They cost us nothing."

"What if they do not sell?" she persisted.

He puffed up indignantly. "Not sell! No, that is too unkind. Have I not sold jade for eighteen months and made Galerie Russe the best in Hong Kong? Have I not . . . eh . . . answer me that?"

Nadia tried to soothe his ruffled feathers. "Yes, of course. It is just that Vanya worries, and it is bad for him."

Sulking he said, "It is like that boy to worry when there is no need. I think he is worried by his own shadow."

Nadia jumped immediately to her twin's defense. "You do not deal with the books, try to balance the accounts, as he does."

"Ha! He is not here to do it, is he?"

She seized her chance with silent thanks to him. "That is why I am here today. Vanya will be away a long time, so I shall come in to replace him until he is well enough to return."

Uncle Misha was dumbstruck, but it was only what she expected and was ready with her next line. "I did it when we started the gallery, I can do so again. The doctor told me it might be several months before Vanya can take up his old life again. It is too much to expect you to do everything single-handed."

"No, I will not hear of it. A female in business? No, my dear, you are not a shopgirl, but a lady."

"I am also a Brusilov," she said quietly, "and for generations we have faced adversity with unity. Vanya is the brother of my blood, born of the same breath. Who else would help him now?"

"But . . . no, it cannot be done. Think of the disgrace, think of how it will look."

"The office is upstairs. Nobody will see who works there. As for the disgrace, better by far to concentrate your thoughts on who would have wished to kill Vanya. He has no idea, and the police think he is hiding the truth."

It was the cue for a change of approach, and Nadia was taken unawares by it. Her uncle grew agitated. "He does not know? You do not know? How can you not know? First Boris, then Andrei . . . now the son of Andrei. That is what they said . . . all the family."

She stared at him in disbelief. "You cannot mean that. Follow us from Russia to kill the next Brusilov? It is a year and a half. How would they get here?"

"Your mama—they watched and followed. But they will return now for young Constantin. We shall be safe."

Nadia was appalled by what he said. For her uncle nowhere would ever be far enough away from Russia to feel safe. Now she understood the vodka fumes, the nervous excitement, the boasting.

Her approach was almost that which she used with Aunt Marie. "They were peasants—starving and penniless. They could not come all this way to Hong Kong. Just think of how much it cost us, and you will see that it is not possible. We are safe. The men who attacked Vanya were Chinese, you know."

For a moment he gazed at her with glazed eyes, then humped his shoulders miserably. "It was the only explanation. Who else would do such a thing?"

"You cannot think?" she asked hoping he might shed some light on it.

"Of course I cannot think." He turned away to seek comfort in his beloved jade. "It is terrible, *golubchik*, that men kill each other.

205

Your papa . . . he enjoyed it. Yes . . . yes, he enjoyed it. I remember his face when he came in that day after the massacre at the Winter Palace. It *glowed*. When Boris told us how the order had been given and the soldiers obeyed to a man, he looked exultant." Then he said something so terrible Nadia could not believe he meant it. "He did it for her. I watched them together as he told how he had galloped through the crowd with saber swinging. He offered the deed to her as a gift of love, and she worshiped him for it."

There was silence, and Nadia was torn between repugnance for a man who could imagine such a thing, and extreme pity for someone who had been unfortunate enough to marry into a family whose men were invariably strong. Next minute he had swung round and taken her into an embrace. When he pulled away his eyes were full of tears. "Forgive me . . . there has been so much . . . your poor aunt. I should not have said what I did. You are innocent yet of what can govern a man and woman." He patted her hand. "I am a fool—they all think it, I know. But *here* I feel things more acutely than most men." He put a hand over his heart. "Fools who can cry at the sight of beauty seldom shape the world, *golubchik*, but they see more of life than those who are busy being great. I thank God every day that you are not like her. Do not . . ." he grew embarrassed, ". . . do not let him go to her." A gentle smile completed his contrition. "You see, I knew that first day that your heart was captured. Why else did you think I insisted that he should come to dinner?" The smile broadened. "I am not always so foolish, eh? But knowing did not help when Anna came back. I can do nothing except tell you to hold him, come what may. Anna will always be Anna . . . but Andrew is *not* Andrei, and she will fail. Perhaps I have not done well by Marie's children, but this I know and tell you truly."

Feeling unable to cope with an uncle who was bewildering her like a conjuror who changes an original article into a series of others before the eyes, Nadia moved slowly across the room deep in thought. He kept beside her, silent also. Without knowing she began mounting the stairs to the mezzanine floor, and when they reached Ivan's office it seemed to be accepted that she had achieved her wish to stand in for her twin brother.

The door swung back, but Nadia was taken by surprise to see someone sitting at the desk. The surprise was mutual, and it was a moment before the gray-clad Chinese rose to his feet and bowed.

"Greetings, Miss Brusilova. I regret I was not informed of your visit. I would have had ready that which Mr. Brusilov requests."

She smiled faintly at Ho Fatt. "I fear my brother is too ill to concern himself with business." She looked pointedly at the open desk covered with papers. "Was there something you wanted from my uncle?" Walking across to the desk she was very put out to see an open account book, several letters of crested notepaper, invitation cards. The pen beside the ledger was wet with ink, and the last figures entered on the page were also. A quick glance at the triangular face of the comprador found it bare of expression.

"What have you been doing here?" It came out sharply, in the manner she would use to an erring household servant, and so swift as to be imagination she thought a flash of black fire appeared in his eyes before vanishing again. He did not answer, simply looked at Uncle Misha as if the question had been directed at him.

"I do not always manage to get up to the office," he mumbled. "So many inquiries from purchasers ... and there is the unpacking and visits to value jade. Ho Fatt knows what is required in the office. He keeps it tidy and up to date."

It was only too obvious the man was doing more than keeping the office tidy, and Nadia was angry. Her uncle had protested at her intention to help, yet appeared to have left a Chinese employee with access to confidential financial details, letters of great importance, and ledgers recording all the family business. In consequence her voice was even sharper as she said, "He has his normal work, also. How can he have time to do this?"

Uncle Misha spread his hands weakly. "He knows about this part of the business. Vanya always said he could not manage without him."

"I know—he said the same to me. But accounts, letters from clients, invitations to luncheons should be dealt with by one of us. Such things are not part of a comprador's duties, however invaluable he might be." She turned to Ho Fatt. "You should not have been asked to do this."

207

"I did not have to ask," put in Uncle Misha. "The day after Vanya was attacked, Ho Fatt took over."

"I see."

The Chinese inclined his head slightly, not enough to constitute a bow, but sufficiently to suggest he had received a compliment.

"When two men become three, the third is not missed."

"It is impossible for two men to become three," she said with firm reason, "especially for several months on end. I have decided to do the accounts and paperwork for my brother. I assisted him when we opened the gallery, so I know what is required."

The Chinaman's face was still impassive, but there was no mistaking the change in his eyes this time. Dark vicious passion lit them from behind and burned to deny the blandness of his expression. She was shaken by the look, and strangely afraid.

"If it is seen that I am replaced by . . . yourself . . . I shall lose face before those who must obey me," he told her.

Some of her Brusilov pride rose to cover her sudden spurt of fear. "But you are not being replaced; it is my brother. *You* will continue as before."

"It cannot be as it was before," he insisted. "When a man has once changed, he may change again, but never back to the first man."

"My dear," interceded Uncle Misha pleadingly, "do you think it wise to pursue this? Ho Fatt is very capable. I have left everything to him and had no worries. We work well together, eh?"

The Chinese bowed. "Just so, sir."

"Then I hope you will continue to do so tomorrow when I take some of the extra work from you both," Nadia told them firmly, then added for her own satisfaction, "we have a saying, also. *The troika runs best with a full team of horses.*" She smiled serenely at Ho Fatt. "You will see how true that is."

Her smile nearly wavered at the poisoned glance he shot her before bowing himself out, and her hand was trembling as it took up a letter from the desk.

"Now, let us see what this is about."

"There, I told you it would not do for you to begin working

here," grumbled Uncle Misha in despair. "He was upset, I could tell."

"I cannot think why," she said sharply. "His daughter works for Andrew."

"That is a rather different matter. She is there in a subservient capacity. To the Chinese, women are inferior creatures. To have you giving him instructions will be an affront."

She looked up from the letter she was pretending to read. "In this colony East and West must live side by side. I have accepted their smells, their endless noisy processions, their pagan temples, their firecrackers at New Year . . . their attempt to kill my twin brother. Just this once, I am afraid, Ho Fatt will have to accept *my* way."

The return of the photograph posed Andrew a tricky problem; Nadia's accompanying note posed a worse one. For two days he battled with conscience, common sense, and a love that refused to die. He wanted to see her: *It would reopen old wounds.* He had distinct orders to be friendly with the Brusilovs: *What use was it when he was being forced into Anna's company?* It would be an excuse to survey the gallery again: *There was nothing there, he knew.*

Strangely it was the thought of the Brusilovs' fate that made up Andrew's mind to see Nadia again. Whatever the outcome, he knew in his heart she was unaware of what her brother was doing, as was Misha Zubov. They were both being innocently implicated in an international gamble simply by being at Galerie Russe.

When he entered shortly after midday he was acutely disappointed not to find Nadia in the little office alcove. But Misha, snoring loudly with a silk handkerchief over his face, did not awaken when Andrew shook him lightly by the shoulder. It was more than tiredness that kept him so deeply slumbrous. Leaving him, Andrew asked one of the supervisors if Miss Brusilova intended coming to the gallery that day, and was surprised when told she was up in the office.

He stood for a moment or two watching her through the window. She was on the far side of the room wrestling with the handle of a door that appeared to be jammed. The fierce attack

209

she used plus the gentle dishevelment of her hair reminded him of the first time he had come upon her, stamping her foot and venting Russian oaths in the shrubbery. He went in without knocking.

"May I assist you?" He said it in French, as he had that day, somehow caught in that other moment.

She spun round and stood with her back against the door, her hands splayed against the varnished wood, and there was that same instant committal in the widening of her eyes that he had seen that first day.

Dear God, he thought, she is mine and I cannot take her. Is *anything* worth that?

"It was good of you to send the photograph," he said at last. "It was the only picture of my loyal horse, and I valued it."

"I know," she said softly, answering with her intense gaze all the things he could not ask her. "That was how I guessed you had not parted with it knowingly. Aunt Marie found it in . . . her . . . room. She did not know the significance of what she did by taking it."

He took a deep steadying breath. "How is your aunt?"

"Like a child."

He absorbed that for a moment. "Life has not been very kind to her, poor soul."

"No."

They stood too caught by their own emotions to make cohesive conversation, until she said, "There are no words to thank you for what you did."

"Then don't attempt to find any," he said quickly. "I have just come from the hospital. He is in a rare mood after being refused another pillow. He intends to ask you to insist that he gets one."

She smiled faintly. "Poor Vanya, he does not take kindly to such treatment. He always sees it as an attempt to deny his authority. All his life he has struggled to gain it, and now there is no one to overrule him, he sees it in the slightest things. He has not found life easy, you know, and all this is an extra burden." She waved a hand at the office. "The life of a merchant is not his destiny. I tell him he will be greater than his father, one day." Her voice thickened. "I truly believe it."

Her innocence was a weight upon him, and he walked further into the room as if movement would ease it. "What are you doing up here?"

"Working." She came toward him, a slender figure in a dress of palest green, tucked across the bodice and trimmed with fine white lace. The color highlighted the bronze lights in her hair and the sun tints on her skin from spending so much time in her garden.

He forgot revolution and betrayal. "Is it possible for a woman to do accounts?"

She smiled. "Of course. Are not all housekeepers women? They must run their establishment with economy."

"But this is a little more than that, surely?" he protested.

"Why?" She was before him now and using the steady trustful gaze of the past. "There are but ten digits, no matter how one uses them. What is there for a woman to fear?"

He smiled back at her. "You are quite remarkable."

"Not at all," she told him gently, "just someone using basic knowledge to adapt to something usually done by gentlemen. And I have this to help me."

It was an abacus, something he had never used but saw each day in Chinese shops, the beads flying up and down the wires as quick fingers reckoned what the customer owed.

"You understand that thing?" he asked.

"Oh, yes. In Russia they are used extensively. Shall I show you?"

"Yes, please."

He watched her fingers and thought how slender and graceful their movements on the beads. He listened as she explained and was charmed anew by the softly accented voice. He let his gaze wander over the piled coiffeur, noting the softness of her neck above the lace collar, and how tiny bronze curls lay against it. He smelled the fragrance of her skin—wild roses in sun-drenched hedgerows—and felt her nearness as a physical pain.

Suddenly, she was looking up at him and her face was bare of any pretense. "You do not make an attentive pupil," she whispered.

"I know."

211

The kiss was gentle, experimental. His hands were on her shoulders; hers against his chest. They touched no more than that, yet claimed each other back instantly.

"You should not have to do this," he told her in rough tones, still holding her shoulders.

"I have missed you, Andrew," she confessed with generosity. "And so has Uncle Misha."

"Uncle Misha is downstairs sleeping off the effects of too much vodka, while you are here in this heat struggling with accounts." He let go her shoulders and took her hand in his. "Ink-stained already. I'll shake him awake when I leave and give him my opinion."

She looked down at the ink marks on her hands. "The bottle spilled over. I was trying to find more when you came in. The storeroom seems to be locked and I cannot find the key. Vanya told me yesterday the key is in his desk. I have looked, but it is not there. I was trying to open the door. I can do nothing until it is." She half-smiled. "Do you know how to break open a door, Andrew?"

"I know one rather drastic method, but I'd rather try something gentler first."

With his arm around her back he led her across to the door, then squatted to see how heavy a lock there was. "Mmm! I really need a knife to have any chance."

She brought him a letter opener, but it was too fine and ornamental to be of any use. For a while he prodded ineffectively, then stood and looked around at the size of the office.

"If you feel it necessary, I can shoot off the lock. It means you'll have to get a carpenter to make a small repair." He frowned in sudden thought. "There's no jade in there, I hope?"

"No, it is just for the office. Vanya keeps all his supplies and ledgers where he can soon get at them." She studied his expression. "Can you really do such a thing?"

"Yes, we opened many things in South Africa by that method. Well?"

It took only a second or two for her to decide. "It will have to be opened. The key is somehow lost, and I cannot bother Vanya with such things."

212

He made her stand outside while he did it, then they went together into the storeroom that held all the normal supplies of an office, plus one or two stout boxes usually containing deeds.

"Here is your ink," he said, taking down a large bottle from the shelf. "I'll fill the inkwells for you . . . and I suggest you use some of this blotting paper for your fingers," he added teasingly.

He went over to the desk with the big stone bottle, his mind full of nothing more than the pleasure of being with her again. He was in the midst of carefully tipping ink into the pewter containers on the desk when she called out, "Andrew, do you understand Chinese?"

"Mmm . . . not all that well, and then only one or two dialects," he told her over his shoulder. "Why?"

Her perfume filled his nostrils as she drew near. "Do you know what is written here?"

A small sheet of red paper covered with black Chinese symbols appeared on the desk beneath his gaze, and he cast a cursory glance at it.

"Andrew . . . *the ink!*"

A pool of black was spreading across the desk, and he put the bottle upright with hands that were unsteady. Nadia was going swiftly to the storeroom and returning with blotting paper, grumbling lightheartedly over their carelessness.

"It was my fault. I should not have shown you that when you were pouring. Now, we shall have to . . . Andrew, what is it?"

He had to ask the question. "Where did you get this?"

"In the storeroom. There is a box full of them." She looked from his face to the paper, then back to his face. "What is it . . . you look so . . . Andrew, is something wrong?"

At that moment the door crashed open and Misha almost fell into the room. His face was yellow with fear, and he was shaking from head to foot. For a minute or so Nadia spoke to him in rapid Russian, trying to calm him and reply to the jumble of sentences that fell from his lips.

Andrew slid the paper into his pocket. It had grown unbearably hot and he was now aware of the smell of the pistol shot.

"He thought I was being harmed," said Nadia through the storm clouds in his brain. "He lives in fear of revolutionaries."

ELEVEN

The discovery of revolutionary pamphlets in a private locked cupboard in Ivan Brusilov's office was all the proof needed to condemn him. But he was very ill in hospital, so those few who were working on the case decided to do nothing and watch. They wanted to catch the whole organization in the act of moving them from the colony into China, and alerted their chain of investigators up-country.

The Governor was delighted when Sir Goodwin told him of the development and spoke to Andrew of his satisfaction. Neither senior man appeared to notice how silent and drawn the young administrator looked. Nor, when they told him to intensify his investigation of Madame Brusilova, did it occur to them that they might be asking too much of him.

Meanwhile, the young police officer employed on the task of finding Ivan's attackers was still kept in ignorance of the true picture. He went about his job methodically and in accordance with normal practice. Following on the case of Wah, who had unwittingly sold fakes as genuine pieces, it seemed more than likely that the Russian was caught up in something similar that would make money fast. His Chinese rivals had plainly felt he was treading on their toes. That, or he had fallen foul of the Triads over some doubtful dealings. Either way, the police officer set about trying to break down the protests of innocence made by the wounded man.

Now that he was fully conscious all the time Ivan found himself as obsessed with the mystery as his English inquisitor. At first, he had been too full of pain and shock to think straight, but the continuing days spent flat on his back left him with nothing to do but tease his brain with a long list of problems.

Andrew Stanton had been to see him several times and said he was keeping an eye on the case personally. He was not so obvious with his questions as the police officer, but there was no mistaking his casual inquiries about business transactions. Ivan could tell him no more than the other man, and said the attackers must have mistaken him for another—what other explanation could there be? Andrew had not looked convinced.

He felt a strange reluctance to ask the Englishman about Mei-Leng when he came to visit, but questioned Nadia on the subject. She was very offhand about Andrew, and Ivan suspected all was not well between them, for which he was very thankful. But Nadia did ask Ho Fatt about his daughter, and it appeared she was still away nursing the sick uncle on the mainland.

Ivan fretted over her, although he could do nothing if she were back. He could not seem to forget the way she had been afterward. In the calm of aftermath he acknowledged that he had overridden her early protests with some force, but she had responded after a while—responded with such exciting fervor it had driven him on. She had made him a man. He longed to feel that mastery again with her. Also, a little niggle of conscience told him he should reassure her. She had run away into the trees that day, and he had crashed around trying to find her until, his energy spent, he had given up the chase and gone back to his horse alone.

Thinking of it all again that evening his spirits sank very low. One morning with her had shown him the heights he could reach, then she had vanished and everything had begun to move like a landslide. His mother was hounding Andrew Stanton into

215

complete surrender; he knew they were meeting because Andrew spoke of things about Russia only Anna could have told him. If she took him in place of the real Andrei, life would be unimaginable.

Daily he thanked God for his twin sister. She soothed him with comforting words on his staunchness in turning his back on death and making a recovery, she assured him that Aunt Marie was cared for and happy. She wrote the letters to the young ones in Russia, keeping the harmony of the family split far apart. Now, she had taken over the book work at the gallery which had fallen behind since his accident. It offended his pride that she should do such a thing, but she had made him see that it was the only answer until he was better, and that none of the customers would know there was a girl up in the office.

All the same, he was particularly despondent when his uncle walked in to inquire after his progress a few minutes after darkness fell. For some reason the sight of the sad moist blue eyes already glazed with inebriation set Ivan on edge.

"Well, well, my boy, how is it coming along?" he asked, putting on the white bedcover an untidy bunch of flowers that immediately shed petals everywhere.

"Too slowly for my liking. It is frustrating to lie here day after day. Do you know, they will not even let me sit out yet."

"Ummm . . . ummm," mused Uncle Misha. "It was bad, Vanya, very bad. You are fortunate to be alive at all. If Andrew had not. . . ."

"Yes yes, I know what he did," Ivan interrupted testily. "Every visitor I have tells me of it."

"But not Andrew himself" was the stern comment. He lodged himself on the corner of the bed which made the mattress sink to a degree that jerked the patient uncomfortably. "Instead of trying to become a replica of your father you should model yourself on that man. You are not so very different from him underneath all that absurd pride."

Ivan was stung. "I am a Brusilov."

"Perhaps you should think of yourself merely as a man."

"Ha! Is that what the Czar thinks? Where would the great

216

families be if the name and honor of those already gone were not maintained?"

Uncle Misha gave a crooked vodka-induced smile. "You are not the Czar, boy—just a jade merchant."

The twinge of pain brought on by the jerking bed added fire to Ivan's tongue. "Not for much longer, from what I hear."

"Eh, what does that mean?"

"You know the state of our capital. We cannot afford to buy jade at the rate you are doing at the moment."

"How do you know this? Nadia is coming to you with tales," cried Uncle Misha, getting out his colored handkerchief and mopping his face.

"No. You forget my signature has to be on the checks. She brings them to me. I shall not sign any more, I warn you. We cannot buy and not sell."

"Not sell . . . not sell! Of course we sell. It is simply that business is black everywhere. It is the hot season. People do not go out," he ended feebly. "Today . . . yes, today, I sold an elegant trinket box."

"A few hundred dollars, no more. You are buying pieces worth thousands."

Uncle Misha rose in agitation. "Are we Galerie Russe or not, hey? Do we stock our gracious premises with trifling trinkets that can be bought in a back-street Chinese bazaar? Is that what you want, young Brusilov? Ho Fatt hears of excellent pieces and advises me immediately. My judgment has made our name, I will remind you. You think it beneath you to own a gallery of beautiful things. Then will you be more content to own a trinket shop?"

"I will never be happy in Hong Kong," Ivan flung at him in a temper that rose alarmingly. He looked with contempt at the crumpled suit and the sagging face with a moustache glistening with the beads of saliva that always appeared during his uncle's impassioned speeches. He saw the man his family had metaphorically swept under the carpet from the day he entered it. He saw him wearing the yellow sheen of fear and screaming at the driver to whip up the horses.

217

"By bringing us all here you have destroyed us. If you cannot see that, if it is not on your conscience, may the Lord forgive you." His vehemence put a strain on his chest that accelerated his breathing and aggravated the healing knife wounds, but his anger was too strong to be halted. "Katya is gone forever, your own wife is beyond recall. Nadia is being torn apart by a man you think I should copy; Mama has abandoned us again for that same man. I am here like this, and financial ruin is on its way—all because you brought us to this infernal island." He felt the breath begin to rattle in his throat, and his voice grew hoarse with effort. "You are a coward. You know it every time Mama looks at you."

For a few moments Uncle Misha sat in silence. Then he picked up his hat with a hand that shook. "Few men are proud of their lives, but if they can see their own weaknesses there is a little that is worthwhile in them. The fool who knows he is a fool is greater than the one who does not."

He went out without another word, but Ivan noticed the sparkle of tears on his face as the light from the corridor caught him before the door closed. He turned his head restlessly on the pillow, his outburst having increased his melancholy. For a swift moment he wished his assailants had succeeded. If he could not live like his father, he could have died like him.

It had been a day full of alarms that came one on top of the other. Andrew went from the Kowloon ferry, where several dignitaries were arriving after a harrowing tour of the railway pushing its way through the New Territories, to the home of the French Consul where several ruffians were thought to be lurking in the grounds.

No sooner was he back in his office than there came news of a pirate junk captured by the water police and carrying several passengers from a vessel it had sunk up near Shanghai a week earlier. And while he was still at the docks word came of a new emergency. There had been a fracas at a brothel when two prostitutes claimed the same man as client. The girls came to blows and, both being high on opium, it ended with the death of one from a knife wound by the other. The client was a member of the administration and not in a fit state to give evidence.

Andrew was told to get down there double-quick and get the man out with as little fuss as possible. When he saw who it was he wished anyone but himself had been given the duty.

Unsteady with drink and shock, Gerard Brotherton was slumped in a chair in a corner of the room draped with violet-blue curtains and gold tassels of tawdry cord. His handsome face was gray; his hands were shaking. Andrew got him away from the fast-gathering crowds with smooth expertise, cutting short the man's profuse thanks that would be forgotten when the shock wore off.

As he returned to write his report of discreet half-truths a wave of bitterness engulfed him. Brotherton could consort with as many Chinese whores as he wished, and indulge in any excess of their trade so long as he kept it apart from his social life, yet he himself was shunned over an honorable association with a Russian family. Lechery was acceptable; marriage to a high-born foreigner was not! What a sham it all was, he thought as he signed his report with a vicious flourish.

He finished his paperwork regretting the absence of Mei-Leng for so long, then went from the office for his horse. The ride home was long, and he set off lost in thoughts. By handing over the pamphlet found in Galerie Russe he had ended all right to any kind of contact with Nadia. It had been a straight case of betrayal knowingly carried out. He no longer had any official need to visit the gallery, and the hurt she might suffer at his absence would help her to withstand the truth about him when she and her family were accused. He had passed the stage of cursing his decision to see her again, and now found it easier to accept the Chinese belief that everything was part of a greater plan.

The shock of finding such damning evidence in Ivan's private office had shaken his self-assurance. He would have staked his life on the boy's innocence. How could his judgment have been so wrong? In asking himself that question so many times he had been forced back to memories of Cissie and his defiance of parents who had seen immediately what she was. Such thoughts had begun to eat away at his confidence until he faced the prospect that he might also be wrong about Nadia, and Misha

Zubov. Were they laughing at his simple trust in them? As he was betraying their trust by seeing Anna?

Every meeting with her left him restless, caught in a web of suppressed excitement against his will. If she was merely beautiful the attraction would have been containable: if she was just rapacious he could have handled it. What she wanted from him was something so tremendous he could not begin to accept it, much less fight it. It lay somewhere between adoration and dedication—deeper than allegiance, more total than worship, more eternal than death.

But that was not all. She gave to him all she commanded in return. Her life was lived for him, around him. In his hands she had placed the total of her senses, her soul. It bound him to her, and the harder he struggled to break free the tighter the bonds became. It placed upon him the responsibility for her continuing life. Love, that sweet true emotion, did not enter into it. Her mesmeric assumption of his total surrender made him breathless, tantalized, bewitched. Each time they met he went with resolution and fell deeper beneath the sorcery.

She spoke of Andrei, then called him by that same name. He was fair, his eyes were blue, he had been a soldier—a cavalryman—he had served his ruler. Andrei had been all those things. *Andrei Brusilov.* When he was with her he began to take on that other identity. She called him Andrei in her husky Russian voice, and he answered as that man, felt as that man, *was* that man. After each meeting it took him longer to shake off the feeling of having lost himself somewhere. Worse, he returned to it in moments when dusk brought a sense of metamorphosis, or when the seduction of his isolated bay at midnight kept him awake and on his terrace.

But unlike Andrei Brusilov, Andrew went unwillingly into those realms and could still return from them. When he did he knew he was engaging in a battle he must win, or merge into the oblivion of another man forever.

Following his orders he had managed to question Anna on her friendship with Orlov and had discovered that the Russian had used his influence to organize the carriage of the Brusilov jewels by diplomatic courier. Today Andrew decided to change his tactics. They usually met at a place she named, and she always won the first skirmish before he was even armed. Deciding he would stand a better chance on his home ground he had invited her to supper that evening. As host, he could control the situation. She could not take him by surprise in his own home, and he had to find out whether her association with Orlov had deeper overtones than mere national affiliation. Was he receiving Brusilov money from her to help the Russian cause?

He strode into the house shouting to Kim that he would take a dip first, and attacked the sea with more energy than wisdom. He emerged exultant, but out of breath, bringing Kim hurrying with refreshment and fresh amazement at the antics of Englishmen. The breathlessness lasted while he bathed and dressed, and he suddenly had doubts as to the wisdom of inviting Anna Brusilova to this place of such witchery.

The boat he owned had been sent to Victoria for her, and he went down onto the beach when he saw the lights approaching. Why had the dusk not brought such beguiling softness of air and silky shimmery water when Nadia had been there with him? At the recollection of her sweet face wild with passion as she accused him of treachery, and the wind that had whipped her hair across wet cheeks, his sense of mastery began to fade.

The little craft drew alongside the small jetty as he walked onto the staging to help his guest alight. The tide was low, so he was forced to go onto one knee to take her hand, and tried to dismiss the instant suggestion of submission in the action. When she stood beside him he kissed her fingers, but darkness fortunately hid her eyes, and it was only her soft, "Andrei, *nenaglyadny moy*," that boosted his pulse beat.

They walked in silence across the sand to the long flight of steps leading to the terrace where Andrew had told Kim to serve supper. Lantern light, he felt, would dim her brilliant glance and hide his reactions to her. His body was tense, however, and his senses acutely heightened by the perfume drift as she walked, the seductive rustle of silk, the velvet hood that lay across her cheek in a dark line against pale skin. It was all there in a flash—a feeling of escorting a Czarina to the steps of some great basilica.

Anna went in to the sitting room, loosening the strings of her cloak, but before he knew it she had walked quickly forward leaving the dark velvet to slide to the floor behind her.

"But you have changed it!" she exclaimed, stopping before a cabinet on which were two carved figures of Zulu warriors.

"Changed? Oh . . . those figures have simply been moved from the mantel. I am surprised you noticed."

She swung round. "I remember everything about this house, Andrei," she said passionately. *"Everything."*

He was picking up her cloak and caught the full blaze of beauty aroused as he looked up at her. The dress of deep violet paper-taffeta cut across her shoulders in a graceful shallow curve to fall into a deep plunging vee to her waist at the back. It clung to her body as far as the hips, then was swept back into a cluster of godets caught together by a spray of silken violets. Around her left wrist was a wrought-silver bracelet set with palest green jade and diamonds; a magnificent matching tiered necklace lay against her breast.

"You must not change anything," she said. "I think of you here, imagine your every movement. There is not a moment when I am not with you, Andrei. It was always like that. It *will* always be like that."

He breathed quicker to take in air that would steady him, and dragged his gaze away from a face that showed him a bizarre paradise. "I changed nothing, it was Kim." Taking a grip on himself, he walked away to pick up one of the wooden figures. "These came from South Africa."

"They are savage and beautiful . . . like you, Andrei."

It was his turn to swing round. *"Savage?* No, you are wrong."

"I am right," she told him dreamily. "I see it in the way you move, how you speak. It is there in your soul, deep in your soul, but it is there."

Like Andrei. He forced his mind from that thought and moved determinedly to an antlered head on the wall. "This is a sable antelope. They run in great herds across the plains of Africa."

"Did you kill that beast?"

"Yes, one of our fellows organized a. . . ."

"Savage . . . did I not say you were?" She had come to him and her smile accepted his apology even though he had not intended

222

to make one. "He killed me a bear, once," she went on in her soft dreamy tone. "Its noble head bowed beneath his boot when the *okhotnik* brought it in, and when he lay full stretch beside it the creature was immense in comparison. He lay there laughing up at me, and never was he more magnificent." Her hand touched his sleeve. "You laugh and he laughs, Andrei."

He saw the danger quickly and was starting an organized retreat when she gave a great sigh.

"Those are from South Africa, also?"

He followed her glance to the swords on the wall. "One was my grandfather's in India, the other mine. I used them in the war, yes."

"Bring them down for me."

Glad of the change of subject, he took down his own sword and let her admire it, drawing it carefully from the scabbard to show her the engraving on the blade. Then he began to take down the heavier antique scabbard that had belonged to his grandfather. As he turned back to her he felt a sharp needle-point in the hollow of his throat. Anna had his sword in her hand.

With the sharp prick of the point on his skin came a rush of excitement from the pit of his stomach to heat his body and set his senses swirling. He was trapped with his back against the wall and the pressure on his throat was sufficient to keep him still. It was bizarre, heady, and he knew the exquisite fear of the mountaineer who knows snow blindness might deceive his judgment.

"The sword is the noblest of weapons, Andrei," she breathed in her husky Russian voice. "It is used to bring men to their knees, but it can also elevate them to the highest honor."

The brilliance of her eyes did both as she locked her gaze to his, and the breath was driven from him by the adoration and triumph that blazed across her features. Time wavered and tilted, landscapes of snow and veldt intermingled, hoofbeats thundered in his head as her image blurred. His body felt on fire, throbbing with excitement of a wilder nature than he had ever known. As the sword-point pressed harder against the vulnerability of his throat the fire became a raging inferno and the excitement mounted higher and higher.

When it became more than he could contain, shockingly the point pierced his skin and a trickle of blood ran in warm insinuation down his throat. The sword was lowered, but he stayed where he was knowing that had been the most magnificent moment of his life.

A voice somewhere announced that supper was ready, but the terrace could have been the keep of a Russian castle. In the moving light from the lanterns her face alternately glowed and became shadowed, tormenting him with half-visions from the past as she spoke of St. Petersburg and the vast summer estates where he had hunted for boar and the great red deer.

He recalled the pulse beats as he had galloped after the creatures that zigzagged across the ground, eyes wild and proud antlers crashing through the undergrowth. He told her of the thrill when the great beast was brought down to lie at his feet, but he stumbled over his words when describing the evening of celebration. The hunting lodge kept fading into a lamplit tent, the full tankards of ale into brandy in tin mess cups.

They drank wine, and he watched her oblique eyes change from silver to dark shimmering diamonds like those that lay against her breast. She asked him about the regiment and the grand military reviews ending with a thundering cavalry charge with men and horses wild with the cry of battle.

In an instant he recalled with vividness the physical exhilaration of a horse between his knees and the wind rushing past his ears, men's voices shouting with rough bravado, sabers glittering in the sunlight. He found himself telling of the excitement of battle, the fear on the faces of the men who went down beneath his slicing sword, the savage satisfaction of thrusting the blade into someone who had just killed the comrade alongside. He spoke of the shrill screams of the horses, the long agonized cries of men dying violently, the thunder of guns that spurred him on and on.

All the time her soft accented voice led him along the path of incitement. His own feeling of splendor was thrown back in the luminous worship of her eyes, his supreme masculinity lit the sensual lines of her face, his voice grew as husky with emotion as hers. It was not long before he was back as he had been with the sword at his throat, and she went to him urging him down the steps and onto the beach where a great silver moon flooded the bay with bedeviling light.

"Enchantress of the night," breathed Andrew at the moon. "You were cruel to me once."

"Tell me, Andrei. Tell me how cruel!"

He felt bewildered for a moment. Why had he said that?

"Tell me about the moon, Andrei."

It came through a mist to him, the memory of a black, black night and a mind broken by a girl who had betrayed him. He found it easy to speak of how he had felt climbing onto the box of his carriage, whipping up the horses and driving hell-for-leather into oblivion caught in the madness of passion.

When he finished he was breathing hard, and she was crying, not with sadness, but with supplication. He gazed back at her, at the silver tears on her cheeks, at her mouth parted in breathless anticipation, at her head thrown back to challenge the moon who had forsaken him that night.

"The moon is not cruel tonight, Andrei," she whispered. "See, she has put a path upon the sea for us."

He turned his head automatically and saw a broad shining pathway from the beach running out across the pewter sea. When he turned back she was moving away to where the moon-path began. In stunned immobility he watched as she reached the tide line and continued without hesitation along the broad stripe of moonshine. It was all there in shattering force as she went, a tall slender majestic figure in silken dress and diamonds, further and further into the sea.

The tide of ecstasy and desire that had tossed him to and fro could no longer be stemmed, and he cried out her name as he flung off his jacket and raced into the water. It was silky-calm, but in his urgency to reach her he crashed forward sending up great spumes of spray that glittered like shooting stars in the brilliant light from the moon. It struck his fevered body with chill shock, but he hardly noticed. She was at the limit of her depth when he reached her and caught her slender waist.

"Anna . . . *Anna!*" he cried, pulling her against him.

"*Andrei.*" Her face turned up to his was alive with the glory of that moment, and he swept her up in his arms like a man demented. The wet silk clung to her body and wrapped itself around his arms, her hair had been loosened by the water and streamed down in dark swaths. But he was aware only of the diamonds flashing around her throat, and the pleasure of his hands on the bareness of her back, as he struggled through the shifting sand on the edge of the shore until they were clear of the water.

Then he was kissing her, holding her against him with the savage strength born of shock while he bruised her mouth and throat and shoulders with kisses meant to punish her for tormenting him. She moaned his name against his mouth, filled his mind with Russian words, drove him deeper into the fires of possession as her hands moved against his shoulders and in his hair.

Master of her but not of himself, he took her up in his arms again and strode to the steps. He had no knowledge of where they led—a castle, a hunting lodge, a house with a room that hung over the sea? He walked with his head thrown back, sighing with the exhaustion of the journey he had traveled that night, and when someone barred his path, he ordered him away in a voice that was harsh with the limits of endurance.

The man said, "Has there been an accident? Are you all right, sir?" Then louder, "Mr. Stanton . . . are you all right?"

The room was swaying, the night had become unbearably cold. The sound of the sea was in his ears. Brightness dazzled him. He could not think where he was.

"Frightfully much better to put the lady here, sir," came the voice, and Andrew suddenly knew that it was Kim, his houseboy. "There is someone waiting urgently to see you."

Caught in the grips of sudden terrible desolation Andrew gazed at the surrounding room, then at the Chinese boy. "Someone waiting?" he echoed with difficulty.

"Yes, sir. A police constable. He has some frightfully nasty news for you."

The darkness of the night-washed hillside, the bobbing lanterns, the musky heaviness of close tropical undergrowth contributed to Andrew's lethargy. He moved with drugged slowness, stumbling now and then over roots and stones that made the path unworthy of its description. His whole body ached, alternating from extreme chill to unnatural heat. His head swam.

The excited chatter of the constable was a mere background of irritating noise as the dreams and visions still battled within Andrew. He wanted to sleep, close his eyes and surrender. This nighttime ascent of a hill, walking beside a man in uniform, was too reminiscent of South Africa, yet the memory became a hunt in the foothills of the Urals. He wanted to remember neither and shook his head to drive them out.

The climb became steeper. The lanterns gave insufficient light, and their progress slowed. Beneath the trees the moon could not penetrate, but soon they would break out into clearer ground and take benefit from the clear natural moonlight. Just as he was seeing once more that shining ribbon across the sea, Andrew caught sight of the hut in a clearing several hundred yards ahead and remembered why he was there.

"Is that it?" he asked the constable.

"Yes, sir."

"Are you quite certain about this? You haven't got me out on a wild goose chase?"

"No, sir. Bad solly you come, but your house velly near. I no likee. Too muchee bad *fung shui* here now. You come quick takee look."

Yes, Andrew mused, if what he says is true no one will come near this place again. The man had been walking back across the hills to his home village after making a routine check on the fishing community in the bay, and his path took him past the death hut near the summit. It was one of the places on Hong Kong island where men and women near the end of their time on this earth were sent by relatives who could no longer provide food for them. They were given a bowl of water, then left to die in solitary dignity, making room in the household for infant sons who had more claim to the food. To western eyes it was barbaric, as were many Chinese customs, but was accepted as common sense by the young relatives who sent them and by the old people themselves.

This particular evening the young policeman had noticed something lying on the grass near the hut and, on investigating, had run headlong down the hill knowing Andrew to be the nearest source of help. He was badly frightened and stopped now they were near the spot, refusing to go nearer. Andrew knew better than to order him to do so, and took the man's lantern for extra light.

Crossing the stretch of grass toward the hut his mind was on the scene back at his house. He had left Anna to be taken back in his boat when she was ready, but could not remember exchanging any words with her before he left. Several stiff brandies had warmed and steadied him, but added to his general air of bewilderment at the arrival of Kim with a policeman.

He was close to the hut now and saw the dark shape lying as the Chinese had described it, just a few feet away from the door that was open. The smell of death was around the place, and there was a strange sense of pagan stillness that touched his western soul. He found himself advancing almost on tiptoe lest he disturb the spirits.

The body was small, dressed in yellow silk that swamped the sticklike limbs and wasted trunk. As the constable had said, the clothes were not those of an old person, and the hair hanging free from restriction was untouched by gray threads. It was a young girl up here in a place meant for those who had lived out their gift of life.

Setting one lantern on the grass, he held the other higher and gently turned the body over. It was no weight at all. For a long time he knelt there while trying to accept what he saw. The face was hollow-cheeked and skeletal, the bones of her neck stood out clearly against the skin, and her eyes gazed at him as they had on many occasions—only never blindly like this. The dead girl was Mei-Leng.

TWELVE

There had been two weeks of exceptionally hot weather. Hong Kong island melted beneath the power of the sun, and water grew scarce. The supplies in the reservoirs were dangerously low, and those Chinese living in villages dependent on farming looked at the wilting crops and prayed earnestly to the rain god. Soothsayers were pessimistic. All reached the same conclusion and looked grave. No rain would come yet and, when it did, ships would sail over the crops.

The farmers took it to mean that Tanka people would be so hungry they would steal their food that flourished in the rains. The boat dwellers themselves read into it a suggestion that the farmers would steal their boats to negotiate their flooded fields. The hatred between those who lived on land and those who crammed into the boat villages intensified.

Wise men saw more sinister implications in the findings, and hurriedly changed their fortune forecasts for the next few months, charging a little more for the extra work involved. In general, there was amongst the Chinese a feeling of bad joss in the air. Wise men blamed the Canton-Kowloon railway. If the great gods had intended men to travel across China in iron beasts they would have put a railway there long ago. The barbarian westerners had made them angry.

The British, free from such pagan beliefs, wore their pith helmets and spine protectors with their tight-fitting formal suits and sweated profusely as they held endless meetings to discuss a possible emergency situation to come. Reservoirs were inspected and efforts were made to restrict the flow of refugees making for the security of the British-ruled territory from a China that was savagely ruled by warlords. Agricultural experts viewed the crops and wrote gloomy reports on the prospects of starvation, naturalists expressed their fears of insect plagues, and medical officers were bowed under with another outbreak of cholera and dysentery amongst the sampan colony hugging the coast.

The premises of Galerie Russe were as cool as possible in temperatures of well over one hundred degrees, but Nadia found it extremely trying, nevertheless. Her dress of pale yellow shantung silk clung to her back in uncomfortable fashion, and she wished her maid had not laced her corsets so tightly that morning. The pile of curls on top of her head seemed to generate heat until her brains felt cooked, and she found it hard to concentrate on the rows of figures. During the past few days she had spent only the mornings in Ivan's office, but that particular day she intended to remain for the afternoon also.

She put down her pen after making a third mistake and leaned back in the high wooden chair, dabbing at her brow with a cologne-scented handkerchief. Was it any wonder she could not sit calmly at the accounts when everything within her was raw? Anna Brusilova had her Andrei. Last night she had gone to his house, and still had not returned that morning.

What could she do? Nothing would induce her to return to live under the same roof as her mother, yet what would happen to Aunt Marie if she was abandoned? And what of her own future?

She knew Andrew had been cold-shouldered by his own set because of his association with them all. Now it was all too obvious that it had been his passion for her mother that they would not accept. It would be more than ever impossible now they had become lovers.

Her eyes fastened on the figures in the ledger she had crossed out because they were wrong. She had not counted the cost to herself of loving Andrew, or she would never have sent that secret invitation to him so many months ago. Now she had to make the ledger of her life balance somehow or go under.

She heard the door open behind her and took a moment composing herself before she turned. She did not want Uncle Misha to guess what she felt. "I did not expect you back so. . . ." She stopped dead.

Andrew was standing in the doorway. He looked pale, strained, and very shaken—as well he might, she thought with an inward cry.

"I'm . . . sorry," he said slowly. "Your man downstairs told me your uncle was here."

"No." The single word came through stiff lips.

"I see." He stood there off guard, his eyes dark with some kind of incomprehensible message—as if last night had not happened. She turned away, hating him.

"Do you know where I can find him?"

"No."

She heard his long sigh from where she stood. "It is extremely urgent."

Her head went up to stare at a picture on the wall, but she kept her back to him. "He has gone to value a piece of jade, somewhere on the Peak."

"I see." He waited a moment, then asked, "Do you know when he will be back?"

"No."

She heard a movement, then the door clicked. She swung round, but he had not gone—merely closed the door behind him and moved toward her. He was fighting to stay calm, she saw that, but it only made her more contemptuous.

"My uncle will not see you. He is not a Brusilov, but feels as we do."

"To hell with the Brusilovs," he said in flash anger. "I am concerned with people, not names. You have made your opinions clear—more than clear—but despite that I am trying to help you . . . help the whole family."

"Help us?" she cried passionately. "You have just broken us, dragged us down, tarred us with the brush of your own dishonor."

He turned even paler, but she had to strike the final blow. "She was there all night at your house. You dare not deny it."

"No . . . but there. . . ."

Hearing him admit it, cancel any lingering hope she might be wrong, took the rest of her control and left her the victim of all her hurt and anguish. She was no longer Nadia Brusilova, just a woman rejected in the cruelest possible way.

"You spoke so bravely about fighting back," she flung at him breathlessly before he could finish. "I did not believe it then, I do not believe it now. There was no fight; you surrendered that first evening." She moved round gripping the top of the desk convulsively. "I wish you luck of her. She will consume you piece by piece. I have seen it before, remember. But the real Andrei was a man of her caliber. You are just a weak imitation."

It was a long long moment before he spoke, and when he did the words were not what she expected. "Even the tie of mere friendship cannot survive such utter contempt. You will have to accept my official status as my reason for remaining against your wishes, and I speak to you as the only member of the family present. Personal consideration for your sex does not enter into this." He moved away, shifting the white helmet from one hand to the other as his only sign of pressure, but when he turned back to face her with his news she realized he looked almost ill.

"At about eleven last night I was asked by a Chinese constable to accompany him back to a hilltop death hut where he believed he had found a case that needed investigation. I found the body of a young girl who had starved to death. It was Mei-Leng, daughter of your comprador. I arranged for the body to be taken into Victoria, then discussed the situation with a friend of mine in the police force. Tests were carried out that showed there was no other cause of death, and it seems the girl had not been shackled in any way. We have to conclude that she remained in that abominable place deliberately, knowing that she would die."

He wiped the sweat from his brow with the back of his wrist and continued, "Ritual suicide is not uncommon, but still has to

232

be investigated for motives of pressure or blackmail. It is not my department, but the girl was employed by me so I am naturally involved. However, when I returned to my house this morning Kim came to me with some startling information which he thought I should know as a fr . . . as I was acquainted with your family. I knew nothing of it, but my servants all did, of course." He took a breath, then made himself say, "It appears your brother and Mei-Leng were in the habit of meeting on the headland near my house on the days she came to work for me. They were seen together on the last day she spent in her village. Were you aware of their friendship?"

"No . . . no, I cannot believe . . ." she stammered, unable to cope with what was happening that morning. The heat was making her feel faint. "Vanya and Ho Fatt's daughter? It is ridiculous!"

He gave her a measured look. "Even a Brusilov is vulnerable."

She turned away, unable to meet his eyes.

"You believe servants' gossip?"

"There is always some truth in it. Your brother was very anxious when Mei-Leng went away."

She turned back quickly. "Anxious, yes. For your sake. He felt the responsibility of sending her to work for you. That was all there could be in his anxiety."

His face had grown inexpressibly cold. "Women do not fully understand why men behave the way they do. We are not the saints they choose to make us."

She flared up. "If that is all you have come to tell me, I see no reason for you to remain."

He walked to the door. "The police will question my servants about Mei-Leng, and they will say what they know." He gave the information in businesslike manner. "After that, your brother will also be questioned."

His inference penetrated her mounting air of unreality. "Why? I do not understand all this. I asked Ho Fatt only a few days ago and he said his daughter was nursing a sick uncle."

"That is what he said when told of the discovery."

"Well then!"

He frowned. "It takes a very long time for a healthy young

233

person to die of starvation. I doubt she ever left Hong Kong island." He put on his helmet and opened the door. Suddenly, there was a hint of emotional roughness in his voice and a glimpse of the old barricaded vulnerability about his jawline. "Your brother has been very ill. Someone should tell him about the tragedy before it is done in thoughtless official manner. If he cared anything for that girl, it will be an unpleasant shock." He turned to go.

"Andrew!" It came from her throat as part plea, part command, and halted him on the mezzanine floor outside.

"This all happened last night?"

"Yes."

"Then . . . you were not at your house."

Standing outside the room his face was shadowed by the brim of his white helmet, but she heard the finality in his words and was glad not to see his expression.

"Does it matter? The belief of treachery is equal to the deed."

He went along the gallery and down the curving stairs to cross the main room which was now deserted. Nadia ran out onto the upper floor in time to see the doorman bow to him, then his tall figure was out of sight. She gazed down at the cold immobile jade figures that had seen the passing of centuries. That moment was but a pulse beat in the stretch of eternity, but to her it was her whole lifetime.

The rest of that day was hectic. Andrew's police officer friend took up a large part of his morning with questions about Mei-Leng.

"Pretty grisly, don't you think?" he asked Andrew. "The father said she was about seventeen which, allowing for their acceptance of being a year old on the day they were born, makes her not much more than a child."

"Only to our way of thinking, Chris," pointed out Andrew. "They take on the role of motherhood by the time they are seven, in many cases. The mother dies and they bring up a family of six others. Show me a Chinese girl of fourteen who hasn't the wisdom of our grandmothers."

"Mmm," mused Chris Smethwick, "my grandmother is potty,

234

has been since the age of sixty. But I know what you mean."

"This girl was slightly different, though. Well-educated insofar as the father could manage it. Spoke English and Portuguese well—no pidgin speech. Although, like her father, she spoke in the ancient Chinese manner: riddles, proverbs, symbolic phrases. Easy enough to understand once you got used to it, but she read and understood exceptionally well. Ho Fatt saw the fact as a furtherment of his own standing. He had no intention of losing face by having an ignorant child, albeit a daughter."

"Tell me about the father," invited Chris taking a sip of his lime juice and soda.

"Secretive, clever, an acute businessman," began Andrew as he rose from his desk to push the window higher. "I wish to God these damned fans rotated a bit quicker. I can never decide whether opening a window is an advantage or not. It only lets in more hot air."

"Quite enough in this building as it is," joked the police officer. "I sometimes wish I had joined the Royal Navy. There's always a breeze at sea."

"Yes. My house is a dashed sight cooler than any place in Victoria."

"Wise man. Is that why you chose to live out there?"

"That . . . and various other reasons." He was still at the window. The sun was striking the sea and putting a blinding stripe across the blue surface, like a road stretching to the mainland. *A moon-path.* He put his hand up to his eyes. The heat was making him giddy. He had had no sleep.

"Are you all right, Andrew?"

"Eh?" He turned, saw Chris Smethwick, and remembered where he was. "Yes . . . yes, I'm fine."

"You look bloody awful, if you don't mind my saying." The dark-haired young man leaned forward in his chair. "Look, old chap, this girl Mei-Leng—she wasn't your mistress, by any chance?"

Andrew flared up instantly. "Oh, not you, too! I've already had half the service giving me cool winks and man-of-the-world advice on how the Chinese prefer it. She was sixteen, dammit, and a timid little virgin."

"No . . . she wasn't."

Andrew was startled. "No? Are you certain?"

"The doc put it in his report."

"Pregnant?"

Chris shook his head. "It might have been an explanation of her suicide if she had been. Perhaps the lover let her down—took up with someone else. *Hell hath no fury* . . . and all that! Women will put up with God only knows, but the moment another woman comes upon the scene they turn into viragos."

Before he knew it Andrew had slammed his hand on the desk and shouted, "As you're such an expert on women, what are you hounding me for? Go out and solve your bloody case on your own."

Chris Smethwick looked startled, but kept cool. "Sorry . . . sorry. It must have been a bit of a shock finding the girl was someone you knew. Let's leave it a day or two, shall we?"

"No." He walked round the desk and put a hand on his friend's shoulder. "No, you have a job to do; and I can probably help by telling you about the girl. She was very strictly Chinese. Her father had improved his station in life quite considerably over the past fifteen years, worked his way up to become a skillful comprador. Strangely enough, I met a man in Macao not long ago who had once employed him before he brought his daughter across to Hong Kong."

"And?"

Andrew shrugged and went back to sit in his chair. "He felt Ho Fatt was an opportunist, anti-European, of course, a little too eager to gain responsibility. *Power* was the word he used, but I think it was a little too strong. He has reached the summit of most men's ambitions."

"With your friends at Galerie Russe?"

"Yes," agreed Andrew heavily, seeing again Nadia's face as she turned on him that morning. "But he is one of the old-style Chinese despite his close associations with the western world, and proud of his heritage. Consequently, he brought up the girl in strict observance of their culture. She treated men with reverence and obedience. Whenever I asked her to do something she treated it as an imperial order . . . which was rather uncomforta-

236

ble, at times. Her father was regarded as the heaven and earth. Every word he spoke was a pearl of wisdom, everything he did was impeccable."

"Mmm, thought the world of him, did she?"

Andrew smiled grimly. "You know better than that, Chris. Reverence can be born of fear as often as love, and Mei-Leng believed what she had been taught with blind obedience." He sighed. "I like the Chinese personality when it is at its most relaxed, but I have to admit men like Ho Fatt are beyond my understanding. That little girl was gentle, trusting, and very beautiful. Her sensitive nature made her compassionate beyond her years. It makes my blood boil to see sweet little creatures like her turned into skivvies—outcasts from the benefit of humanity." He caught sight of his friend's face. "Oh, for God's sake stop looking at me like that! Why does everyone imagine I am some kind of lecher who cannot resist taking every woman in sight to his bed?" In his anger he got to his feet, knocking his chair over.

Chris rose, too. "Take my advice and get some sleep, Andrew. I know when a person is reaching the end of his tether, and if I were not your friend I might think you were starting to crack up."

Andrew felt the room closing in on him. "Imagine what the hell you like."

The other man went out, and Andrew crossed to the window, where he hung out of it trying to banish the feeling of being slowly trapped.

At midnight he had still not slept. For several hours he lay beneath the mosquito netting staring across at that side of the room that revealed the whole of the night sky and the sea below. He had once reveled in the view, in the pure enjoyment of lying virtually beneath the stars. It had reminded him of nights in South Africa when they had bivouacked beneath the great sky of the Transvaal and lay in awed silence gazing at the immensity of the universe.

On that night he wished he could blot out the scene. He tried drawing the curtains across it, but the utter darkness had him back in the throes of feeling trapped. He lit the lamp, but the

237

empty space on his chest of drawers mocked him. Anna had taken the photograph again . . . and this time the significance was too stark for his conscience.

Heavy-headed and aching all over he eventually dragged himself from the bed, put on a dressing gown, and went downstairs. It was eerily silent. No lights or murmurings around the servants' quarters. They had all gone, except Kim. When he had returned from his office late that afternoon, the Chinese houseboy had come out to greet him very upset. The servants had disappeared, he said, before he could talk to them. They had been uneasy all the morning after the policeman had been to talk to them, and all had agreed there was a bad *fung shui* in the bay. They had gone to work there with reluctance because of the suicide of the Javanese artist, but now there had been a second suicide—a Chinese this time—there was no doubt the spirits of the bay were angry and vengeful because the house had been built there.

Perhaps there was something in *fung shui,* thought Andrew as he looked out through the folding glass doors that led to his terrace. Maybe there was a curse on this bay since a foreign barbarian ripped out part of the hillside to build his bizarre and beautiful house. Over to the left where the shacks of the fishing village clustered, all was quiet. The usual lights of the boats bobbing on the water were absent; the shacks were deserted. The entire village population had melted away. Andrew was now alone in the bay, except for a young lad who believed in the one God, but Chinese enough to walk wide-eyed with apprehension about the place.

A moonshaft entered the room and lit the brandy decanter on the cocktail cabinet with a beckoning light. He went across and poured a stiff drink, but had taken no more than one pull at it before he could almost hear his aunt and uncle warning him about living in such isolated surroundings. *Solitude leads to loneliness and that leads to drinking. Before you know it, you will be back like you were before you came to Hong Kong.* In defiance of the thought he tossed back the drink and poured another.

It was when his head was back to drink the next glassful that the dark shadow of crossed swords on the wall caught his eye.

Instantly, he was pierced by a shaft of excitement, and the tiny cut in his throat began to throb with remembered pressure. He turned with a quick evasive movement, but she was out on the terrace also.

His breathing accelerated. He could have taken the sword from her at any time, but she had challenged him to stand defiant before the fatal blade. In meeting that challenge he had started on a dangerous headlong gallop through his darker self. He recalled the lanterns swinging their light across her face with compelling rhythm. Who knew what he had said to her, but it had filled him with the wild exultant fire of aggressive masculinity. Yet it seemed to him now that she had told him what to say, *made* him confess to her the deeper thoughts that lurked out of reach of his real self.

He gripped his glass tighter. This morning when Nadia had accused him he had reacted like an innocent man. Yet, God knew where he might have traveled if Kim had not stopped him. He was as guilty as she suggested. *Her own mother!*

He poured another drink, then another as floating recollections of himself and Anna on the beach tormented him. He loved Nadia totally; how could he have been so near to betraying that love? How had last night happened?

Then, he remembered the sword, her blazing possessive eyes, her husky voice calling him Andrei. He had lost the battle in that moment. Like the Boers, Anna used surprise and ignored the basic rules of combat. She was like no other woman he knew, used weapons they would not be aware of possessing. She had stayed all night in the hope that he would return. She would never give up until he was hers body and soul—or had shown that he could withstand any assault she made upon him.

Taking the decanter he walked down onto the beach. The night was hot, giving no sign that the following day would be any cooler. Sitting on the sand he began dedicatedly lowering the level of the liquid in the cut-glass decanter.

The sea was rolling in in long lines of waves that could have been fields of maize in the Transvaal, bending in the wind. Or was it the corn in the fields of his own summer estates? Anna would know. She would tell him of all the things they had done that set the blood rushing and the pulse pounding with triumph.

He stood up, and the scene tilted as he nearly fell. He laughed loudly, and all the others laughed with him, all those who had helped him kill a bear to lay at her feet. He could see her silver-green eyes laughing up into his, promising him a sacrifice on the altar of his masculinity. Then, he saw the moon-path on the sea, leading across to the mainland like a silver-gold track to the great plains of Russia. That was where he should be. She would be waiting for him, and he would live in the heights of existence, seeing only her.

He emptied the remaining brandy into his glass and drank it in one mammoth draught. "To Anna Brusilova," he cried drunkenly. "To the victor!" Then he hurled the glass into an imaginary hearth, Russian style.

For a formal dinner party it was small by their usual standards. Nadia could remember the great dining hall in St. Petersburg where it was not uncommon for fifty guests to sit at the long table, ladies in rich dresses, and jewels with long histories of family possession; gentlemen in noble uniforms or formal suits enlivened by colorful orders of honor. The Brusilov family had been well represented. Grandfather, Grandmother, Mama and Papa, Aunt Marie with her husband carefully subdued, Ivan and herself. At the last two or three Katya had been allowed to join them. That made nine in all.

That night there were three. Anna at the head of the table, herself at the foot, and Uncle Misha somewhere in the middle, as if he were a guest. Nadia felt he was being insulted and should have taken Ivan's place instead of herself, but her mood did not allow her time for prolonged protests of that nature. It was hard enough trying to concentrate on their seven guests and remember all her French which protocol demanded as the language of the evening.

The Russian diplomat and his wife were elderly and stiff, the French comte, his wife and two daughters Nadia found too disparaging of Hong Kong for her liking. The remaining two aristocrats from Paris, although young and personable, were too disparaging of the English.

Nadia dreaded the long evening ahead. It was sure to be an ordeal. Uncle Misha was already flushed with alcohol and surprisingly morose. Instead of worrying over what he might say, it was his silence that caused concern, for once. It left the brunt of the conversation to herself and her mother. Feeling the way she did made Nadia dull company, a fact she saw reflected in the eyes of their guests. Dull company and out of looks. She knew her pointed face was pinched and pale, her eyes too large with lack of sleep, her mouth too tight to smile freely.

It tightened further as she looked at the woman at the head of the table. In a dress of kingfisher-blue shot-silk and with the Brusilov opals around her neck, Anna made a striking picture. The ladies plainly disliked but envied her, as most females did; the gentlemen, old and young alike, found her regal and unbelievably beautiful. But none of them looked at her as Andrew did . . . because she did not wish them to.

How she wished all the guests would go home. There was so much unhappiness in their house now it seemed almost indecent to hold a dinner party. Aunt Marie was growing slyer and had to be watched all the time for her own safety's sake. Uncle Misha was spending a fortune on jade pieces negotiated for them by Ho Fatt, and appeared to have a plentiful supply of vodka at the gallery to compensate for the lack of visitors. The gallery was losing money, and Anna was spending it fast. As for Ivan, he lay weak and despairing in his hospital bed, unable to do anything to help the situation. The only bright spot in his day was her visit, but it had been very brief that afternoon because of the dinner party. With deliberation she had made no mention of the girl Mei-Leng. Ivan had looked tired and dispirited, in no mood to hear dismal news. She did not for one moment believe Andrew's servants. It was quite incredible to imagine her brother would have any kind of friendship with that little Chinese girl she had seen only once at Andrew's house. They might have seen him looking at her that evening and imagined they were friends rather than acquainted through Ho Fatt. Anyone who knew Ivan's very real pride would know just how far from the truth their belief could be. He hated Hong Kong, was intolerant of the pagan Chinese, and knew his place as Brusilov of Petersburg. He could hardly bring himself to acknowledge an Englishman as a friend, much less a little Chinese servant.

The Russian man had come to the end of his boring speech on the climate of South America, and the servants were bringing a final course of sweet trifles onto the table. Nadia sighed. There was still the rest of the evening to endure before she could go to her bed.

"I think Mademoiselle must have her thoughts on someone more fortunate than myself," said a soft voice beside her, and she looked up into an amused face. "Twice I have asked if you intend to visit the City Hall next week for the opera, and twice I have had the painful pleasure of seeing dreams flit across a face that is not even aware of my presence."

She frowned. "I beg your pardon, Monsieur. If I do go to the opera next week, I grant you the right to leave my questions unanswered, during the interval."

The Frenchman laughed. "To be the recipient of that much attention from you will quite make my evening, I assure you."

Nadia had the grace to feel guilty. It was not his fault that her world had no room in it for opera and flirtations at the moment. He was rather handsome and had been doing his best to entertain her all evening . . . something no one else did, these days. She took a deep breath and tried to smile with warmth.

"Perhaps Monsieur has been *distrait,* at times?"

"*Ah oui,* but I make it the rule to put an end to such a feeling as soon as possible."

She did smile then. "How does one achieve such success?"

Saucy brown eyes shone with laughter, as he picked up his glass. "With champagne, and a beautiful companion. Here is the champagne . . . and do you find me beautiful enough, mademoiselle?"

She took up her glass in reply. "Here is the champagne . . . and you are very beautiful, monsieur."

"Then let us celebrate our success."

Just at the moment of putting the glass to her lips, the doors burst open with disturbing noise. The room fell immediately silent. Ivan stood just inside the room, white-faced, wild-eyed, and swaying on his feet. He had on the dark trousers he had worn at the Dragon Boat Festival, and the hospital nightshirt was tucked into them. It opened at the neck showing his bandaged chest. The effort of his journey had put a streak of crimson freshly upon the white bandage.

Nadia rose to her feet in horrified alarm. It was a scene being repeated: Papa staggering in covered in blood and white with shock. A swift silent prayer was on her lips as her twin brother looked across the room at her.

"*Sestrushka,* I have to talk to you. For pity's sake, I must talk to you," he said in a voice touched by hysteria.

THIRTEEN

Since acquiring the New Territories nine years before in an effort to increase their stronghold against the encroaching interest in France, Russia, Germany, and America, the British administrators of Hong Kong had found their relations with the Viceroy of Kwangtung, which was the neighboring region on the mainland, of the greatest importance. While both sides strove to present a placid friendly face, the thoughts behind the masks were often hostile in personal and official form.

For years, the mandarins, as a group, had been rigidly adherent to the old ways in their hatred of the western barbarians. They did not want other eastern races in China, much less white devils who were licentious, immoral, overbearing, and greedy for land. What was worse, they brought with them their womenfolk who exposed their bosoms and arms in shameless manner, then proceeded to bow before them, kiss and fondle their hands in public, swing them around in their arms to music, and generally worship them. It was the final insult when mandarins and senior officials of the Imperial Court were expected to accept the presence of these females when they visited British residences.

The Viceroy of Kwangtung and the Governor of Hong Kong knew it was essential to keep relations steady between them, but each walked a tightrope with aggression on one side and fatal weakness on the other. They had to judge to a nicety the balance between friendship and stern adherence to principles.

The intense heat wave had still not broken when Andrew left for a meeting between both sides two weeks after the discovery of Mei-Leng's death. It was an evening reception to which ladies were invited, and he thought grimly of all those acceptable English wives who would unite to preclude the presence of a Russian aristocrat from their elite circle.

The meal was western in style, with careful deference to Chinese tastes. The guests sat on gilt chairs around the table, adding an exotic touch with their colorful robes and circular mandarin hats.

Andrew was fairly low in the seating order, but found himself placed next to one of the Viceroy's staff. Any member of the service who spoke one of the Chinese dialects was invariably used to impress and entertain the visitors, but this time the Chinese minister was so anxious to air his English Andrew was not called upon to use his knowledge.

The meal ended, and the assembly of guests in formal evening wear like himself, gold-encrusted uniforms, rich brocade jackets and skirts, or graceful silks and satins, moved into one of the elegant reception rooms. Overhead fans were lazily rotating at a speed that did little more than stir the fronds of the potted ferns, as fragrant tea was served in little delicate cups in honor of the guests to whom the taking of port and cigars was a foreign ritual.

Andrew thought ironically that it was typical of his countrymen to manage to suggest there was nothing more delightful after a heavy meal on a stifling evening than to stand around in thick tight official dress drinking pale herbal tea that chased around the stomach after the mixture of wines which the guests had not touched.

He recalled an army friend telling him of his father who, with

245

brother officers, had been invited to a banquet by one of the Khans in Afghanistan. The ruler deliberately set the meal on the floor obliging the guests to kneel on cushions to eat, as was the custom. The British officers had manfully knelt in skin-tight uniforms, while spurs on their boots had jabbed them at every attempt to rest back on their heels, and eaten dishes of rich and indigestible nature with a nonchalance that hid their inner feelings. Arriving back at camp they were all heartily sick, but dignity had been preserved and the Khan left nonplussed.

A rush of strong feeling took him by surprise. The people around him were his countrymen. He had fought a war on their behalf. They represented some of the finest families in England. The ladies had produced men and boys who now filled England's universities and public schools. They could be so splendid. Why were they also so shortsighted at times?

"Feeling the repercussions, old chap?" asked Gerard Brotherton at his elbow. "Can't say I didn't warn you."

Andrew looked at him with dislike, his mood sharpening his tongue. "The one consolation is that you have been severely reprimanded for that affair."

"Yes . . . a blow, to be sure. Unfortunately, I have no uncle in high places." He indicated Andrew's cup. "How do you manage to get that stuff down?"

"Same way you do."

Brotherton smiled. "I doubt it. I tip one of the stewards to lace mine with brandy. You see," he went on, "if one breaks the rules it has to be done discreetly. No one gets hurt and one 'saves face.'"

"As I saved yours not so long ago, *old chap*," Andrew reminded him dryly. "Your discretion slipped a bit then, didn't it?" Adopting the other man's lazy drawl he went on, "If you must have two women at once, you should ensure they are both friendly."

Having felt he had put Brotherton in his place, he made to move off, but floating after him came the soft question, "How about your two . . . are they friendly?"

Every instinct to turn and attack was forcibly held back. He had hit out once before at a party and become the butt for everyone's mirth; he was wiser and more mature now. But it was an effort to remain calm. He withstood the turned backs of half a dozen ladies with no more than a cynical smile until he came face to face with Lady Halder in a situation that gave no time for discreet avoidance.

"Good evening, Aunt Maude," he said.

"*Andrew!*" Her hands fluttered nervously and her eyes looked from left to right for some form of rescue.

"How are you?" he inquired politely. "Are the headaches improving?"

To his dismay her eyes filled with tears and she seemed quite overcome. Since they were near one of the doors to the terrace Andrew gently persuaded her outside, masculine dread of a "scene" prompting his action. But once there he could think of nothing to say that would fill the silence.

"I'm sorry, Andrew," said Lady Halder eventually, having recovered her composure. "It was the unexpectedness of seeing you."

"I have been here all the evening."

"Yes, I know . . . but this puts me in a very awkward position."

"Would you rather I had walked past you as if you were not there?" he asked stiffly. At her tense silence he added with bitterness, "Why does everyone behave as if I had cheated at cards, or deserted in the face of the enemy?"

"Andrew . . . *please*," she begged him. "It is such a dreadful business. I have been extremely upset, you know." She turned to him and the light from one of the lanterns lit the diamond flower on her shoulder. "Your poor mother! She is my sister . . . what am I to say to her? I have been unable to write to her for several months, because she is sure to guess something is wrong if I make no mention of you. What have you told them? You do write, don't you?"

"Of course. I mentioned that I had met a lovely girl I wished to marry, but that she was Russian and it might mean I have to resign from the service."

"And . . . the *other?*"

"What *other*, Aunt Maude?" he asked with dangerous quiet.

"That . . . that . . . *woman*." She put up a handkerchief to dab at her eyes. "If it were just the young one I daresay people might have forgiven, in time, but . . . oh, if you knew how ill I have been over it all—how your uncle has suffered. It is not easy to sit on my committee knowing all my ladies have been discussing your . . . *exploits* . . . just before I walked in."

"I'm sorry," he murmured tonelessly. "I will write to my father and explain what has happened. There is no need for you to feel unable to contact Mother. She will understand it is no fault of yours. As for your social life, it will get back to normal just as soon as some other disaster befalls the colony, or one of its members. I shall be forgotten within minutes. In the meantime I will try to avoid embarrassing you with scenes like this." He hesitated, then felt some word was needed by way of thanks. "I do appreciate all you did for me when I first arrived."

She dabbed quickly at her eyes again and put a gloved hand on his sleeve. "I am fond of you, dear, you know that. I did my utmost to present the right kind of young woman to you, but I suppose you take after your grandfather. He led Mother a merry dance in India." She began to move away. "If it weren't for my committees . . . you do understand, Andrew?"

"Perhaps better than you do yourself," he said heavily.

After she had gone he stayed on in the lamplit atmosphere of the terrace, smoking and valuing the solitude until a colleague found him there and said he was wanted by the Governor to discuss the incident of the beheaded revolutionaries with the Chinese Viceroy.

"Be tactful, for God's sake," warned the young man. "So far, the old boy is very sweet. Don't upset him at this stage."

"Which old boy do you mean, ours or theirs?"

"Both, to be on the safe side. Brotherton is already smoothing the way for you."

"Ha!" said Andrew. "He could smooth a nutmeg grater with words, but he was damned useless when confronted with the situation."

"Mm. A theorist, young Brotherton. He'll get to the top . . . if he doesn't go to the dogs first."

"Like me?" He could not resist saying it.

"No, not like you, Andrew. You didn't go to the dogs, I rather think they came to you."

The mandarin was short and squat, with a full face, slit eyes, and a graying moustache. One did not find it easy to gauge his mood, but he was very courteous and listened intently to all Andrew had to say when he tried to explain how it was the British had laws for their new territory, but could not see they were upheld. The Viceroy heard him out with polite interest, but shot in some awkward questions that showed he knew Andrew was covering up for someone. At the end of the conversation he smiled.

"A worthy defense, Mr. Stanton." He turned to the Governor. "A true diplomat, Your Excellency. You are fortunate to have such a man on your staff."

"Yes, indeed," beamed the Governor. "You will be pleased to hear that it is Mr. Stanton who is presently engaged on uncovering the movement of revolutionary literature through Hong Kong. I gave you the interesting facts of our progress in that direction."

"Ah!" The slitted eyes moved round to look at Andrew again. "A million pities Mr. Stanton was not in charge of your police boats. That junk would never have got through as easily as it did." He smiled with the knowledge that he had made his host feel uncomfortable, and said to Andrew, "Congratulations, Mr. Stanton. I trust you will accompany His Excellency when he next visits my province. I look forward to renewing your acquaintance."

That was the end of the interview, but his praise had left Andrew untouched. The Chinaman had no idea what success had cost.

When it was possible to drink more than tea Andrew downed two brandies very quickly, then took his time over another while chatting to a newly appointed officer of the water police and his wife. They knew nothing of his "exploits" and were interested in all he told them of their new environment. He was glad to give the man a resumé of the type of problem he was likely to come across, and amused them with anecdotes of those who lived on the waters of Hong Kong harbor. They, in turn, gave their impressions of a place they thought as hot as Hades and quite as infernal. When the wife admitted a passion for jade, Andrew unhesitatingly suggested she visit Galerie Russe and have a chat with Misha Zubov, who was a close friend.

The woman was delighted with the recommendation, and all was going swimmingly until her husband mentioned Sir Goodwin, saying that his father was a great friend.

"I really am obliged to present myself. Do you know Sir. Goodwin, Mr. Stanton?"

"He is my uncle."

"Good lord, what a coincidence!"

"Yes, isn't it! He's the tall sandy-haired man with Sir Frederick Maysey."

"Would you be kind enough to introduce us?"

"Of course," replied Andrew woodenly.

They moved across the room and the woman looked around her at the moving assembly of colorful dignified colonists, the splendid Englishness of Government House, the exotic costumes of the Chinese visitors, and the myriad moths fluttering in the fall of light from each doorway onto the terrace. She fanned herself in the oppressive heat of the Hong Kong night.

"I suppose one grows used to living here," she reflected, "but at the moment, it all seems very unreal." She looked at Andrew with a smile. "Did you ever feel that way, Mr. Stanton?"

"Frequently," was his reply. "I still do, at times."

For the first time since arriving in Hong Kong, Nadia longed for the snows of Russia. As the rickshaw traveled the short distance to Galerie Russe the heat slammed down on Nadia's head, even at eight in the morning. There would be no letup today; perhaps it would even be worse.

She let her gaze wander inattentively over the steamy scene while her inner eye saw white roads glistening in the lamplight; trees beautified and enchanted by the snow pattern lying along their branches; troikas gliding to the tinkle of bells, leaving in their wake twin tracks cutting through the crisp spread of snow.

The sense of bereftness that assailed her in that moment made

Nadia turn her head into the privacy of the sunshade angled over her shoulder. Was that where she truly belonged . . . back there with her younger brother and sisters? No, she could not return to that life as it had been; she was not the same person.

Her mother and Andrew were still locked in battle, she knew. The contest was exhausting her. Each time Mama returned, Nadia looked for the signs of victory on her face. They were never there . . . but neither was defeat. Deep in her heart she longed for the end of it, whatever the outcome might be. The extension of suspense, the uncertainty of what really passed between the two, the guilt she felt at the withdrawal of her faith in Andrew were all wearing her down. Her future depended on the outcome. If Mama won, a return to Russia with the family was unthinkable. But if her mother lost her Andrei, he was also lost to Nadia and she could not remain in Hong Kong where he was.

How was it possible to feel so alone in the midst of family and friends? Yet, she was alone. The gulf between herself and Ivan had widened again. She cared for him, saw that he received the medical attention he should have had in the hospital, and took charge of his business affairs as far as she was able, but that Chinese girl had put a screen of incompatibility between them.

She had succored him from their youth, knowing him to be introspective, uncertain, shadowed constantly by the inescapable necessity of taking their father's place. She had seen how the self-absorption of their parents had defeated his every attempt to become assertive and confident, and understood with great sympathy the burden placed prematurely upon his shoulders by the murder of their father and grandfather.

But *this* she could not accept. Each time she thought of the dinner party and his wild desperation, something inside her clenched too tightly. Was there nothing of the Brusilovs to be saved? At a time when she needed a foundation on which to rebuild her own life, they were all going to pieces around her. Not one had any thought for her except as a prop. Was it any wonder she felt so bereft?

The gallery was empty, except for the black-coated supervisors who bade her a subdued good morning. Uncle Misha plainly had not yet put in an appearance. Sleeping off his inebriation, she thought grimly. The disturbance of his return in the early hours with several companions in similar state had awakened her, and kept her tossing and turning wishing it were possible to escape from reality with the aid of vodka. How could she condemn her uncle for doing what she could not?

The sympathetic understanding vanished rapidly when she went into Ivan's office to sort through the letters and accounts and saw a crate of bottles in the corner. Drinking in the clubs and hotels was one thing; having a supply at the gallery was quite another. Customers were few. Effusive unsteadiness would drive even those away.

As her hands slit the envelopes with the silver paper knife her brain was seething with protest against all kinds of things. Did her uncle want the gallery—that of which he was so proud—to fail? Lately there had been an absence of English visitors. She could guess why, and the knowledge made her determined not to let them succeed in bringing down a business that had been so good. But it was a last-stand kind of determination, a defiance in the face of something that had already happened. With Uncle Misha fuddled by vodka those visitors unaffected by the scandal of Andrew Stanton and Anna Brusilova might also decide to shun the premises. An inebriated proprietor gave no impression of dependability when large sums of money were involved.

All the envelopes contained accounts to be settled. There was not a single bank draft among them. She pushed them aside angrily and went to stare down into the gallery. An elegant couple had just entered the main room. There was something about them that suggested they were English, so they could only be from one of the ships en route to Australia, or so newly arrived in the colony they had not had time to hear the gossip. Whichever was the case, it was to be hoped they would return later, for there was no one in the gallery to discuss the sale of anything to which they took a fancy.

Her gaze traveled over the cases and their splendid contents. During the past weeks she had come to delight in Galerie Russe— its gracious atmosphere, the hushed quality of the rooms, the works of art that represented men's vision and craft over

252

hundreds of years. It was hard to understand her twin's feeling that being a jade merchant was beneath his dignity. There was something about the smooth stone that suggested more than dignity—grandeur!

All at once, she felt pride in standing above the showrooms, knowing they were part of her life. If and when she had to leave Hong Kong it would be part of her sadness to say goodbye to something she had watched from birth to death. In the moment of turning away she saw her uncle come through the entrance and hurry toward the couple, flapping his wide cream hat to cool himself. The redness of his face was not only due to the heat, and Nadia fervently hoped he was in a fit state to conduct the negotiations of sale, if need be.

Back in the office she bent her mind to the accounts, pushing her hair up in an attempt to cool her forehead and rolling back the sleeves of her delicately starched blouse. For half an hour she worked, a frown creasing her damp forehead and her fingers growing smudgy with ink. But that half hour only deepened her worries. On the desk were papers of purchase amounting to thousands of dollars which, together with the up-to-date balance, showed they had no more in hand than the cost of one of their less valuable pieces of jade. True, within the walls of the gallery was a massive fortune, but a business could not exist if it sold none of its stock. They *must* cease buying at the present rate.

It was hopeless talking to Uncle Misha on the subject. He could not resist beautiful things. Nadia suspected he was happier when they did not sell because he hated parting with any piece, but what they were virtually doing was amassing a priceless extension to their own family collection of jade, and Ivan could not afford it.

For fully ten minutes Nadia sat battling with herself before sending for the comprador, who had been the negotiator for the expensive items recently acquired. For some days she had put off speaking to Ho Fatt—ever since Ivan told her about Mei-Leng, in fact. At the time of the tragedy she had expressed to him her sincere condolences, which he had received as impassively as if she had told him it was raining. Now, however, she felt unwilling

253

to face him; felt her brother's sins personally. It was uncomfortable to feel guilty in front of a person one employed. It took away one's sense of dignity.

However, he had to be faced sometime, and she waited with a quickened heartbeat for him to answer her summons. That he delayed an unforgivable length of time increased her distaste for the interview, but she declined to let him see she had even noticed how long he had left between her summons and his arrival.

His bow was barely that, but his voice was as respectful as usual when he bade her good morning.

"I have been going through these bills of sale and find we doubled our expenditure last month," she told him in what she hoped was a crisp tone. "We now have more pieces than we can display in the showrooms. Will you *not* arrange for any more negotiations on our behalf until our existing stock is considerably lowered?"

The man might well not have heard from all the interest he showed. "You must stop the purchase of further pieces," she repeated sharply. "Do you understand that?"

The black eyes brightened, then went black again. "With respect, Mr. Zubov gives his instructions. A man can serve only one master."

"Mr. Zubov does not see the accounts. They are the only master a man can serve when running a business."

"When a great man sees the world within reach he does not count the cost."

"Then he will soon be a foolish man," she retorted, finding her customary assurance shaken by thoughts of her brother's deeds. "At present, my uncle has much to worry him. He is not aware of the need for reductions in stock. It is best that he does not see the world, then he will not yearn for it."

"A man will always yearn for what is beyond his reach," he said in the strange monotone he used.

It was impossible! The small figure in long gray gown might look like a picture from a storybook of the East, but he was making her argue, try to put her case, when he was paid to do as he was told. She knew he resented her presence in a masculine

254

role, but he was just an employee who had to observe the commands of those he served. She would not dream of arguing with a household servant, so why was she doing so with him?

She rose from her chair and walked the length of the room hoping the action would give her more authority. The man always made her feel uneasy; today, there was something almost sinister about his quietness.

Turning to face him she said sharply, "Figures do not lie. We shall buy no more jade until our sales have increased. I am taking my brother's place here, and it is his wish that you engage in no more negotiations, for the present. Since he owns Galerie Russe, his word is final."

The Chinaman very slowly inclined his head in a gesture that touched on Nadia's raw conscience. It was almost insulting in its reluctance to be a bow, and it led to her calling him back when he reached the door.

"How did this get here?" she asked indicating the crate of vodka in the corner. "Do you know anything about it?"

For a rare moment the triangular face registered contempt. "Those who seek in their souls and find darkness turn to the dragons of light, who will consume them one by one."

He went before she was aware of it, leaving her trembling with something she dared not name, and she was still shaken when her uncle burst into the office with the news that he had just arranged the sale of an expensive Ming vase to an Englishman and his lady whom Andrew had sent to the gallery on recommendation.

It came at the wrong time—that evidence of Andrew's continued concern for them all—and she found herself in tears.

Uncle Misha visibly drooped. "I thought it would please you."

"Yes," she nodded, "but if they had been sent by anyone but him."

"Aah," he sighed in understanding and took her hand to pat it fondly. "You cannot accept him as a friend? No, of course you cannot. But that is what he wishes to be, despite all else."

"How can he wish it after all we have done to him?" she asked in distress.

"How can you love him after all he has done to you?" He smiled a little lopsidedly and tapped his chest. "It is what is in

255

here that overrules what is in there," he told her, gently touching her curls. "If you had been my true daughter, I should have said you took from me your sensitivity. As it is, you must be a changeling child, for your parents were not only insensitive, they were brutal in the extreme."

She stopped her tears. *"Brutal?"*

He looked abashed. "My tongue . . . it runs away with me sometimes. Those times have gone and you, thankfully, were an innocent child." He looked critically at her. "You are too thin. All this work in such heat is not good . . . no, I did not like it from the start. Close the books . . . go home, at once. I cannot have wilting flowers in my gallery. No . . . no, I cannot have that." He kissed her cheek almost shyly. "Go home, *golubchik*. If you also fall ill what shall I do then . . . hey?"

"I do not wish to go home," she told him bleakly, knowing it was better to be where she was than see her mother go to a meeting with Andrew. In her present mood she was liable to rush at her with unsheathed claws.

"Mmm," said her uncle thoughtfully. "Well, then let us both pay a visit to our beautiful children downstairs. They like to be admired, you know . . . yes, to be admired. Come." He put an arm lightly behind her. "Come and tell them how exquisite you think them all."

She went, and so great were his persuasive powers she forgot to lecture him on his extravagance. She also forgot about the vodka until she was in the rickshaw setting off for home. Taking his advice, after all, she left the gallery early. If she sat at the far end of the garden in the shade of the trees it might be possible not to notice Mama setting out perhaps for another meeting with Andrew. As far as she knew, they had not met at the house at the bay since that one night, but could not decide whether it was a sign of Andrew's strength or weakness that he would not take her there.

It was at the thought of a man's weakness that she remembered the vodka, but decided against turning back. What could she do about it? Her uncle would find his solace somewhere, whatever she did.

Turning from something that caused her heartache, she grew

aware that they were not taking the usual route home and asked the rickshaw boy why. He mumbled something about "too muchee lion dance," and she sat back in her seat again. Another of the celebrations that demanded two men in a shaggy-silk body with a monstrous head in vivid-featured caricature of an eastern-style lion. Thank heaven he was bypassing it. Crashing cymbals and gongs were the last things her nerves could stand.

She looked at the sky that was white with heat and longed for a cool breeze. The whole colony had been warned that water was dangerously low in the reservoirs, and that the weather was not expected to break just yet. Cholera was still raging in the New Territories, and cockroach plagues were filling the shanties down by the waterfront. When she thought of the squalid rat-ridden homes of the poorest Chinese, and the sampans in bobbing communities, she shuddered. How could human beings live under such conditions, and in heat such as this?

From all reports they preferred it to living in China, for they poured over the border in hundreds for the safety of the colony. Andrew had told them. . . . The recollection came to a halt as memory of the speaker overshadowed the theme, and the pain returned. No, she could not go home to go through the torture of wondering if *this time* the triumph of victory would be blazoned across Mama's face when she returned.

She sat forward in the seat and gazed around her, newly aware that she did not recognize her surroundings. The road was narrow and mean. The shops on either side were dark caverns. Some contained the odorous ingredients of Chinese meals: dangling dried fish in great vertical rows, rattan bowls full of shiny beans, dried vegetables, herbs, odds and ends of shriveled bloodless meat.

"Where are we?" she cried to the rickshaw boy, but he made no answer.

The stifling heat combined with the stench of rotting vegetables, bad drainage, and the unmistakable smell of the East made her feel faint. Perspiration broke out over her body, and a strange sense of alarm took hold of her. Convinced that she was far from the midlevels, she shouted again to the rickshaw boy.

"This is not where I told you to go. Where are we?"

As if she had not spoken, his feet pounded the ground even faster. The rickshaw swayed and jolted over the uneven surface, throwing her against the sides. The road seemed to stretch on forever in a narrowing path overhung with banners covered in calligraphic writing, and washing on bamboo poles. Growing afraid Nadia looked around her as she clutched the sides of the rickshaw. There was not another white person in sight. Every face around her was Chinese.

FOURTEEN

The letter from Russia came like a douche of cold water. For the past two weeks he had thought of nothing but the stifling nightmare ambience of Hong Kong. Every day, every hour had been dominated by the smells of parched vegetation, the sound of servants' alien voices below his verandah; distant gongs and firecrackers, joss sticks burning slowly in numerous temples filled with grotesque idols, the high-pitched excitement when yet another snake was caught in the garden.

Sitting propped with pillows in a chair by the open shutters Ivan lived through those two weeks in the agony of his continued life in *her* world. He could go nowhere to escape it. If he shut out the view of Hong Kong's graceful buildings and shanty communities he stifled in tropical heat in a room filled with reminders: a lacquer screen, carved chest, cloisonné enameled vases, hand-painted lamps.

If he closed his eyes he heard the eternal crickets in the undergrowth, the shuffle of coolies approaching the house to deliver great cubes of ice, eggs, vegetables, all in pans hanging from a bamboo pole across their shoulders. He heard the rich

259

song of birds with brilliant plumes, the laughter of little black-haired children as they played with a *Chien-Tzu,* kicking the homemade shuttlecock up and up, never letting it drop to the ground for fear of being out.

When he placed his hands over his ears and lay in darkness he still sweated in the severe tropical heat as mental visions of Mei-Leng tore open the wounds in his chest to expose his guilt. He could not eat or sleep, could not rest, could not escape her. She was in everything around him. Her world remained to accuse him; her people swarmed wherever he looked.

Why, why, *why?* He had only done what men had done since the beginning of creation. In Russia, in Hong Kong, in every country in the world, men discovered their manhood or tried to hold on to it when it was beginning to fail. In his homeland he would have taken peasant girls, waitresses, other men's wives if he could be discreet about it. Here, the Tanka girls brazenly offered their services in loud invitation, and the brothels were filled with prostitutes of all colors and creeds, only too willing to satisfy any desires a man could have. Yet, while he told himself all that, he knew deep within his soul that he was guilty. He had known it the minute it was over and he saw her face.

That day a letter had arrived from his brother Constantin, with little notes enclosed from the young sisters, too. The affection tinged with respect for the brother soon to become head of the family increased Ivan's feelings of being trapped in Hong Kong by his own deeds. Young Catherine would soon be the age of Mei-Leng. How would he feel about a man who had . . . ?

He moved painfully in the chair, and his thoughts winged away over the top of the palms to the hills beyond. Sweat stood on his brow and moistened his hands. The supporting pillows created heat around his body, but it was nothing to the furnace of horror that was created every time he thought of how she had died.

Day after day, while he had been filled with resentment over his way of life, she had been sitting up in that terrible place of death growing weaker and weaker in the grips of hunger. While he had regretted his failure to give her some reward for that morning, she had been so near, so close to rescue from her purgatory.

Putting his head in his hands he felt the tears spring to his eyes. So beautiful, so meek, so perfect. The softness of her skin, the petal-fresh quality of her whole appearance, the tiny feet in black slippers that skipped over the ground to keep up with his long strides. The sound of her lilting voice. *One is always sad to lose the moon and sun. It is only possible to look from afar but that does not make the day and night any less black when they have gone.*

They had gone for him now. If he had not been certain as he looked at her face after his passion, he was now. What she had felt for him was worship. She had been no Tanka girl, no Russian peasant ready to roll in the hay with her noble master. Mei-Leng had loved him in the way of her ancient culture. He was the honored Master—a man of wisdom and great virtue—and she served him devotedly. But it was honorable service as a companion and, later, as a legal wife. There were concubines for sexual satisfaction. That was their way, and the accepted belief of a girl brought up in strict observance of her culture. By taking her so casually in the long grass of a secluded spot he had degraded her and broken her heart. He, who had always been so full of pride, only recognized hers when it was too late.

When the police officer had come to him that night the ghastly shock of such news had been more than he could stand alone in his hospital room. With a strength found in desperation he had somehow gained the house without collapsing, and reached out to his twin to share his burden.

He lifted his head and brushed back the tears with his hand. His words that night had separated him from his twin as finally as a surgeon's knife parting Siamese twins. Too passionate to notice her reaction at the time, he saw it in her eyes every time she looked at him now. Something had been lost between them that would never come back. Finally, he was alone.

The struggle to equal his father was over and lost. Papa would have been strong enough to dismiss a little Chinese girl from his mind without another thought; Ivan knew he would never forget her. Mama would never now turn to her son: She had her new Andrei. He was free of her forever. Nadia was now a woman in her own right. They might still feel each other's pain, know each other's inner thoughts, but the shared heartbeat had divided and taken on different rhythms. In seven weeks he would come of age and his future now rested with him alone. The shackles had fallen off. He was needed by no one in Hong Kong, and the place mocked and accused him. He must now learn to be Ivan Brusilov. *It is sad to lose the moon and sun.*

The afternoon wore past as he waited for Nadia to come with her daily report on the gallery, but his thoughts were far away from accounts, jade ornaments, and business matters. So far away that the commotion did not, at first, register with him. When it did he felt initially irritated by the raised voices, then disturbed by the realization that they were speaking Russian.

Fully alert within seconds he located the sounds as coming from his mother's room further along the verandah, and recognized the voices as those of her and Aunt Marie raised in anger. *Aunt Marie!* What was she doing there? In concern he called to his servant, but the boy had gone to the kitchen to fetch tea.

The voices rose higher, and he recognized the hysteria in his aunt's words. Looking around angrily he wondered where the servants had gone. What had happened to the woman who was employed to look after the invalid? How had his aunt slipped away from her and got into Mama's room?

On the point of rising, Ivan saw his mother walk onto the verandah fifty yards to his left and look back into the room. She was dressed in sherry-colored silk, with a large hat of deep cream-shaded georgette which suggested she had just returned from an outing. Her words told him she had discovered her sister-in-law in her room when she entered.

"Even a locked door does not keep you out . . . nor in. You move about the house like a rodent. Take her away, at once. Take her away, I tell you," ordered Anna apparently to a servant also inside the room.

But Aunt Marie appeared in the doorway alone. There was no Chinese servant in sight. She looked white-faced and stronger than any woman should be.

"Give it up, it does not belong to you," she cried like a child in a tantrum over a borrowed toy. "Give it to me!"

By way of answer Anna turned her back on the other woman, and Ivan could then see she held something in her hand that glistened in the late afternoon sun. He hardly had time to identify it before Aunt Marie gave a howl of rage and rushed out with hands outstretched to push at the back turned to her.

Anna jerked forward under the impact. What she held flew from her hands into the garden below, and she was clinging desperately to the stone balustrade in severe danger of following it as the demented woman pounded at her with clenched fists. Acting under instinct Ivan began to hurry forward, using the balustrade as a support.

"Stop . . . for the sake of God, stop that!"

In the grips of her dementia, Aunt Marie heard and saw nothing but the subject of her long-standing hatred, and she went on pounding until Ivan reached her. Her strength was beyond that of his, and in the whirligig madness of those few moments he was aware that Anna was free and standing against one of the pillars.

Gasping and panting Ivan mastered his aunt and held her against the door jamb while waves of giddiness assailed him. Gradually he became aware that she was crying in short whimpering sobs.

"It belongs to Nadia. She took it before. She always takes things that belong to someone else."

"Be quiet," he said wearily, propping himself on the hands that held her. "Be still and quiet!"

Conscious of jabs in his stomach and chest where his wounds were trying to heal, he peered into the dimness of the room. His mother's maid and the woman employed to watch Aunt Marie were cowering wide-eyed in separate corners. Angrily he barked orders at them, but they had no intention of obeying until they were completely reassured that the fight was over. They came slowly to help Aunt Marie back to her room. She was still whimpering, and clutched Ivan's sleeve as she went.

"We must get rid of the worm in the apple," she implored him.

He simply prised her fingers open and nodded to the Chinese women to take her away. After they had gone he stood for a moment to recover, then turned to his mother. She stood against the pillar looking pale and incredibly beautiful, as if she had withstood the forces of tyranny. She stared at him with nonrecognition in her eyes and said nothing.

He took four paces and leaned on the stonework to look down into the garden just below. On the flowerbed lay the silver-framed photograph he had seen at Andrew Stanton's house on the night of his dreadful dinner party.

He turned his head, seeing his mother as she really was for the first time. Why had he ever striven to reach standards set by such a woman?

"My aunt was right. It belongs to someone else, and I shall return it to him." With some effort he moved past her. "I think you are touched by the same fever as she . . . but yours is a madness I cannot accept."

Not far above Nadia's face was a ceiling of rotten and crumbling wood which showed the straw outer covering. She could see the swarms of shiny insects moving over and through it giving the impression that the whole surface was moving. The smell of damp decay was unpleasantly strong. It mingled with the lingering odor of fish and friend vegetable stalks. There was only a dim light from a lantern somewhere behind her. It threw the corners of the small room into darkness, but there was hardly likely to be anything worth seeing there.

Alarm was diluted by lethargy. They had made her drink something, then left her lying on what felt like a wooden shelf. She could not move. Her whole body felt leaden, and it was difficult to hold on to her thoughts when the ceiling moved up and down to the accompaniment of drums in her ears. Sleep was urging itself upon her, but there was enough will still in her to deny it.

The moving colony of insects on the wood began to merge into a shifting pattern of nothing-in-particular until she floated on a billowing sea that tossed and swung her in sickening manner. There were hands gripping her. They were doing the tossing, and it hurt her arms and legs. Her head was hanging back, and lights were beginning to grow all around her.

There was noise. Loud screeching voices, music, horrible laughter. They all echoed and merged with each other, and still she was tossed and swung by the hands holding her with a fierce grip. She tried to move her lips to form a protest, but nothing happened. Then fear rose above lethargy to identify itself . . . but it could only lie in her heart unexpressed.

A nightmare began. The lights became blinding and multicolored. She seemed to be surrounded by walls that were covered in red, blue, and yellow lights, walls that gleamed like mirrors. It was suffocatingly hot, and faces swam about her disconnected from bodies. They were horrible faces: men and women laughing down at her and shouting in high shrieks. They were all around her as her eyes swiveled round as far as they could in each direction.

The tossing had stopped. She was lying on a hard surface that was isolated from anything else, like a raft in the midst of an ocean. There were thumps and screams above her, and terrible inhuman roars. She felt sick, and bruised, and terrified. Yet she could do nothing but lie immobile while things swam about at will.

The faces above her converged into a grotesque cluster that cackled with laughter so deafening it hurt her ears. Next minute, hands were upon her again, pulling at her hair and clothes, like a pack of wolves tearing at a petrified, sacrificial lamb. Her head lolled from side to side as the tugging hands pulled at her scalp so fiercely that her eyes began to water. She remembered vaguely an afternoon in the sun when she had looked up at a man in a garden through eyes watering from the tugging of hair caught on a branch. Oh, Andrew . . . *Andrew!*

Then other hands ripped the dainty blouse from her and began on the cambric camisole beneath. Her skirt was sliding down over her hips as the bodice fell away leaving her upper body naked. The tears overflowed onto her cheeks as the remainder of her clothes were removed. It was the worst nightmare of her life, but she could not awaken from it. The degradation would be eternal. Those faces would be above her always; the shrieks forever in her ears. When they began to touch her bare limbs and bosom the whole scene began twirling into a vortex of brilliant colors and black rushing winds into which she fell, and went on falling until the colors vanished and left only darkness.

At two in the morning Andrew was in his darkened sitting room with a glass of brandy in his hand. He looked at it ruefully. It replaced sleep on too many occasions lately. All the same, he drank it and poured another, walking toward the folding doors to gaze out at the night. The moon was blurred and hazy, but he was not that drunk. His lunar-friend had been that way most of the time it had been so hot.

"What am I to do, my dear?" he asked her in a murmur. "Not that I trust you. You have led me to disaster before now."

He pounded his brain once more in futile conjecture. There seemed to be no evidence of Anna's spending apart from jewels and exquisite clothes. Orlov appeared no more than a friend—inasmuch of a friend as anyone could be to a woman like Anna—and merely formed one of the Russian set in the colony. What more could he do? Apart from breaking into Orlov's home and studying his financial documents, there was no evidence that any Brusilov money had been passed through him for political activities.

He wanted the end of the affair. Each meeting with Anna was wearing him down. They could not expect him to go on seeing her in the name of duty . . . yet how could he explain to men like Sir Goodwin and Chris Smethwick the manner in which a ghost was taking him over? He leaned on the stone handrail staring into the distance, so lost in thoughts of life and death that it was some time before his gaze wandered from the far distance to notice a dark shadow on the sand at the foot of his steps.

His heart jumped a beat, for it looked like a person lying there deathly still. Surely it could not be Kim? The Portuguese cook he now employed was fat, and this person looked small. With strange unwillingness he began to move down the steps, finding the situation bizarre and unnerving.

As he drew closer it seemed even more bizarre for the figure was dressed in some kind of long robe and tall hat. It definitely was not Kim, but how had it come to be on the beach? Now the fisherfolk had gone there was no other sign of life in the bay, and visitors were deterred by the *fung shui*.

Reaching the beach he looked down at the figure, thinking back of the evening he had found Mei-Leng. This body was also facedown, and it took an effort to put out a hand and turn it over. It rolled round easily, and he recoiled in instinctive horror. He had seen death in some terrible forms, but nothing had prepared him for a chalk-white face, the features painted on with grotesque emphasis of blood-red mouth, black-lined slanting eyes of vivid green, and brows that swept up into the hairline with thick strokes. It was macabre, terrible, and he stood shocked, unable to bring himself to touch it again until his brain grew coherent enough to tell him where he had seen such a thing before.

Even then, he had to force himself to take some action. Bathed in the cold sweat of aftershock he stooped down to inspect the figure, then realized the body was warm to the touch—living warm! There was no hesitation then. Lifting it from the sand he hurried up the steps to his sitting room, laid it on the sofa, then went to light the lamps.

Turning back to the figure his heart froze again at the lurid sight. The white-faced girls of the Cantonese opera—how often had he seen them posturing, heard their shrill shrieking voices? This one was dressed in peach-colored robes embroidered with gold thread and flashing colored beads in a heavy cape pattern across the shoulders. Her hands were also chalk-white with fingernails painted bright scarlet. Her feet were normal size, but bound to represent the tiny crippled feet of ancient Chinese women. It was not a tall hat on her head, but her own hair twisted and shaped into a pagoda of bun-shapes that were intertwined with gold ornaments, pearl ropes, and scarlet tassels that hung round the painted mask of a face like an extraordinary, brilliant fringe.

The whole effect still gave him the feeling that he saw a lifesized puppet that had crossed the borderline from doll to human in a travesty of science, but he leaned across to take one of her wrists in his fingers. She was alive, but the pulse beat was very slow. Tentatively he felt her body but could find no wound or symptom that would account for her unconscious state. The vivid green eyelids were fast closed. It was impossible for him to tell how deep was her coma, but there was no doubt she was under the influence of a drug.

Fetching a rug he threw it over her, then went to make some

strong black coffee, as much for himself as for the victim. Glad of the excuse to leave the presence of something that prickled the back of his neck, he wondered how on earth she had come to be on his beach. In that state she must have been dumped by others. Why? Chinese avoided the place like the plague now; they would not come there from choice. Did they hope to punish the girl by leaving her in a spot ruled by angry dragons? Who could tell? The oriental mind worked in ways that appeared devious to a westerner. Knowing that, he decided not to call in Kim who was decidedly jumpy these days. An incident like this might complete his half-formed fear of the place.

Back in the sitting room he drank a full cup of the coffee to steady himself, while he looked at the still figure on his sofa. If he could get some coffee down her throat it might help, but he had no idea which drug she had taken, or in what quantity. It was a hell of a situation—a drugged Chinese girl at such an hour and no doctor within miles! He had enough to cope with, at present. Why did they have to dump her at *his* steps?

The question pressed down on him as he poured a little of the dark liquid into a cup to take to her, and he frowned. Yes, why at *his* steps? A girl from a Cantonese opera. What possible reason could there be to leave a girl in her full costume on a beach where she could only be found by one man, and he an Englishman dealing with law and order?

The more he considered the question the more involved it became . . . and the more sinister. He drew a chair up to the sofa and sat looking at the girl, still reluctant to touch her. Perhaps it was the association of her appearance with those open-air dramas he had seen and disliked, or maybe it was the ominous flavor of her presence in his sitting room at such an hour. He could not rid himself of the notion that there was more in the incident than he realized.

Then, in the act of sliding a hand beneath her head to give her the coffee, every muscle, every pulse beat froze, and the breath rushed from him with sickening force. The prickling on the back of his neck increased as his mind fought against what he saw. It was unthinkable . . . appalling. It could not be. Above that painted unreal face, beneath the tassels, pearls, and gold ornaments he had just noticed the most terrible thing of all. This "Chinese" girl had hair of a beautiful bronze shade.

The coffee slopped all over the carpet as he set the cup down and went in a frenzy for a towel and bowl. Almost fearfully he wiped at the white mask with the wet towel, his hands shaking as he did so. The skin beneath was pale—European.

A rage of frightening proportions began to flare in him as the mask flaked away, and he was sick with the need to tear away the jeweled ornaments and tassels, the richly embroidered robe, the hideous fingernails—everything that made a travesty of the girl he knew and loved.

Black thoughts drove into his brain as he gathered her up in his arms and walked blindly up the stairs to his bedroom, where he lowered her onto the bed.

When her feet were free he turned his attention to the embroidered fastenings of the robe. The desire to rip the costume from her almost mastered him, but it slid down over her shoulders once he had loosened it. She was naked beneath it. He thought of other eyes looking at the sweet soft perfection of her breasts, the smooth creaminess of her shoulders, the slender curving waist, the flat stomach, and youthful rounded thighs—he thought of their hands touching her . . . her humiliation . . . and something inside him broke.

Gathering her up he held her inert body against him with protective yet savage possession while his lashes grew wet. Drawing the coverlet up around her nakedness he rocked her in his arms as his grief and fury ran riot. The ornaments in her hair scratched his face, and he began removing them one by one, throwing them down with vicious revolt against what they represented. He took off the tassels and beads, then carefully unwound the pagoda of buns until her hair flowed freely over her shoulders. He stroked it with a cherishing gesture as he spoke of his love and need for her in a voice that was thick and harsh. Only when every trace of the creature they had made of her had gone did he start the long business of bringing her out of her unnatural state.

It was at least an hour later before she was anywhere near coherent. He had coaxed coffee between her immobile lips, spilling more on the bedcover than went down her throat. He had bathed her face gently with cold water over and over again. He had chafed her feet and hands, warmed her body against his own, moved her limbs continuously in an effort to make the blood circulate more quickly.

All the time he concentrated on such things the rage inside him was contained, but when her eyelids finally fluttered to remain open, it pounded through him again making him unable to speak to her. She simply looked at him through eyes dark and dilated until she knew him.

In an instant she was against him, pressing her body on his in the instinctive need for protection. Her voice was wild and touched with hysteria. Her hands gripped his solid strength with convulsive movements.

"They were *laughing*," she moaned, and he felt her anguish in his own body as he held her fiercely. "There were faces everywhere . . . lights—brilliant lights. I could not move. It was horrible . . . *horrible*. They were touching me . . . taking off . . . my clothes. They were *laughing*." Her voice broke as she began to weep, and her desperate pressing body set him talking feverishly as he stroked and kissed her hair.

"Hold on to me. I'll never let you go again, I swear." He felt her heart thudding against his, and passion ran riot. Cradling her head with one hand he buried his face in the soft hair that lay against the warmth of her neck. "I was wrong—oh God, I was so wrong," he groaned. "Nothing else matters but loving you. I shall take you away from here—from all this. We'll start a new life and to hell with everything else."

When she spoke her voice against his shoulder was muffled and thick with tears. "Tell me that again, Andrew."

"I love you, *I love you*," he said savagely. "I should have listened to my heart that first day. There'll be no peace without you." He tilted up her face and melted at the sight of her tearstained humiliation. "Whoever did this to you will pay for it, I swear."

She reached up to touch his face with hesitant fingers. "It has brought you back to me, *serdechko moyo*, that is all that matters."

The movement caused the coverlet to slip from her shoulders, and she became aware of her nakedness for the first time.

Automatically she clutched the material across her breasts with a quick movement, then glanced up into his face with the echo of humiliation putting faint color on her pale cheeks and sparkling her eyes with tears.

"Don't," he said swiftly, covering the hand at her breast with his. "I saw you only with the eyes of love, and found you beautiful."

Her color deepened as she looked around his room that was washed in yellow light from the lamp. "So many times I have imagined being here alone with you." Her glance swung back to his. "Now it has happened it is all wrong."

He knew that in other circumstances he would have taken her, shown her it could never be wrong between them, but tonight he could do nothing.

"Andrew, I . . . how did you find me? I can remember nothing after those terrible . . . how did I get here to your house?"

He took a long breath to steady himself. "I don't know. You were on the beach at the foot of my steps. You could have been there for some time. It is three-thirty A.M." He gave her time to absorb that, then went on, "They must have brought you by boat. You have been drugged."

Now they were speaking of such things she began shivering, and he drew the bedcover tightly around her shoulders and held it there for warmth.

"Can you tell me what happened?" he asked gently. "What do you remember?"

She looked up at him, then put her head down on his shoulder. "I love you, Andrew." It was said in a voice thick and unsteady, and he tightened his hold around her, waiting until she was ready to go on.

"It was when I left the gallery. I was not paying attention in the rickshaw. He said there was a lion dance and went a different way. I was thinking—about you and Mama," she explained, and he swallowed his quick rise of guilt.

"He took me to a place I did not know—Chinese—and I grew afraid. There were many people in the street, yet they did nothing to help me when I was seized and taken into a little filthy shop with bottles all around the shelves. They made me drink

271

something." Her head dropped until she was resting her cheek against his hand that held hers. "Andrew, I thought I was going to *die.*"

He felt the rage begin to rise in him again as she nestled against his body. "Do you know what they gave you?"

"No. It tasted bitter, and I felt giddy almost immediately. I was in a room—squalid and very hot, with insects everywhere. I could see a little, but could not move. I felt very sick."

He rested his cheek on her bent head. "Did they say anything to you—say why they were doing it?"

"The first ones said nothing. I think they carried me to the other place. I remember swaying as if in a boat, and their hands tightly around my arms and legs."

She described the other place, and he knew the screaming, the thumps, the brilliant colored lights, the terrible voices and faces represented the Cantonese opera. They must have taken her to the dressing rooms beneath the bamboo staging while the performance was taking place. There was only one such company in Hong Kong at present, and he knew where it was.

Nadia stopped in her narrative at that point, and he had to force himself to ask, "Is that where they took your clothes off?"

It was a moment before she answered him. "They tore at them—a whole group of people. Men and women," she added with some distress. "They *tore* them off. They pulled at my hair like savages. They were laughing all the time. It was . . . horrible!"

He felt himself tauten to snapping point. God, he would choke the life from them if he caught them! "Did they . . . did they . . . ?" He could not finish the question.

Her head was suddenly flung back and she looked up at him in the full shock of that day. With her bronze hair hanging loose and flowing around her shoulders, her eyes huge and dark with the haunting of uncertainty, she looked as tempestuously sensuous as Anna.

"Forgive me," she whispered. "That is all I remember. I . . . I shall never know."

But I shall, he cried within. When I take my wife in love and passion, *I* shall know.

272

FIFTEEN

A tropical night is never entirely silent, but the bullfrogs, the crickets, the sinister rustling of creatures in the undergrowth were subdued by the thundering of hooves as Andrew put his horse at the road above his bay during that time an hour or so before dawn. A very good horseman, he nevertheless rode like a madman from the moment he left his house.

With every mile his mood grew cooler until his anger was icy-cold and deadly, as it had been once in South Africa when riding out to avenge the death of a close friend. He knew exactly what he was doing, was fully in command of himself and his horse, was pitched at the top of all his faculties. All the same, nothing and no one would stop him from carrying out his purpose by the dawn that would end that terrible night.

The heat that hung heavily between the dust road and the overhanging foliage rushed past his ears, and his breathing became labored in the humid blanket of air. He felt the thin shirt sticking to his back and the breeches clinging to his calves with uncomfortable tightness, but the sensations registered only in a tiny part of his brain. Occupying most of it was the reason for wearing his gunbelt.

Why had it not been obvious to him before? So lost in his own morass of emotions he had stretched his brain no further than imagining Ivan Brusilov had earned the anger of a business enemy. Even when he had found the girl dead, and the young Russian's friendship with her had come to light, he still had not linked all the facts into a chain.

The rapacious young fool! With all the Tanka girls and popular establishments abounding, what madness had led him to seduce a girl like Mei-Leng? Did he know so little about Chinese that he was unaware of the consequences of such an act? Did he know so little of the poor young creature he had taken so selfishly that he could not guess the shame she would feel? Lastly, and most deadly of all, did he truly understand so little of his comprador's code of honor that he could expose his entire family to the danger of vengeance?

Andrew leaped his horse over a darker shape on the darkness of the road. It was possibly a dead dog, or an aged wild boar that had been attacked and driven from the herd by the younger virile males. The laws of a harsh society! So it was with the Chinese. Mei-Leng was a virtuous middle-class girl who had been brought up to obey the harsh laws of her culture.

Andrew urged his mount to go faster, even though the way ahead was still black. Beneath the trees even the shrouded moonlight gave him no help. But his sense of urgency dictated that he must bend low and fly through the night. Time was of the essence. He had not been expected to find Nadia until the morning, by which time Ho Fatt would be on his way.

At the thought of what the Chinese had paid others to do to the sister of the man who had insulted and degraded him, Andrew cursed himself for his lack of perception. He only wished young Brusilov had seen the body he had found lying on the grass that night. It would have haunted him for the rest of his days and taught him more about life than all his twenty years so far. In effect, Ivan's deed had caused Ho Fatt to kill his own daughter.

But it could not end there. Such loss of face demanded more—

the death of the European who had perpetrated such an insult against Eastern culture. That same culture, however, ruled that no second attempt could be made upon a life if the first failed. The only course left open was to take revenge on the family of the guilty one, and if such revenge could also include the person who had foiled the murder attempt, then so much the better.

Andrew was too good a rider to whip his horse needlessly, but he longed to take his crop to something if it would only get him to that village quicker. He had left Nadia tucked up in his bed, with Kim standing guard in the house for the remainder of the night. She had been frightened for him, and very upset over what he had told her, but it had been due to her long confession that he had jumped to the truth. Weepy and emotional from the effect of the drugs, she had poured out all her misery over himself and her mother, the worries over the finances of the gallery, and her estrangement with Ivan due to his seduction of a Chinese girl.

At that last, everything had fallen into place—the attack on Ivan, the tragic death of Mei-Leng, and the oriental bizarreness of what had been done to Nadia that night. There was only one person who could be linked with all three events, only one person who would know the movements and relationships of the Brusilov family well enough to plan such a revenge. The man who worked for western masters he hated: the man Andrew had been told wanted power.

Reining in sharply he went up to the outskirts of the village with some caution. The man would not be expecting him, but Ho Fatt had a cold calculating temperament and would not go easily to certain imprisonment and possible death. The house stood apart, as befitted the man's importance, at the approach to the village. It seemed quiet and sleeping, as still and inanimate as the stone gryphons on the slightly raised terrace leading to a door of carved complexity, but Andrew slid from the saddle and approached the house with great care, revolver in hand.

The door handle turned easily, and he went in immediately assailed by the odor of camphorwood and joss sticks. Pale light fell in a bar into the darkness of the room, showing the stone floor and carved-wood table and chairs beneath a great ornamental lantern of painted glass, blackwood, and scarlet and gold tassels. It was silent and eerily deserted.

Andrew moved across the floor, cursing the squeak of his riding boots. A bead curtain led to another chamber from which came the strong smell of joss sticks burning, although there was no lamp alight. He cocked the gun and took a firm grip on it before putting out a hand to lift the curtain. The room was deserted. He knew then that he was too late. Ho Fatt was on his way from Hong Kong.

Wasting no time in searching the room he knew the man could not be long on his way, for the joss sticks were still burning near the top where he had prayed at the little altar for favorable fortune on his journey. Andrew knew there were only two ways to leave the island—the Kowloon ferry or a small private boat—and he would need help with both.

He swung into the saddle and raced off in the direction of Victoria. Unless he could have men posted in time for the first ferry the Chinaman would slip away into the vastness of the New Territories and, with the usual closing of Chinese ranks, would remain there undetected forever. Already he could see a faint lightening of the sky to the east, and he had some miles to go yet. He had pushed the horse to its limits on leaving his own house and, in the sweltering humidity, dared not attempt to gallop the beast all the way to the city. As it was, a light lathering was appearing on the dark flanks and its breathing was labored.

He had known horses literally galloped to death in the temperatures of South Africa, yet the urgency of the moment dictated breakneck speed. As he was grappling with the decision it came to him that there was a way through the woods that would take him just above the midlevels and save time. In the darkness it was risky, for he was not too familiar with the path, but it was worth the risk for the opportunity to shave some minutes from the journey, and he swerved from the dimness of the well-defined road into the treed obscurity at the point where the woodland path began.

The horse was not happy at the change of surroundings, nor at the new uncertain footing, but plunged gamely on. Andrew made little attempt to guide the beast, knowing the animal could sense its way through the trees better than he could.

They had settled into a rhythm: the dull thud of hooves on leaf mold, the snorting breath of the horse, his own jerky gasps of air as the exertion had his lungs fighting for oxygen in that cloistered atmosphere, and the snappings of twigs and offshoots as they passed. Thorns had already caught at the legs of his breeches and torn the flesh of his thigh, and twice he had ducked quickly to avoid a low branch. The horse might know well enough where he might pass, but the rider must look to his own safe passage.

It was remarkably lighter. Andrew turned his head to the east. Dawn was coming up fast. But the swift glance was his undoing, for he turned back just as a heavy horizontal branch caught at his chest and sent him crashing backward to the ground. Rolling over with the agony of the blow, he heard the onward rush of the horse with a groan of hopelessness.

But his mind soon rose above it, telling him that the beast would pull up when it became aware the rider was no longer in the saddle urging it on. Winded and gasping with the pain in his chest he staggered to his feet and lurched after the horse.

The effort of climbing back into the saddle made him cry out with pain that shot through his chest and back, but he dragged himself into a position that would allow him to set the beast forward again. It was getting light enough to see his own way, and all he could think of was the first ferry to Kowloon.

The remainder of that ride was an impression of gray-green foliage, unbearable heat, and stabbing agony in his ribs, but he broke out onto the road again above the Brusilov house knowing he had saved time by his action. There were lights on in the familiar rooms, and he thought it would not hurt Ivan to be distracted with worry over his sister for a while longer, as long as it took him to reach a police station and send a man up to the house.

At the headquarters he dropped from the saddle, throwing the reins to a groom before making his way into the building. There he had a stroke of luck. The officer on duty was Chris Smethwick, who had been investigating the suicide of Mei-Leng. He would know enough of the case for the briefest of explanations to suffice.

The police officer's look of surprise quickly changed to consternation.

"Good God . . . Andrew!" He came around the desk to him. "Has someone set about you?"

Andrew knew he must look filthy and exhausted. He gave a concise account of what had happened and what he wanted.

One messenger was dispatched to the Brusilov house, then came Andrew's demand for a detachment to be sent to the site of the Cantonese opera company.

"My God, don't you see, Chris, we have probably been on the wrong track all the way along. That boy was attacked because he seduced Mei-Leng, that was all."

"But the pamphlets in his office," protested Chris.

"That office was used by Ho Fatt during the first day or two of Brusilov's absence. He is Chinese, ambitious, and hates his western masters. Who else would be riper for the attractions of a revolution that would give him all the things he wants? And isn't he the obvious person to arrange for that case of leaflets to be loaded onto the junk—a comprador who deals with transactions with Chinese merchants or carriers? Miss Brusilova was taken to the opera site at his instigation; I'll wager you'll find it worth searching their premises. I always said the Brusilovs were innocent."

Chris looked doubtful, but complied with the request. When Andrew told him he wanted a squad to go with him to the Kowloon ferry, he made his first protest.

"You can have the men, but you are not fit to go, yourself."

"Watch me," retorted Andrew grimly.

"You are dead beat and in pain" was the second protest.

"I'm the only one who can identify him," shouted Andrew.

"Oh, very well," said Chris with great unwillingness. "Watch your step, Andrew. No woman is worth dying for."

The small squad of Chinese policemen formed up and ran down the road to the jetty where the ferry left for Kowloon, but Andrew took another horse from the stables, deciding he wanted to be mounted if Ho Fatt should decide to make a run for it. He knew it was quite possible Ho Fatt had gone across on a small boat and the chances of catching him, in that circumstance, were

278

remote, for there were hundreds of tiny craft crisscrossing between the island and the mainland. But he was taking a chance on his guess being right. Ho Fatt would not expect Nadia to be found until about now, and certainly would not have considered the possibility of himself jumping to the truth immediately after listening to her account. Delivering Nadia to the steps of his house in that guise was, to the oriental mind, an act designed to disgust the man who put her on a European pedestal. The notion of true mutual love, as known to westerners, was unacceptable to a man of Ho Fatt's culture. Because of that, Andrew believed that the man would leave Hong Kong in the full confidence that he was supremely safe.

Blake Pier stood at the end of Pedder Street, and the square area before it was already busy with sedan chairmen and rickshaw boys waiting for early customers. The inevitable foodstalls were there, and the smell of hot oil was already filling the air. Coolies were throwing seawater from buckets on the dust surface, then sweeping it clean. They carried out their task with all the expressionless uninterest of road sweepers, and those of their countrymen standing around waiting to cross on the ferry watched them with equal lack of expression.

A quick glance told Andrew Ho Fatt was not there yet, so he stationed the policemen around the pier while he remained beside a small wooden pavilion on the pier approach ready to give a signal if he saw their quarry. They were to allow him onto the thatch-covered pier, then encircle him in such a way as to exclude prospective passengers. He was not to be allowed onto the ferry, for there would be a stampede amongst the Chinese if they saw policemen swarming onto the boat.

They were barely in time. Andrew could see the little steamboat approaching with its predominance of European passengers bound for offices and warehouses on the island. He fixed his eyes on the street leading down to where he stood.

Then he saw him, a small figure in a gray gown and round black hat. Strength and courage, plus the rage of revenge flooded back into his mind and body. With the flash memory of a white painted face, bound feet, and bronze hair twisted about with tassels and ornaments, he felt his blood pounding in his ears and

279

the coldness of purpose blot out pain and exhaustion.

Through the pillars of the small pavilion he watched the quarry approach in the midst of a group of laughing soldiers. How like him to use those men he hated as his protection! Andrew gave the arranged hand signal to the waiting policemen, and unfastened the leather holster on his belt. In the act of drawing his pistol a voice called his name, and he looked up swiftly to see an army friend giving him a cheery wave.

"Can't stop, old chap," the man called. "Party went on later than I thought, and the Colonel is on the warpath."

It was disaster! The gray-clad figure was already moving away, and Andrew gave a frantic signal to his men to spread out around the area before setting off at a run after the man. Back up the street he went and vanished into a narrow alleyway while Andrew crashed up the slope through the throng intent on catching the ferry. The alley was no more than a man's width between two high walls, and full of those who inhabited the mean rooms built within them. Ho Fatt raced with nimble feet, leaping over crawling babies, chickens, and buckets of refuse, but Andrew's broad body and greater weight made passage more difficult for him. He leaped obstacles where he could, but was brought to a scrambling crawl in order to sidle past a pile of baskets containing squawking poultry.

But soon he was out and caught sight of the Chinese running like a bobbing skittle down the stepped street back toward the waterfront. Andrew raced after him, taking the shallow steps three at a time, which caused excruciating pain in his chest. But he knew the only chance of catching him was by personal pursuit. The policemen would have lost their opportunities now the crowds were pouring onto the pier.

The whole of Hong Kong had awakened, and there were masses of people everywhere cramming into the streets for early shopping and early vending. Pursuit was hampered by coolies with their wares swinging from bamboo poles across their shoulders, and Andrew could see Ho Fatt entangled in one at the bottom of the street. Trying to take advantage of the fact, Andrew leaped the steps with reckless speed and came to grief himself when a child with a kite on a long string walked straight into his path. Twisting desperately he fetched up against a barrow that caught his hip a heavy blow.

Fighting to get his breath, he pushed himself away and pressed on down the steep street, having lost sight of Ho Fatt. His wild progress hardly caused a ripple in the sea of Chinese bent on their own affairs. They were used to the madness of western barbarians and did their best to ignore it. At the bottom, he looked quickly in both directions, then spotted the gray gown way off along the waterfront, heading for a sampan colony where concealment would be all too easy.

All along the waterfront there was a busy passage of sedan chairs, rickshaws, and horses, but it was level and easier ground for the athletic Englishman. It was difficult to see Ho Fatt, but there was no doubt the distance between them was lessening.

Ho Fatt ran down some steps and out along the rickety double planking that served as a path-over-water for the inhabitants of the sampan colony. It was broken and rotten, wavering on bamboo stilt supports and ran between hundreds and hundreds of tiny covered boats to give access to land for the sea-dwellers.

The planking ran way out to the center of the hostile colony, and Andrew's heart sank. Not only was he too heavy to run with any speed over the fragile wood, he was a foreigner. In his filthy shirt and breeches, brandishing a revolver, he represented all they distrusted. Men had ventured into the heart of such places and never been seen again.

Even so, he slowed his pace only because of the narrowness of the footway. The blanketing stench that rose up around him was almost suffocating after a heat wave lasting into its third week, and the faces that peered from the dark interiors beneath the curving rattan hoods were listless and gaunt and hostile.

It did not make him any easier to acknowledge that he had no chance now of arresting Ho Fatt; he would have to kill him. His fate at the hands of these people after he had shot one of their countrymen would be grim indeed, but still he jogged on across the swaying planks that wound in so many curves he could never hold his quarry in sight long enough to take a shot.

Then, rounding a curve, Andrew saw the Chinaman caught and held by a leg that had gone through the wood. Knowing this might be his only opportunity he gambled on the chance of not doing the same. Running with dangerous haste he was about to take aim when something gripped his calf with such ferocity he yelled with pain and twisted to shake off the pi-dog that had its teeth so firmly embedded in his calf. Andrew shot it through the head without hesitation. It dropped without a sound, and he stood holding his leg while the agony of the bite took its toll of his fast-failing strength.

The sound of that shot had brought out hundreds of Chinese who followed him with their eyes as he limped on toward the Chinese who had managed to free himself and was on the run again.

After that Andrew lost all sense of everything but the pain that now consumed his body, the gray-clad man ahead, and the boat colony that was now closely surrounding him. He ran limping past flapping rags of washing; past naked children, and mothers with eyes sunken into yellow resigned faces; past men with limbs like sticks who barely had the strength to hold the pipe they smoked; past dangling dried fish and cooking pots containing soggy bloated rice.

Then, just when Andrew thought he could run no more, the small figure ahead tripped on the uneven planks and fell forward slipping between the swaying walkway and bobbing boats.

In less than ten seconds Andrew was there staring down into the much-laden water where the figure had disappeared. But they were far from shore now, and a passing junk beyond had created a wash that set the entire water colony of boats rocking and bobbing against each other. The gap closed, leaving Ho Fatt beneath a solid wooden layer that covered the surface for miles— a layer that would ensure he never came up from the filty depths.

Andrew felt sick. His mind played with pictures of what was happening down there and he stood like a man in shock, the revolver hanging from his hand forgotten. The violently rocking boats increased his feeling of sickness, and he seemed to be swaying with them. His legs folded beneath him and he found himself lying precariously across the narrow walkway with the morning sun blinding him. Now it was over, pain ruled him and he wanted oblivion. For some while he drifted between awareness and blessed relief until, seemingly far away, he heard the high-pitched bold voice of a Tanka girl asking the usual question. He began to laugh softly. It was the last bizarre touch in an episode that had contained all Hong Kong could offer by way of oriental grotesqueness.

While the sampan colonies, the farming communities, the fisherfolk, and those who existed in the crowded cockroach-infested cubicles of lower Hong Kong faced the fatal prospects of the continuing drought, life for those on the midlevels and Victoria Peak also seemed doomed to certain hardships. The reservoirs were at emergency level and water supplies were restricted. A bad harvest would have little effect on the lavish tables of the wealthy, but no amount of money could buy water in Hong Kong, nor could it protect them from the disease and stench caused by dry nullahs in which refuse and sewage remained uncleared by rushing storm waters.

The administration was deeply worried and worked almost around the clock to devise emergency routines. Medical and sanitation experts knew they were fighting impossible odds, but called upon all the Chinese doctors and nurses they had trained in an attempt to lessen the dangers of an epidemic. The civil department made frantic arrangements to supply food to the Chinese population if their worst fears came to be realized.

The continuing insupportable heat took its toll of the aged and sick besides making tempers inflammable. But anger was not the only emotion to run high in the soaring temperatures of those days, and Nadia found herself possessed with a desire for Andrew that gave her no rest night or day.

In the three days since her abduction the love she felt for him had taken on a predominantly sexual aspect. The fearfulness of that night had been subjugated by his presence, and she longed for physical subjugation also. Each time she thought of herself naked before his eyes, of his hands touching her while she had been unconscious of his presence, she was consumed by a fire of excitement.

Even when Ivan had come for her with rickshaws, her maid, and clothes, her brother's defiance of his physical condition to do

283

so in no way compared with the heroic quality of the man who was somewhere out in Hong Kong in defense of them all.

A police officer who said he was a friend of Andrew's came to the house that afternoon to see her and Ivan, and his account of the morning's activities had heightened Nadia's passions further. The opera company had moved on during the night, but their boat was being followed. Ho Fatt was presumed dead. The chances of ever recovering his body were negligible, but several witnesses had seen him go under the water and there was no way he could have survived. Andrew was being kept overnight in the hospital with two cracked ribs and a severe bite in his leg from a wild dog.

During that night Nadia had been unable to sleep for the desire to reach out to him, give herself in return for his dedication. The blanketing heat that dampened her skin and put the heaviness of drugs back in her head only increased the ache for fulfillment in his hands. Ivan's persistent probing questions about that night drove her to distraction, and they quarreled in mutual testiness, hitting out at each other in a situation that, for the first time, their close affinity could do nothing to dispel. Her brother's very obviously tortured spirits only increased her longing to make him suffer more—for Andrew's sake. Consequently, she told him to leave her alone while she still felt unwell, and he unhappily complied.

Andrew sent a note to assure her that he had recovered and left the hospital. It was full of tender phrases, declarations of love, reaffirmation of his intention to make her his wife as soon as possible, but she wanted passion instead of reassurance, dominance rather than tenderness, sweeping ravishment in place of wedding plans.

And so, for three days she moved listlessly about the house, ruled by sexual awareness she had not realized was possible. At some time in the midst of those throbbing hours she neared understanding of what Andrew was fighting against with Anna, but her own driving desire overwhelmed all other considerations and turned her away from final enlightenment.

But there was a deeper, more persistent, need that plagued her during those three days and, eventually, she sent a message to

284

her doctor asking him to pay her a visit as soon as he was able.

On that third evening Ivan begged her to join them at the dinner table, and she softened at the sight of his strained white face. But it was hardly a warm family gathering. Anna sat at one end of the long table in a gown of exquisite apricot silken lace highlighted by a pendant of topaz set in heavy gold. Her aloofness that evening held a suppressed hysteria, and Nadia guessed why with a quick flare of apprehension.

At the end of the meal Nadia was on the point of excusing herself when Ivan took her arm to lead her into the salon.

"*Sestrushka,* forgive me. Play something for us all . . . *please.* Something of our homeland," he begged as she made to refuse. "Music will bridge any gap, do you not agree?"

So she played a little Tchaikovsky, but the heat was not conducive to a good performance, and she ended her recital very quickly.

Ivan stood and went across to her as she left the piano, taking her hands. "I should not have asked you when you have been unwell. But there has been so much. . . ." He broke off looking very uncomfortable. "We cannot dwell on such things forever. We must make a new start. We *must!*"

"Yes," she said.

"In six weeks we come of age," he went on rather louder. "We shall hold a grand dinner party to celebrate . . . then I shall begin planning our return to Russia to reunite the family. It has been split long enough."

A stunned silence followed his sudden momentous decision uttered in so casual and unsuitable a manner. Nadia was thrown into a fever of protest she could not begin to put into words, and she halted as thunderstruck as the others in the room.

Uncle Misha was the first to react. "No," he panted as he tried to struggle from his chair. "It is out of the question. You cannot . . . we cannot . . . the gallery . . . all we have achieved at . . . the gallery. Vanya, no . . . you cannot, you cannot."

"I shall sell the gallery. It is decided. There is no more to be said. The Brusilovs shall be merchants no longer."

"But . . . but the Zubovs, my boy." His full face was pathetically crumpled as he finally got to his feet and stood finding a steady balance for his unwieldy body. "Think of the Zubovs."

Ivan stiffened. Nadia could feel his hostility from her place next to him.

"The Zubovs did not think of the Brusilovs when the decision was made to come here." His voice was colder than his sister had ever known it, and she sensed a different man in him, a man she did not recognize nor even like. He was cold, calculating, and his tone held an edge of brutal disinterest. Like Papa, she thought with surprise. He seems more like Andrei than Ivan.

Uncle Misha had begun to shake, and Nadia could not help feeling a rush of sympathy for him. His jade "children" were all he had left now.

"There was no choice but to leave Russia. We were all in danger," he said. "We cannot go back there."

"We cannot stay here," snapped Ivan. "We have all been touched by madness in this place—except you," he added pointedly.

The older man paled. "You can say that? Vanya, I loved little Katya . . . yes, as my own child. It touched me . . . *bozhe moy*, it touched me . . . in my way, you know." He put a hand to his head. "And . . . and my dear wife—Mama, I called her, because it pleased her. Do you think it does not touch me each time I see her look at me like . . . like. . . ." He almost broke down. "She calls me Sergei, Peter . . . any name but my own. Can you say I have not been touched by the madness?"

"Then you too should be glad to leave this place" was the unemotional answer. "However, the Zubovs must make their own decision. The Brusilovs will go. I have decided. Galerie Russe will be sold as it stands."

"No . . . Vanya, no," he pleaded with tears in his eyes. "It is my creation—my one creation that really lives."

Ivan gave a contemptuous exclamation. "A creation I never wanted. I felt nothing for it but dislike and resentment."

"Then . . . then wash your hands of it, if you wish," said Uncle Misha eagerly as he came toward his nephew in shambling gait. "I will remain as the manager . . . eh? We are known here . . . have a good name in the colony. It will prosper, but you will have none of the irksome worries. What do you say . . . eh?"

"How long do you think it would last?" said Ivan coldly. "It has needed my sister, a girl, to manage the business side while I have been ill . . . and we have still lost money. Without her and without a comprador how long do you think Galerie Zubov will last before it falls around your ears, and I am ruined?"

Nadia put her hand on her brother's arm in protest at what he was doing, but he paid no heed. "So you were touched by Katya's death; you mourn for my father's sister? You are to blame for both. If you had not fled in fear from our homeland they would be alive and well in our house in Petersburg with the splendor of the Brusilov heritage around them. I shall take my aunt back—she has Brusilov blood—but you may stay here with my blessing. Perhaps another merchant will need a 'manager.' One who will pay you in vodka!"

"*Vanya!*" cried Nadia, appalled at his cruelty, and he turned to her fully in the grip of his anger.

"You told me the day would come when it would be clear to me what I must do—when I would step into the shoes of my father. We are returning to our homeland. It is my decision."

"No," she whispered. "No, *bratishka*. I am going with Andrew, wherever he wishes to take me."

For a moment of challenge they held each other's glance, their childhood, their spiritual affinity, everything that had ever been between them hanging on a delicate thread that needed only a breath to break it finally. Then a movement, rustling silk, and the click of a door took their attention. They both turned. Anna had gone out of the room.

SIXTEEN

By asking Andrew to meet him in the club Ivan hoped to add weight to his words. Although the doors of many British institutions were closed to him in this colony, the club of which he was a member restricted its list to Europeans of high birth or exceptional influence. Such a reminder of his status would surely impress the Englishman who was a member of a race much concerned with rank and class.

His recovery was speeding up, but he still had times when weakness invaded him, and he prayed that morning would not be one of them. He needed physical strength in addition to strength of purpose for the coming interview. He had rehearsed it thoroughly, and went over it again in the rickshaw that took him through the center of Victoria.

The rickshaw boy ran slowly in a temperature of 112°. Ivan, beneath the hood he insisted on being raised, sweltered in the formal suit and sun helmet, his starched collar chafing his neck as it clung to his clammy skin. There were few white men about; no western women at all.

It would not be necessary to look at such a scene for much

longer. In November he would celebrate his majority, and those six weeks would be ample time in which to recover sufficiently to make his plans. He would be in Russia by Christmas!

As head of the family it was now plain to him what must be done. They would all be taken back to Russia to take up their rightful places in society, and all this would be forgotten. He knew now he must be Ivan, son of Andrei. He must be Brusilov of Petersburg. Papa had given his orders in cold ruthless tones, and they had been obeyed. He had always decided what the family must do, and they had done it without question.

He deliberately arrived at the precise time he had mentioned to his guest, sending his rickshaw boy around the square one more time in order to achieve this. He felt that such punctiliousness would show neither deference to Andrew Stanton, nor bad manners in arriving late, but to his annoyance he found the other man had not arrived. Twenty minutes passed before he spotted Andrew in his starched white suit come through the inner doors and stand with his helmet beneath his arm looking for a sign of his host.

Ivan deliberately took his time in going over to him. "I was beginning to think you unable to keep the appointment," he said stiffly.

"I apologize for being so late," said Andrew holding out his hand. "How are you feeling now?"

For a moment Ivan considered a stiff bow in place of a handshake, then decided against it. It would not do to be churlish. "Much improved, I am glad to say." He indicated the bar with an outstretched arm. "And you? I see you are limping." Politeness demanded the inquiry.

"Oh, that . . . yes," was the easy answer. "A damned cur sunk its teeth into me and it seems to have affected my muscles. My ribs are still strapped, so I'm pretty comfortable, on the whole." He accepted Ivan's offer of a drink, then went on to explain that he had been delayed by an official matter. "Unfortunately it was to do with a job I instigated several months ago, and no one else knew quite how to deal with it. Still," he said heavily, "they will have to manage when I go."

It was too soon. Ivan did not want to get on to that subject just yet, so he let the remark hang in the air and went on to speak of the critical situation facing the colony. Andrew was informative on the subject, and Ivan rose the minute his guest had finished the drink.

"Perhaps we should have luncheon now. We are both busy men. . . ."

Andrew went to the washroom and joined Ivan at the door to the dining room several minutes later. "This is very impressive," he said, looking at the murals executed by an Italian. "I have always thought so."

Ivan was taken aback. "You have been here before?"

"On numerous occasions." He glanced down at him. "I have been in Hong Kong nearly five years, you know."

There it was, that indefinable attitude that suggested superior experience in addition to greater maturity. That this man should patronize him, under the circumstances, was intolerable. However, he determined to keep his dignity while laying the ghost of Andrew Stanton once and for all.

They sat at a table in an alcove. Ivan had asked for it especially, so that their conversation would be private, and they had no sooner given their order than he began.

"I asked you to meet me here because I felt you would not care to come to the house." It was meant as a cutting comment on how he had abused their hospitality, but he seemed unabashed.

"No. How is Nadia now . . . fully recovered, I hope?" It was full of concern and Ivan was thrown for a moment, murmuring something noncommittal before getting back to his rehearsed speech.

"As the head of my family it is my duty, I feel, to express our indebtedness to you for your prompt action on several occasions."

This time he was interrupted by the steward bringing their soup, and he shook out the starched napkin with an angry flick of his wrist. Andrew studied him with a slight frown.

"I believe you were aware of our gratitude for calling the doctor during the tragic illness of my young sister, but I think I have not touched on the service you rendered me at the Dragon

Boat Festival, and again this week in the bringing to book of my comprador for the deed."

It had sounded very civil and dignified in his room at home, but now the words seemed stilted. He sighed inwardly. It was imperative that he discharge the obligations with fitting courtesy, but in a manner that did not suggest servility to a man about to be put down in true Brusilov style.

"If you asked me here simply to say that, you really need not have bothered," said Andrew. "On two of the occasions I was on official duty and acted accordingly."

"But I insist," he said with irritation. "I could not leave Hong Kong without doing so on behalf of my family." He had not intended that information to be disclosed so quickly, but Andrew seized on it immediately.

"You have decided to go back to Russia, then?"

"Naturally. If it had been left to me, we would never have come here. My uncle made a coward's decision."

Andrew's blue eyes grew speculative. "You were *nineteen*— surely old enough to have refused to come?"

With his spoon raised he was obliged to return it to the soup bowl before he spilled the contents. "I ... I ... it was not as simple as that," he snapped at a man who had never seen his parents murdered before his eyes. "Half one's family killed in an afternoon! How could I be expected to make sane decisions at such a time?"

"It was probably the same for your uncle. He had a family thrown into his care—the lives of four people to consider."

"How dare you make comments on something you cannot begin to understand? What a man feels when he witnesses violent death is something only he knows," Ivan said with more passion than he wished.

But Andrew narrowed his eyes as he said, "If you imagine you are the only one to go through such an experience, you are even more immature than I thought."

Ivan felt color flood his face. He had forgotten Andrew Stanton had fought in a three-year war. The reminder now served to bring out all the defensive aggression that put

291

paid to a calmness the Englishman retained.

"Do not patronize me! Out here your people enjoy their posture of superiority, but it is a very tiny colony populated, in the most part, by ignorant pagan people on the verge of starvation. Hong Kong would be swallowed up in the Brusilov summer estate."

"And England with it, no doubt," was the caustic reply. "You have never been able to accept your role here, have you? Galerie Russe is an achievement many envy, but has it not once occurred to you that the greatest credit for it goes to your uncle? Apart from the money you sank into it, none of which you have had to earn, your talent for keeping books in orderly fashion could just as well have been used in a match factory. It was his artistic flair and a great love and study of jade that has made your life in Hong Kong bearable."

Ivan leaned back in his chair and made no demur when the steward removed his half-filled soup plate and replaced it with some fish. He had started out with everything on his side, yet this man was speaking to him as if he were no more than a boy.

"Yes, our life has been very tolerable as far as comfort is concerned," he admitted stiffly, "but nowhere approaching that which we led in Russia. I think you have no conception of our place in society. I am taking my family back to claim that place."

"You will not be taking Nadia. She has agreed to become my wife." It was said calmly, but with a hint of challenge.

Part of his prepared mandate came back to him, and he flung it across the table with as much of his father's manner as he could muster.

"My sister is no longer responsible for her actions. I will never give my permission for such an alliance."

"I was not intending to ask you for it. She will be twenty-one next month, and free to do as she wishes."

"No!" It was sharp, expressing all his envy and dislike of the man across the table. "She is Russian, of noble birth. Her obligation to her family is heavy upon her. Unlike your English girls, who appear to do as they please, the young women of our great families are obedient."

"I see" was the quiet reply. "Have you told her of this?"

Andrew had played into his hands, and confidence returned with the flow of remembered words. "There is no need. You will withdraw any offer you have made to my sister, and undertake to have no further contact with her for the remainder of the time she is in Hong Kong. You have done her reputation irreparable harm. I rely on your instincts as a gentleman, if you have any left, to spare her further distress—to spare the whole family further distress." He was well into his stride now and leaned forward to emphasize his command. "Apart from the scandalous meetings you are conducting with her mother throughout all this, what is society to deduce when they hear my sister was left unclothed on your doorstep at night and remained in your house until midmorning in that state? It is my duty to protect her from you until I can take her away to Russia where, thank God, none of this will affect her any longer. You may conduct your affairs how you please, but they will no longer include any Brusilov, that I swear."

It was said, and he was well pleased. Andrew looked considerably affected.

"My meetings with your mother have ceased" was all Andrew said.

"Indeed?" said Ivan, hardly believing him.

"But before you pronounce on another man's behavior, I suggest you look to your own. You sneer at my countrymen for running this colony, but you have never shown the slightest interest in its complexity. The majority of these Chinese might be ignorant and on the brink of starvation, in our eyes they are certainly pagan, but they will *not* serve any master. They are extremely proud, with a culture that extends back beyond mine . . . or yours. It is because we do our best to respect that that this colony flourishes."

Andrew's eyes were aflame with anger, and Ivan could not help seeing the pride and breeding in a man about whom he really knew very little. Ivan's moment of triumph vanished as Andrew continued.

"You are puffed up with ridiculous arrogance. You have

293

witnessed tragedy and let it teach you nothing. You have achieved success but will not acknowledge it. You speak endlessly of your noble family, but it is *you* who have brought them down." His hand holding the glass pepperpot brought it down on the table with a sharp rap. "There have been times when I longed to shake you by the scruff of the neck, but now I know the full truth I would like to drag you to Mei-Leng's grave and force you down on your knees before it. Brusilov you might be, but if you had taken any interest in the people around you you would know that even the Czar of Russia does not take an honorable well-bred Chinese girl and use her as a whore."

He took a visible grip on his anger. "You left Ho Fatt no alternative. The instrument of his disgrace had to be removed; the insult avenged. You had brought down his honored name. Yours had to be similarly brought down. You, as the offender, had to die—but I prevented that. Unfortunately the sight of your bleeding body turned your aunt's simple mind."

He heard nothing but Andrew's voice. Saw nothing but the contempt on his face.

"Attention turned to Nadia, the next in the Brusilov family. Chinese have devious minds, and Ho Fatt carried out a plan that would also punish me for preventing his murder of you. It was grotesque and obscene, as he meant it to be. You had turned his daughter into a western barbarian by your act, so he took the sister you have just so nobly sworn to protect and turned her into a pagan Chinese. She was not left unclothed on my doorstep, as I let her believe, but in ancient Chinese robes, with her feet bound, her hair bedecked with golden ornaments, and her face painted dead-white like the girls in streetside theaters." His voice had grown harsh. "God knows what else they did to her . . . but it is on your conscience—all of it. Go back to Russia, Ivan Andreyevich Brusilov, but before you stride your summer estates with imperious boots and don the noble uniform of a cavalry regiment in service of the Czar, take a hard long look at yourself and see if you are worthy of the name you brandish with such pride." He stood up, throwing his napkin on the table. "Now, if you will forgive me, I find my appetite has completely gone."

He limped away between the tables, a tall impressive figure in a room containing some of the most important men in Hong Kong. Ivan stared at the doors after he had gone, and continued sitting at his table until a steward asked if the other gentleman was returning.

Without a word he got up and left the club, hearing none of the greetings from fellow members. He was hardly aware of the rickshaw that took him to the house, nor of Nadia's greeting as she passed him on the stairs.

Like a man in a trance he took off the formal suit and put on a soft silk Russian shirt, and breeches. Then he let himself out at the back of the house and went round to the stables. He knew the road so well and rode like the wind, despite the heat. With every mile he felt his spirit crumble, and he began to gasp with sobs of desperation. Let him not be too late!

Then he saw it in a grove of good *fung shui*—the temple of Kwan Yin, goddess of mercy. It was a small stone building embellished with an intricately carved frieze on the edge of the roof, heavy carving down the pillars, colorfully picked out in scarlet, green, and gold. The sight of that place where he had sought a girl with a face like the people of Russia put such pain inside him he broke completely.

Flinging himself from his horse, he stumbled into the dim interior, hung about with scarlet silken prayer banners, and faced the altar where Kwan Yin gazed down at him with passive yellow features. She did not appear to look at him with mercy, so he lit candles with hands that shook. The memory of that other time was so strong he could almost feel Mei-Leng's presence beside him.

He remembered she had knelt before the goddess—a tiny figure in brocaded coat and silk trousers—so he went down on his knees, also. But he could not pray. With eyes closed he saw the flowers and fruit, the gifts of chickens and rice, and her shy attempts to include him in the rejoicing by offering him titbits with ebony sticks.

Dropping back onto his heels he flung his arms around his upper body in a desperate effort to ease the agony inside him. Bending forward he rocked back and forth while trying to come to terms with his own destruction. Time passed. Sweat poured down his face, and his kneeling position became part of the penance. No other worshipers entered, for they feared a mad spirit had taken possession of the temple.

He stayed there until darkness descended over the island, then left, remembering to dedicate a gift to the goddess in gratitude. It was a ring he took from his finger—a ring engraved with the proud Brusilov emblem.

Andrew's office was only at the far end of the same street, but he took a rickshaw from Ivan's club to reach it. Not only was he too incensed to walk in that heat, his leg was still extremely painful.

But when he paid the fare and limped up the steps to his office he could not settle to work. The brush with the young Russian had brought his problems to the surface once more, and he sat in the wooden swivel chair, twisting a pencil around in his fingers.

He had not seen Nadia since that night and longed to do so, but calling at the house was out of the question. A sense of frustration enveloped him. She was isolated by those who were selfish and blind at a time when she most needed him. He tried not to think of the possible implications of her ordeal, but it was impossible to forget the look on her face on admitting she did not know the answer to the question he could not bring himself to ask.

Ho Fatt was dead, but revenge had not been sweet enough for Andrew. Nothing would compensate for what he had caused to be done to a young innocent girl. Yet, even as he raged anew, he had to see the oriental justification for the act. Curse young Brusilov to hell! He had taken the pride and honor from Mei-Leng. Had his sister been similarly assaulted? Andrew put his head in his hands. God forgive him, but if Nadia bore a Chinese bastard he would drown it, like many another unwanted child of the East.

He must arrange a meeting with her to discuss their future. All they had done was exchange letters. He could not go there, neither could she go to his house. He had been in hospital; she had needed time to recover from her terrible experience. But letters were not enough. Somehow he must find a way of being alone with her, show his love and desire to protect her.

Then, despite all efforts, he found thoughts of Anna filling his mind. She had contacted him several times since his pursuit of Ho Fatt—every day, in fact. They had been excited vibrant letters overflowing with pride and desire aroused by his deed, but he had resolutely ignored them. He knew he was acknowledging defeat by his withdrawal, but it was not to be compared with complete submission. Young Brusilov had spoken of taking the family back to Russia. Did the plan include Anna? He must believe it did if he was to have any peace of mind.

His soliloquy was interrupted by a messenger summoning him to Sir Goodwin's office. He told the man he would be along shortly, and rose with heavy unwillingness. He had hoped for a little more time to marshal his plans, but it was as well to get it over as soon as possible. His uncle would need time to reorganize.

Entering his uncle's office he was surprised to find another man with Sir Goodwin, one he recognized. It was the marine police officer he had met at Government House.

Andrew smiled a greeting. "Hallo, are you settling in all right? I hope you found my advice useful."

The man did not smile back. He looked strained, and a quick glance at Sir Goodwin told Andrew social pleasantries were out of place.

"You sent for me, sir?"

"Regrettably, yes" was the bluff answer. "Captain Marchbanks has come to me with a distressing story, in which it appears you are involved."

"No," put in the man quickly, "I did not suggest. . . ."

"A distressing story . . . I don't understand," said Andrew, looking from one man to the other.

"At the reception for the Viceroy of Kwangtung you met Captain Marchbanks and his wife?" asked Sir Goodwin.

"Yes."

"You also suggested to Mrs. Marchbanks that she buy some jade at Galerie Russe?"

"No, I suggested that she should visit the gallery and have a chat with Misha Zubov, who is an expert." Some premonition of disaster prompted him to ask swiftly, "Has anything happened to him?"

Captain Marchbanks shook his head. "Not unless you count this incident as a mental aberration. He sold to my wife a fake Ming vase."

Andrew took the news like a blow to the chest. "No, there must be some mistake."

"An extremely clever piece of work, but definitely a fake." The man looked uncomfortable. "Look here, Stanton, I'm not accusing you of anything, but I want to get to the bottom of it. There is no doubt in my mind that you recommended the gallery in good faith. We both went, and I admit the premises are very imposing. Zubov spoke with authority on jade, but it was quite apparent he had been drinking prior to our visit. Don't misunderstand me," he added hastily, "there was nothing offensive about him, but one does not expect the proprietor of such a place . . . still the Russians are notorious for their insobriety. A colorful race, at the best of times."

"The family has been through several tragedies recently," put in Andrew tonelessly, trying to accept what was being told to him.

"That has nothing to do with selling jade," said Sir Goodwin firmly. "If a man runs a business of that caliber he cannot allow personal or family matters to affect his honesty."

"Are you certain you are not mistaken over this?" Andrew asked desperately.

"I would not stir up a hornet's nest, if I was not. My wife bought a vase which Zubov assured us was Ming. She paid a very considerable price for it and was delighted with her purchase, until she proudly showed it to Valentine Bowaters. He has a formidable collection himself and is something of a fanatic on the subject. He very naturally studied the piece with great deliberation and gave his opinion that it could not be genuine."

"He could be wrong," said Andrew. "A second opinion. . . ."

"He sought a second opinion" was the quiet answer. "The piece was studied in a laboratory. There is no possible doubt."

Andrew stared at the man. He *knew* Misha Zubov would never knowingly sell a fake piece of jade. He loved the green stone with dedication, valued his own judgment on it. Apart from that, he was a man of shining honesty despite his many faults.

"A very unstable family, the Brusilovs," Sir Goodwin was saying. "I am surprised Bowaters did not put you in the picture where they are concerned."

"He spoke highly of Zubov—said he knew what he was talking about when it came to jade. It is because he believes we were unwittingly deceived that I am reluctant to take the matter further before I discussed it with you and Mr. Stanton. The man is a European, and this is a serious charge. Presumably, there has never been any trouble of this nature before, or you would never have recommended the gallery, Mr. Stanton."

"No, of course not," muttered Andrew.

"But there has been a great deal of trouble connected with that family," persisted Sir Goodwin. "Zubov's wife has lost her wits after an attack on young Brusilov during which he was nearly killed by Triads, and the sister was abducted and drugged by Chinese four nights ago. Not really the kind of people who enhance a colony such as this."

"Good lord, I had no idea," said a startled Marchbanks.

While he spoke, Andrew had been collecting his thoughts. Sir Goodwin's rundown of the troubles of the Russian family had set up a sequence in his brain that suddenly made sense. First Ivan, then Nadia. Aunt Marie had suffered after witnessing the scene at the Dragon Boat Festival; he, himself, had suffered on finding Nadia at the foot of his steps. That left only two—Uncle Misha and Anna. The ruin of one would affect the other . . . and revenge would, at last, be complete!

"A moment, please," he said, still slightly thoughtful. "I am certain I can shed some light on this matter."

"You can? That is why I came," said the visitor. "If it had been some damned Chinese rogue I should have had no hesitation in charging him, but one hardly likes to. . . ."

"It *was* some damned Chinese rogue," Andrew told him. "Are you prepared to listen to a story that might astound you, yet prepare you for something you are sure to come up against time and time again in this colony?"

At the man's nod he began to tell the story of a man who had been made to lose face, knowing it was the only way of saving the family to which he had become inextricably linked. Marchbanks listened intently, showing incredulity that changed to concern as the story unfolded. Andrew put all the honesty he could into the telling of it, and concluded with, "So I think you must agree that the comprador most certainly planted that fake piece knowing that it would be bought sooner or later and bring about his final piece of vengeance. Ho Fatt would be the first to appreciate the hand of wrath reaching out beyond the grave."

Marchbanks was silent for a moment, then said, "The whole thing is macabre. It's like something from the Middle Ages."

Andrew shook his head. "It is something from the beginning of time when Chinese culture was first conceived. I admit Zubov should have spotted it, but he had no reason to distrust the Chinaman, and various family problems led him to drink more than was wise. However, he was as much a victim as you and your wife. If you would allow me to take back your jade vase and ensure the return of your purchase price, I guarantee nothing will be sold from the gallery until every piece in it is examined and proved genuine. Will you agree?"

"I suppose that is fair enough," said the police officer, at last. "But I think I should like to choose the expert to examine their stock."

"Of course," agreed Andrew gladly. "I'm certain you will find nothing amiss with the remainder. It's very good of you, Captain Marchbanks. Thank you for your reasonable and understanding approach to a sensitive affair."

"Just a moment," said Sir Goodwin, who had been quiet for so long Andrew had forgotten his presence. "I think you two gentlemen have lost sight of the fact that we are not dealing with an innocent victim, but a family business that is up to its eyes in debt due to a young seducer and a man who was too inebriated to know what he was selling." He fixed a foxy eye on Andrew. "Your somewhat emotional melodrama was meant to protect a family that has already had its share of protection from the administrators of this colony. You stand there now with strapping around your ribs and a nasty wound in your leg, all for the sake of people who have brought Russian instability and excesses to a well-run community. I do not see why this man should be allowed to escape his punishment."

"They would be ruined," cried Andrew hotly.

"Quite . . . they would then leave Hong Kong. It would be an easy way of ridding the colony of their presence."

"There is an easier way. Brusilov has decided to return to Russia as soon as possible. By Christmas they will be gone . . . and will leave behind no trace of scandal. Unless you insist that Captain Marchbanks presses this charge," said Andrew pointedly.

"Going, eh?" Sir Goodwin's thin face had gone pinker. "In that case . . . you are sure?" he put in quickly.

"Quite."

The older man smiled at Captain Marchbanks. "Then I suggest you allow my nephew to deal with the matter as he described. No need to raise a dust when the family is leaving for good. Gives the colony a bad name, you know—Europeans passing fakes. . . ." He shook his head. "A bad business. Sets a bad example to the Chinese. Much better sweep it under the carpet, eh?"

Something seemed to explode in Andrew, and the short while it took to arrange things with Marchbanks did nothing to help the pent-up anger. Only when the visitor had left did he turn to his uncle and, with emotions hardly held in check, tell him he wanted a serious interview with him regarding the case he had been on.

Sir Goodwin looked evasive. "Well, I had been meaning to have an official discussion with Captain Smethwick, but you have been ill. Today is your first day back. I will arrange something for next week."

"No," said Andrew coldly. "In view of what has just happened I want to discuss it now."

One look at Andrew's face was enough to persuade his uncle to agree, although it was with obvious reluctance. "It can only be unofficial, of course."

"The Brusilov family is free of all suspicion with regard to the revolutionary activities, I understand?" began Andrew brusquely.

"Er . . . yes." Sir Goodwin sat and invited Andrew to take the chair across the desk from him. "Sit down, boy, you look dashed under the weather."

Andrew sat, but continued his questions. "It is confirmed that

301

Ho Fatt was the agent, using the premises of Galerie Russe for storing the material as it was shipped into Hong Kong?"

"Yes. It was very convenient. Amidst so many packing cases several more went unnoticed. He was also able to arrange shipment to the mainland with any known revolutionary sympathizer. The capture of that junk was a disaster. It meant he had to find another means of getting the pamphlets to their destination."

"And found the perfect answer," completed Andrew tautly. "What better than a traveling Cantonese opera company? They went from village to village with their show, and handed the leaflets to the headmen as they went. No danger of ships being searched, and no risk of being detected. A company that reenacted the history of old China, the perfect group to inflame with promises of a China for the Chinese, as it once was."

Sir Goodwin fiddled with his blotter. "That was quick thinking on your part, Andrew, to send men to the opera site. They were due to move on within an hour of the police visit. Once they had boarded the ship, it would have been more difficult to locate those boxes of pamphlets. I understand Ho Fatt locked them in a storeroom of Brusilov's office, not knowing the sister would take it into her head to play accountant. As it happens, young Brusilov did himself and us a good turn by his dreadful conduct with that Chinese girl. We must just be thankful that our investigation had gone no further."

"Would you explain that, sir."

Sir Goodwin rose and studied the view from the window. "The Viceroy of Kwangtung will now be satisfied that we have the Empire's interests at heart, and relations will improve correspondingly. But you do see, my boy, that if it ever leaked out that we were investigating a prominent Russian family for political motives, our relations with the Russians would be seriously damaged. They would not take kindly to English interference in the private lives of their nationals. Orlov would be the first to send a strong protest, and with things as they are in China, we cannot afford to upset them. Thank God they are leaving the colony shortly."

Andrew felt his anger building. "What of my part in all this . . .

the betrayal of people I regarded as friends? What of the snubs and insults to which I have been subjected? You and Chris assured me everything would return to normal when the truth was known. Now, you are saying it must never be known."

"You are no fool, Andrew," said Sir Goodwin. "You must see why it can never be known. The family has been told a convincing story that will insure they have no suspicion that their comprador was involved in anything more than revenge for his daughter. Orlov has sent a personal note of gratitude for your service to his countrymen. The matter is now closed." He walked forward and put a hand on his nephew's shoulder. "You did your duty, my boy, that is all that can be asked of any man. They will be gone by Christmas, you say. It is time to start rebuilding your life here. Naturally, I shall do my utmost to dispel this present attitude you are facing. With your aunt and I showing open approval, Chris Smethwick doing his part toward your social reinstatement, and the Governor letting it be known that you are highly regarded, I feel sure it will not be too long before opinions begin to change. This is a fickle society, Andrew. People are ready to condemn, I agree, but they also forgive when they see a man mending his ways." He stepped around his desk to the tray containing brandy and glasses. "As soon as another scandal or excitement hits the colony, these past months will be forgotten. By that time, you will most likely be settled with a nice English girl in mind." He turned round holding out a glass. "Here, you look a bit seedy. As for your career, I daresay there might be promotion in the offing, to make up for your . . . shall we say . . . *discomforts,* of late."

In one movement Andrew was on his feet and the glass of brandy flying across the room. "By God, I would not believe it unless I were here as the recipient of this face-saving monologue. It is not only the Chinese who dread to 'lose face,' is it?" he roared. "My career is over. I had already decided I had had enough of a profession that played such dirty games and intended to give you my resignation. Now I have been privileged to discover just how the administrative mind works, my decision is irrevocable." He paced the room, kicking the brandy glass out of the way with his foot. "People do not matter, do they? You turn your face to the sun whichever direction it might shine. I was sacrificed on the altar of Anglo-Chinese relations, along with a family who might, to your eyes, seem unconventional and eccentric. But they are warm, generous, and full of greater understanding than you will ever have. They were my friends." He came back and slammed his fist on the desk. "Orlov is a villain plotting diplomatic greediness; now, Orlov must not be offended. You will never know what all this has cost me, and I will never attempt to tell you because it would be a waste of time. I tell you, Zubov has more understanding of what life is all about than you ever could." He went to the door and jerked it open. "One thing on which I heartily agree with you is that this story should never leak out . . . not because of our relations with Russia, but because I never want my wife to know what I was prepared to do to her and her family."

The heat that day held a stormy quality. It reminded Nadia of Russia where it was possible to watch the following day's storm gather in the distance on the summer estate, and send peasants rushing to gather the grapes and the harvest before the wind and rain could ruin them.

She remembered quite vividly that molten stillness of heat that made her long hair cling to her damp neck and face as she played with Ivan in the careless happy atmosphere of the country. She had seen dark patches beneath the armpits of the girls' blouses and men's shirts, and smelled the pungent sweat as she and her brother had sat on the back of a cart watching their peasants working.

There had been a mysterious suggestion of something she did not understand then which sent a strange excitement through her—glances from man to girl across a forkful of hay; young girls handing down fruit from their ladders to lads waiting below who whispered in their ears to turn their cheeks pinker; and running happily through the barn to find couples who appeared to be fighting in the piled hay. Yet it was not fighting, for they both laughed throughout the struggle and emerged later looking the best of friends.

How innocent a child is to the truth about life, she thought as she sat dreaming at her window . . . and how innocent I am still.

Those ordinary people of Russia knew the secrets of passion from an early age. In a few weeks she would be twenty-one, and the memory of those days in the fields of the summer estate made her long for the relief of union with Andrew, who would teach her all the shades of passion.

Shifting restlessly she looked again at the watch pinned to her blouse. The doctor was due to arrive at any time, and she would know the truth about herself. Nervousness beset her again at the thought of what she must ask him to do. If only she had a mother who cared, or if her aunt were still as she used to be, it would be such a comfort. As it was, she was quite alone. Even her brother had gone out against all her advice. Lunch at his club, he had told her, but he had returned since and gone out again. She passed him on the stairs, noting how ill he still looked. Now dusk was approaching and he was still away from the house. Uncle Misha had come back from the gallery very early and gone straight to his study, according to the servant who brought her tea.

Unable to remain alone any longer she left her room and wandered along the upper corridor, then down the sweeping staircase. Ivan was leaving this house, leaving Hong Kong within a few weeks. It was a house of unhappiness in a land of tears, he said. She knew he meant to go, but what would happen to her aunt and uncle . . . and what about Mama? A lurch of apprehension always accompanied that thought. She could not forget how her mother had walked from the room after her statement that she was going with Andrew wherever he wished to take her. It did not seem possible that she would go back with Ivan and surrender Andrew so easily.

As for herself, she would begin a new life away from her family, but where and under what circumstances she had yet to discover. She would be Nadia Stanton, and that was all that mattered.

Her glance took in the large circular hall that was of such beautiful design, and she knew she would miss this house they had entered with such pleasure, despite the sadness it had witnessed since their arrival. It had seen the breakup of the family, yet the true break would come only when they left it.

Crossing the hall she noticed an envelope lying on the silver tray by the entrance, the tray used by servants to deliver messages and letters arriving by hand. She went to it quickly, hoping for a note from Andrew and mentally cursing the servant for not giving it to her as soon as it came.

It was addressed to her, but by her first name only and in her uncle's handwriting. Frowning she opened it and scanned the few lines.

Take care of my poor wife—Mama, as she loved to be called. This is my final blow to the Brusilov family. They will find it impossible to forgive, but I shall harm them no more.

Mikhail Sergeyevich Zubov

The absurd use of his full name at the end of such words made alarm pump through her with such force she felt faint. Dear God, what had he done? Dropping the note she clutched her long skirts and ran the length of the corridor to the study, only to find the door locked.

"*Dyadya! Dyadya!*" she cried, pounding on the thick wood with her fists. Then she remembered the verandah and rushed back to the hall where an open door led to the lower verandah. He was lying across his desk. By his outstretched hand was a small bottle that had contained pills, and in the other a little book of his own poems he had paid to have printed, that was dogeared from the author's study of it. Nadia stopped short, unable to bring herself to approach his still figure. He looked so pathetic. In falling he had knocked over a pot of ink that had soaked into his hair and moustache.

Her sadness was greater than at the death of her father or sister, for they had been strong through life. Uncle Misha had never known strength, yet had striven so much harder for it. Perhaps her own comprehensive love for Andrew now allowed her to see deeper into the hearts and minds of others; in his way, her uncle had been more worthy than many who had died in prouder manner.

The tears flowed fast down her cheeks as she quietly unlocked the study door and left. There was someone in the hall. He came to her quickly.

"Miss Brusilova, I had no idea you were in such distress, or I would have come earlier. Please allow me to assist you to your room."

She looked up at the doctor through her tears. "Please, I think it is to the study you should come. My reason for asking you does not seem important, at this moment."

SEVENTEEN

Mikhail Sergeyevich Zubov did not act out of character when trying to kill himself. His attempt failed. He could not have known a doctor had been summoned to attend his niece at the precise time the pills began to take effect, and was early enough to counteract their deadly poison. After an exhausting night of stomach pumps, emetics, face-slapping, and forced walking, Uncle Misha was declared safe and well.

Nadia, who had sat up all night and most of the morning with her silent twin, was too drained to feel even relief at the news. Brother and sister exchanged a long look that contained wariness more than anything else, then went in to see their uncle at the invitation of the doctor. He spoke softly to Nadia about attempting to discover the reason for the patient's terrible decision, and she had time to wonder why he asked her and not her brother.

Not that Ivan gave any appearance of being better fitted for the task. He looked almost as ill as Uncle Misha. He had returned strangely chastened last night and, when she had gone to him with the news, shrunk a little more. He went to the bedside now and stood looking down at the pathetic figure with ink-dyed patches in his fair hair and moustache.

Nadia sat on the side of the bed and took up one of his hands from the coverlet. *"Dyadya* . . . why?" she asked softly.

His eyes filled, and he drew his hand away. "Even in this I was a fool."

"You are with us still. That cannot be the action of a foolish man." Her glance strayed to the photograph of Aunt Marie beside the bed. "I would have done as you asked, but did you really wish to leave her?"

He turned to look at the picture. "It is a mercy that she will never know." Then he seemed to find his courage, but it was to Ivan that he spoke. "Take your family back to Russia, Vanya. Take them soon. I have brought disgrace upon myself, but Hong Kong will condemn the Brusilovs for it." He grew agitated. "I, who prided myself on the gifts of an artist, I am no more than a puffed-up creature who dared to venture into the world of the dilettante. How they will scoff and scorn! *Ay-ay-ay*, Mikhail Sergeyevich Zubov is no more than a rascal, a charlatan they will say." His shaggy piebald head wagged sadly from side to side. "How was it I did not see . . . how could my eyes have missed? So beautiful it was." He looked quickly at Nadia. "You remember the day I sold it so . . . so unwilling to let it go." The eyes still moist with tears slid back to gaze at Ivan. "It should have been Ming . . . it *should* have been."

"What are you saying?" asked Ivan in a curiously flat voice. "That you have mistaken the value of a vase?"

"Mistaken? If it were only. . . ." He spread his hands in a gesture of hopelessness. "To Andrew's friends . . . I sold a . . . a *fake.*"

Nadia was prepared to hear anything but that. The shock made her tongue sharp. "No, I do not believe it. Who has said such a thing? Surely not Andrew?"

"Not Andrew. He came to tell me. He is a good man, that one. The friend will do nothing. We must return the money he paid, and he wishes to send an expert to study all the pieces we have at the gallery. Andrew says there will be no more. He thinks Ho Fatt needed but one piece to complete his revenge." He looked at the twins. "Why should that Chinaman have wished to harm me?

Always we worked well together."

Nadia squeezed his hand, but could not answer his question. It was for her brother to answer, if he ever could.

Misha was close to tears again. "My children that I love as my own, I have done you all possible harm by bringing you here, I know that I have. I could not risk to do more." The voice broke. "Yet, still am I here."

For a moment or two he moved his head from side to side on the pillow, overcome by his own failures. "How will I ever face Andrew again? Already for this family he has done more than any man should. I valued him as a friend, you know. . . ." He gazed up at Nadia through tear-filled eyes. "When he hears of this he will know I am not worthy of his friendship."

"*Chepukha!*" said Nadia thickly. "Andrew himself has been as close to despair as you are now, and would understand. But he will never know. No one will ever know, except the doctor, and he will not speak on professional matters to anyone. Is that not right, Vanya?"

Ivan appeared unable to answer, just gripped the older man's shoulder in a fierce gesture of kinship and understanding before going from the room.

"He goes," murmured the invalid. "So great is his disgust of me."

"Not of you, *dyadya*, but of himself, I think," she said slowly, watching her twin. "It is not so terrible, what you have done. Many a man has more to lie heavily on his conscience in the days ahead." Patting his hand fondly she stood up. "The doctor says you must rest."

She left and went to her room to get some sleep, but it evaded her. All her affection for Ivan had returned as she watched him walk alone in his misery from her uncle's room. She realized it was for life, their bond. It might be stretched to the limits, but it would never break. Her heart was too full of compassion.

After an hour, she put on a wrapper and went in search of her brother. But he had gone and a servant said that he had taken a rickshaw to Galerie Russe.

Nadia was disappointed. "Did he give a time for his return?"

"No, missee, no time come back."

She was turning away when the man added something that turned her stomach over to leave her breathless.

"Madame missee go way, no come back tomollow."

She spun round. "Did she tell you that? Are you certain?"

Such was the aggression of her tone the man bowed apologetically. "So solly. Madame missee go long way . . . all plentee muchee take go."

"How . . . how long ago did she leave?" It was not much more than a whisper, so fearful was she of the answer.

The man shrugged, having the usual oriental disregard of time. "Long time go. Go Wan Chai."

The road that led to Andrew's house in the bay! She forgot Ivan, forgot Uncle Misha, and ran up the stairs holding her long skirts free of her flying feet. No, no, she cried silently, knowing this had had to come, yet finding it impossible to accept now it was upon her. Andrew had sworn not to meet her mother again, but what could he do if she appeared at his house? Rushing into her room she snatched up her clothes with desperate haste, dressed, then took up a net purse containing some money before racing out again, along the upper corridor and down the broad shallow staircase. Once she missed her footing and saved herself from a fall by grasping the banister, but she went on, not slowing at the front entrance for a servant to summon a rickshaw, knowing it would be quicker to run down the drive where several waited in the road.

Heart pumping fast, wet with perspiration, and breathless with urgency she gave her orders to the man, and he set off with a steady stride. Dear God help me, she prayed. Andrew accused us of never having tried to fight her. Give me the strength to do so now.

September 18th, 1906—my first day as a retired colonial administrator, thought Andrew caustically as he stripped off his shirt. When I first came to Hong Kong I believed I would be gray-haired, covered with honors, and surrounded by my grandchildren on that auspicious day.

He walked to the washstand and splashed his face with water, taking care not to dampen the strapping around his ribs. Then, he gave himself a stern lecture. Be thankful for what you have, Stanton. There was a time when each day brought the risk of maiming or death. You have a strong able body, no lack of wits, and a girl any man would envy. All you have to decide is what best to do with all those blessings.

Picking up a towel he rubbed at his hair and face. The early morning gallop had done him good but left his body uncomfortably overheated. He had best sit down for a while with a cool drink. It would also give his leg a chance to calm down a little. It was throbbing painfully, as it always did when he first put his weight on it in the morning.

"Damned cur!" he muttered as he crossed his room, then pulled up short at what he saw from his floor-to-ceiling window. His own small boat had been cut loose from the landing stage and was being towed out to sea by another. He could see quite clearly the rope fixing them together, and the Chinese boatman who sat with eastern unconcern at his robbery.

"What the hell . . . the thieving rogue!" he exploded, and left the room at a limping run. "Kim!" he yelled as he descended the stairs, hoping the boy was within earshot. He heard no answering shout. Cursing his absence when he needed a fast pair of legs to run on his behalf, he burst into the sitting room full of the frustrated certainty that he would be unable to stop the theft. There, all thoughts of stolen boats were slammed from his mind by the impact of what he saw.

She stood in the center of the room making a pillar of color against the dark furniture. If she had looked superb before, today she was magnificent. She was the Czarina, the Queen of the Snows, the mistress of the keys to dark bastions. The dress of vivid shimmering green stiff silk clung to her body before sweeping away in a train that rippled in waves of shaded color behind her. It hung across her upper arms to reveal shoulders of enticing beauty, and dipped in dizzying fashion between the swell of her breasts. Against her skin blazed a tiered necklace of matched emeralds that were echoed in cold fiery drops at her ears and in a massive solitaire on her right hand. Glossy black hair piled in masses high on her head, arranged in regal fashion that emphasized the obliqueness of her brilliant eyes, and the passionate Slavic lines of her face.

She did not smile, but her whole being lit into vital animation as her glance traveled lingeringly over his face, throat, bare torso, and well-fitting riding breeches.

"Andrei, you are magnificent," she said with soft excitement. "Cruel and magnificent."

Suspended in that unheralded moment he drew breath painfully. "How did you get here?" The words were husky and echoed his shock.

"You have punished me, and I suffered. Have you any idea how I suffered from your cruel neglect?" Incredibly, there were tears high on her cheeks, quivering like jewels as the light caught them. "I die . . . yes, I die when I am not with you. But I always forgive," she whispered. "You know I always will, *serdechko moyo*."

He had sworn to Nadia never to see Anna again, but had not foreseen this situation. As usual, she had taken him by storm, caught him before he had time to build his defenses, faced him with all guns blazing and no preliminary skirmishes. Sensing acute danger, his first instinct was to walk from the room, walk from the house before he forgot the present and became captive in the past.

"I have sent your boat away, turned your horses loose. Your servant is in his quarters. We are prisoners here—as we used to be, Andrei. We are here now until I have melted the snows within you, until you know that I have forgiven you. See, I have brought the wine of our reunion." Taking a bottle from a silver ice bucket she poured pale liquid into two of his heavy crystal glasses, then held one out to him.

He knew then that this must be the ultimate battle. He either fought to its conclusion, whatever it might be, or literally ran from her along the road he had so manfully galloped last week for the sake of the girl he loved so deeply. There was no escape, and Anna knew it. Crossing the carpet he reached her and took the glass she held out in challenge, supremely conscious that he was not even dressed for battle. He had accepted the bait when all odds were against him!

She took up her glass, linked her arm through his to drink in intimate fashion, then held him there, his face but a few inches

313

from her own. He controlled his breathing with difficulty.

"Nenaglyadny moy," she murmured, her warm breath caressing his mouth. He did not need to understand the Russian endearment, for her eyes said all he tried not to acknowledge as she continued to hold his gaze. They drank the heady wine, locked in battle as surely as they were by the intertwining of their arms.

Slowly, tantalizingly, they took the wine sip by sip, standing only inches apart, the softness of her white arm against the taut brown muscles of his. Seconds passed, and the blood began to pound in his temples. Sweet perfume mingled with the bouquet of the wine to assail his senses, the emeralds winked and flashed through the paleness of the liquid, the brilliant silver-green of her eyes tormented him with promises and memories, and her breath stirred against his bare chest as she spoke in soft Russian between each sip. He watched her sensual lips as they caressed the edge of the crystal glass each time she drank, and the wine-sheen on them when she lowered it. Excitement mounted within him.

God help me, I am losing ground already, he thought wildly, and tried to concentrate on Nadia, their future, anything but Anna's mouth and eyes as he matched her sip for sip.

The glasses emptied, and she refilled hers to hand to him, then his which she took up. Reminding him of the need to drink from the glass touched by the lips of the other, she tipped back her head and emptied the contents in one long graceful movement. At the end, she dashed the glass into the fireplace where it shattered into silvery fragments.

She was looking at him, challenging him to do the same. The magnetic depths of her eyes told him he had done it all before, that this was only the beginning. He knew that ahead of him lay the snow that flashed past beneath the racing *troika*, the dark forests of Russia, the solitary stronghold where the heights of a life he had once known were waiting him. But he must not think of that—only of Nadia.

"Drink, Andrei," she commanded in the soft dreamy tones that always set his senses throbbing, and he fought to hold his own against her subtle attack.

With his head tilted back he felt the vulnerability of his throat, and thought fatally of the swords on his wall with that increase of pulse rate the danger of battle always brought. If she should take one of them down and hold him again a prisoner of the weapon! The glass was empty, and he straightened before flinging it into the hearth.

The action aroused in him a strange aggression that renewed his confidence. He could easily win a drinking contest. She had mistaken her weapons, this time. Seizing two more glasses he filled them and held one out to her. She took it, kissed the rim, then put it to his lips, tipping it so swiftly the wine began to run down his chin before he had time to put his head back. The relentless pouring forced him to arch back further and further as he took the wine down in great draughts until the glass was empty.

Before he had time to straighten and orientate himself her hand covered his eyes, while the other pressed the glass into his right hand. His heartbeat lurched. He knew very well what he must do now. In the past he had played this dangerous game with her, and the penalty was unavoidable and bizarre. But she was urging him on with words of enticement in his ear, and the softness of her skin was against his bare back. With an air of defiance he hurled the glass where he thought the hearth should be. There was a crash of breaking crystal, but also of china. He had missed!

In a flash there was more wine running over his lips, so fast he had to fight to swallow it. The chill trickle traveled down his throat and chest like a sensuous finger moving over his skin. It filled his brain with thoughts of seduction and desire. He began to see the flashing emeralds even through the darkness over his eyes . . . then her eyes, vivid, possessing him, giving him her body and soul.

Suddenly, it was there again, that tangle of memories that swung from snowscapes to barren plains, from colorful swaggering uniformed men to khaki and bloodstained bandages. Dizzy, his mind confused and throbbing, his temperature mounted until he felt on fire. Her voice was speaking urgently in his ear, her hand was sliding down his arm to the hand holding another glass. Hardly knowing what he was doing, he flung it as hard as he

315

could and heard the crash of more ornaments.

The noise broke into his visions, and he struggled back from them just as another spurt of wine touched his mouth. Jerking his head away the movement uncovered his eyes, and the present returned. His room looked a shambles. The glass-fronted china cabinet was broken, some of its contents shattered; and a pair of slender porcelain vases from his mantel were piled in pieces with a mound of glass. God in heaven, what was he doing? He knew the rules of this particular game; they were designed to ensure he could not possibly win. He must go now, before she tightened that invisible thread that would bind him hand and foot.

He turned in a daze, but she was there telling him how it had been, how it would be again. The emeralds moved on creamy skin and swung in winking drops from her ears. Another great emerald on her hand caught his attention and held it as her finger traced the runnel of wine down his bare chest with a touch that made him long for the feel of her hands on his whole body. But the jewels did not match the brilliance of her eyes, and the glory of the passion within them.

Rocketing up to the heights of existence he remembered a moon-path on the sea, and her in his arms. His brain was filled with sensations of pursuit and capture, strength and weakness, challenge and submission. *Andrei and Anna.*

"No . . . dear God, no," he breathed, and moved away from her like a man in a daze.

"Andrei," came the command, but he was out on the terrace gripping the solidity of the stone as he fought to come out of the past.

She was there behind him, her hands caressing his shoulders while that husky whisper told him of the nights they had spent together, of the agony and ecstasy of all they had done, would do again. He seemed to hear the wild wind that howled across the barren Russian plains, and the coldness of snows invaded his limbs and torso. He was rocking with the motion of the *troika* as it raced toward the hunting lodge, and he knew he would be lost once it reached the heavy door. If he entered he would never come out. *La Belle Dame sans Merci.*

He swung round. "I am not your Andrei!" he said with

desperation. "He is gone forever . . . *forever.*"

"No-o," she cried, and her words had a hollow sound as if from a great distance. Then she was kissing him, pressed against his body as she had been on so many occasions when he had been cruel to her, the pain of her plea for forgiveness turning into the pain of wanting her, forcing her to kneel at his feet, finding himself kneeling at her feet. Traveling in the realms of dark sensual memories he heard the crashing of crystal glasses all around him, and felt the wine pouring over his body once more.

The cold wine brought a return of his senses, and he pushed her away, holding her with hands that were wet and shaking.

"No," he said hoarsely. "Nothing you do will make me become Andrei. He is gone."

The wine was flooding over her, too, sliding over her shoulders making them gleam with silver runnels. She was laughing into his eyes, a low sensuous sound through the crashing of glass all around him. Then, suddenly, he lost his balance and fell against the wall, loosing his hold on her. She was gone, and he could hardly see through the torrent of wine. It soaked him, plastering the breeches to his legs and sliding off his body in great silver waves. Blinking to clear his vision he searched desperately for her and saw that she was standing by the terrace balustrade, pressing back against it, superbly outlined by the clinging material of her dress. The tumult of noise mingled with the pounding in his head, and the baptism of wine suggested a surrender that beckoned with tantalizing power.

For a long moment he stood struggling between the delights of a phantom identity and an inner voice that told him to deny it. Somewhere there was the sound of his name being repeated over and over again. *Andrew. Andrew. Andrew.*

He shook his head and began to move away from the terrace, but was sent crashing backward into a wall with a force that winded him and brought a sickening pain to the side of his head. Then she was there pummeling him with her fists.

"*Andrew* . . . think what you are doing. *Andrew.*"

It had grown bitterly cold. It was raining—not a gentle refreshing shower, but a battering deluge of water that hit him as a solid weight. It was not wine; nor was it shattering crystal glasses

317

all around him. Utter desolation crept over him leaving his body icy.

He saw her face clear then, a pale pointed face with greeny-brown eyes, large and dark with desperation, and bronze hair plastered to her head. Next minute she was kissing him, holding his head down to hers with fingers cruelly entwined in his hair. He felt the tugging at his skull, and her cold wet mouth drawing all the bewilderment from him. He knew this girl. He loved her. Her fingers loosened the grip in his hair, and she said softly against his throat, "I will not let her take you, Andrew."

The minute the words were out she was flung with tremendous force against the wall beside him, and he stared across the terrace, unable to believe what he saw. It had grown unnaturally dark. Up on the headland the trees against the purple-red sky were bending over with their topmost branches sweeping the ground, and from over the top of them came flying debris of all kinds from pieces of thatch, pots and pans, chickens, beehives, clothing, and huge severed branches—all caught up and whipped across the bay to crash into the opposite headland. The sea was copper-colored, bubbling and frothing like a giant cauldron on the boil, throwing up spume with greater force than the rain that thundered down upon it. The deserted fishing village just visible through the red mist of obscurity was half flattened and, at that moment, a mat shed rose from its place and traveled whole across his field of vision until it crumpled into splinters against the hillside behind to his right.

"Typhoon!" he breathed.

Acting under instinct he grabbed the girl beside him and moved along the wall of the house until they were standing inside the sitting room. The folding doors were slamming back and forth, the glass long having smashed into piles on the flagstones of the terrace.

Then he saw Anna. She was clinging to the pillar, a vivid splash of emerald against the stone, her long black hair streaming out behind her in the tempest. Through the sheets of rain he could see her face turned to him, and he thought once more of wild nights when storms had raged within them both. He ran out but was immediately thrown back into the room when one of the cane

318

chairs hurtled through the opening and caught him full in the chest before continuing to smash into the china cabinet he had already damaged. Wheezing with the pain in his ribs he got to his feet and staggered through the doorway, holding himself steady for a moment before pushing out into the torrents to fight his way across to the pillar.

With the rain almost blinding him it was not easy to find her and, when he did, she looked up at him with exultation in her eyes, turning her face to the storm without a trace of fear.

"This day was made for us, Andrei," she said, but the words were whipped away and he only half-heard them.

"This is a typhoon," he yelled against the gale. "We are all in danger."

But she still stood facing the elements. He thought of Nadia inside the house and knew he must get back to her. Just then, he flung his arms around Anna and protected her with his body as he watched the little landing stage he had used fold up like a pair of nutcrackers then sail toward them. It hit the pillar at the opposite end of the terrace and broke into a hundred small pieces.

The tumult was incredible. The wind shrieked and roared all around them, sending everything in its path smacking against the only things solid enough to withstand the blast. All the glass had long since gone; furniture and woodwork were being torn apart with terrible splitting sounds.

He looked up at the hillside into which his house was built. Trees were being torn from the ground near the crest and crashing down the slope. All kinds of debris littered the undergrowth, and the rains were beginning to form cascades that swept stones and rocks down through the inner scrub. They were in danger where they were.

Directly above him lay a greater hazard, however. The great glass wall of his bedroom had been blown into splinters, leaving an open three-sided box which would never withstand the tempest that could be trapped in it at any moment.

The pillar to which they clung began to tremble, reawakening in him the need for safety, but when he looked down at Anna she was laughing up at him, as savage and merciless as the elements.

319

"Anna, for God's sake, we shall be killed if we stay here." Then, as she continued to laugh at the battering rain and wind, he saw that flare of animal excitement in her eyes. "That's what you want, isn't it?" he breathed, shocked and revulsed.

Just then a figure crashed into him and held his arm with a fierce clasp.

"Andrew," cried the girl with desperation.

"Go back," he yelled. "I left you safely inside. Go back."

"No." Her face was streaming with rain and tears. "I will not go anywhere unless I take you with me."

Her hair was falling from its pins in long sodden strands, and her face seemed paler than ever . . . so different from Anna's. She is afraid, he thought, with a rush of feeling.

"It's all right," he assured her. "I know who I am now." With that he forced Anna's arms from the pillar and wrapped them around his body, before taking the other girl in a tight clasp and forcing both women to the ground. There, he began moving forward on his hands and knees, shielding the two women as best he could with his greater weight against the buffets of wind and rain.

They had almost reached the house when there was a tremendous slam of wind followed by a rending crack. His worst fears were realized. Overhead, his bedroom disintegrated under the strain, stone and mortar flying up into the air or crumbling like paper to fall onto the terrace with a choking cloud of dust. Flinging himself across the two women he felt sharp edges cutting into the flesh of his back, and painful blows to the hands covering his head. There was a final sickening pain in his injured leg before the shower ceased.

He lifted his head cautiously. The terrace was now a formidable spread of masonry, splintered wood, and glass. His bed hung twisted and broken across the balustrade, sodden with rain and shifting ominously in the shrieking wind. The danger swept all remaining bewilderment from his mind as he saw the pressing need to leave their present position. He had known typhoons before, but never like this one, and experience told him the height had yet to be reached. When it was, there was every chance that the entire house would collapse.

It was pointless shouting to the two women, for the noise all around them drowned any other human sound. There was only one place where they might be safe, if he could get them there. The icehouse was a small stone cellar in the hillside across the side courtyard. Battened down there the danger would be minimal, but to reach it meant crossing an open square fully exposed to the bay.

The rain had settled the dust very quickly, and he began urging the women forward on their stomachs, clambering across the rubble as best they could while he protected them on the windward side until they reached the sitting room. Dragging them to their feet he urged them forward. There was a mass of broken china and glass, with furniture driven into a great broken pile in one corner. The swords had dropped from the wall to lie somewhere beneath the debris of the storm.

Out in the hall there was a similar picture. A weird moaning filled the stairwell, and the walls were creaking ominously beneath the strain. The staircase was already half-hanging from the upper floor that was now open to the elements. Lightning regret pierced him through, but danger overrode sentiment to send him swiftly propelling them through the kitchen regions to the courtyard door. It was swinging back and forth, the wire gauze caved in as if it had been kicked with a great boot. He halted there, holding the wrists of the women, fighting for breath.

It was all of thirty yards to the icehouse and, even as he watched, a tumbling, cartwheeling metal bar was sent across the open stretch to thud against the hillside. It was a tethering bar; the stables must have gone. It meant there would be even less protection as they crossed, but the risk had to be taken before the walls crashed down on them.

In the relative quiet of the house he said brief authoritative words to them, glancing at both faces—one white and terrified, the other glowing with supreme ecstasy as her eyes deified him.

"We must go now," he said through a throat dry with dust, and took their arms in a firm hold. "You know what you must do?"

They nodded, and he tried to look reassuring. The iron rail edging the path to the icehouse was three feet from the ground.

It made a frail anchorage but ten yards from the icehouse the rail had broken, smashed away by masonry from the house, leaving a gap to be crossed without any support whatsoever. It was still their only chance, and it had to be taken.

The minute they set foot outside the door it was like all hell let loose. The rain still fell in a fury, the roaring of the sea had increased, and the wind caught at them even in the semi-lee of the house. But he pushed the women to the nearby rail where they did as he had told them, gripping the iron bar and bending low across it. He then put a hand each side of them and used his greater height to bend over them both in protective fashion, facing into the wind and moving sideways as they edged hand over hand.

It was slow and difficult. The rail was slippery, wet from the rain, and the path was liquid mud making it hard to keep their footing. The minute they left the lee of the house they were hit by the full force of the wind, and Andrew knew they would be lucky to survive a typhoon of such proportions.

Foot by foot they moved forward, the women several times being saved by his strength when their hands slipped and he held them steady. It was a terrible strain on his arms, holding himself and them against the force of the wind that sent bushes, bars, planks, and broken furniture hurtling past as easily as bubbles caught in a breeze.

Turning his head he squinted through the rain. They would soon be coming to the gap. All they could do was put their faith in the Almighty. At that moment Nadia slipped, clinging desperately to the bar as she knelt in the muddy sand, and he braced himself, feet apart, before loosing hold of the bar to haul her up. Instantly, he was swung back by a huge gust, the strain on the remaining hand becoming intolerable. Grimacing with pain he felt his fingers slipping on the wet metal, overbalanced onto one knee and thankfully caught at the upright support at that point. Mentally thanking God that the women did not panic, he used their long skirts as partial hold to regain their original position and began urging them on again.

All too soon the railing ended, and a ten-yard stretch of open path lay between them and the steps to the icehouse, where a single span still stood. Nadia hesitated, but he pushed her down onto her knees with rough urgency. She knew what to do; he had told them both most carefully before they set out. To stand without support was impossible, so they had to get as close to the ground as possible, which meant crawling on their stomachs through the oozing muddy sand.

The girl turned to face him just once, still not sure of him, then lay flat as he had ordered her. Down went Anna behind him, and he lay between them, gripping Nadia's waistband and having his own gripped by Anna. In that fashion they began to claw their way across the open gap, digging their fingers into the soft runny surface in hope of finding some kind of purchase. Spread flat they were at the full mercy of the rain that thundered down upon them like sharp missiles, and Andrew felt the rawness of the cuts on his back and the pressure on his bound ribs as he snaked along.

A miscellany of things was hurtling over them—pots, barrels, garden tools—all blown from the outhouses that had crumbled already. He wished he could protect the women more, but it was impossible with two. He was doing all he could now, but Nadia was almost swimming in mud, her long hair dragging in it, and the pale skirt and blouse, filthy and so sodden that the weight of them was slowing her down. He should have told them to strip off their outer clothes . . . but time was pressing. At any moment he expected the house to go.

They were halfway across when a ladder somersaulted past catching him a blow on the back. His face went down in the mud as he gritted his teeth against the pain, but it could not have been more than several seconds before he realized the hold on his belt had gone. His heart missed a beat, and he twisted his head in dread of what he might see.

Anna's arm had been hit by the flying ladder. It was covered in blood and, apparently, useless. In her agony she had rolled away, slipping in the mud some feet away from him.

"Hold on, for God's sake," he yelled hoarsely, knowing she was now alone and helpless, but his words never reached her in the raging wind.

Nadia turned her head to look back at him, staring as he began shouting like a madman to Anna. He dared not lose his hold on Nadia or she would also be in danger, but he flung himself around, stretching out a hand to the isolated woman. She was well out of reach and slipping further as the force of the wind began to make itself felt on her slight body.

"Anna, dig your hands in! *Anna!*" Frantic, helpless, he clawed his way toward her, shifting his hold on Nadia to her ankle in an effort to close the gap. But their fingers were still a foot apart.

Blinking the rain from his eyes he shouted to her to edge forward, desperation making his voice harsh. Using all his strength he stretched to his fullest, gasping with the pain it brought him. His fingers were but a few inches from hers.

"Anna, come on . . . come on!"

He knew she did not hear his words, but the wind blew hers to him to increase his desperation.

"Andrei . . . Andrei." Her fingers were moving in the mud, but getting no nearer.

"Anna . . . Anna," he moaned, trying to inch his fingers nearer as he saw the adoration flaring in her eyes at his struggle. She was willing him to go to her, reveling in the strength that enabled him to rise to such effort.

Then, above the wild desperation of the moment, he grew aware of a new sound, a sound so deep, so terrifying it pushed all else from his mind. A great subterrestrial thundering grew and grew, bringing with it a gray pall that rolled toward them like the onset of the end of the world.

Paralyzed, he stared out at the bay. Beyond the pall, driving it ahead was a great wall of water, the top of which vanished into gray obscurity. It was dark copper in color and moved with the thunder of an earthquake. It reached the two headlands and swallowed them up, spewing up broken junks and flotsam, turning day into night, land into ocean.

It was only a split second, yet it was the whole of his life— eternity. The fingers were so near, reaching for his. He looked at the brilliant silver-green eyes and his brain spun; the world tipped. He felt again the heights of existence, and he wanted to die at that moment spread at her feet.

But the roar was still in his ears, and he looked again at the death-wave. There was no time, no time for life above and beyond life. It would destroy him as surely as that wall of water. Like a man possessed he turned away and began scrambling over the mud dragging Nadia with him, feeling none of his physical agony, only the agony of loss that tore at the darker regions of his soul. They would now stay forever subdued.

"Andrei!" The wind carried the sound to him like a voice from another world, but he had his world—the only possible world for any man who was not Andrei Brusilov—there in his sight as he drew nearer the rail by the icehouse.

Driving himself on he hauled Nadia to her feet and folded her hands around the iron bar. Then he took the leather belt from his waist and strapped her to the metal support, looking round swiftly at the sea advancing upon them.

Nadia looked up at him through the advance pall of spray, and he saw all her life, her pain and her love for him written on her white face. Wrapping his arms around her he twisted his wrists into the leather belt behind her back. Only then dared he look back. The small figure in emerald-green rose from the ground into a kneeling position, then shakily to her feet, standing in the full fury of the typhoon. She was there but a moment before the tempest caught her and hurled her like a doll across the open ground.

Just then, the wave hit the hillside below the house. The earth shook and trembled, then a great umbrella of water shot high into the air over their heads to crash down on everything on that level. Andrew was in a swirling darkness of ocean that dragged and pounded him swelling his lungs beyond endurance and pulling his arms almost from their sockets as they were held by his lashed wrists.

Then it was gone, retreating in a tumult of suction that was as great as its advancing roar. He stood gasping, finding the punishment of the wind almost pleasant after the smothering water. Looking down at the girl sagging against him he felt a great sense of release. She was unconscious, but alive. He untwisted his lacerated wrists and held her close to him in the continuing storm, as he gazed out over the bay.

His house was no more than a broken tangled mass of stone

and wood strewn right across the sand to the edge of the boiling foam of sea. Of Anna Brusilova there was no sign.

"Dear God ... oh, dear God," he breathed. "Surely the dragons of this bay have now been fully appeased!"

EPILOGUE

The typhoon on September 18 in that year of 1906 was the most severe onslaught by the elements ever recorded in the colony's history to that date. It struck Hong Kong without warning and raged for less than two hours, but around ten thousand people lost their lives, thousands more were made homeless, and hardly a building on the island escaped damage.

The meager harvest was flooded and spoiled as the whipped-up sea invaded the land. The waterfront was devastated and smashed by great vessels that were spewed onto the sheds and warehouses, littering the coast with broken hulls, spilled cargoes, masts and rigging, sodden coal, and human bodies. Their prows jammed in the entrances of narrow streets, their huge iron structures smashed down the jetties and copings as they rose from the waters and attacked the land. Over two thousand Chinese vessels were lost, one hundred and forty-one European ships.

The soothsayers were proved right. Boats did sail over the crops, but farmers and sea-dwellers alike suffered from it. Sampan colonies turned into vast areas of floating debris in which

327

bobbed the drowned bodies of adults, babies, and animals, all victims of the vengeance of the serpents and other spirits of the sea. Farming communities were wiped from the face of the earth, their spirits forced to wander forever in search of a resting place. In Victoria itself, hundreds were killed when buildings collapsed upon them.

The Chinese accepted it, as they always did, as the work of angry spirits and beasts. The British rulers might rate it "an act of God" but, as *they* always did, felt He intended that they should do something to alleviate the misery resulting from it. Disaster plans were put into operation. Medical services did their best to cope with appalling injuries and rampant disease. Fears of a return of the plague rose as rats came from their lairs in thousands, and dysentery cases grew alarmingly when starving Chinese ate anything they could find amongst the ruins of their hovels.

Welfare and church bodies did their utmost to give shelter and some kind of meal to those in need, opening emergency centers for the orphans found wandering in a daze. It was virtually impossible to identify them in many cases, so they were given a number on a label tied to their cotton shifts.

The task of clearing the devastation was put in hand immediately, and Europeans as well as wealthy Asians contributed funds to cover the astronomical cost of relief for the suffering population.

At such a time, personal considerations were put aside: The colony had a new sensation on its hands. Andrew Stanton was accepted with open arms by the department from which he had made a final break on the day before the typhoon. Injured himself, he was nevertheless able to give valuable assistance to a severly overworked group of people at a time when it was most needed. Without a home or possessions he gratefully took an offer from Chris Smethwick to share his small house which had merely lost windows and part of the roof. He also had to borrow clothes from his friend, for all he had in Hong Kong were the breeches and riding boots he was wearing when the typhoon hit the island.

Driving himself hard he was only that way able to come to terms with all that had happened on that tragic day . . . and if he was haunted now and again by the memory of his moment of decision it was merely a sign of his human weakness. The final battle with Anna had gone to him, after all, but it had left him with no pride in the victory. Perhaps it was the only way such a contest could have ended, the only possible outcome for a battle for possession that was animal, dramatic, almost shocking in nature. The end, the severing of the hold on him, had been as cruelly ruthless as anything Anna and Andrei Brusilov had ever contemplated in their bizarre relationship. She had escaped violent death once; Andrew felt she would glory in the manner in which she had finally gone to the man with whom she was so totally obsessed.

The destruction of his house left him with nothing except money in the bank. Of Kim, the cheery houseboy, of the Portuguese cook, and his horses there was no sign. All the things he valued were gone, lost beneath the great spread of stones covering the beach. No coolies would ever clear it. The *fung shui* saw to that. One day he might go back himself, but even he felt it would be best to let the dragons rest in peace in that bay.

Nadia kept him going through those first days. The knowledge of her love turned his mind away from what was past and onto the future, so that instead of lying awake tormented by all that had been lost, he searched his mind for the best way to handle his future with her.

The Brusilov family, in partial mourning for Anna, found a great deal to do in those first weeks following the typhoon. Galerie Russe, escaping heavy damage, had to be made secure again. All the windows and display cases had smashed, and a corner of the building broken, but every item remained in its place. Food, clothing, and medicines disappeared from shops in an orgy of looting, but of what use were great lumps of green stone to the starving homeless?

The twins and Misha Zubov spent a great deal of time listing and locking away all the pieces ready for the proposed sale of the business. That done, Nadia began the unwelcome task of sorting her mother's possessions. She looked at the ivory miniature of her father for a long time before wrapping it carefully for her grandmother back in Russia. With Anna Brusilova gone forever, it might give the old lady a little consolation for the loss of her son to that terrible liaison that took him so brutally from her.

The jewels were packed in their velvet-lined cases for Ivan to take on his journey. They would be given to his wife when the time came. A pang shot through Nadia as she looked at the flashing opulent stones. Her every instinct was to shut them away in the family vaults: They held too much of her mother's personality in their secret depths. She was afraid the girl Ivan took as a bride would either assume the aura of Anna Brusilova or be overshadowed by the gems forever.

She halted in the midst of her task and tried to picture the girl who would become the next Madame Brusilova of St. Petersburg. Gentle, quiet, and passionately in love with Ivan? Who could say? He was a changed man—yes, a man and not a boy, any longer. If he also had a haunted look in his eyes, it appeared to strengthen his new determination rather than make it waver. In her heart she knew she had been right all along. He would be greater than his father, in time. Ivan might possess the pride and arrogance of the Brusilovs but he was also ruled by human compassion. The mixture would prove victorious.

The twins' coming of age was to be celebrated quietly with a family dinner party rather than the grand affair Ivan had intended. Their mother's death dictated the event, but they both preferred it that way, as it happened. The dinner party was to include Andrew. Ivan had sent a formal invitation, and Nadia knew he had now accepted an alliance between herself and the Englishman to whom they all owed so much.

It was a further sign of his acceptance that he and his uncle tactfully delayed their arrival in the salon that evening to allow her time with Andrew when he arrived. While waiting for him she thought reflectively of other occasions when they had looked at each other across the room, unable to speak of their love; of Katya's provocative chatter; of Aunt Marie moving happily amongst her "children"; of her mother appearing at the threshold of the room, holding Andrew in thrall. Then she shook away the memories as a servant announced him, and went forward full of joy. She had to tell him of the happy result of her doctor's visit the day before.

330

He was in evening dress, a tall striking man who no longer resembled Andrei Brusilov. He kissed her and offered congratulations, and she was woman enough to sense that he was full of some deep tranquillity that was not yet ready to be broken by lively company.

"You look very grand tonight," she teased gently, slipping her arm through his and moving out to the verandah.

A faint smile touched his mouth. "The tailor only just finished in time. Tonight, of all nights, I could not appear in borrowed clothes."

"For me, it would not have mattered, but Vanya is sure to have been offended," she told him, smiling back.

They went together onto the wide stone verandah and stopped by the balustrade, looking out into the night. The spread of lights was reduced to just a few. Repairs were still being done, and there were things of more pressing importance in the task of recovery. But there was a moon, clear and silver-gold, to flood the reviving colony and put a pathway across the sea.

They stood silently for a moment or two, lost in their separate thoughts, then Andrew said, "The night is so soft and beautiful. Did that ever happen?"

Nadia remained quiet beside him. He needed no word from her, just her nearness in the tropical evening.

"I resigned from the department on the day before the typhoon," he said into the night. "I am only helping them while this emergency lasts."

"Andrew, no," she protested. "You have done too much for us already."

He looked down at her. "The decision was the only one I could make . . . and I cannot tell you how glad I am to leave something that made too many demands on me."

She saw the strain of the past months etched on his face and wondered what he had sacrificed for their sakes. But the vulnerability, the wariness had gone, and the tightness of his jaw was due to determination, not defensiveness. She tried to think of a way to thank him, but he went on. "I am a fairly wealthy man and have found a solution to most of our problems. After several meetings with your brother it has been agreed that I shall buy the

331

gallery and continue to run it with the aid of a business manager. The negotiations for purchase were begun yesterday, and Ivan has given us the present stock as your dowry. He said it must be something really fitting for a Brusilov."

Her throat thickened painfully, and the words she wanted to say would not be spoken. All she could do was take Andrew's hands and grip them tightly.

"Of course, I should also need Uncle Misha as my buyer and consultant. Do you think he would agree to remain at Galerie Russe?" he asked her.

She gazed up into his face shadowed by the overhanging roof and recognized the man he really was, the man he could have been if he had never met her along that path.

"You are doing this for us . . . but Andrew, you must not. You could never be a jade merchant. It would make you miserable!"

He took her hands to his mouth and kissed them tenderly. "I know. It is an alarming thought. Thankfully, I have been saved from that fate by Chris Smethwick, who viewed the prospect with as much horror as you have just shown. Through him, I have been offered a senior post with the police department. They are short of trained officers and are less rigorous about the private lives of their men." He smiled with deep pleasure. "It also means I shall be dealing with Chinese people themselves, and not with those stiff-shirted diplomats who are trying to seize their country from them . . . much more rewarding work. If I accept. . . ."

"Of course you will accept," she cried joyously. "In no time, you will be chief of police. I know it, if they do not."

She stood on tiptoe to kiss him and found herself caught in a fierce hold while he turned her impulsive embrace into a lengthy and breathless expression of his need for her. Then he held her away from him, and she saw the blue fire in his eyes as the lamplight caught them.

"Don't you think this is the right time and place for the formal proposal of marriage I have never yet made?" he asked.

"And if I should refuse?" she teased lightly, but was stricken by the bleak and frightening tension that crossed his face.

"I should hit another wall, but this time I should not survive."

Filled with an overwhelming love that longed to blot out those things in his past that had nearly broken him, she put her fingers lightly against his mouth.

"*Serdechko moyo,* when a woman has fought for a man and won, she never lets him go again. You will find that out."